The Heart's Citadel

The Cresswell Inheritance
BOOK TWO

The Heart's Citadel

Anita Burgh

ORION

First published in Great Britain in 2005 by Orion,
an imprint of the Orion Publishing Group Ltd.

1 3 5 7 9 10 8 6 4 2

A CIP catalogue record for this book
is available from the British Library.

ISBN 0 75286 071 2 (hardback) 0 75287 197 8 (trade paperback)

Typeset by Deltatype Ltd, Birkenhead, Merseyside
Printed in Great Britain by Clays Ltd, St Ives plc

All the characters in this book are fictitious, and any resemblance
to actual persons living or dead is purely coincidental.

The Orion Publishing Group Ltd
Orion House
5 Upper Saint Martin's Lane
London, WC2H 9EA

www.orionbooks.co.uk

For my granddaughter, Hannah Leith, with love

Acknowledgements

I would like to thank my editor, Jane Wood, for her understanding during a difficult year. I would also like to thank Jane Collier, and Anne and Andrew Johnston, for their kind permission to use an image of their hotel, Bibury Court, my favourite watering-hole, for the cover of this book.

The pound in 1914 is equal to £58.68p in today's currency.

Love is a breach in the walls, a broken gate,
Where that comes in that shall not go again;
Love sells the proud heart's citadel to Fate.

Rupert Brooke 1887–1915
Collected Poems 1916

CHARACTERS

The Cresswell Family
Sir Mortimer (Mortie) Cresswell
Coral – his wife
Penelope – his mother
Morts – his son
Felix – his son
Lettice Hamilton – his daughter
Hugo Hamilton – her husband
Charlotte – their daughter
Georgia – their daughter
Hannah Cresswell – Mortie's sister
Agnes Beatty – Hannah's companion
Oliver Cresswell – Mortie's brother
Esmeralda – Oliver's wife

The Cresswell Family's Staff
Edward Whitaker – butler
Hilda – pastry cook & Edward's wife
Eve Gilroy – cook
Philomel Herbert – housekeeper
Rowan Marshall – maid
Willow Marshall – kitchen maid
Freddie – footman
Charlie Beasley – head gamekeeper & Melanie's father
Robert Robertson – head gardener
Fred Robertson – gardener
Sol Pepper – boiler man
Ferdie – coachman
Lavender Potts – Hannah's maid
Bridget – Esmeralda's maid
Gussie Fuller – Esmeralda's housekeeper

Milner – Esmeralda's butler

Others

Stanislas von Ehrlich (Stan Eldridge) – Esmeralda's father
Melanie Joynston – owner of the Cresswell Arms
Richard Joynston – her husband
Zephaniah Topsham – Melanie's son
Dolly Topsham – his wife
Apollo – their son
Cordelia – their daughter
Xenia – Melanie's daughter
Timmy – Melanie's son
May Snodland – Dolly's maid
Charlie – May's son
Ramsey Poldown – a neighbour
Reverend Fogget – vicar
Simon – his son
Emily Sprite – plants woman
Fanny Petty – suffragette
Inspector Steedman – Barlton Police
Miss Rowntree – Barlton Police
Dulcie Prestwick – hotelier
Henry Battle – lawyer
Matron Wilbur – Barlton Memorial Hospital
Sister Westall – Barlton Memorial Hospital
Lady Sylvia Ferguson – VAD
Major Frobisher Fellowes – Medical Officer
Sergeant Bob Turner – army cook
Flossie Marshall – cook at Cresswell Arms
Alf – her husband
Oak – her son
Petroc Cornish

Animals

Cariad – Hannah's dog
Blossom – Esmeralda's dog

Chapter One

August 1913

1

It was the rhythmic booming of a drum that attracted Esmeralda Cresswell's attention. Curiosity getting the better of her, she stopped pouring the tea and approached the window, which was a good ten feet high, every inch of the glass gleaming in the bright sunshine. She positioned herself by the heavy curtains, of blue and gold brocade, so that she was not seen. Below, the shrill chattering of a crowd of women sounded as if a flock of starlings were approaching their roost. They were marching down Gold Street, arm in arm, their expressions verging, she thought, on belligerence.

The drummer changed the rhythm, and in unison they broke into song. They were somewhat off key, more raucous than tuneful, but the melody was familiar. It was their version of 'Onward Christian Soldiers':

> *Forward, sister women!*
> *Onward ever more,*
> *Bondage is behind you,*
> *Freedom is before ...*

She much preferred the original words, she decided. Not that she or her husband often attended church to sing them. They were of different religions – she a Catholic, he Church of England – which might have been a problem had faith been of importance to either of them, but since neither felt the need for divine comfort, it wasn't.

A shout from the throng made her jump. She had scant sympathy for the women – to whom she could never imagine herself referring as *sisters*. All her life she had acquired what she wanted with smiles and sweetness – well, most things – and could not see the point of screaming and shouting for change. And *bondage*! What an extreme word to use, with its implications of slavery. Did she lack freedom? 'No, I don't,' she said aloud, to the empty room, and giggled at her silliness. 'At least, I don't think I do ...' She decided it was a thought she was better off not pursuing.

Instead, to distract herself, she patted the pale yellow silk of her skirt, rearranging its folds until she was content that it was perfect. Then she checked the tiny pearl buttons on the sleeve of her matching jacket – so sweet. The women in the street were all drab. Why did they feel they had to wear dull, serviceable browns and greys to be taken seriously? Surely more people would notice if they looked pretty. Oh, how she loathed the colour brown and would never wear it.

Freedom. What did it really mean?

The noise was fading as the group made their way towards the high street. Esmeralda opened her minuscule bag, checked that she was still alone, then dabbed a little perfume on her wrists – he always expected her to smell nice.

A prisoner was not free, certainly. Her canaries in their cages weren't, and neither were the animals in the zoo. But women? Why, within limits she could do as she liked. She frowned. Well, almost … But those limits, undefined but understood, were acceptable. No husband wanted his wife running about willy-nilly without him knowing where she was. And of course she must entertain for him, even if frequently she had nothing in common with his guests – it was her duty. Perhaps those women had confused bondage with duty.

To be sure, she wouldn't want to change her life. Again the tiny frown marred her pretty face, the pale but perfect complexion. Well, that was what she told herself and everyone else. If only she could turn the clock back to when her life had been truly perfect. She sighed. Whenever she visited the wishing tree on the hill at Cresswell – which was not often since it was at the top of a steep climb – she circled it three times, just as Oliver had shown her, and wished that he and her father could be friends. Of course, there had been another wish … She gave herself a little shake – there was no point in thinking of that.

It was hard that the two men she loved most in the world would not speak to each other. If they found themselves in the same room, which occasionally happened since their social circle was small, one would leave hurriedly, usually Oliver, insisting that she accompany him. She wished he would stand his ground, and took pride in her father's refusal to budge, which immediately made her feel disloyal to her husband. How complicated they made it all.

Sometimes she found herself wondering why, if they really loved her, they hurt her in this way. Perhaps their feud was more important than she was. 'What a silly idea,' she said, and laughed to make it go away, but it didn't.

The falling-out had happened long ago. They had argued about land, which was so absurd when both men had so much of it. That she and Oliver had eloped had not helped matters, but they had been so much in love – and still were, she told herself hurriedly – that her father would not have been able to stop her marrying him. Of course, she had thought, and still did, that her father, then forty, had been too old to understand how she felt. Perhaps he had never loved – if he had, he could not have forgotten how all-consuming it was. She was sure that if she lived to her eighties she would never forget what it was like to love.

All that had happened ten years ago. It had taken her two of those years to persuade her husband that she needed to see her father. Even then she had lied to achieve it, which made her blush, even now: she had claimed her father's cold was pneumonia and that he was about to be given the last rites.

But what else could she have done? She loved her father.

After that, when Oliver was away she would go to her father's house. A couple of times he had arrived unannounced at hers, and she had had to swear the staff to secrecy, which she found demeaning. She did not like lying to her husband but felt it expedient to cover where she had been and whom she had seen. It was Oliver's fault, not hers, that she had to do so.

Three years ago she had taken her courage in both hands and had told him she had met her father in Barlton and that they had taken tea together. To her astonishment Oliver had simply shrugged and said he hoped she wouldn't expect him to join them if it happened again. They had even laughed. Now she met her father once a fortnight but she had not told Oliver how frequently they saw each other.

Perhaps the need for lies and subterfuge were signs that she was not as free as she had thought. What a horrible idea!

From the noise below it was evident that the women were returning. The group was larger now, joined by several other chapters of the movement, judging from the increase in banners. She stood up the better to see. The leaders of the march were wearing sashes in the now familiar colours. Purple showed their loyalty to the king – but it was a strange loyalty that made for such problems in the king's streets and for the poor constabulary; white was for purity, but when she looked at the twisted, angry faces there didn't seem much of that; and green was for hope, and they were certainly in need of that, she thought. Others sported rosettes on their collars in the same colours with no thought of whether they co-ordinated with their clothing. They stretched across the entire road,

3

making it impossible for others to move in the opposite direction. Now an elderly man wearing a top hat waved his umbrella at the marchers and shouted at them angrily. They moved on relentlessly, pushing him backwards. Esmeralda feared for his safety, convinced that nothing would stop this juggernaut of humanity. Should he fall, he would be trampled.

'Votes for women!' they bellowed.

'Justice for all!' yelled one.

'Votes for women!'

A gang of ragamuffins were darting in and out of the group, laughing, pulling faces and enjoying the spectacle. What fun they were having in their innocence. Well, not so innocent, she thought, as she observed a child snatch a purse and disappear into the hubbub, ignoring the victim's howls of indignation.

Esmeralda placed her white kid-gloved hands over her ears. She wished their voices were not so high-pitched and offensive. Then she saw someone she knew. 'Oh, no!' she exclaimed. 'Oh, Hannah!' Her sister-in-law was marching along, chanting in such an unseemly way, bringing shame on her family, Agnes Beatty beside her.

Years ago, Miss Beatty had been Esmeralda's companion but now she was Hannah's. As a child she had been in awe of Agnes, and more than a little afraid of her. Now, as an adult, she did not like her and knew she never had, that she had confused respect with liking. Agnes had such a superior air, and a rather supercilious smile often flitted about her mouth, as if she was a keeper of secrets. It made her seem so haughty. She had often wondered if her father and Agnes had been sweethearts, but then, given their age, she had dismissed the idea as ludicrous. There was something threatening about her, too, although Esmeralda had never been able to put her finger on what it was. Oliver loathed the woman but would never tell her why – 'Not for your pretty little ears,' he was wont to say. It annoyed her when he spoke to her like that, as if she was still the child he had married rather than a woman of twenty-eight. She would never tell him, that was not her way.

'Oh, Hannah, don't!' Involuntarily she banged on the window, which, given the noise below, was pointless – Hannah could not possibly have heard her. Two large policemen barred the way and to Esmeralda's horror, Hannah was arguing with them now. 'Hannah!'

As word of their presence sped through the group, the noise increased, and those at the back pressed forward. At least Hannah was no longer the only one involved in the altercation – a much larger woman had thrust her way to the front. Her face was distorted with fury, reddening with every word. One policeman wagged a finger at her – perhaps the worst thing he could have done; the woman, who was taller than him, knocked off his helmet.

The crowd surged forward, laughing. They swept the two constables out of the way and turned into the small park opposite the hotel where, Esmeralda knew, the mayor was inaugurating the new bandstand. The pretty edifice had been built in honour of King Edward VII, but he had died before it was finished and now it was to be dedicated to the new king. Such a shame, thought Esmeralda. The old king had had about him such an aura of glamour, which the new one lacked, worthy though he was.

Unfortunately she had never met either king. Oliver did not like society, preferring the quiet life they led here in Devon. When she had been talking to her sister-in-law, Coral Cresswell, she thought wistfully of what fun it might be to go to London in the Season and to Court especially. Coral knew everyone who counted – she was the daughter of a viscount, as she never tired of telling them. Oliver was a second son, which was one of the reasons why Esmeralda's father had objected to their union. He'd wanted a titled spouse for his daughter, and the better social position that would have given her – and himself. She knew her father had wished she could have had Oliver's brother, Sir Mortie Cresswell, but he was already married to Coral – and he was so corpulent that she shuddered at the thought. By contrast, Oliver was a fine figure of a man even though he was now in his forties.

The women continued into the park. Surely they were not intending to disrupt the ceremony? How rude – and it was much more likely to anger people than gain them support. Still the children played about them. Filthy, in rags. No doubt their mothers had no idea where they were and probably did not even care. Esmeralda felt sad as she watched them. How easy it was for some to have children – from the state of those little ones, they were not even loved. She longed, with a gnawing desperation, for a child of her own but so far had not been blessed. This time, perhaps … She stroked her flat stomach. She must cling to hope. She had resolved not to tell anyone of her suspicions, even Oliver. That way, if what seemed inevitable happened, only she would know and only she would be sad.

'How courageous they are.'

Esmeralda's hand fluttered to her heart. 'Why, Lady Prestwick, you made me jump!'

'I'm so sorry, Mrs Cresswell. I always make so much noise when I enter

5

a room, or so my dear husband assures me.' Dulcie Prestwick, owner of the hotel, laughed as she looked out of the window. 'They've had a good turnout, don't you think? And I saw Hannah well in evidence.'

'So silly of her.' Esmeralda turned from the window now that the women were out of sight.

'Do you think so? They march for all women after all.'

'I never asked them to do so for me. It causes such disruption to everyone.'

'But only for a short time, and they will march triumphantly into history.' Dulcie flung out her arms expansively, which made her appear even larger. 'I envy them.'

'You do?'

'I long to be with them.'

'Really?' Esmeralda was curious. She respected Lady Prestwick more than any other woman she knew. 'Then why did you not join them?'

'I fear I have to confess to hypocrisy. Many of my clients at the hotel do not approve of the suffragettes, and I bow to their views since I need them. To mix a metaphor, I must sell my soul for a mess of pottage. I can support the marchers only in spirit and despise myself for my weakness.'

'But you're so clever – can you not make them change their minds?'

'I fear I should waste my time if I tried, for they are old and set in their ways.'

'But I'm not old – or set. I'm sorry to disappoint you, Lady Prestwick, but I think they're noisy and silly. And I don't feel I'm in *bondage*.'

'Maybe we're not but many of our sisters are.' Dulcie spoke with a smile but Esmeralda felt she was being admonished.

'But what do I know of politics? Nothing.' She waved her hand vaguely.

'Dear Mrs Cresswell, as with most things, we have to learn. Knowledge liberates us all ...' As Dulcie spoke she glanced about the room, checking apparently that all was in order. She swooped on the tea tray. 'You need fresh tea. Shall I send up the champagne now?'

'That would be most kind. Thank you.' She watched Dulcie leave the room, nimble and light-footed for one so large. She liked her, although many didn't but only confessed it behind her back. Dulcie was a conundrum to local society. For a start she was in trade, that most despised social class – Esmeralda often wondered if this betrayed fear at the way in which the social order had changed. Why, the old king had counted grocers among his friends. Dulcie did not work as such, but used her

6

brain – always perplexing to those who felt it nigh on sinful for a woman to be clever – and she was very rich, one of the richest people in the vicinity, and money, in these progressive times was taking on a glamour, even an acceptance, of its own. To complicate the puzzle further, she was married to a baron and thus had a title, which put her above all others in the neighbourhood, even the Cresswells. And where a title was involved everything else went out of the window – everyone loves a lord. Dulcie had confessed that she had once seen her husband nearly mown down by a stampede of elderly women, hobbling on sticks, eager to speak to him. And, of course, she was always with him, so if they wanted to talk to Theo they had to accept his Dulcie too. To Esmeralda, none of it mattered a fig: she liked or disliked people for themselves – who or what they were never bothered her.

Esmeralda flicked open the jewelled case of the watch she wore on a gold chain round her neck. Once again, she looked about her to make sure she was alone, then took from her bag a pair of spectacles with which she quickly checked the time, then put them away. He was late, and her father was never late.

She wondered if she should worry. Perhaps he'd had an accident or a seizure – always a possibility at his age and in this heat. There were magazines aplenty and a shelf of novels in a corner of the private sitting-room, but she could not risk anyone seeing her in her spectacles so instead she tapped her feet impatiently. It was a mystery to her why she could see for miles but could not make out the words on the page in front of her.

'My little bat.' Oliver teased her. She hated it when he called her that. It was so insensitive of him not to realise how her need for the hateful glasses distressed her.

She sighed. Oliver thought she had gone to Exeter. 'Well, it's his fault,' she said defiantly, and moved back to her seat in the middle of the room. He could be so pigheaded. What difference did it make to him if she saw her father twice a month rather than the once to which he had agreed? Perhaps if she gave him the son and heir he so longed for he might relent altogether.

'Bloody women! Stupid sheep!'

'Papa!' She was hurtling across the room towards the father she adored, all guilt about her husband forgotten. 'You are so late.'

He hugged her. She loved the smell of him, a heady mixture of sandalwood, pomade and cigar smoke – it made her feel safe, and no one else in the whole world smelt as he did. 'Always such a lovely welcome you give me, dear daughter.'

'Because I'm always so happy to see you.'

He turned her head slightly to the light. 'You look pale, my sweet.'

'It's just the heat.'

'You must take care of yourself else …' He did not finish the sentence.

'Else I won't make you a grandpapa. Is that what you were going to say?'

'No, as a matter of fact I wasn't. I would never speak of such a delicate matter with you. But I often wonder …' another unfinished sentence.

'What?'

'Whose fault …'

'What fault?'

'Nothing, my darling.'

'Why were you so late?'

'Blame the suffragettes. If I had my way they'd be flung into jail and horsewhipped.'

'Silly, Papa, you don't mean that.'

'I most certainly do. If they cause a breach of the peace, I hope they come up in front of my Bench. I'd force-feed the damn lot of them.'

'You'd never hurt a lady.' Conveniently she had forgotten, or rather told herself she had forgotten, how he had attacked her when she had insisted on marrying Oliver.

'I wouldn't call them ladies.'

'Hannah Cresswell is among them.'

'So?'

He was steely-eyed now and Esmeralda wished she hadn't mentioned the name. 'And Lady Prestwick would have liked to join them.'

'Which only proves my point. She is certainly no lady.'

'Perhaps not by breeding but she behaves like one and she has such deep sensibilities about all manner of things.'

'Tush! Have I simply come here to argue with you about a group of foolish women? They need husbands, that's their problem. Ah, the champagne.' A waiter had arrived.

'Oliver agrees with you,' she said once they were alone.

'Then perhaps I shall have to consider where I stand on this issue. It would never do for me to agree with your husband!'

She was chilled by his cold tone, then saw that he was laughing. 'Oh, you monster, you're teasing me!' And she kissed him: at least he could joke now about the impossible position in which he and Oliver placed her.

Hannah Cresswell felt stupid, which she often did. It always made her fret. All her meticulous planning for the demonstration had gone wrong. Even the weather had conspired against them. It had been overcast and chilly this morning, so she had donned her navy blue gabardine suit. Now she could feel sweat trickling down her back and soaking the shields she had carefully placed in her armpits to protect her favourite white linen blouse. She feared she might smell – a horror that was always with her because she had such a sensitive nose and presumed everyone else did. She was always wary of dousing herself with perfume, as her sister-in-law, Coral did, for fear that people might think she was covering up one smell with another – that was what old Nanny Wishart used to say.

'The lack of organisation was diabolical.' Clad in ivory linen and not in the least dishevelled, Agnes Beatty stabbed her parasol on the pavement, venting her annoyance.

Not now, please. Just for once, Agnes, keep your opinions to yourself, Hannah thought, and had to look about guiltily to be sure that she had not actually said the words. She was lagging behind now, trying to straighten her hat, which had been knocked askew in the mêleé. She tripped on the uneven paving and, as she grabbed at a railing to steady herself, was glad that Agnes had not noticed. If she had, Hannah would have felt even more stupid than she did already. Her dark hair had escaped from its customary bun and tendrils were floating about as if enjoying their new-found freedom.

'You look a frightful mess.' Agnes had turned and was looking her up and down with the expression that made Hannah feel as if she was ten years old instead of fifty-two next birthday.

'I'm fully aware that I do.' She winced as she grazed her scalp with the sharp point of her hatpin. She stood still, placed her large, cumbersome tapestry bag on the flagstones, and attempted to tame her hair and hat. That done, she had to run to catch up with her companion. But not fast enough – Agnes had already turned again to find she wasn't with her.

'Did you want me to appear as stupid as you? I've been talking to myself. Heaven only knows what passers-by must have thought of me.'

'Sorry.' But Hannah was grinning.

'And what is there to be amused about?'

'When that happens to me I always find it funny.'

'Well, I don't.' Agnes had set off again purposefully. Hannah poked out her tongue at the ramrod straight back, then giggled. How undignified, she thought. But Agnes provoked her so, with her conviction that she was always right and Hannah always wrong.

'I don't like to be humiliated.'

'I doubt anyone would dare try to.' Hannah murmured, under her breath.

'What did you say?'

'Nothing.'

'Don't be childish. Of course you did and I demand to know what it was.'

'Oh, for goodness' sake, Agnes, you're making such a fuss.' Hannah felt almost triumphant at the irritation she was sure had registered in her voice.

'I don't want anyone to think I'm an imbecile.' It was not the response that Hannah had expected.

They carried on at a cracking pace. Hannah was conscious that, as usual, she walked a few steps behind as she had seen native women in photographs follow their husbands. Perhaps people thought she did it out of deference, but the truth was that she liked to look at everything about her, unlike Agnes.

It was inconsiderate of Agnes to walk so fast today when she must be aware of how hot and uncomfortable Hannah felt. She was such a bully, Hannah thought. But was not she herself at fault for allowing it? How did one stop a tyrant? Gracious! What a strong word. But that was what Agnes was. People observing them would think that Agnes was the mistress of the house and Hannah her impecunious companion, rather than the other way round.

In the past ten years Agnes had stormed off more than five times after an argument – or, at least, when Hannah had stood her ground and refused to do whatever Agnes had wanted. Three times Hannah had begged her to return and twice Agnes had reappeared of her own accord – without apology.

Those had been her chances to be rid of the woman, and she had failed each time – for fear of loneliness. And, of course, there was Agnes's lack of money: Hannah was kind and would never willingly expose anyone to discomfort; without her help, Agnes's life would be hard.

There was another, darker reason why she didn't ask Agnes to leave: the threat of blackmail. Agnes had never blatantly threatened her, but she had hinted at it. And if she did not have such a plan, why, when she was dependent on Hannah, did she risk being so difficult? Hannah knew she would never be entirely happy while Agnes was with her. Not that she expected constant happiness – that was a fool's dream – but she'd like to be happy sometimes. It was only when she was away from Agnes that she was relaxed and content.

When Hannah thought of the things they had done to each other in the early days, she blushed. Fortunately *that* had died away. There were times when she wondered if Agnes had seduced her only to have a hold over her, for their lovemaking had lasted barely a year. While Hannah had taken pleasure in it, she had known deep in her heart that it was not what she really wanted. But at the time she had decided that sometimes one had to accept second best to assuage loneliness.

'Where are you going?' Agnes asked, as Hannah turned right off the high street.

'I'm going to the police station to see if there is anything I can do for Mrs Petty. I feel responsible for her.'

'That is most unwise. Such places are not for us.'

'Or for Mrs Petty. A more respectable woman it would be hard to find.'

'You choose the most unfortunate companions. To refer to someone such as she as respectable – well, really, Hannah! Have you lost your wits?' Agnes looked insufferably superior, and Hannah felt a surge of fury.

'It was you who started the altercation,' Agnes went on. 'Had Fanny Petty not come to your rescue it would be you languishing in a cell. So, her fate is your fault.'

'Which is why it is my duty to go and see her.'

'Leave well alone is my advice.'

'As you keep saying. But I can't.'

'You didn't ask her to knock off the constable's helmet. She behaved in a most reprehensible manner.'

'We all did, so we should be treated in the same way.'

'You screaming at the constabulary to get off the flowerbeds hardly helped. It caused the whole meeting to descend into anarchy.'

'It had taken the gardeners hours of painstaking work to plant Barlton's civic crest in that way. As a gardener I could not stand by and watch the policemen ruin it.'

'It was a miracle you weren't arrested.'

'I wish I had been. Then I could look the others in the face. And why do you always judge me so harshly?'

'I? Judge you? What nonsense.'

The anger swelled. 'At least I did something! Unlike you!'

'Well, really!'

'Just for once I would be grateful if you would stop criticising me. I find it most irksome.' Without looking at Agnes, she set off along Painters' Row. There was a spring in her step and she felt unusually elated.

'What does that mean?' Agnes caught up with her.

Hannah stopped dead and faced her. 'It means that you're very good at telling others what to do while doing nothing yourself.' *Where* was she getting the courage from? Hannah wondered. The events of the day must have fuelled her spirit.

'That is an unkind thing to say. I have been a stalwart of the chapter.'

'In giving orders to the rest of us.' She felt quite drunk with new-found pluck.

'Well, really! I shall go home. Immediately. You do as you wish.'

'Then you'll have to take the bus. I've told Alf to meet me at the railway station in two hours.' She felt triumphant at the look of annoyance on Agnes's face. 'Excuse me, I've matters to attend to.' And with that Hannah continued resolutely on her way.

The bag, still full of pamphlets that she had not distributed, weighed heavy and her arm ached. She shifted it to her left hand. Arguing with Agnes had been silly: now a bad day would become worse. But the woman's smugness had goaded her into it, she told herself.

She was in Gold Street already, she saw with a start. That was what thinking did for one – it made one unaware of where one was. Ten years ago when Agnes, thrown out by the unspeakable von Ehrlich, had first come to live with her it had all been so different. Then Agnes had been her wise soulmate – she had not been able to do enough for her when Hannah had been at her lowest, grieving for her father; now she wondered if she would have survived without Agnes's help. She often tried to pinpoint when Agnes had changed. Perhaps it had started on that day when Hannah had admired a man. Certainly her comments on his handsomeness – he had been a stranger in a tea-room in which they had been sitting – had made Agnes snap and descend into a sulk that she had only shaken off when Hannah purchased her an aquamarine brooch she had admired in a jeweller's window.

She leant against the wall to allow a woman with a perambulator to pass her. Such a pretty baby, she thought.

Despite Agnes's disapproval she knew she looked at men with interest and, if she was honest, still longed for one to love her, even if it was too late now for children. Just to be held and cuddled in the depths of the night …

She was opposite Dulcie Prestwick's hotel, the Victoria, and the entrance to the park where the demonstration had unfurled. They hadn't meant to disrupt the mayor's ceremonial opening of the bandstand – or, at least, not to the extent that the band had fled in terror from the placard-waving women. She laughed at the memory of the man with the large bass drum falling, then being run over by his instrument, which had rolled down the hill and into the lake and startled the swans.

'Coo-eee.'

Hannah looked across to the hotel. Dulcie was manoeuvring herself down the marble steps, hanging on to the shiny brass handrail. She really should lose some weight, Hannah thought. It couldn't possibly be healthy for her to be so heavy and it made walking so difficult. Hannah glanced away, and glimpsed her sister-in-law in an upstairs window. She waved. The figure moved behind a curtain and Hannah thought she saw a man behind her. 'Oh, no!'

'Oh, no, what?' Dulcie was beside her.

'I've left my purse at home,' Hannah lied.

'I have plenty of money.' Dulcie patted her bag. 'I suspect you're on the same mission as I.'

'I must do something for Mrs Petty and the others.'

'How many were arrested?'

'Twelve. Everything became somewhat wild.'

'The mayor and lady mayoress came into the hotel for a restorative drink. They were very angry. I found it hard to keep a straight face.'

'I offered to pay for the damage.'

'That was good of you.'

'I felt it was my fault. I was trying to protect the flowerbeds.'

Dulcie laughed. 'How typical of you, dear Hannah. And where is Miss Beatty?'

'In a huff with me.'

'Sometimes, Hannah, I think you have the patience of a dozen saints where that woman is concerned.'

'She can be a little dogmatic.' She blushed at her disloyalty. 'I think I saw Esmeralda upstairs?' She could not bring herself to mention the man.

'You were mistaken, Hannah dear.' As Dulcie spoke, she was fiddling with her bag, her gloves, her collar, her brooch. Hannah wished she could believe her, but Dulcie's agitation belied her words.

'You chose not to return your Sapphic sister-in-law's wave?' Stanislas von Ehrlich was delighted that Hannah must have seen him – in fact, he had made certain she did.

'I didn't want her to see me. You must understand why.'

'I can't think of anything more normal than that a daughter should wish to spend time with her father.'

'Oh, Papa, she mustn't know we meet as often as we do. If only …' Her voice trailed off.

'*If only* what? If only I would make friends with your husband?'

She did not answer. Her father was playing games with her, she knew. There had been a time when she had dared to believe he meant it when he suggested such things, but not now. 'What does Sapphic mean?' she asked.

Stanislas laughed. 'If you don't know I don't think it is proper that I should tell you.'

'If it is an improper word, perhaps you should not have used it.' She smiled sweetly at him, pleased that for once she had got the better of him. Her father laughed again and spilt some of his champagne.

'You are looking tired, my dove,' he said, as he dabbed at his trousers.

'I can't think why – I don't feel tired.'

He felt in his inside pocket and produced a brown envelope, which he placed on the tea table between them. 'Thank you,' she said simply.

'You never seem overjoyed with my presents to you.'

'Because I feel such guilt in accepting them. It is a betrayal of my husband.'

'If he keeps you short of money then he is the cause of the deception.'

'He does not. I have everything I need.'

'But not sufficient for you to be kept in the fashion I desire for you. Which, my dearest, is what you want too.'

Esmeralda blushed. She knew she was vain, and loved the best of everything. The money Oliver gave her did not cover half of her dressmaker's bills. It was lucky that he, like most men, had no idea what her wardrobe cost. 'I like pretty things.'

'And you shall continue to have them. But you didn't answer when I said you looked tired. Are you ailing?'

'No.' It was not strictly true. 'But I have been a little out of sorts lately. I've been thinking of going to Buxton for a treatment.'

'Why Buxton? Are you rheumatic?'

She laughed at the idea. 'Not in the least.'

'Why not Baden-Baden?'

'I like Buxton.' She blushed. She could not bring herself to tell him that her friend Sylvia Hornwell had conceived a child after she had taken the waters there. She could never discuss such matters with her father – or her husband.

'You go alone?'

'Oliver will be too busy to accompany me.'

'How sad.'

She didn't respond. She knew he was trying to provoke her.

3

'Such a frightening place.' Dulcie Prestwick shifted her weight on the hard wooden chair, searching for comfort. It was unlikely that she would find it for the chair was hard and the seat narrow.

Dulcie and Hannah were in a waiting room at Barlton police station. The desk sergeant, an acquaintance, had welcomed them warmly and offered tea while they waited for the inspector. He had ushered them into this room. 'You'll be better off in here, ladies, away from the *hoi polloi*.' He had smiled proudly at his use of the expression: he was a regular visitor of the library Dulcie had founded.

'You are too kind, Sergeant Milton. How are your wife and children?'

'Doing nicely, Lady Prestwick, and I'm proud to say another on the way.'

'Congratulations, Sergeant.' She waited until the door had closed behind him to add, 'These men! Such inconsiderate, selfish creatures. That will be the sixth or perhaps the seventh, and his wife is a frail little creature. It makes me so angry.'

'But, then, if babies come ...'

'The man should have more self-control and, if not, he should take measures to protect his wife.'

Hannah felt herself blushing at the turn in the conversation. Dulcie was a dear soul but sometimes, without warning, she reverted to her outspoken lower-class ways, which was always embarrassing.

'I often wonder if I shouldn't instigate a learning programme for them,' Dulcie went on.

'Would anyone attend?' Hannah could not think of anything more awful than talking about such matters, especially to strangers.

'The women would.'

They lapsed into silence. Hannah looked askance at the tea in thick china cups on chipped saucers.

'Be grateful for the saucer, Hannah, my dear.' Dulcie smiled.

Hannah studied the depressing green paint on the upper walls. 'It's another world, isn't it?' She consulted her watch. They'd been here half an hour already.

'Those need a good scrub,' Dulcie said, indicating the yellowish tiles below the paint.

'At least the windows are not barred.' Hannah pulled her coat round her. The room, despite the heat of the day, was chilly.

'Not in here perhaps but they will be elsewhere.' Dulcie shifted again on her chair. 'That it should have come to this.'

'Everything happened so fast. And I had never expected to see our police so violent.'

'But you've been on demonstrations before that became unpleasant for our friends. Don't you remember how brutal it all was when Mrs Pankhurst was arrested?'

'But that wasn't here. I had never expected to see such ferocity in dear old Barlton. Why, I've known the constable who arrested Mrs Petty since he was a small boy.'

'Small boys have a habit of turning into large men.' Dulcie smiled.

'And although I have witnessed violence I was never involved in it. I've always been such a coward.'

'My dear Hannah. I've always regarded you as a woman of courage.'

'Then I've misled you. I'm always afraid.'

'It takes pluck to join a demonstration, especially when you are fearful.'

Hannah twisted her fingers in her lap. Eventually Dulcie took one of the restless hands.

'I feel it's all my fault,' Hannah said.

'What nonsense. Those women went of their own free will, because they wanted to.'

'Agnes said it was my fault.' There was a catch in Hannah's voice. 'She considers that I incited Fanny Petty to attack the policeman, and caused the meeting to disintegrate. But, Dulcie, I was only trying to protect the flowers.'

'Miss Beatty likes to blame others. Never, of course, herself.'

'Oh, she didn't do anything.'

'Did she not? She was at the demonstration, which means she was in part responsible too.'

'Do you know what dear Fanny said to me? That if anyone was going to be in trouble it was better that it was one of her sort rather than me. Wasn't that too sweet of her?'

'Far too sweet. Why should she suffer for others?'

'That was what I thought.' This was not strictly the truth. Hannah had been relieved that Fanny had been arrested rather than herself. She feared she would crumble at the sight of a cell. Fanny had a strength that she lacked, Hannah thought. Now she knew she would torture herself over her failings – and Agnes would make sure she did. 'Had I known—'

She stopped. A woman had screamed – a bloodcurdling sound that echoed and was magnified as it bounced off the tiled walls. In the distance a door slammed. They heard the pounding of heavy boots on concrete floors. 'Dulcie, you don't think ...'

'Probably not, my dear. I'm sure there are other *guests* of the constabulary here.'

'I wish I had never been involved.'

'But you did right. Have we not discussed the question many times over the years?'

'But always in such a civilised way. To think that any of us could be reduced to such ranting! I was ashamed of the spectacle we made of ourselves.' She shuddered at the memory. The door opened abruptly.

'*Lady* Prestwick, I'm so sorry to keep you waiting. It's been a busy day. Miss ...' A uniformed inspector, portly, red-faced and finely whiskered entered the room, acknowledging Hannah with a nod. A woman with a large bunch of keys swinging from her waistband followed him. She had a coarse, pockmarked face, and was certainly not the type of person Hannah would have cared to cross. He took a seat and the woman stood behind him, as if she was guarding him. He placed his hands on the table in front of him.

'And you are? I have not had the pleasure ...' Dulcie asked.

'Inspector Steedman, at your service. *Lady* Prestwick.'

Hannah did not like the way he addressed Dulcie, emphasising her title. It was almost as though he was sneering at her. Perhaps he had been told of Dulcie's modest past and that she had married well. To Hannah, Dulcie's origins were irrelevant.

'You must be newly arrived here,' Dulcie went on.

'That is most certainly the case, *Lady* Prestwick.'

'And where were you before?'

'Here and there.' He looked uncomfortable, and Hannah wondered if he had done something wrong where he had previously been. He coughed. She noticed that crumbs nestled in his moustache, which made him seem less fierce.

'And what can I do for you this fine day?' he enquired.

'We were concerned for some friends of ours, Inspector. They have been taken into custody here ... to be charged,' Dulcie whispered, as if afraid to being overheard.

'Friends of yours, *Lady* Prestwick? Well, well, well. You do surprise me.'

'I'm sorry?'

'I wouldn't have expected a *lady* of your standing to be involved with riffraff like that.'

'Officer!'

'You may not like my choice of words, *Lady* Prestwick, but riffraff and no better than they ought to be.'

'You know, Inspector *Studman* ...'

'Steedman, *Lady* Prestwick.'

'So silly of me, Inspector. But I'm never sure what that expression means. Are you?' Dulcie bestowed a sweet smile upon him, which evidently confused the policeman for he coughed again.

'Inspector Steedman. You speak of our friends.' Hannah felt she should contribute.

'Not something I'd be boasting about if I was you, Miss ...' He looked at her questioningly.

'How remiss of me, Inspector *Stedman*. This is Miss Cresswell, the sister of Sir Mortimer, whom I'm sure you know.'

'I fear I have not had that pleasure. You were saying, Miss Cresswell?'

'I'm sorry, Inspector, but I don't like your tone.'

'Hannah,' Dulcie said, with a warning inflection.

'And what do you intend to do about it?' he asked.

'I shall report you to your superiors. Those women have been un-necessarily detained and, if charged, wrongly so.'

'Cresswell. Now, that name rings a bell.' He tapped his head with a wide fat finger, grinning unpleasantly. 'Would you say this was the lady we were looking for, Miss Rowntree?'

The woman with the keys walked up to Hannah and pushed her face towards her. Hannah reeled back from the fetid breath that issued forth. 'Yes, Inspector, no doubt of it.'

'What do you mean?' Hannah's stomach clenched with fear.

'Miss Rowntree was attacked in the park by a madwoman who bit her arm. Show her your arm, Miss Rowntree.'

The woman rolled back her sleeve to show toothmarks.

'And kicked her viciously in the shins.'

'I'm sorry if that was so, but it had nothing to do with me.'

'But Miss Rowntree says differently, don't you?'

'That's her. That's the one what did it. That's the one what was urging them on.'

'I never did any such thing!' Hannah was on her feet. The chair she had been sitting on clattered to the floor.

'Not, so fast, Miss Cresswell. There's the matter of your caution …'

4

Lettice Hamilton sat on a window-seat in the drawing room at Cresswell Manor, her childhood home. Here, she could make the most of the late-afternoon light, which flooded in through the long casement windows as she worked on an intricate piece of petit-point depicting her husband's coat-of-arms. It wasn't that she enjoyed sewing, but it concentrated her mind so that she didn't have to think of other things. And this embroidery would please Hugo, she hoped, since little she did managed to do so.

She looked out of the window at the view she had known all her life and which she longed for when she was at her husband's house. She never thought of it as her home. This was home and always would be – not that she would confess it to a living soul for fear it might reach Hugo's ears.

The gardens below were a riot of colour, thanks mainly to Aunt Hannah. Lettice's mother, Coral, had no enthusiasm for horticulture. Her interests were restricted to fashion and gossip. Lettice could consider her mother dispassionately since she rarely thought of her in that role.

Coral had shown scant interest in Lettice and her elder brother when they were children, and not much more now that they were adults. When Lettice had had children of her own, her mother's attitude to her own had mystified her: Lettice would have given her life for Charlotte and Georgina, while her own mother would never have countenanced such a notion. Yet Coral adored her youngest child, Felix, on whom she lavished love and attention. Lettice did not resent this; she was glad that, finally, her mother had found love for one of her children.

Aunt Hannah and old Nanny Wishart had cared for Lettice and her brother, Young Mortimer, throughout their childhood, and it was to her aunt that Lettice had always turned because her mother was rarely at home. To Lettice and Young Mortimer, Hannah was their loving aunt although her mother and grandmother were at pains to tell them, even now, that she was a *half*-aunt only – as if that might make her less important to their lives. They were constantly told that Hannah's mother, their grandfather's first wife, had died, as if this was some sin and made her a lesser person. If anything, this had made them love her more. They knew she loved them.

Lettice's parents were happiest pursuing their life in London and visiting friends in their country homes. Their routine never varied: they went to the Durhams for one week, the Fitzwilliams another, then Derbyshire, Lancashire, London for the season, and Scotland in August. Then they started at the beginning again. They knew where they would be, when, and with whom, for the rest of their lives. Only illness altered their round of entertaining and being entertained, which was why they were here now in August. Lettice's grandmother had been taken ill.

Penelope Cresswell was someone else Lettice did not much care for. She felt guilty that she could not love her grandmother, but she had been afraid of her for too long to change now. It had been a relief when, as an adult, she had discovered that she was not alone, that no one was fond of Penelope. Guilt was such an awkward emotion. She finished with the red silk, tied it off neatly and, with her small silver scissors, cut her needle free.

She opened her sewing box and dithered over which part of the crest to move on to. She loved looking at the glorious colours of her silks, neatly laid out in the padded box. She selected one of cobalt blue, threaded her needle again and began to sew.

It had always puzzled her why anyone should be so unpleasant. A few years back it had occurred to her that her grandmother enjoyed being disliked and arousing fear in others. Why else make the cutting remarks that could spoil a day, destroy hard-found self-confidence? As Lettice had matured, she had wondered if Penelope was like this because of some deep sadness then rejected the idea: Lettice had cause to be melancholic yet she would never hurt anyone.

It was sad in a way that Penelope hadn't grasped that, for several years, no one had been scared of her; they regarded her now as a silly old woman. Lettice had observed the maids giggling and pulling faces behind her grandmother's back. Not that she had let them know she had seen – after all, why should she be cross when they were only doing what she had longed to do when she was young?

The door opened and her brothers, Felix and Morts, peered in.

'The coast is clear,' Lettice said, with laughter in her voice.

'God, I'm bored.' Felix, barely fifteen, flopped on to the sofa.

'I bore myself,' his brother admonished him, and was rewarded by a well-aimed cushion flying through the air. He grabbed it and threw it back.

'Stop it, both of you. You're behaving like stable-boys. You'll break something and then we'll all be in trouble.' But she was laughing.

'Wish I *was* a stable lad,' Felix said, with an exaggerated sigh.

'So that you could whistle?'

'Something like that.' Felix grinned.

'No, Lettice, he would like to smoke, drink himself senseless – and worse.'

'I thought he did that already.'

Lettice loved both brothers but Morts was her favourite. When he was younger he was called Young Mortimer but now that he was in his twenties everyone agreed that 'Morts' was more suitable. He was only two years older than her while Felix was nearly twelve years younger – almost from another generation.

The brothers were as difference as chalk and cheese. Morts was serious about everything and Felix the opposite. The elder brother had sailed through school and university, insisted on making his own way in the world and was a successful stockbroker – not that their mother cared to admit it: respectable as the profession was, she felt it was too close for comfort to trade. Felix had to be dragged to his books, and if he ever showed any intention to work Lettice was sure she would faint.

Morts was kind, thoughtful and sensitive, qualities not shared by her younger brother. It was just as well that Morts would inherit everything – Felix would ruin it all, given half a chance.

'How is Grandmama?'

'Haven't you seen her today, Felix?'

'He's only been up a couple of hours. Lazy goat.'

'Felix, you shouldn't waste your life. You're sleeping it away.'

'Not you as well!' Felix got up and banged out of the room.

'I worry about him.' Lettice laid aside her embroidery.

'Who and what don't you worry about?' Morts kissed the top of her head.

'Dear brother.' She put up her hand and took his. 'I wish I saw you more often.'

'I do too, but …' She knew he had stopped himself saying, '*you are married to Hugo Hamilton*'. 'I wish I could feel sorry for Grandmama, but I can't,' he said instead.

'I was thinking the same thing. It's so different from when Grandpapa Cresswell was dying. Do you remember?'

'It was as if life would never be the same again. And, in a way, it wasn't.'

'We loved him … And we don't love her. But we shouldn't be talking like this, should we?'

'Is it surprising? She has sneered at everything either of us has ever done, made us feel failures.'

'Only Felix will be sorry.'

'Felix!' Morts laughed. 'He probably won't notice.'

'You're hard on him.'

'With reason. He's clever and never uses his brain. He's good on a horse and with a gun, but never has the energy to do either. I fear he will never work – and who will have to support him and any wife he chooses? I, of course.'

'You'll do it willingly.'

'Don't be so sure.'

He watched as Lettice folded away her work. 'That's a fine thing you're making.'

'It's for Hugo's birthday, if I finish it in time.'

'Is he coming here?'

'I doubt it. You know how he feels about family gatherings.'

'Good.'

'Darling, don't say that.'

'It's how I feel.'

'But it puts me in a difficult position.'

'Have you ever thought that it might do you good to moan about him with someone you can trust?'

Lettice longed to unburden herself, to tell of the bullying, the unkindness, but loyalty won.

'It's tragic, really, isn't it? You are so miserable with Hugo and I wasn't allowed to be idyllically happy with Clemmie.'

'Oh, Morts, don't.' Tears pricked her eyes as he spoke of his wife, who had died two years ago, giving birth to their son, who had also died. At the time she had feared for her brother's sanity – his grief had overwhelmed him.

'It will never get better, only easier to manage.' His voice was thick with emotion. 'I can talk about her now, at least, and enjoy it. You see, Lettice, if we don't talk about her then she's really gone from our hearts and that would never do.'

'She was such a dear, sweet creature and the perfect wife for you.' She squeezed his hand tight.

The butler entered the room. 'Yes, Whitaker?' Morts said.

'There's a *person* here insists she sees Sir Mortimer.'

Lettice hid a smile. Only Whitaker could imbue the word with such disdain.

'Then you'd better find him.'

'I've looked everywhere without success, sir.'

'Gracious, Whitaker! Have we lost Papa?' Lettice said. Her father had hidden so that he could sleep undisturbed – it was hardly surprising that Felix was the same. 'What about my mother?'

'Lady Cresswell is unwell and cannot be disturbed.'

'Who is this person?'

'The daughter of an employee who no longer works here. I gather he's now potman at the Cresswell Arms.'

'Show her in, then, Whitaker. We'll deal with it.' Morts waited for the butler to leave. 'Do you know where Papa is?'

'The old nursery. It's one of his favourite places. He told me where he would be in case there's a change in Grandmama's condition.'

'Cunning of him. How long can you stay, Lettice?'

'I shall remain here until I'm no longer needed.'

'Won't Hugo want you back?'

'He understands,' she said, although she doubted that he did.

Morts did not respond for the butler had returned – with a most beautiful young girl. Morts's mouth hung open.

'I'm sorry to bother you, but I didn't know who else to turn to,' the girl said, with a worried frown.

'Would you *mind*? I have not introduced you. Manners!' Whitaker said to her sternly.

'It's no bother, Miss … ?' Morts, Lettice saw, was staring at the girl as if he were bewitched.

'Might I introduce Rowan Marshall, sir? Rowan, this is Mrs Hamilton, and this is Mr Mortimer Cresswell.'

She stepped forward and shook their hands, which took them and the butler aback.

23

'How do you do?' She had a lovely voice, soft, and heavy with the local accent. She was obviously a serving girl, thought Lettice, for her clothes were stained and of poor quality. The same could not be said of the curly blonde hair, the perfect creamy complexion, the wide crystal-clear blue eyes and the red lips.

'How can we help you?'

'I was sent to Mr Oliver's with a message, but he wasn't there and no one knew when he would be back so I thought I'd best come here to see Sir Mortimer.'

'He's not available, I'm afraid. Perhaps you could talk to us?'

'It might be all right,' she said uncertainly.

'Of course it will, you silly girl. Mr Morts is his son.' Whitaker had lost his customary imperturbable patience.

'It's your aunt, Miss Hannah Cresswell. She's gone and got herself arrested. She's in the clink.'

Five minutes later, Rowan, Hannah, Morts and Whitaker were standing in the nursery in front of Sir Mortimer – Mortie to his family and friends. He had paused on the point of ramming a scone, with jam and clotted cream, into his mouth to study the young woman.

'I tried to take the message, Sir Mortimer, so that none of you were disturbed, but the young woman was insistent.' Whitaker was agitated.

'Quite so, Whitaker. Well, girl, has the cat got your tongue? Explain.' Mortie turned his attention to Rowan.

'I was told to speak to Mr Oliver personally – no one else. But since I couldn't I talked to your son.'

'Of course. And you are?'

'Rowan Marshall, sir. My mother cooks for Mrs Joynston down at the pub and my dad sometimes drives Miss Hannah.'

'Is it your mother who makes the steak and oyster pie?' Mortie's piggy eyes gleamed with interest.

'It is, sir.'

'Who told you of my sister's predicament?'

'Lady Prestwick told Mrs Joynston and she told me as I was to tell you that Miss Hannah was locked up.'

There was a flurry at the door as Coral sailed in. Whatever had ailed her had disappeared for she looked in the pink of health.

'Mortie, what is happening? Who on earth is this?'

'Rowan, milady.' She gave a little bob.

'Is it true what I hear?' There was a tinge of hysteria in Coral's voice.

'Who told you?' Mortie asked.

'All of the servants are gossiping.'

'It weren't me. I didn't tell no one anything,' Rowan put in.

Mortie answered his wife's question: 'It appears to be the case.'

'We can't keep this from your mother, Mortie. So, girl, tell me, what has occurred?'

'It's Miss Cresswell, milady. She threw a policeman into the fountain, bit another and knocked the helmet off a third.' Rowan clapped a hand over her mouth, as if to suppress a giggle.

'Control yourself!' Whitaker admonished her.

'Feed her, Whitaker. Send a message to my brother.' The normally indolent Mortie was on his feet now, waving his napkin with agitation. He began to pace the floor. 'That Beatty woman is behind this, mark my words,' he thundered.

'The shame of it! Has she no consideration for others?' Coral screeched. 'Think of poor Lettice.'

'Why? She's not in prison too.'

'Don't be stupid, Mortie. What good will it do the family if Lettice's aunt is incarcerated in Barlton jail?'

'Quite so. Silly woman.'

'We can't stay here, that's for sure. We must return to Scotland.'

'But why?'

'The shame, Mortie! I can't survive it – I shall be ill.' She sank into a chair to rock back and forth.

And what would Hugo have to say? Lettice wondered. No doubt he would insist that she left too – but she wouldn't, she told herself.

5

Dolly Topsham, short, fair and attractive, was a blur of movement as she always was at six in the morning. 'Where's your book satchel? How many times do I have to tell you?'

'Sorry, Mum. I know I should get it ready in the evening.' Apollo grinned up at her. Her son's dark eyes, with the long lashes that girls envied, were full of mischief. Dolly fought back the grin that was twitching at the corners of her mouth. Try as she might, she could never stay cross with her first-born who, at ten, was showing signs of the handsome, charming man he would become.

'Then why don't you?' As she spoke Dolly was brushing her daughter Cordelia's hair. Dolly had chosen her children's names: since hers was so simple, she had been determined that her offspring, like her husband Zephaniah, should glory in uncommon ones. However, Apollo had soon become Pol, and Cordelia was always called Del. Such a pity. Dolly was the only person who used their full names but only when she was cross with them.

Their names had always caused comment, but so, too, did their colouring: Apollo was dark and Cordelia was blonde and blue-eyed so no one could believe they were brother and sister. Dolly had weathered the gossip: she knew that Zeph was their father, as he did, and no one else mattered in her world.

'Do I have to go?' Cordelia grumbled.

'Yes.'

'You're hurting me.'

'Then you should brush it yourself. At eight years old you're quite capable of it.' She heard her annoyance in her voice. She was rarely angry with her son but she was frequently so with Cordelia. Dolly was sure the child went out of her way to be irritating. Not that she loved her any less … Dolly paused, brush in the air. That wasn't true. Shame made her pull Cordelia's hair harder and her daughter yelped. 'Sorry,' she said. She loved Apollo most – she knew she shouldn't but at least her husband favoured Cordelia. They had never discussed it. Their emotions were not the sort of subject she and Zeph talked about.

She finished Cordelia's hair, then cut doorsteps of fresh bread, baked that morning, and covered them liberally with the beef dripping of which she always kept a bowl in the meat safe. She cut the bread into squares and pushed the plates towards the children, then poured milk into two white tin mugs; the blue enamel rims were badly chipped.

'Be quick,' she ordered. She turned to the washing-up in the sink, scattered soda crystals over it and added water from the kettle, which was boiling on the hob. She turned off the gas, an expensive luxury at which she still marvelled even after a year in the house. Zeph often talked, too wistfully for comfort, of moving back to the countryside; Dolly could think of nothing worse. When she had left Cresswell she could have danced with glee. Life on the estate had been so dull that gossip was the main entertainment. It eddied and flowed about the cottages like a malevolent miasma.

She swished the soda suds around, left the plates to soak and ran up the stairs to make the beds. Small though the house was, the children each had a room – a matter of pride to her. When she had lived with her parents she and her siblings had only been able to dream of privacy. They had been squashed into two rooms, five in one, three in the other, in the small damp cottage that had been included in her father's wage for working as boilerman at Cresswell Manor. And what had happened when he'd hurt his back? Been shoved out, that was what. There was such injustice in the world.

From the cupboard on the landing she collected a clean pillow-slip. Cordelia's ear had been weeping again – she'd take her to the doctor this evening. That was something else she could afford and her parents couldn't. It had all been different in old Sir Mortimer's day: he'd have made sure that Sol, her father, had seen the local doctor and he would never have thrown them out – but his son was different. He took no interest in the estate or what happened to the people who worked for him. It was her father's bad luck that in slipping on a lump of coke he had hurt himself so badly he could barely stand now.

It was bad luck, too, that Sir Mortie's younger brother, Oliver, who normally managed the estate, had been away at the time. When he'd returned, he'd tried to put things right for them: he had offered them a cottage on his land, but Sol Pepper had his pride and, despite his wife's pleas, had told him where he could put it. Dolly knew she would never again feel the same about the Cresswells – unlike her brother, also called Sol. He had taken over their father's job and the cottage! Dolly had vowed never to speak to him again, and she hadn't, not even at their father's funeral two years ago. She couldn't countenance such disloyalty.

She patted the pillows straight and covered the bed with the counterpane she had crocheted. Had it not been for Zeph's mother, Melanie, they would all have ended up in Queer Street. She was a good woman, Melanie Joynston. A sad one too. Her first husband had been a drunkard who beat her mercilessly. He'd been murdered, over ten years ago by Melanie's brother, rumour had it. It was one of those tales that wouldn't go away, and Dolly felt sorry for Zeph and Melanie whenever it was resurrected. Her own father had been a witness to the crime, which was deemed an accident: once, in his cups, he'd burst into tears and told her he was destined for damnation, but he never said why and he never repeated it.

Dolly had only once, in the early days, mentioned it to Zeph, who had shouted at her for being a gossiping woman. But that didn't stop her thinking about it and wondering if his reaction had confirmed the rumours.

Now Melanie was married to another drunkard, but fortunately he didn't hit her. He was an educated man who, as far as she could make out, did nothing. Dolly, who had had no education to speak of, thought it sinful that he did not use the chances in life he had been given, but Melanie never complained and worked hard in her inn, from morning to night. 'He helps me,' she would say, if Zeph mentioned it. Zeph loathed and despised the man as much as Dolly did.

Once the children's rooms were finished, Dolly had made her own bed and was now dusting the dressing-table, a recent acquisition of which she was particularly proud. She never dared mention Xenia, Zeph's twin sister, to him either. Whenever her name came up, a shuttered look appeared on his face and he would walk away or change the subject. Rumours had abounded about her too – that she was a kept woman, or worse. Dolly was consumed with curiosity and longed to meet her sister-in-law. All she knew for certain was that Xenia had left in a rage for London.

Of course, in the circumstances, Dolly could feel sorry for her and for Zeph. They were related to the Cresswells, but born on the wrong side of the blanket so it didn't count. It must be hard to see that family with all their riches and not have much yourself, she thought. Perhaps that was why Xenia had left.

It was Melanie who had offered Dolly's parents one of the many houses she owned in Cresswell-by-the-Sea – known to all as Cress. She had been left the Cresswell Arms by old Sir Mortimer – the gossip *that* had inspired! Many in the village had decided he must be the twins' father, but it wasn't so. His eldest son, Mortie, was, but Zeph had made Dolly promise never to tell, and she hadn't. No doubt it was the old man's way of settling the debt, and quite right too. But Melanie was a clever woman, and she had saved and bought more property as homes for her ever-increasing staff or to let.

Sol Pepper had been unable to work after his accident but Dolly had insisted that rent must be paid to Melanie and that she would pay it. When her father had died of cancer, she had continued to pay it for her mother. In some ways she was grateful to the accident – not, of course, that her father was hurt or that he was dead, but because it had given her the opportunity to work too.

When she had first married Zeph and had Apollo, she had wallowed in blissful idleness, but after Cordelia was born she had hankered for work and some money of her own. But she had married a proud man who did not want his wife to work. She had argued and pleaded because his

28

wage as a clerk to the local solicitor was not enough for a family of four to have any little treats but had been unable to sway him. He had only relented when she had insisted on working to pay her parents' rent. He understood her need to help. Without that, she would not have been the businesswoman she was today and they would not be living in this house with a bedroom for each child. She looked with satisfaction around her room, with its fine mahogany wardrobe and matching washstand. Curtains billowed at the window, the same colour as the eiderdown on the bed. She lived in style.

Back in the kitchen, she finished washing and drying the dishes and scoured the bowl. 'Everyone ready?' The chores done – the parlour could wait until her return – Dolly crammed a straw hat on to her head and ushered her children through the back door and down the path between the rows of vegetables Zeph tended. She closed the gate behind them and they made their way, Dolly shooing her children along the alley, across the road and down the hill. She pushed them in front of her to the doorway of a dilapidated large house and rang the bell.

'You're early, Mrs Topsham.' The shabby figure who opened the door smiled broadly at the children.

'I don't think we are, Mr Wilmot, but they're eager as always.' She prodded Apollo to make sure he was.

'In you come, fledglings. See you at noon, Mrs Topsham.' The door closed quickly, as if he wanted her gone. She never worried about the children when they were with Henry Wilmot and his wife Florence. She tripped down the steps. She'd had such a fight with Zeph to get them into the only private tutor in town.

'School is enough for them. You'll tire them out with all this education.'

'That's easy for you to say. You've had a good one, learnt a lot. We can't afford anything as fine as you had, but it's our duty to help them as much as we can.'

'What's the point in Del having extra tuition?'

'Because she's clever.' This was true, but more importantly Dolly would not have been able to do as much as she did during the school holidays if she had to worry about her daughter.

It always puzzled her why Zeph, with the advantages he'd had, shouldn't want the same for them. He had won a scholarship to Blundells at Tiverton – not that he'd done much with it, still stuck now in that solicitor's office in Barlton without advancement or any time to make his own way. He didn't seem to understand. Dolly had had to teach herself to read and write, never having paid much attention at school, and she was proud of her achievements, but she longed to know more. Her children would have the best.

She was hurrying along the lower end of Barlton now, down by the harbour. She liked this part of the town, with its bustle and noise. Not that she would want to live there. No, her aim was to be rich enough one day to move up on to the hill above the town where the best villas were. How this was to be achieved, when Zeph had so little ambition, she did not know.

He had changed so much in the years she had known him. He'd once been so full of life and curiosity. Often now she thought he was like a scarecrow who had had the stuffing knocked out of him. When they had been courting he was all for going in with his mother and forgetting the solicitor's but then something had happened to him. He had become bitter and, these days, was more often depressed than happy.

'That's what comes of shotgun weddings,' her elder sister Maud had said, with a sneer.

'Rubbish. He wanted to marry me as much as I wanted him.'

'If that's what you reckon, look at the sky and watch out for them pigs.'

'You're jealous, that's what,' Dolly had shouted. Maud and Dolly had never got on and Maud had been jealous when Dolly had got a position at the manor and she'd had to stay behind to help their mother with the younger ones.

'You hoped to get him yourself.'

'Me? With a bookworm? No, thank you. Give me a man with fire in his belly.'

'Like your *Cyril*?'

The argument had sallied back and forth until their mother had intervened. 'Takes two,' she'd said. 'He had his pleasure and now he can shoulder the consequences!' But Dolly had never forgiven her sister and had avoided her for years.

She frowned as she walked along. Maud had been too close to the truth for comfort, that was sure. The same thought had crossed her own mind. She had been tortured with guilt that she was the cause of his depression, that she and Apollo blighted any dreams he might have had.

Still, she couldn't regret having her son. And she had been punished. Marriage was not the bed of roses she had thought it as a girl. She loved her husband, but she had wondered for a long time if he loved her.

As always a cluster of familiar faces was waiting for her, and a woman she didn't recognise.

'Morning, ladies.'

'Morning, Mrs Topsham,' they chorused, as she fitted the key into the door of her office, bent down to pick up the post on the doormat and let them in.

'Kettle, first,' she said, filling it from the tap that hung precariously over the tiny sink in the back room. There was no gas hob here but she had a Primus stove. She lit it gingerly, never sure if it might blow up in her face. 'Now,' she bustled back, 'I've only three jobs today. Who was here first?'

'I was.' A small, slim woman with a desperate expression, whom Dolly had not seen before, held up her hand.

'You never was, it were me.' Ida Flower, a large woman with a matching voice, shoved her aside.

'Right, Ida. A Mrs Greenstock, up Pennsylvania way, needs a cleaner for four hours.' She handed Ida the docket on which she had written the address and the rate. When the work was completed to Mrs Greenstock's satisfaction she would sign that it had been done, then Dolly would pay Ida and invoice the employer. 'Phyllis, the Victoria Hotel needs a chambermaid just for this morning. June, the laundry needs a presser.' June pulled a face: none of them liked working in the laundry where the conditions were hard and the work even harder, but she took the docket.

Disgruntled, the other women moved out of the tiny office into the sunshine. 'Who are you?' Dolly asked the stranger, who was the last to leave.

'May Snodland, ma'am.'

'You needn't "ma'am" me.' She laughed. '"Dolly" will do. Now, tell me a bit about yourself.'

'Me? Why?' May looked even more nervous. Dolly wondered if she had something to hide.

'I like to meet people before I send them out. I need to know about you.'

'I'm a hard worker.' This was said with a hint of defiance. Dolly liked that: downtrodden people made her feel guilty, although she had never understood why. She noticed the woman spoke with an educated accent, which put her in mind of Zeph's – a lovely voice he had.

'I'm sure you are. But I have to find out if I like you and if you're honest. I have to guard my reputation.'

'I've done nothing wrong.' Defensive again. 'I live down by the harbour …' She was glancing about her as she spoke. There was not much to look at in the drab room: an old kitchen table with a drawer, which was Dolly's desk; a rush-seated chair that had seen better days; a cupboard in which she kept her cleaning materials; and a small rickety table with a vase of flowers to make the room look a little more cheerful. There was also a high-backed leather chair, reserved for any clients who might call in. A peg rug, which she hoped to change for a nice Turkey carpet one day, lay on the floor.

'May, I'm sure you haven't, but you must understand my position. The people who let us into their homes, they trust me to send them honest, upright women. So *I* have to be able to trust *you*, don't you see?' She smiled, trying to coax some response. There was something about the woman, despite her attitude, that made Dolly feel sorry for her.

'I'm sorry …' To Dolly's consternation, May burst into tears.

'You'd best sit down a minute.' She allowed the woman to sit on the hallowed chair. The kettle was boiling now and she made them both a cup of tea. 'Sugar?' she called, and when there was no response she took it into the office anyway. There she found May, her head slumped on her arms, shaking with sobs. 'Oh, my dear, it can't be that bad.'

'But it is. You don't understand …' And the sobbing began again.

'If you don't tell me, how can I?' Dolly asked reasonably.

She waited, sipping her tea, until the crying subsided. 'Now, get it off your chest, whatever it is.'

It was a sorry tale and not an uncommon one. There was no Mr Snodland, but there was a child of three, no money, a landlord who was threatening her, she was near starvation and had no idea how she was going to manage. She implied she was widowed though Dolly wondered if she lied and it was shame making her so upset.

'Where's your little boy now?'

'In my room. I tied him to his bed.' May slapped her hand over her mouth to suppress a cry of anguish.

'Then you'd better go and get him. Bring him here.'

'You mean … ?'

'Yes, and hurry up before I change my mind.'

While Dolly waited, she opened her mail. It amazed her daily how rapidly her business was expanding. There were four enquiries for helpers and, most interestingly, one was for a nurse to attend an invalid overnight – she'd not had such a request before.

The last advertisement in the *Barlton Echo* had produced twenty-five responses so far. She would place another next week. She pulled a sheet of paper towards her and began to plan it:

THY – Temporary Help for You. In need of help in your home? Then let us remove your worries. Anywhere, anytime, any job. Our staff are guaranteed honest and hardworking; personally checked by the Proprietress.

She would have liked to add her name but Zeph had forbidden it: he was worried that clients at the solicitor's would connect them. Dolly forbore to tell him that several of them were already on her books. Then she picked up her pen again. 'Nursing assistance a speciality.' There.

'You're a big boy,' she said, as May returned with her son. 'What's your name?'

'Charlie.'

'Well, Charlie, are you going to help me?' She took her keys out of her handbag. 'May, I live at number five Walnut Road. If you would be so kind as to clean the house for me and prepare the vegetables for dinner, I'll be back around noon.'

'Mrs Topsham, how can I thank you?'

'By doing a good job.'

She watched the woman leave. Perhaps she had been foolhardy – what if she was a thief? Somehow, she doubted it. She pulled her writing pad to her. She had no nurses yet but that didn't stop her replying confidently: it shouldn't be hard to find one. She put a list of her charges in the envelope with the letter.

She smiled to herself as she worked. It had been such a simple idea, which Zeph had doubted would work. He'd been wrong. When she had begun work to pay her parents' rent she had gone out cleaning herself. It had brought in money but she had found that she could easily have worked for twenty-four hours every day of the year, such was the shortage of maids. Finding good staff was hard: girls preferred to work in factories now, no longer prepared to put up with the petty rules and regulations that employers insisted their indoor servants observe. But Dolly had also realised that there was a great pool of women who had children and needed money but couldn't work when a child was ill. They were the women she sent out. After nearly two years of hard work, her business was flourishing. And today was another milestone: 'Fancy me having someone to clean my house!' she said aloud, and laughed.

6

The Cresswell Arms had stood for the past three hundred years in Cresswell-by-the-Sea, which was too large to be a village and too small to be a town. It stood on the harbour quay, buffeted by sea winds to such an extent that the hanging sign, depicting the arms of the Cresswell family, had to be repaired or replaced regularly. The windows were small, to keep out the draughts from those winds, so that even when the sun shone the lights were on in the bars. It was built of the same local granite as the cottages that huddled about it so the harbour wall, the cobblestones and the houses appeared to have evolved from the soil.

Over the centuries the original inn, which had been the front room of a fisherman's cottage, had grown, much as the village had. The one room had become two, then three. No one was sure when the back had been developed into a coaching inn with a traditional balcony over an inner courtyard. Now, in the twentieth century, it had developed into a complex arrangement of inn, restaurant, hotel and stables, which did not suit all of its clients.

'Her's talking of making more bedrooms.' Sol Pepper, the estate boilerman and plumber, looked soulfully into his tankard of scrumpy.

'What's her want them for? Ain't she making enough money?' Robert Robertson, the estate carpenter, was stuffing tobacco thoughtfully into the bowl of his pipe.

'Greedy, that's what her is,' Fred, his younger brother, put in.

'That's not a kind thing to say of her. Her works hard. Her's a businesswoman, sees a chance and goes for it. Good luck to her.'

'You'm would say that, Sol. She's seen you and yours all right, what with your mum's cottage and all. What has she done for the rest of us?'

'I'm related, don't forget that. Makes a difference.' Slowly he began to scatter tobacco from a pouch on to a cigarette paper and rolled it painstakingly, then licked the gum with the tip of his tongue. 'Our Dolly's been a good daughter-in-law to her, and housing our mum and all shows she regards us as family. Don't make no difference to the price she charges me for me cider.' He grinned. 'And as for you two, you carry on like old women, with your moaning. 'As she got to say thank you for the rest of 'er life? Anyway, as far as my old dad told me, you 'aven't done so badly from our Melanie. Never forget that.'

'Nor should she. Not with what we know,' Robert said, in his deep, loud voice.

'Your bloody big mouth,' Sol muttered, and nodded towards a stranger, who was staring morosely into his tankard.

'Said nothing what anyone would understand, now, have I?' Robert whispered.

'Her's kept this bar for us much as it was. We should be grateful for that.'

'Sol, why does everyone think it's us what should be grateful all the time? That layabout husband of hers said the same to me the other day. I put him right, I did!' Robert was blustering. He often did.

'You'm didn't say aught, did ee? Not to that idiot?' Fred looked worried.

'Course I bloody didn't. I wouldn't, not to someone as weak in the head as 'e is. God knows who he might blab to when 'e's drunk. And that's most days, as well you know.'

'He's a lucky bastard, when you think about it. Rich widow woman and her owning a pub into the bargain. Every man's dream come true, if you ask me.' Robert looked quite sad at Richard Joynston's good fortune.

'Wonder how much he's nicked from her so far. And do you think her knows?' Fred tapped the side of his nose.

'Course her bloody knows. Her's a smart woman. Our Dolly says as her Zeph gets furious just thinking about it.' Sol always enjoyed showing the others that he was on the inside track.

'Thought your Dolly didn't speak to you.'

'Course she does,' he lied.

'Then if her knows, why she put up with him?' Fred persisted.

'Maybe he's got a big ... Not like yours, Fred.' Sol gave him a playful push.

'Doubt if he could do much with it, the state he is most nights.' Fred pushed him back.

'I wouldn't mind being his stand-in and that's for sure.' Robert roared with laughter, an awesome sound to those hearing it for the first time: it rumbled from the lower regions of his gut, growing in momentum and volume.

'Seriously though. Our Dolly says as to how her Zeph is worried about his mum and that parasite. Reckon he'd like to come back here and give her a hand and stop his tricks,' Sol continued, as if he knew everything when, in fact, he could only repeat what his mother had gleaned from his sister Maud.

'Then where is he?' Fred made an exaggerated play of looking about the smoke-filled room.

'Our Dolly put paid to that. Said as her wasn't going to move from Barlton, and that was sure.'

'What sort of man lets his missus boss him like that? Sounds to me as if her could do with a good strapping,' said Fred, who famously avoided hurting so much as a snail.

'That's no way to treat a maid. Our Dolly's never had a hand laid on her,' declared Sol.

'Probably her should have. Then he wouldn't be having the trouble he is with her … What did you do that for?' Fred glared angrily at his brother who had kicked him in the shins. 'Evening, Mr Beasley.' He looked flustered as he welcomed Henry Beasley, their landlady's father, to the bar.

'Evening to you all. There's the smell of autumn in the air and that be sure.'

'How are you keeping, Mr Beasley? Time on your hands now you'm retired?'

'So I'm told, though I've no idea where it's going. I can't imagine how I ever found the time to work – the days don't seem long enough.'

'I'm glad to hear that, Mr Beasley. It's best to keep busy. When my dad retired he was dead afore six months was up. Me mum's nagging did for him, to be sure.'

'Hear from that son of yours, Mr Beasley?'

'Funny you should ask, Robbie. Got a letter only yesterday. Married he is now, with five grandchildren for me what I've never seen.'

'It's a long way and costs a pretty penny to get to that there Canada.'

'Could I?' The older man indicated the tankards on the table.

The three spoke in unison: 'That'd be most kind'; 'Thankee'; 'I wouldn't say no.'

Henry Beasley strode over to the long bar, which had replaced the trestle table that had once stood here.

Robert shoved his brother again. 'Talking about young Beasley!'

'Do you mind? Stop pushing me. I was behaving natural, like. It looks worse if we never mention him at all.'

Melanie's father was returning with the drinks. 'If we sit elsewhere?' he asked, and without waiting for a reply he carried the tray of glasses to a table at the other side of the bar. 'I never like to sit here, not where Bernard …' He nodded towards the spot on the floor where his son-in-law had died in a brawl. 'Seems disrespectful.' Everyone assumed a suitably doleful expression. No one was going to disagree with him when free drink was in the offing, but it wasn't just that. Few in the village and

36

on the estate had had any time for Bernard Topsham, a bullying wife-beater. More sense, everyone thought, for him not to want to sit where his own son had beaten out his son-in-law's brains. The very son whom nosy Fred Robertson was talking about.

The death of one and the disappearance of the other was one of the reasons Henry Beasley rarely came this way, but logic had told him long ago that if he avoided his daughter's establishment tongues would wag all the more.

'They told me you were here.' Melanie, a tired-looking woman in her forties, had joined them. She placed a large plate of sliced meat and a basket of bread on the table. 'May I?' She took a seat on the bench beside them, but waved away Sol's offer to buy her a drink.

'You'm looking peaky.'

'That makes me feel a whole lot better, Dad!' She laughed good-naturedly, but pulled her shawl closer to her.

'You've got so thin there won't be anything left of you soon.'

'Too busy to get fat.' She laughed, but did not sound relaxed. 'Are you all right? Being looked after?' she asked the others, to divert her father.

'Couldn't be better, Melanie. Nice cask of ale, this.' Robert held up his glass to her. 'You always are good to us.' He took a sliver of ham from the platter she had placed before them.

'Should always look after your friends.' She smiled.

They all looked up as the door burst open and Alf Marshall hurtled in. 'Evening, all. Have you heard?'

Everyone in the bar focused their attention on him.

'It's Miss Cresswell. Her's in the clink.'

There was uproar as everyone rushed across the wooden floor to him the better to hear.

'Had you heard about this?' her father asked, when he and Melanie were alone.

'Lady Prestwick telephoned earlier, then sent a telegram. Dreadful business.'

'Can't say I'm surprised, not with the company she keeps.'

'Dad!' Melanie frowned. She did not like anyone, even her father, to speak ill of Hannah Cresswell.

''Tis true, though. Not nice, them suffragettes, not proper women, rushing around throwing themselves in front of horses, bombing people. It's not right.'

'I don't think Miss Cresswell has been involved in such activities.' But, seeing the closed expression on her father's face, Melanie knew she could never persuade him otherwise. 'I'm glad they've left us for a minute. I had a letter from young Henry.'

'Your mum and me had one too, but he didn't say as he's written to you.'

Melanie said nothing. Most likely he had written to her separately because he could not know if their parents were speaking to her. And that was half the case, since her mother would not countenance Melanie crossing the threshold of her cottage. She blamed her for Henry's flight so far away.

'He says as he'd like to come home. It'd be nice to see him. As the years slip past I fear I never shall again.'

'You think it would be safe? What if someone talked?'

'Dear Melanie, they've never stopped talking about your brother. What's different now?'

'There are many hereabouts don't like me and are jealous of my good fortune. One might talk to the constables to get back at me.'

'Who would believe them, after all this time? The constable who was here then went down in his fishing-boat, the doctor's dead – they were the important ones involved. Those lads out there have kept mum. I can't see them blabbing, and if they did, they'd be in trouble too for not saying anything before.'

'That's true.' But she sounded doubtful. She had already written back to her brother telling him it was not a good idea to return, but she did not want her father to know it.

'You've never said nothing to no one, not even that husband of yours?'

'Not a living soul. Zeph's asked me, of course, but I just say it's jealousy of us. He believes me. And I wouldn't confide in Richard.' She pursed her lips as she mentioned her husband who, as she spoke, was upstairs and in a sleep so deep it might have been a coma.

'Let him come, I say. Then I shall die a happy man.'

'Get on with you! You'll see us all out.' She laughed, which made her cough.

'If you don't get your chest seen to and take more rest you might be speaking closer to the truth than you know.' He spoke kindly but his concern annoyed her. 'I ain't interfering, maid, just worried about you,' he added.

'There's really no need, Dad.'

'Well, then, what a to-do.' Robert Robertson had returned to them. 'A Cresswell in the nick! Never thought I'd live to see that.' And his rumbustious laugh rang out again.

Chapter Two

August–September 1913

1

That morning Hannah had been sick twice already and expected she would be again. She sat hunched on the mattress rocking back and forth with the pain in her churning stomach. She had never felt so nauseous in her life. Just the sight of the over-milked tea and the grey sludge in the metal bowl made the nausea worse. She pushed it under the bed with her foot so that she need not see it.

During the sleepless night she had identified the smell that had puzzled Dulcie and her yesterday. It was urine. As a result she had refrained from lying down; the mattress stank and was, no doubt, full of bedbugs. She had kept her coat on and sat, huddled for warmth, on a piece of newspaper she had found in the corner of her cell.

The bed was in fact a stone shelf, so narrow that only the slimmest could lie on it without fear of rolling off. Even the poorest estate worker had a better bed than this. The ubiquitous yellowing tiles covered the walls from floor to ceiling, adding to the chill, and the grouting was black with dirt. A meagre streak of light shone through the barred window of the jail, which was too high for her to see out.

Jail. The word made her shudder. Thank heaven her father had not lived to see her shame. The thought brought her up sharp; it was the only time she had ever been glad he was dead.

Why was she here? She had done nothing wrong. The wardress had lied for Hannah knew that Polly Jones had bitten her. Of course she could never betray Polly for she had a young family dependent upon her. But why had the wardress lied? Polly was tiny, and Hannah was tall; Polly had blonde curls, and Hannah's hair was dark and straight. And Hannah was in her fifties while Polly was barely thirty. There could be no question of mistaken identity.

She hoped Polly would not confess. But she might. She was a simple soul yet she had a depth of integrity that was surprising in one of her class, Hannah thought. She knew she was lying to herself. She *longed* to hear that Polly had stepped forward. Polly would be able to deal with this place far better than Hannah – she was used to deprivation, noise and perhaps even bedbugs. Hannah feared that if she was here for another night she would go mad. But what about Polly's family? Well, Hannah could take care of them – if not by moving them into her house by making sure that other cottagers kept an eye on them.

Hannah reproached herself. When had she become so selfish: 'Me! Me! Me!' she said aloud. But it was hard to be rational: since the death of her father and Lettice's marriage, no one had needed her. Now self-pity swamped her. 'Cariad,' she said. Her dog would miss her and the thought made her smile, even if it was sad that only a dog cared about her – not that Cariad would appreciate being considered *only* a dog.

A key grated in the lock. She stood up as the heavy door swung open and a wardress entered. 'If you don't eat you'll get into trouble and you don't want that, do you?' The woman spoke kindly.

'I can't. I feel sick.'

'That's common. Can't be nice, a lady like you in a place like this. But you should try. It's always best to have something in your stomach.' She stood to attention as the wardress from yesterday entered, ominously swinging her bunch of keys like a pendulum.

'Why did you lie about me?' Hannah asked.

'Me? Lie? What an accusation. What do you think of that, Mrs Baker?' she asked the other wardress, who was rigid, her fear of the other woman evident.

'Dreadful, Miss Rowntree.'

Hannah was frightened too and stood straighter, as if a ramrod back might lessen her dread. 'You lied. I have a right to know why.' Her mouth had dried, which made her speech thick.

'*You?* You should have thought of that before you behaved as you did yesterday.' She smiled as she spoke, but it was not a true smile and its falseness made it alarming. The woman was playing with Hannah's fear.

'I suggest you take care how you speak to me. My family is of consequence in these parts.' Even as Hannah made this statement, she wondered if she had made a mistake.

'That might be so, but it doesn't reach into here. Now, eat or there will be another consequence for you to think of.' She twirled on her boots and left.

'You'd best do as her says, Miss Cresswell,' the kinder wardress said, then scuttled away.

Hannah sat down on the bed. She knew what they were threatening her with if she didn't eat, but she couldn't. She wasn't making a protest.

She simply could not put that slop into her mouth.

She wondered how long she would have to stay here and why they would not let her see her solicitor. Perhaps she should have made a fuss, but the last thing she had wanted was to appear difficult.

Think of other things, she told herself, like the plans for Mrs Wallace's new garden near Chudleigh. Autumn planting was approaching rapidly: Hannah needed to finalise her drawing and the watercolour painting she always presented to help her clients make up their minds as to whether they wished to employ her. They usually did. If they rejected her ideas she would be disappointed but it would not be the end of the world: she had no need of the fee she would charge them. She had met other professional gardeners and knew of their need for the money. It made her feel guilty that she deprived them of work but her love of gardening and the excitement she felt at a new commission made it impossible for her to stop. In the years she had been working she had built herself a fine reputation and, best of all, she was admired by others. Even Miss Jekyll had congratulated her on Dulcie Prestwick's garden on Dartmoor when she had visited.

For the Wallaces she had decided on a luxuriant theme, almost a jungle. Mrs Wallace was a fiery Brazilian and Hannah always took into account the character of the owners. She was already experimenting with orchids and ... The door opened again.

'You.' That was all Miss Rowntree said, crooking her finger at Hannah to follow her. She wanted to protest, but knew it would be pointless.

They walked along a corridor lined with cell doors. She could hear sobbing from one, wailing from another. A prisoner was banging on the door and cursing – she admired that woman. Perhaps it was Fanny Petty.

The wardress stopped in front of a door, opened it and pushed Hannah into the room.

'Mr Battle, I am pleased to see you. Zeph too ...' Her voice was filled with relief.

Zephaniah Topsham pulled out a chair for her and she sat down quickly. Suddenly she had felt as if her legs would no longer support her.

'Some water, Miss Cresswell?' Henry Battle asked anxiously.

'Thank you, Mr Battle. I fear I am weak from hunger.'

'That is not a solution, Miss Cresswell.'

'What do you mean, Mr Battle?'

'Refusing to eat, Miss Cresswell.'

'I am fully aware of the consequences if I don't, and I would but the food is dreadful.'

'I thought you might have difficulty with it, Miss Cresswell, so I took the liberty ...' Zeph opened his attaché case and removed a brown-paper bag. 'I'm sorry about the bag, but I stopped at the baker's on my way here.' Then he produced a bottle of ginger beer and smiled shyly as he gave it to her.

'Dear Zeph, how thoughtful of you.' She bit into the bun. 'Such bliss! Oh dear, you must forgive me.' She patted her mouth with her handkerchief.

'We took the liberty of acquiring some ...' Henry Battle coughed discreetly and Zeph picked up a large tapestry bag, which he placed beside her.

'Clothes?' she asked hopefully. 'How?'

'Lady Prestwick contacted Melanie Topsham, who sent Rowan to Mr Cresswell's home but unfortunately he was not in residence. The child, sensibly, went to the manor and informed Sir Mortie. The housekeeper contacted yours and young Rowan travelled to Barlton on the train with the bag.'

'But she's too young to be out and about on her own.'

'Lady Prestwick insisted she stayed at the Victoria and had her put on the train back to Barlton this morning.'

'How kind everyone is. But while I'm happy that they care I'm ashamed that they all know of my predicament.'

'It would be impossible to keep it secret, with the newspapers—'

'The newspapers!' Hannah's eyes widened with shock. 'Reporters!'

'When you appear in court they will be present. Women's suffrage is a subject which interests such as they.' The manner in which he spoke made Hannah realise he did not approve.

'In court?' Her voice rose and her eyes filled with tears. 'I've been stupid. I'd no idea ... Well, of course I feared for my friends. I came here yesterday to see if I might be of use to those who had been arrested and then I was accused of something I had not done and it is all too unfair.' At the end of this breathless tirade, she allowed the tears to fall. Her solicitor and his assistant looked steadfastly at the floor as she dabbed at her eyes with her handkerchief. 'I'm so sorry, but your news quite took the wind out of my sails. I had presumed you had come to take me home.' Her voice broke.

Henry Battle made a play of taking out his notebook and a pencil, which he sharpened with deep concentration. Hannah stared at him with desperation but he avoided her eye and sharpened another pencil instead. Zeph got to his feet and crossed to the other side of the table. Gently he patted her shoulder. 'There, there, Miss Cresswell.'

'I feel so alone, Zeph. Will my brothers be there?'

Zeph glanced at Mr Battle, who was lining up his notepad with the edge of the table.

'I fear they could not come.'

'Not Oliver?'

'His wife tells us he is in London. Of course we have sent a telegraph communication to his club. I'm sure he will be here as soon as he can.'

'And Sir Mortie?'

'His gout,' Zeph interrupted.

'So there is no one?'

'We shall be there.' He patted her again.

'When is this to happen?'

Henry Battle removed his half-hunter from its pocket on his waistcoat and flipped open the lid. 'Less than an hour.'

Hannah's hand shot to her mouth.

'I'm sure when the magistrates see someone of your standing in the dock they will discharge you. So, if you feel up to it, we must proceed now. There is much I need to know.'

Zeph took out his own notebook. Hannah noticed, with a pang of nerves, that he did not seem as confident as his employer.

2

They were being sent up to the court in batches of three. In the waiting room, Hannah took comfort from the presence of the other women. They seemed in remarkably good spirits, given the circumstances, which helped her take a grip on herself: she must not be the one to let them down. Her instinct had been to rush to those who were distressed and put her arms about them, but they were not allowed to touch each other. Miss Rowntree had forbidden them to talk. But once she had flounced off, and someone had noticed that the wardress left in charge was smiling at them, they risked whispering to each other.

'That Rowntree's a cow. Oh, sorry, Miss Cresswell, begging your pardon for my language.'

'Not at all, Fanny. I quite agree. But it's a bit unfair on cows, such delightful creatures!' This made them all laugh and everyone felt better. 'I shall, of course, pay your fines for you.'

'That's very kind of you, Miss.' Fanny Petty, whose arms were as big as a hefty man's, sniffed loudly. There was a general murmur of gratitude.

'It is most kind, Miss Cresswell, but I am in a position to pay my own,' Cynthia Marshall, a local teacher, admitted. Hannah was concerned about her: now that she had been arrested she might lose her position at the school in which she taught.

'Shall we see how things go?' Hannah smiled at her. It was astonishing how much happier – and how much less guilty – she felt in their company and from the knowledge that she was doing something to help them.

'Should we say that you are willing to pay our fines, Miss, when we're in front of the beak? Otherwise they'll never believe we've got the money.'

'I think that would be a good idea, Fanny.'

'That is, if they don't lock us up.'

'Surely not. There was only a little damage.'

'I reckon I'll get sent down for hitting that policeman.'

'Fanny, I feel so responsible for that.'

'I don't see why, Miss Cresswell. You didn't make me march, I did so of my own free will. What have they charged you with, Miss?'

'Biting a wardress.'

'You? What rubbish! You did nothing.'

'They won't believe me.'

'Then who did?' Fanny gazed sternly at the others. There was a long silence.

'I did.' Polly put up her hand.

'Don't confess – you mustn't be locked up and leave your children,' a woman advised her.

'Probably for the best, Polly. They're never going to lock up someone like Miss Cresswell, are they? What are you going to say, Miss?'

'I shall deny it, of course, but please don't worry, Mrs Jones. I shan't say I know who did.' She smiled but her stomach churned and the confidence that had been building a few minutes ago ebbed away.

'It's them mad women in London have got us in this mess.'

'How do you make that out, Fanny?'

'All that violence. Smashing windows, hurling bricks, threatening bombs, and we get the same punishment for a little demonstration.'

'I do hope you're mistaken,' Hannah said, but she was inclined to agree. The movement she believed in was too violent now: there had to be other ways of persuading parliament to give women the vote than by frightening people.

The next four were called and then the next. Each time the names were shouted, Hannah's stomach clenched. The fear of such humiliation added to her mounting terror.

A few minutes after Fanny's group had gone up she heard loud shouting. She hoped Fanny wasn't losing her temper and arguing with the magistrates – it would be so unwise. Another group was called. Puzzlingly she was left on her own. She would be last to go up, deprived of the comfort of the others' presence.

'Miss Hannah Cresswell,' a voice boomed down the stairwell.

When she stood Hannah swayed. One of the wardresses took her elbow – to steady her or stop her running away? Hannah was not sure.

She was led up a steep flight of wooden stairs and found herself standing in the dock. She clung to the rail that separated her from the court, which to her horror, was packed. She could see men with pads already scribbling away. At least she had had clean clothes to change into. She adjusted the cameo at the high neck of her blouse, with its leg-o'-mutton sleeves. The knowledge that she looked clean and smart might help her, she thought. It didn't.

The room was dark and oppressive with pitch-pine panelling. The windows were high and dirty. The gas-fired lighting made the atmosphere hot and stuffy. She glanced nervously behind her and, to her joy, Dulcie Prestwick, taking up space for two, waved at her. Beside her Theo, her equally large husband, took up another two spaces. Now they stood and bowed in her direction. She smiled in response, but felt tearful at their kindness to her in being present. She did not notice her brother and his wife at the back.

'All stand,' barked the clerk to the court. There was a scraping of chairs and intermittent coughing as if the exertion of standing was too much for some. Three magistrates entered. They sat, and there was another rustling as the rest of the court followed them. Then the magistrates were in deep conversation. Hannah's nerves were so taut that it seemed they would snap at any moment.

Eventually they looked up and stared at her solemnly. She had hoped she might know them, but they were strangers, old men with large moustaches and high complexions. They would have scant understanding of the suffrage movement. Perhaps they had known her father.

'We are sorry we have kept you waiting, Miss Cresswell. Unfortunately our fellow magistrate had to declare that he knew you and retired.

A replacement had to be found.'

'I understand. Might I enquire who, or is that not allowed?'

'You may. Mr von Ehrlich told us he is an old friend of your family.'

'I understand.' Friend of the family? Arch enemy, more like.

'Now, if we may proceed.'

The clerk of the court stepped forward with a Bible. Hannah took the oath. The first witness called was Miss Rowntree.

Hannah had difficulty in controlling herself as the lies poured out of the hateful woman. They were worse today. She was making out Hannah to have been the ring-leader, shouting instructions to the others. And then she accused Hannah of having bitten her and dramatically rolled up her sleeve to show the marks, now blue. The prosecution solicitor sat down. Hannah sat forward on her chair as Henry Battle got to his feet. Now the truth would come out.

'No questions,' she heard him say. There was a murmur in the court-room, which gathered momentum.

'I did not bite that woman. She lies!' Hannah was on her feet and shouting before she could stop herself. Henry Battle swung round and shook his head. 'I'm sorry,' she said, then slumped on to the chair. She realised she had not helped her cause.

The chairman of the magistrates was droning on now. She found it hard to concentrate on what he was saying since the dangerous woman he talked about was not her and never would be. How could she ever be a danger to society? It was ridiculous. It might have been funny if it wasn't so serious. She let her mind wander.

But her concentration returned with a vengeance as she heard the chairman of the magistrates state, 'We have no alternative but to impose a custodial sentence of three months.'

From the public gallery there was a communal gasp of horror and several people shouted, 'No!' But the loudest voice of all was Hannah's.

3

Esmeralda clung to her husband's arm as they made their way out of the fusty court, her shoes click-clacking on the tiled floor. The hall was busy with people but Oliver was wheeling his way through them at speed, apologising politely enough to left and right as they brushed against people, but allowing nothing to impede them. She did not know what to say or how to comfort him. His pallor had drained to a dough-like grey and his mouth, normally full and generous, had become a thin line. Esmeralda knew that look. He was angry, so angry that she knew it would be some time before he would want to speak to her. When he was in a fury, he was best left alone. Esmeralda had to trot to keep up with him, still hanging on to his arm. She was alarmed when she saw whom he was marching towards.

'And where were you?' he spat.

'I beg your pardon?' Agnes Beatty replied, gazing up at Oliver, who towered over her. She was dignified but Esmeralda noted that she had flushed.

'Why were you not in court?' Oliver bellowed.

Esmeralda was embarrassed. At this rate everyone would know their business.

'I couldn't bring myself to attend.'

'And how do you think we, her family, felt to see her in the dock like a common criminal? Do you think I wished to be there?'

'I have no idea.' Agnes searched in her small jet bag for her handker-chief.

'I blame you. If it were not for your malign influence she would never have done anything so foolhardy as to march with those women.'

'You insult your sister, Mr Cresswell. She is a grown woman and makes her own decisions. I can assure you I had no influence on her. I did not attend today because, in my opinion, Hannah would not like anyone who cared for her to see her. She knew I was in the building because I sent a note to her.' She straightened her long black calfskin gloves, tweaking each finger end to her satisfaction. 'And if we are speaking of absentees, Mr Cresswell, then where was the rest of her family? Now, if you will excuse me ...' She swept away from them, head held high, black and white parasol clicking on the tiled floor.

As Esmeralda watched her former companion, she had to admire her even though she had not liked the way she had bested Oliver – it was not good for a man to have a woman defeat him verbally.

What Agnes Beatty had said was not strictly true, but Esmeralda had been too appalled by the interchange to interrupt. Esmeralda's nephew, Morts, had been at the back of the court, a few seats along from where Oliver and Esmeralda had sat, but evidently Oliver had not seen him. He had been looking as pale and wan as his uncle was. At the end he had rushed out of the court even faster than they had.

'Why didn't Mortie come?' Esmeralda asked.

'He's gone to Scotland to a grouse moor.'

'But he doesn't shoot.'

'No, but he enjoys eating them.' Normally such a comment would have made both of them laugh, but not today. 'Coral's gone with him. Apparently he wanted to be here but she refused to delay their plans.' She heard the defensive note in his voice – he disliked any criticism of his family, even by her, and rightly so. But his principles did not stop him making disparaging remarks about her father.

'Surely your mother hasn't gone too? She's far too poorly.'

'Lettice has stayed to care for her.'

'Such a dear child,' she said. She wondered whether the girl had chosen to care for her grandmother to avoid returning to her husband. Nothing had been said, but whenever Hugo was mentioned a guarded look came over Lettice's face.

Suddenly, as the crowd parted, she spied her father to the left of them in the cavernous hall. She twisted to the right so that her husband turned too. She didn't want them to see each other and certainly not when Stanislas was in deep conversation with the wardress who had said such awful things about Hannah. 'Let's have luncheon at Lady Prestwick's hotel.' She pulled at Oliver's hand.

'How can you think of such a thing at a time like this?' he said crossly.

'Because we have to eat. We would not be much help to Hannah if we became ill,' she replied patiently. 'In any case I arranged a table with the head waiter, certain that Hannah would be joining us. I've also invited Mr Battle. I think we should speak with him, don't you?'

'Much use he was.'

'But perhaps Hannah can appeal, or whatever prisoners do.'

'You can be so tactless. Why call her a prisoner? Such a distasteful word.'

'I couldn't think how else to refer to her. I'm sorry.' And a prisoner was what Hannah was.

'Since you've arranged it …' Oliver began to walk towards the large door that led out on to the street.

'Uncle!' Morts was hurrying towards them. 'This is a disaster. What can we do?'

While her husband was engaged with his nephew, Esmeralda turned in time to see her father handing the horrible woman an envelope. Her heart sank. She knew those envelopes and what they contained. She also knew her father. She could bet her fortune that he was behind poor Hannah's incarceration.

Rowan looked out of the window of the train that was carrying her home to Barlton. Fields, hedges, houses, cows and sheep flew past her. She had had no idea such speed was possible. She had seen trains before but always from the outside. Being inside was a different experience. She felt she would be happy to sit where she was for ever as the world whirled by.

What an amazing time she had had since yesterday. She had seen things she had not known existed, luxury she could not have imagined. The rooms she had been in, first at Cresswell Manor and then at the Victoria Hotel, had been enormous, so large that she was sure her parents' cottage would have fitted in three or even four times.

When she had been shown into the Cresswells' living room – no, she corrected herself, it was the sitting room – only two people had occupied the vast space. It might feel very lonely. She thought of the clutter and noise in her own living room when only half of them were there. Which, she wondered, did she prefer? Why, her whole family in the Cresswells' room – that would be perfect. On her return from the house, when she had excitedly told her mother what she had seen, Flossie had told her they had yet another room, called a drawing room, which they also sat in and was even bigger.

From Barlton station, Rowan had been directed to the Victoria Hotel. And that was another surprise: she'd expected it to be like the Cresswell Arms, but it was another grand house with such a lovely staircase sweeping up from the busy hallway. She wouldn't have liked to clean the brass banister – it must take hours. Everywhere she had looked there were ladies in silks and satins and both places had smelt so sweet. Her home stank, no matter how hard they scrubbed it.

If she thought about it, it really wasn't fair. Why should some have all that luxury and others nothing? She yawned. She wouldn't say no if it was offered to her so she shouldn't begrudge it to others.

Lady Prestwick had been very kind, insisting that she ate as much as she wanted. The food was good, but her mother's was better, she'd decided. The room she had been put in to sleep, high in the eaves of the building, was lovely. A bed all to herself while at home she had to share with three of her sisters. She had been impressed that this morning she had summoned the courage to ask Lady Prestwick if there was any possibility of a job. 'I'd be happy to do anything,' she'd said.

'Have you any experience of cleaning?'

'With eight brothers and sisters I know a lot about it.' She'd managed to laugh.

'The cleaning here is somewhat different.' Dulcie Prestwick had smiled, and Rowan couldn't imagine why she had been frightened of her.

'I'm a quick learner.'

'I'm sure you are, my dear. How old are you?'

'Fifteen – I'll soon be sixteen.' Well, next November wasn't that far away.

'Then you must discuss it with your mother first. If she agrees, I'm sure we can find a position for you, perhaps in the kitchens or as a trainee chambermaid. I would have to ask my housekeeper what she needs. Let me know what your mother says …'

Rowan hugged herself with excitement. Surely her mother wouldn't stand in her way.

Ten minutes later the train ground to a standstill at Cresswell-by-the-Sea. Rowan climbed down reluctantly, hoping someone might see her. Then she ran along the harbour and burst into the kitchen of the Cresswell Arms in search of her mother, yelling her name.

Everything about Flossie Marshall was large. Her breasts, her rear, her face, her hair and, above all, her personality. She was, as always, hauling the large pots and pans on and off the hob in the pub's cavernous kitchen. A lesser person might have complained at the amount she had to do but not Flossie – she loved her work, the customers, her employer Melanie Joynston, her husband Alf, and her eight children, all named after trees. Her own little forest, she called them.

'Running from the policeman, are you?' She grinned at her daughter, admiring, as she did all the time, Rowan's beauty, and marvelling that she had produced her. 'Did you ever see such excitement, Melanie?' she asked, as her employer entered the kitchen.

'Hello, Rowan. I hear you've been to Barlton. On your own?'

'It was wonderful! So many people and carriages and cars!'

'Did you see Miss Cresswell? How is the poor soul?'

'No, I didn't. I gave the parcel what Lavender, her maid, gave me to Lady Prestwick. Oh, Mum, she's such a kind lady and she said—'

'Do you know if she's been before the magistrates?'

'Yes, this morning. Her's been sent down for three months. That's what's happened.'

'Dear God. She'll never survive prison.' Melanie clutched at her neck, an unconscious gesture she often made when she was upset.

'It shouldn't be allowed.' Flossie began to beat her batter vehemently. 'Still, if you go marching through the streets making a right hullabaloo then you have to take the consequences, don't you?'

'Mum, Lady Prestwick said—'

'I blame that Miss Beatty. I don't think Hannah would ever have become involved in such matters if it hadn't been for her,' Melanie interrupted.

'I'm not so sure.' Flossie dabbed at a splash of batter that landed on her ample bosom.

'Mummmm!'

'You do interrupt,' Flossie reproved her.

'But I've something important to ask you.'

'What is it?'

'I've asked Lady Prestwick if I might work for her and she's said yes!' She was jumping up and down with excitement.

'No.'

'Mum?' Rowan stopped.

'Nothing more to say.' Flossie went over to the range.

A family argument was about to erupt and Melanie left the room.

'But, Mum, I could earn good money.'

'You can do that here.'

'But here isn't there. It was so lovely.'

'That don't alter the fact that the work will be just as hard, if not harder. And I'm not having you putting yourself at risk.'

'What risk?'

'White-slave traffickers, that's what. The towns are rife with them. And men with dishonourable intentions.'

'I can take care of myself.'

'Well, I don't think so. You seem to have no idea how pretty you are. And that puts you in constant danger from lecherous men who'd like to do you no good.'

'Mum!' Rowan blushed furiously.

'Well, it's true. In any case, I don't want you ending up like me.'

'But I'd like to be like you. You're always so happy, and you love Dad and all of us.'

'That's true. But I'd like you to have an easier life.'

'But if some man liked me, it would be easier, wouldn't it?'

'That makes me even more determined not to let you go.'

Rowan burst into tears.

'And the waterworks aren't going to make me change my mind.'

'I love you. I like being here with you and Mrs Joynston, but I want to make my own way. Can't you see that?' Her mother paused. Rowan stood breathless, waiting. Flossie had once told her that she had left home at thirteen because she had longed to be her own mistress.

'All right …' Flossie said slowly.

'Mum!' The jumping started again.

'Not Barlton. You're not going there on your own. But I'll have a word with the housekeeper up at the big house.'

Rowan's shoulders slumped. But it was better than nothing – and then she thought of Morts Cresswell and her face was lit with a wide smile.

4

'How is she?' Eve Gilroy was larding a fillet of beef, laid out on the pine table in front of her. Although the sash windows along one wall were open, it was still steaming hot in the enormous kitchen at Cresswell Manor.

'Still complaining. I don't know if I can take much more.' Philomel Herbert sank on to one of the kitchen chairs sighing deeply. She was in her early forties, an attractive woman – or she would have been if she ceased frowning and her turned-down mouth smiled.

'It's what you're paid for,' Eve said, with a sniff. She missed her friend Gussie Fuller, who had once been housekeeper at the manor. Philomel was aware that she was not accepted by the others as her replacement, and she resented the atmosphere that Eve created: it was not her fault that, broken-hearted, after Whitaker, the butler, had married the pastry cook, Gussie had fled to work for Sir Mortie's brother.

Philomel would have been even more disgruntled, had she known that Eve thought of her, and always referred to her, as *the usurper*. She thought Philomel an outlandish name for a housekeeper and called her Phil instead, since she knew it annoyed. 'Wet the bed again, has she?'

'I've no idea. That's for the nurse. She's asking for a bowl of oxtail soup.'

'She'll get what's she's given.'

'I hardly think that's the right attitude, Eve. She's the mother of your employer.'

'Well, it would take me at least five hours to make a *potage de queue de boeuf*.' She rattled this off with no semblance of a French accent but as Philomel spoke not one word of that – to Eve – barbaric language, she could display her superiority. Philomel was the fourth housekeeper she had had to endure since her friend had left, the other three beaten by

Lady Penelope's difficult, demanding character, and Eve's intransigent attitude towards them – as if it was their fault Gussie had gone.

'What am I to say?'

'She'll have the consommé. I arranged the menu with the other Lady Cresswell before she went to Scotland.'

'It's so confusing when there are two mistresses. It never makes for a happy household.'

'You should have been here when Miss Cresswell was mistress. Now, *there* was someone who knew how a house should be run, and considerate with it.'

'I wonder how she fared today. Silly woman.'

Eve threw her larding needle on to the table and stood with arms akimbo. 'If there's one thing she isn't it's silly. How dare you speak of the daughter of the house in that manner? Why, you don't even know her.'

'Sorry, I'm sure,' Philomel whined. The accent of the estuary she had come from still lurked in her voice, despite her best efforts to rid herself of it. Gussie, in Eve's opinion, was beautifully spoken. 'Where's Hilda?'

'How would I know?'

'I must say I've never worked in a house where the pastry cook was married to the butler. I mean, what sort of example does it set the maids and footmen?'

Eve slapped the beef into a metal pan and coated it with dripping. She did not answer for the simple reason that, for once, she was in agreement with her, not that she was going to let her know it.

'Do you know a Rowan Marshall?'

'I do. Why?'

'Her mother telephoned and asked if there was work for her here. That's another thing. She *telephoned*! I ask you! What are the lower classes coming to?'

'She'll have been using her employer's telephone, that's for sure. You'd be wise to take her on. Her family's the most hardworking I've come across in a month of Sundays. She might unsettle the footmen, but she's a good girl. When she comes, ask her if Willow fancies a job too. I could do with more help.'

'Shouldn't you ask Lady Cresswell first?'

'Why? Neither of them's that bothered.'

'Who isn't bothered with whom or what?' Edward Whitaker asked, as he strode into the kitchen. Such a manly man, Eve thought, as she often did. He had been the love of her life until he had betrayed her with Hilda. They had expected Eve to leave with Gussie, but her revenge had been to stay. There was no way that the pastry cook would take her position.

'Phil here wondered if I shouldn't ask Lady Coral if I might have a new kitchenmaid.'

'She wouldn't be interested. We're left to our own devices very much, Mrs Herbert, and I like it that way. Any tea, Eve?'

She knew she moved with too much alacrity to get it for him but she could not help herself. She loved him, she always would, even though he was married to another. It was strange how for years she had tried to persuade him to call her Eve but it was only after he had married Hilda that he had done so. Carefully she heated the Crown Derby teapot. Hope burned in her heart: she had sensed that Hilda was not happy in her marriage, which pleased Eve no end.

'We've Mr and Mrs Oliver dining here tonight, Eve. Sorry news about Miss Cresswell, isn't it?'

'Three months, the coachman said. Surely it's not true.'

'I very much fear it is.'

'Was Mr von Ehrlich on the bench? As soon as I heard the news I thought he was behind this viciousness.'

'I'm surprised the man hasn't changed his name. It would be expedient with there being so much antagonism towards the Germans,' Whitaker declared.

'And with reason. They're a bunch of bullies, if you ask me. But there won't be a war – I'd bet a half-crown there won't,' Philomel put in.

'I fear you would lose your money, Mrs Herbert. One of the footmen had to go home for his father's funeral, to Wapping, said the anti-German feeling was running very high.'

'Well, I still think it's all too silly. Who is he anyway? And why should he harm Miss Hannah?'

'He's Mrs Oliver's father. He and Mr Oliver had a disagreement about some land and now he hates this family. He tried to ruin old Sir Mortimer.'

'What a scandalous family this is.'

'Really, Mrs Herbert! I would prefer that you didn't speak in such a way. I find it offensive.'

Philomel coloured. 'I had no wish to offend, Mr Whitaker.'

'Quite.'

'Then you should watch what you say, shouldn't you?' Eve could not resist putting her oar in.

Zeph Topsham was tired as he made his way home. It had been a dreadful day. As long as he lived he would never forget the sheer terror on poor Hannah Cresswell's face as sentence was pronounced.

It was wrong. All wrong. It had taken all his self-control not to shout out when that idiot Battle had said he had no questions for that wretched wardress who had evidently been lying. He had believed Hannah when she had told them what had happened on the day of the demonstration, so why hadn't Henry Battle?

He had tried to discuss the outcome with him but all he would say was 'The law has spoken.' 'Only because you didn't, you fool,' he'd longed to retort.

Of course Hannah Cresswell, of all people, had not done what she was accused of. It might have been foolish of her to attend the march but Zeph admired her spirit. For some time he had thought it illogical that he was ineligible to vote since he was not a householder, and from that he had found sympathy for that other disenfranchised group: women. Such opinions, he knew, did not go down well with Mr Battle who was so set in his ways Zeph often expected him to bring back quill pens. But Mr Battle should not have allowed his personal opinions to get in the way of today's case. It had been unprofessional of him.

Zeph was tired of working for him. The promotion never came, the time to study was never given. He knew now, for sure, that he would always remain a humble clerk, not the solicitor he had dreamt of becoming.

It might, of course, have been possible had he not married so young, but it had taken the two of them to make the baby and Dolly was a good loving wife. He should have been happy but he wasn't. He didn't love Dolly as he had hoped he would. He liked and admired her, but there was no great passion and they had so little in common. That was not Dolly's fault: she was bright, but she had not been educated. He had planned to teach her himself, but with the children she hadn't had the time or the inclination for learning. Now that she had her business there was little chance that she ever would. He had hated her starting it but she was a success and the extra money came in more than handy.

He knew he had to do something. His work and his unsatisfactory home life were wearing him down – he could manage one but not both. Something had to change.

He had ideas, not formulated yet but he was mulling them over. Last week he had gone, on his own, on a rare visit to his mother. What he had found concerned him; she looked too tired. When he had tried to discuss her health with her she had maintained that she was fine and not to fuss. But Flossie had told him otherwise. 'She tries to hide it but I sometimes sees her wincing with a pain in her side, Zeph. And she gets so breathless. There's something not right. And there are days when she has to drag herself around.'

There was a lot else that was not right. Her waster of a husband, for a start. She worked hard at the inn and Zeph would have been interested to know what percentage of the profits his stepfather drank. He was drunk every evening and slept it off during the day. The profits bore no relation to the amount of business they did, so Zeph feared that Richard was also stealing from her. When he had mentioned this, as vaguely as he could, his mother had been cross with him and explained away the deficiency as relating to a bank loan she had taken out on some properties. And that was another cause for worry: she'd never borrowed before – if you have to borrow you can't afford it, she was fond of saying. Her reaction only made him certain that his suspicions were real and that she was worried too – he could not remember a time when his mother had been angry with him.

It was a mystery to him how someone as sweet and loving could have chosen two such dreadful husbands. But at least this one, Richard, did not beat her.

There was an obvious solution to this and his other problems. He should move back and take over running the business for her. The problem was how to suggest it to his mother and Dolly. When he tried, he had failed miserably.

Dolly had not been pleased. 'No.' She had conveyed a fine degree of indignation with that one word.

'I beg your pardon?'

'I'm not moving and that's that. It would be going backwards.'

'But I'm your husband. Surely if I say we go then we go.'

'You can say it all you want but I'm staying put. You go.'

'On my own? What sort of wife are you? What about those vows you made?'

'I might ask what sort of husband you are.'

'And what does that mean?'

'It means that I'm the one who earns the most money so I have a say in where we live.'

'So, your business is more important than my mother and my concern for her?'

'My business is doing well. You know it is.'

'Yes, but we could manage without.'

'You dare say that?' Dolly had swung round to face him, eyes blazing. 'Don't you dare sneer at what I've achieved, the money I bring into this family.'

'Dolly, don't *you* say things you'll regret. You're not being fair.'

'And are you? You're like this because you're ashamed you can't keep us properly. You're a failure.' At this point she had been screaming.

He was shocked: they never argued and Dolly was always so happy. Why was she speaking to him like this? But she was right – as she so often was.

'My business is our only hope for the future,' she went on. 'There's no relying on you for good prospects, is there?'

'And what does *that* mean?'

'It means you're useless, Zeph. All you're good at is moaning.' She had stormed from the room.

That had been a week ago. He turned into his own road. Half-way along he reached their house, paid for, he was acutely aware, by Dolly. He put the key into the lock of his front door – Mr Grips the landlord's door. His monthly visit to collect the rent filled Zeph and Dolly with fear in case he observed something not to his liking and asked them to leave. Of course they didn't own their home, as Dolly had been at pains to point out to him when he had gone to bed that night. They had lain in the dark with their backs to each other.

She had apologised in the morning, as had he, but it was too late: something had changed. Nothing could be the same again.

He went along the passageway to the kitchen.

'Oh, you made me jump!' a voice exclaimed.

'Who are you?' he asked the young woman, as an unfamiliar emotion surged through him.

'Mrs Topsham's employing me,' replied May Snodland.

'Oh, I see.' He stood transfixed, staring at her. 'I'm sorry,' he said eventually. He'd been right. Nothing was *ever* going to be the same again.

5

Two weeks later, Hannah was still refusing the food placed three times a day in her cell. During the first week she had not wanted to eat the disgusting fare and, in any case, the pains in her stomach were almost unbearable, but there had been times when she had been tempted. Now she found a perverse pride in her willpower to starve herself, which gave her the strength to continue. It was as well that she had little to do for the least exertion made her dizzy. She had never been a big eater but was surprised by how swiftly her body had reacted to the lack of food.

The cruellest thing was that all her dreams were of steak and kidney pies, a knife breaking the crust and pungent steam rising to her nostrils, sides of beef, steak dripping with blood. She woke to find none of it existed. And how strange that all of her dreams were of meat – cakes and puddings never appeared.

In the second week she felt better: the hunger pangs had lessened, but she was weaker. It was as well that she had no duties to perform – she doubted she could summon the energy to do anything. She was luckier than some of the other women, who were working long hours sewing prison clothes or, even worse, separating the hemp, which tore their fingers to shreds.

At the outset she had made a fuss, demanding that she be treated the same as the others, but was told in no uncertain terms to 'shut up'. Now she was glad she had not succeeded.

In her new environment she had learned the importance of maintaining her supply of drinking water. They were each given a small jugful in the morning to last the day and she always asked for more. It was the only request that was met. She knew that she could live a long time without food, months, the others had told her, but without water she would be dead in days.

One of her greatest fears was that her breath smelt, and she spent much time exhaling into her palm to see if it did. At first it had not bothered her but one day, whispering to Fanny, she had had to stop herself shrinking back from the poor creature, and then she noticed that others were suffering too. Her appeal for tooth powder and a brush had fallen on deaf ears.

Having accustomed herself to the squalid mattress and covers, she slept as much as she could. She was no longer aware of the smell. Her nails were breaking and her skin was dry and flaking. Her normally shiny hair was dull and lacklustre. She avoided looking in the small mirror that hung in the washroom: she found the image that she saw reflected in it was too depressing. They were not allowed mirrors of their own in case they used them to harm themselves. Until now Hannah had regarded those who succumbed to suicide as selfish but she had come to understand how easy it was to contemplate ending it all.

To Hannah the washroom was a place of horror. It was furnished with rows of baths on either side. Down the middle the duck-boarding was permanently wet and gave off the musty odour of rot. There were curtains at each cubicle but they were never allowed to pull them tight. It was abhorrent to Hannah that anyone might see her naked body as they passed by and she always pulled her curtain, but the wardress made a point of pulling it back.

They were allowed one bath a week. There was a system of sorts whereby, if you were in the wardresses' good books, you used the water first. Those who had annoyed them went last. By that time, at least three others had bathed in the water, which was cloudy and cold. Hannah was firmly in the latter group. When she had her first bath she had been faced with the choice between dirty water or remaining unwashed. She had closed her eyes and made herself slip into the bath.

For even more personal ablutions Hannah was faced with another choice: there was a bucket in her cell, which appalled her – if she used it, she had to live with the odour – or the lavatory by the bathroom, in which she could be viewed by all and sundry for the door had to remain open. 'A precaution,' she had been told, but she did not believe it. There was nothing there with which they could harm themselves. No, Hannah was sure it was done to humiliate them further. To make them more quiescent. Well, she had decided, it was not going to work with her. Now, fourteen days on, she feared it was.

Quite soon she had formed a routine for herself. She was woken at five with the arrival of her breakfast tray, clattering on to the stone floor. She would not allow herself to look at the congealing porridge for fear she might succumb. It's wallpaper paste, she would tell herself. But if she placed it under her bed out of sight, a wardress would appear within minutes to pull it out again.

So, for breakfast she would remember a stanza of one of Lord Tennyson's poems. 'Childe Harold' was her favourite. As a child she had complained when her governess had insisted she learn great swathes of poetry by heart. Now she was grateful to her.

The removal of the food was always accompanied by a lecture on the risk she was taking. Whichever wardress gave it, it was always in the same words. They had obviously learnt it by rote but, from their bored expressions, they were not rewarded with the same degree of pleasure as she was with her poetry.

'I am beholden to warn you that if you don't eat no responsibility can be taken for the state of your health. In consequence, if you persist, we shall have no alternative but to ensure that you do.'

As she listened to the monotonous dirge she began to think they had no idea what they were saying to her, that long ago they had stopped thinking about what it meant. Afterwards she always thanked them for it seemed the polite thing to do. She felt it important to maintain the courtesies or she might become as coarse and unfeeling as they. Not that she was afraid. She knew that the public outcry at force-feeding of suffragettes had led to a new policy. It was why they were weighed each day. Once they had lost a certain percentage of their weight – irritatingly, she could not find out what it was – they were sent home until it was restored, whereupon they returned to complete their sentence.

Hannah had a plan. She would be sent home where she would control her diet and never regain the weight she had lost since she was sentenced. Then she need never come back. She felt elated at the subterfuge and hugged it to her when anyone was being particularly unpleasant to her. She would show them.

She was meticulous about the state of her cell, which she swept out every day when the dustpan and brush were brought to her. That had been one of her little triumphs: she had made such a rumpus that they now allowed her to have it every day instead of once a week.

Once a week. Everything happened thus. The bath. Hair-washing. Cleaning of cells. Visitors were different: that was once a month – too cruel, she felt.

After sweeping her cell she would sit and plan gardens, which stopped her thinking of Cariad, whom she missed with an aching longing – just to stroke her coat once … Gardens! Wonderful gardens. Experimental ones. She would give rein to her imagination, allowing colour combinations that she knew would frighten her more conservative clients. She would dream of propagating new plants, roses as big as soup plates, lilies of varying hues. Soon she realised that some of her ideas were not so outlandish. When she was back in her greenhouses, she would experiment. Until now she had raised plants from other people's seeds and cuttings. Now she would create her own.

'Time is never wasted.' How often had Agnes said that to her? How right she was. Hannah had been sorely hurt that she had not come to visit her, even though she had asked her to come.

'It's not possible, Hannah. You are allowed only one person and we all thought it important that it should be one of your brothers.' Hannah was sitting opposite Oliver on a raffia-seated stool, worn almost through, with a small table between them. The ubiquitous wardress stood impassively by the door, listening to every word. Hannah accepted what he had said, but she was still hurt that Agnes hadn't bothered to write to her. They might have parted with cross words but she would never have abandoned Agnes if their roles had been reversed.

'Not *one* of my brothers, dear Oliver. Just you.' She decided not to think about Agnes any more and put out her hand to touch his.

'No touching,' the woman barked.

'Oh, really!' Oliver was beginning to stand up.

'No, dearest. Don't. You'll make it worse for me.'

He sat again. 'In what way?'

'They have numerous ways of making life a little more uncomfortable than it already is.'

'I shall see the governor.'

'I'd rather you didn't, Oliver.' She smiled at him, but was aware it was more of a rictus. 'Please,' she added, for good measure.

'It's wrong.'

'There is much that is,' she whispered, so that the woman could not hear and had to lean forward to try to catch what they were saying.

'Why, Hannah?'

'Why am I here? I had to do something after poor Emily Davison made her sacrifice at the Derby.'

'Any person mad enough to hurl herself in front of a horse deserves to die.'

'Oliver, please don't. Let's change the subject. I was about to ask about Mortie.'

'He's gone up to Glenkindie – a shooting party. I was disgusted. He should have delayed his trip.'

'Perhaps Coral forbade it. Perhaps she is too ashamed of me to allow him to visit me.'

'You always make excuses for him. It was his own selfishness at work. He has position here – people he could have seen to get you released.'

'Then I presume your mother is much better? He wouldn't have left her.'

'Wouldn't he?'

'Oliver, that is naughty of him. The poor woman!'

'Don't waste your pity on her, Hannah. Illness is making her an even greater monster. If it wasn't for Lettice I don't know what we should do.'

'You shouldn't speak of your mother so, Oliver. And dear Lettice, I worry about her … I fear she's unhappy.'

'Hannah, you should be worrying about yourself. We haven't time to talk about the rest of the family now, we should be discussing you and what's to be done.'

'I didn't bite that woman, Oliver.'

'I didn't for one moment believe you did. I've spoken to Battle, who is worse than useless. We shall appeal.'

'Is that wise? The others here say that if you do sometimes they change the sentence to a longer one, and three months isn't so bad. I shall be out in time for the bulb-planting.'

'The thing is, if you didn't bite her who did?'

'I know who did and I have forbidden her to speak up. She has a young family.'

'Hannah!' He shook his head. 'You're always thinking of others. But why did that wardress accuse you? Who is paying her to say so?'

'I assumed she was mistaken, but it puzzled me because the other woman is a good six inches shorter than me and blonde. But it was such a mêlée … and I don't think I have any enemies.'

'You don't. But I do.'

'You don't mean …'

'Who else? Esmeralda has been behaving strangely and I'm sure she's hiding something – she is usually so open and honest. I think she knows her father is behind this and is too loyal to say so.'

'The poor woman. She's in such an awkward position, between you and her father.'

'I don't agree. Her loyalty should be to me and mine. If you are incarcerated here, and her father is behind it, she is as much to blame as he.'

'No.' Hannah was on her feet, palms flat on the table. 'No,' she repeated even louder. 'You are not to say or think these things. Esmeralda is a wonderful woman and friend. You must not let my misfortune damage your life with her. I forbid it.'

'How can I not be angry?'

'You have no proof, mere conjecture. She might be worried about something else. Her health, perhaps.'

'Then what are we to do? I'll find a new lawyer, one from Exeter.'

'I'd rather you left things as they are, Oliver.'

'Time's up,' the wardress announced.

'I beg your pardon?' Oliver was affronted.

'Please, my dearest brother, don't argue, don't make a fuss, for my sake.' And to prevent further argument she turned and walked swiftly out of the interview room, the wardress two steps behind her.

That visit had been two days ago; now she had nearly four weeks to wait until she saw him again. Still, feeling sorry for herself was not going to help.

The only time she saw the other women was during the half-hour they were allowed out for exercise. They were marshalled into a long line and walked aimlessly round the prison yard with its high walls. Still, she saw the sky, the sun and the birds flying. She often thought of Mr Wilde's poem – *The Ballad of Reading Jail* – and recited it to herself, she had never fully understood it until now. She enjoyed the walking, the whispered conversations. They were not allowed to talk but the wardresses usually turned a deaf ear. The courage of the others shamed her – Fanny was wasting away.

'I had a lot of fat to lose.' She laughed. 'But I ain't risking eating them slops.'

What the authorities didn't understand was that in treating them so badly they were simply ensuring that the women would never give up the fight. All they were asking for was for the right to vote, and to be punished so harshly was out of all proportion to the crime. Another matter was occupying Hannah's mind: when she got out she would do all she could to improve the lot of women in prison. Oh, yes, there was much to fight for.

'Cresswell!'

At the sight of Miss Rowntree, Hannah's stomach lurched.

'Come.'

Meekly, Hannah followed her. They walked along the corridor and up a flight of stone stairs, past the yellowing tiles, the green paint. There was a strong smell of carbolic in the air as they entered the hospital wing. Miss Rowntree pushed open a door, and stood back to allow Hannah to enter, giving her a shove as she did so.

'Won't eat. We'll see about that.'

Hannah looked with horror at the scene in front of her. She felt the contents of her bowels turn to fluid. Fanny lay tied to a chair by heavy leather straps. 'Oh, Miss Cresswell …' Her big brown eyes were full of tears.

'You can't do this,' Hannah looked at the paraphernalia laid out on a small table, which was neatly covered with a white cloth. There was an enamel bowl, a jug and, curled round these items like an obscene red snake, a rubber tube, on which a woman was placing a glass funnel. 'This is no longer allowed.'

'Who says? Well I never. Did you hear that, ladies?' The hated Rown-tree laughed.

'Fanny, give in.'

'I can't do that, Miss Cresswell. Then they've won, haven't they?'

'But, my dear …' Hannah moved towards her but was grabbed and held back. 'It's dangerous.'

'Not when you are as expert as us. We only put the food in the lungs if we want to.' Another jeering. Hannah, who had never before wished to harm anyone, felt such a surge of hatred that she wished she could kill Rowntree.

'Fanny.'

'I'll be all right, Miss. Can't be worse than having a baby.' Fanny tried to smile.

The woman with the red tube approached her.

'There should be a doctor here.'

'I am a doctor.'

'Then you should be ashamed of yourself,' Hannah found the courage to say. Rowntree kicked her calf hard.

As she watched Hannah knew she was witnessing a scene that would haunt her for ever. Fanny screamed and writhed, shaking her head from side to side to avoid the black rubber gag they were forcing into her mouth. It was taking four wardresses and the belts to hold her down. Then the gag went in and Hannah was not sure which was worse – the screaming or the retching.

'You stupid woman, you're making it worse. Just sit still and it will not be so bad,' the doctor ordered, but Fanny still fought. One wardress stood on a stool holding the jug high and a white fluid was poured into the funnel.

'Enjoyed the spectacle, did you? You're next,' Rowntree sneered.

'I'll eat,' Hannah heard herself say and hung her head. The shame, she knew, would never leave her either. She had let them down. She was a coward.

6

When she was young, Penelope Cresswell had been a beauty, but even the most careful or compassionate of observers now would have found it hard to see even a trace of it. She was of such mountainous proportions that it took four people to lift her in her sickbed and care had to be taken when tucking in the sheets that a fold of her skin was not included.

'I have never liked Christmas pudding,' she whined, in what had once been a melodious voice.

'When it is Christmas I shall make sure you are not served it,' Lettice said patiently. It was her turn to sit with her grandmother. That they were all reluctant to be with her was sad, she thought, as she took out her sewing. However, it had occurred to her soon after she arrived that her turn came around more frequently than everyone else's. Still, she did not mind much, which was just as well since, with Coral and Mortie leaving, there was only herself, her brother and the staff left. She liked the days when Esmeralda came to the manor to take her turn, for after a stint her back always ached and she knew it was caused by tension in anticipation of a spiteful tirade.

'Why was I given it for luncheon?'

'You weren't, Grandmama.'

'How dare you contradict me, girl? Are you accusing me of lying?' Although she attempted to heave herself up on her pillows the effort was too much for her and her face became an alarming puce. 'Well, don't just sit there! Help me, you lazy child.'

'Of course, Grandmama.' Lettice stood and puffed up the pillows, knowing she hadn't the strength to lift the old woman. This seemed to satisfy Penelope, who settled back with what sounded almost like a contented sigh.

'I don't like it and no one listens to me.' She pouted, as she had done coquettishly in the past to get what she wanted; she was unaware that now it made her look ridiculous. 'It's rude to contradict your elders.'

'I never would, Grandmama.'

'Then practise what you preach.'

'Yes, Grandmama.'

'I hate Christmas.'

'What a shame. I like it very much. The giving and receiving.'

'No one gave me any presents today.'

'But ...' Lettice thought it better not to proceed.

'When your grandfather was alive I received a bounty of gifts. He loved me so he showered me with baubles. He should never have died and left me. It was so selfish of him.'

'Yes, Grandmama.'

'You mean you think your grandfather was a selfish man?' Penelope frowned ominously.

'I never said he was.'

'Then why did you agree with me?'

'I don't know, Grandmama.'

'You always were weak.'

'Yes, Grandmama.' At least she wasn't lying this time. Her grandmother was right. Lettice *was* weak and despised herself for it.

'Is your delightful husband coming to visit me? I forget his name.'

'Hugo.'

'So? Why can't you ever answer my questions?'

'I'm not sure.' She prayed every night that her husband would not come.

'Tiring of you, is he? I can't say I blame him. He must be bored witless.'

Lettice counted mentally to ten. The woman was so insufferably rude and insensitive. It wasn't her illness making her so, this was how she had always been. She was trying to make her cry and Lettice wouldn't give her the satisfaction of doing so.

'Are you happy?'

'Of course, Grandmama,' Lettice lied.

'I don't believe you.'

'That is your privilege, Grandmama.'

'Grandmama! Grandmama! Yes, Grandmama! Three bags full, Grandmama,' Penelope said, in a singsong voice, hitting the sheet with irritation. 'Does he beat you?'

'No, Grandmama.' He didn't but he shouted, his face a mere inch from hers. He would scream at her, his spittle spraying her face, and she would cower, expecting blows to follow. Sometimes she wished he would hit her just to get the waiting over.

'Then he should. He might knock some sense into you.'

Lettice lowered her head as if concentrating on her embroidery, determined she would not shed the tears that were perilously close.

'I know your aunt has stolen my dog.'

'I always thought it was Aunt Hannah's dog.'

'Because she lies to everyone and says it is. She stole him – can't remember his name.'

'She's called Cariad.'

'Don't be stupid, she's a he.'

'Yes, Grandmama.'

'She took him when your grandfather died. Lied to me and said she didn't have him but I knew she did. She's always hated me, you know. Spiteful woman. Spinsters often are. It's the lack of bodily juices that makes them so. I want the dog back. Now!'

'Yes, Grandmama.'

'He'll be company for me here. You all ignore me, leave me alone for hours at a time. I need company.' She looked suspiciously as if she was about to cry. Lettice passed her a clean handkerchief. 'And tell that ungrateful Hannah it's about time she came to see me.'

'Yes, Grandmama.' They had decided not to tell Penelope what had befallen Hannah, more to protect Hannah than her stepmother.

'Why are you still sitting there? Go and get her.'

'I have to sit with you. I shall go when someone else comes.' Surreptitiously she looked at her watch.

At the sound of the door opening she stowed her sewing with unseemly haste into her work box. 'You'll be needing your lunch, Mrs Hamilton.' Penelope's maid had entered the room.

'Thank you, Colette.' She straightened her skirt as she stood. 'I'll return this afternoon, Grandmama, after your nap.'

'Don't inconvenience yourself. But, then, you never do, do you?'

The maid smiled sympathetically at her.

'Do you know the lies she's been telling me, Colette?' Penelope asked.

'Milady?'

'She said I didn't have Christmas pudding, which I loathe, for luncheon.'

'It was spotted Dick. You ordered it this morning.'

'Was it? You see?' She stared at Lettice with venom. 'And what is more she didn't give me a present and she knows how I love Christmas.'

'No doubt she will when the time comes. But it's September, milady. A long time to the festive season.'

'Then why did she tell me it was?'

'I've no idea, milady.' Colette winked at Lettice. *You go*, she mouthed.

'Get that dog for me, immediately.'

'I shall,' she replied, with no intention of doing any such thing. In any case, her grandmother would have forgotten about it within the hour. Relieved, Lettice rushed from the room.

Rowan Marshall was feeling sick with nerves as she stood in the passage outside the kitchens at Cresswell Manor, waiting to be summoned into the housekeeper's room. She had put on her best dress – well, it wasn't hers but one she shared with her three sisters who were closest to her

67

in size. Consequently the buttons strained across her chest, so she took shallow breaths.

It would be nice to earn some money that was hers alone: she'd be able to buy her own clothes. She'd still have to give some to her mother, but she'd save hard for her own things. She didn't mind: it was the way things were. If she'd been able to work at the hotel she might have made more money …

She fiddled with the hat her mother had insisted she wore to keep her naturally curly hair in some order, but she knew some had escaped – she could feel it. The button boots she wore had large holes in the soles. It had looked like rain when she set out, and she hoped it would hold off until she got home or her feet would be soaked.

Her family was always short of money even though her parents both had good jobs at the Cresswell Arms. Her mother was the best cook in the district, as far as Rowan was concerned, and her father was pot-man, coachman when required, and worked for Miss Hannah too – but they had had eight children. Rowan loved her sisters and brother but she was determined, when she married, to have just two children. She didn't know how you stopped having them but she'd heard rumours and would find out.

The housekeeper's door opened. 'Rowan Marshall?'

'Yes, Miss.'

'Mrs Herbert to you.'

'Sorry.'

Mrs Herbert sat down at her desk. Rowan saw a chair beside it and went to sit on it.

'You stand there.' The housekeeper pointed at a spot on the elegant carpet – lovely it was, full of colour. Rowan took up her stance, hands folded neatly in front of her.

'Why are you looking for a position?'

Rowan thought for a second. She didn't think it would be wise to say she wanted money of her own and to get away from her crowded home. 'I want to help my mother.'

'How does it help her if you are here? I gather you are a large family.'

'Yes, and all those mouths need feeding.' That was a good answer she thought.

'Eight children. Are you the eldest?'

'No, first there's Aspen, then me. Then Willow, Maple, Acacia, Oak, Cherry and Holly.'

'All names of trees. Well, good gracious me.'

68

'Yes. I always say it's better than being called after weeds or bushes.' She giggled but either Mrs Herbert didn't appreciate her little joke or she didn't understand it.

'Your mother might have problems if she has any more.'

'God forbid. But yes, I suppose so. She says she's going to make Dad tie a knot in it.'

'Rowan!' Mrs Herbert looked shocked. 'That is no way to speak.' But she had to look away as a little smile fluttered about her lips. 'So, you want to work here. Why?'

'I don't want to go far away in case my mother needs me.' The woman was frowning, as if this was a problem. 'I'm sure she never will but it would be less worry for me if I was close,' she added hurriedly. 'And Cresswell Manor has always been part of my life. We used to live on the estate and we went to the school here. And, well, I just don't want to go further away...' This was not true but she thought it was probably the right thing to say.

'I have a position as a junior housemaid.'

'A housemaid? That would be wonderful! Me mum said I'd have to start as a scullerymaid – if I was lucky.'

'I am prepared to employ you for a three-month trial. If you are suitable and join us permanently you will be paid fifteen pounds per annum. You will have half a day off each week and one full day a month.'

'Yes, Mrs ...' In her excitement she had forgotten the woman's name.

'Mrs Herbert.'

'Sorry, Mrs Herbert.'

'We shall supply your uniform and the cost will be deducted from your wages. Any damage you cause, or breakages, will also be deducted. Do you understand?'

'Yes, Mrs Herbert.'

'You will not fraternise with the male servants. Nor are you to have followers. Such behaviour will lead to instant dismissal and no testimonials.'

'I won't do nothing like that, Mrs Herbert. I promise.'

The housekeeper looked at Rowan's beautiful face and a somewhat cynical expression crossed her features. 'I hope you keep your promises.' She leant over and pressed a bell.

As if she had been waiting outside a maid entered. Rowan looked at the black dress, the fine lace-trimmed white apron and the neat cap on her head, and nearly exclaimed with excitement.

'Mary, you are to show Rowan to her room. Then take her to Mrs

Jones to be fitted with her uniform.' She turned back to Rowan. 'Return here tomorrow evening. I suggest you go home to collect your things. I hope you will be happy here, and that we shall be satisfied with you and the manner in which you carry out your duties. Thank you. That will be all.'

Outside the door Rowan leapt into the air, clutching her hands to her chest, then hugged Mary until the other girl, red-faced and laughing, pushed her away. 'Here, let me breathe.'

'I'm so excited I could bust.'

'You won't be thinking that at six on Wednesday morning, that's for sure. Here's our staircase. That one's for the men.'

Rowan followed her up a spiralling stone staircase to the top of the house.

'Why are there two staircases?'

'To keep the footmen out of our knickers.' Mary grinned showing her teeth and gums. Rowan hoped *she* didn't do that when she smiled. She must check in the mirror. 'Not that it does.'

'What?'

'Keep them out.'

'Never! But Mrs Herbert said—'

'She says a lot but we ignore it. We're here to have fun.'

She wondered if it was true or if Mary was showing off. She knew one thing: she wasn't going to risk her future with any hanky-panky.

'Here we are.' Mary opened one of the doors on a long dark corridor. They stepped into a plain room with simple striped wallpaper in blue and white. Blue curtains hung at the small mullioned window. On one side was a single bed, the sheets and blankets folded on top. There was a washstand with a basin and a ewer. A curtain hung over a small alcove where she could see a coat-hanger.

'There's only one bed.' Rowan's voice brimmed with her astonishment.

'We don't share here.'

'And this is just for me?'

'It is.'

At which point, to Mary's astonishment, Rowan burst into tears.

Chapter Three

November–December 1913

1

Dolly was tired. Her day had been long and fraught. She had rushed home from her office, later than usual, to prepare her husband's dinner only to find that he was not there.

Normally you could set a watch by Zeph. His routine never varied. It irked Dolly, who found such rigidity dull and unadventurous. And she was worried. Since their argument, over two months ago, their relationship had changed: their easy comfort with each other had been swept away. In the last months each had tried too hard not to upset the other – the naturalness had deserted them. She had read about earthquakes and how they could alter the landscape and felt that that was what had happened to their marriage.

'Where could he have got to?' she asked May Snodland, who had appeared from the stairs. Dolly looked at the clock on the mantelshelf, draped with a tasselled burgundy velvet cover. She stroked it: she had always wanted one and it was newly acquired. The clock, another recent acquisition, showed it had gone half past six. She followed May to the kitchen. 'Where can he be?'

'He rushed in.' May was busying herself at the sink.

'So you've seen him, he's been home?' She was taking off her overcoat.

'Yes. He was in a great hurry. He had to see his mother. He asked me to stay until you returned – to look after the children,' she said unnecessarily.

'That was kind of you.'

May was on the move again, this time going back to the sitting-room. Once again Dolly followed her. 'But it was inconsiderate of him.'

'Oh, I didn't mind. But I put Charlie down in Del's bed – he was so tired. I hope you don't mind.' All the time she spoke she was wandering about the room.

'Of course not. Zeph still thinks the children are babies,' Dolly said to May's back. 'I wish you'd stop fiddling and look at me.' May turned round, but she was staring at the floor. 'But I don't understand why he's gone to his mother. On a Friday too – he always goes to his photographic club,' she said, unaware of the irritation in her voice. She resented his new hobby: it was expensive and she felt he should spend the evenings with his family.

'He said she was unwell.'

'Unwell? What's wrong with her?'

'He didn't say.'

Dolly was folding her scarf neatly. Zeph had mentioned to her last week that he was concerned, and had hinted again that they should move back to Cress. She had refused to discuss it with him. Now she felt ashamed that she had not contacted Melanie, whom she liked. 'He could have popped in to tell me – he'd have had to pass my office to get to the station. He knows I'm often late on a Friday, pay day. Which reminds me.' She had put her purse on the chenille-covered table and now counted out change, which she laid on the tablecloth. 'I don't know how I managed before you came to us. My guardian angel must have sent you.'

'Then I owe the angel a big debt. You're so good to Charlie and me. How many employers would let me bring the little one with me?' She went to collect the sleepy toddler. A few moments later she was back. 'Is it still cold outside?' She stood him on a chair to button his coat.

'It's unseasonably warm. I doubt he'll catch a chill.' She smiled at May, knowing how much she worried. It was hardly surprising – her son was all she had in this world. Life could be so cruel. This thought made Dolly give thanks for the fortunate position she was in. 'You set off home. Where are my children?'

'I asked if they had homework and sent them to their rooms to do it.'

'Poor lambs. I sometimes wonder if I make them work too hard. Their father says I do.'

'They'll be grateful in the long run. You can do nothing worthwhile without education. When the time comes, I wish I could help my son in such a way.'

'Find a rich husband.' Dolly laughed gaily.

She showed May and Charlie out, then hung her hat and coat on the hallstand. The number of wonderful things she was accumulating amazed her. Once a week she bought the house something small – a cup and saucer, a spoon, an ornament. Once every three months she bought it something big, and each item increased her sense of security. She loved her house and everything in it, and somehow, knowing that her labour had enabled her to purchase most of it, filled her with pride. She wondered in what conditions May lived. She'd never enquired, not wanting to hear the answer.

May was a good worker, there was no doubt of that, she thought, as she looked at the gleaming linoleum runner that led like a patterned road to the back of the house where the kitchen and scullery were. 'I'm here,' she called up the stairs, where she planned to have an Axminster carpet one day – it might be some time before she could afford *that*.

In the kitchen she collected the vegetables for supper. Of course there was the tally man: if she used him she could have the carpet whenever she wanted. Still, what if she had an accident, couldn't work? How would she keep up the payments? Zeph would never forgive her.

In the past they would have had bread and jam for their evening meal, with a cake, if she was feeling flush. How grand that they now had a cooked meal every day – although bread and jam was easier. 'Still, girl,' she said to herself. 'You wouldn't have it any other way.' She began to peel the potatoes. Only the other day May had asked her if, God forbid, there was a fire, which of her possessions she would rush to save. She had not known what to answer, but as the clock in the living room chimed the quarter she knew it would have to be that. There was something opulent about a chiming timepiece.

'Hello, my angels.'

'I wish you wouldn't call me that.' Apollo scowled.

'But that's what you are to me. My little miracles.'

He made a retching sound and his mother laughed. 'Do you mind, Del?' she asked her daughter who, with her blonde hair and blue eyes, looked like an angel in a book of paintings. She bent down for her daughter to kiss her.

'What's for tea?' asked Cordelia.

'I'm making carrot soup. And then we've got nice plaice and chips.'

'I hate carrot soup,' said Apollo.

'Is there anything you don't hate?' Her laughter intensified her son's expression of discontent. Why he could be so was a mystery to Dolly, who could only marvel at the change in her fortunes that allowed her to give them so many things she had never had. She hadn't known that half of them even existed because her own family had been so poor. Still, he would probably grow out of his bad-tempered moods – after all, he was only eleven.

She gave the children their tea, amused to note that her boy ate the soup he claimed he hated. There was never any problem feeding Cordelia.

The clock chimed eight, the quarter and finally the half-hour. She tried not to be anxious. Her mother had told her there was no point in worrying about something that hadn't happened; time enough when it did. It was a philosophy she tried to live by.

While she waited she used the time to do some long overdue sewing. Even with May's help she was behind on so many things. When she had first mooted her business idea to Zeph he had resisted, as she had known he would with his male pride. But when she had won the argument it was with the proviso that it did not affect his routine. She had promised it wouldn't – to make her dream come true she would have promised *anything* – but over the last couple of years she had worn herself to a frazzle. Now she was sure that if she had not taken on May she would have had to give up eventually and say goodbye to many more dreams. She smiled to herself as she sewed a button on to one of Zeph's shirts. When she had first employed May she had expected to have to argue with Zeph and justify the cost but, to her surprise, he had never said anything about it. He was a considerate man, unlike many she knew.

Another quarter chimed. Something must be wrong. Was his mother seriously ill? Had there been an accident? She would hate anything to be wrong with Melanie, a good woman, as all who knew her said. And she had had so much to put up with, not only from her errant husbands but her errant daughter too. Melanie had mentioned Xenia to her only once and that was one night when, unusually for both women, they had drunk too much port. That night Melanie had confided in Dolly about her first husband but said nothing about the second. That he was a waster Dolly had learnt from Zeph. But, out of the blue, she had talked of her daughter.

'I never really liked her, you see.' At Dolly's horrified expression, she had added quickly. 'I loved her, but loving and liking are two different things, aren't they?'

'I suppose so.' Dolly had felt uncertain.

'Xenia was not the easiest person to get on with. She was wilful. Beautiful, but headstrong...' She had paused and Dolly had waited for her to continue, virtually holding her breath for she longed to know and Zeph would never discuss his sister. All she had heard was gossip and Dolly had lived long enough to know that the sort of gossip swirling about Cresswell had to be treated with caution. 'I worry about her every day, what she's doing, who she's with, what sort of life she's leading.'

'I'm sure she's all right,' Dolly had said. 'Probably she's married to some nice young man and settled.'

'Xenia can never be settled. There's a wildness in her that ensures she will never be content. And it's my fault.'

Dolly was shocked to see that Melanie was crying and wasn't sure what to do. Her mother-in-law was a private person and she'd never seen her hug anyone or tell them how much she loved them, unlike Dolly, who did so every day of her family's lives.

'I'm sure it's not,' she said finally, not liking to touch her, which was what her instincts told her to do.

'But she knew, you see. From a small child I'm sure she knew how I felt about her and she grew ever further from me ...'

It had taken Dolly a long time to calm her down. When she had asked her husband about his sister he had swung round angrily to face her. 'I don't want to talk about her.'

'But she's your sister.'

'Not any more. I don't care what's happened to her.'

'You don't mean that.'

'Yes, I do.' He had slammed out of the room and she had never dared bring up the subject again. The closest she had got to finding anything out was from the cook, Flossie Marshall.

'No doubt she's someone's fancy woman by now,' Flossie had said, and Dolly had been filled with awe that anybody to whom she was connected could be so wicked and brave.

Then there was his work, which, she was sure was making Zeph unhappy and discontented. Zeph had felt Mr Battle had been less than professional in his treatment of Miss Cresswell, letting his disapproval of the suffragettes cloud his judgment as her solicitor. However, Dolly, unbeknown to Zeph was in total accord – she thought the silly women had got what they deserved.

At the sound of his key in the lock she dropped her sewing. 'Zeph, where have you been? I've been trying not to worry.'

'Didn't May tell you? I had to go and see my mother.'

'But for so long?'

'She has pneumonia.'

'She's not old. It must be a cold.' She was unaware of how uncaring she sounded.

'That's a cruel thing to say.'

'I didn't mean it to be.'

'Then think before you speak. The doctor was there and he confirmed it. I've come back to collect you and the children.'

'What for?'

75

'To be with her, of course.'

'At this time of night? But tomorrow ...' Saturday was always a busy day for her; many women entertained and needed help in the kitchen. And it wasn't just them – the hotel was busy too and often called for extra hands. 'I can't possibly go.' As soon as she said it she regretted it, for the anger deepened on Zeph's face.

'Your duty is to be with my mother.'

'There can't be a train this late.'

'There isn't. I've hired a pony and trap. Instead of standing there arguing, get a move on.'

The children complained at being woken and made to get dressed. Dolly wrapped them up in the back of the trap and climbed up beside her husband.

They sped along, far too fast since Zeph couldn't see where they were going in the pitch dark. If it hadn't been so hurried she would have enjoyed the trip, but instead she was trying to work out how she could get back to Barlton tomorrow. Perhaps if she volunteered to sit up with his mother he might change his mind and let her slip away in the morning.

'... I've discussed it with her,' he was saying.

'Sorry, I didn't quite hear ...' The truth was, she hadn't been listening.

'With ...'

'Discuss what?'

'The move.'

'What move?'

'Have you not heard a word I've said?' Momentarily he took his eyes off the lane ahead.

'I'm sorry.' And she was. This was not normally how she behaved. And her husband was usually equable and kind, not cross and barking at her, as now. Perhaps he hadn't exaggerated and his mother was indeed seriously ill.

'We can't leave her alone with Richard,' he said.

'No.'

'I'm glad you agree. It will be an upheaval but it was inevitable it would happen one day. I've told Mr Battle.'

'Told him what?'

'That we're moving back to Cresswell. My mother needs us.'

'But she's only just become ill.'

'Things have been bad for some time. Richard is permanently drunk.

I saw her last week and we talked about it then. I did try to tell you but, if you remember, you wouldn't discuss it.'

'How could I forget?'

'May has agreed that she can be of use to us there and will move with us.'

Dolly sat upright. 'So May knows about all of this? She never said a word to me. And your mother too? Did it not occur to you that you should talk to me first? I'm your wife.'

'I tried. You weren't prepared to listen. You are my wife. If I go, then you and the children come too. There is no room for argument.'

For once in her life Dolly was speechless.

2

Heavy breathing dominated all other sounds in the room. Flossie sat with her hands in the lap of her apron, which, rushing up from the kitchens, she had not had time to remove. She rubbed them up and down the starched fabric, unable to keep them still. The room was hot since the windows were closed. On the fire, a saucepan of water boiled, steam rising, in a vain attempt to help Melanie's breathing. Across the bed Mavis Pepper sat rigid as stone, unaware that, when the patient's breathing paused hers did too.

It had been Mavis who had called Flossie to the bedside. 'She shouldn't have got like this so sudden.'

'She's so much worse than when Zeph was here,' Flossie fretted.

'He should never have gone. It's not right leaving us alone with her and all the responsibility.'

'I'm sure it won't be long before he's back.'

'Where's the dratted doctor?' Mavis said belligerently.

Flossie stroked the hair from Melanie's eyes and straightened the red flannel blanket they'd placed over her to bring out the fever. She wished Mavis would be quiet: all she'd done was carp ever since she got here, making a bad situation worse. 'Poor dear, she hasn't been right for weeks, coughing and wheezing all over the place, but would she take to her bed? No! Pig-headed is our Melanie. Always has been, always will be.' Flossie chewed her lower lip. 'Still, she'll be all right.' She said this more to give herself courage than because she believed it. She felt restless, so stood up, crossed to the window and peered out. The moon was reflected in the unusually calm water of the bay. At any other time she would have stopped to admire the beauty, but not tonight. She was desperate for the doctor or Zeph to appear. 'I wish he'd come,' she fretted. 'He shouldn't have gone back to Barlton. He'll never forgive himself if anything happens to her.'

'He needs our Dolly here. A sensible girl, her is.'

Flossie, while aware of Dolly's strength of character, felt that Zeph should have sent for Dolly, who could have come on the train – unless ... 'Perhaps he had to go since her wouldn't come herself.' She turned away from the window.

'Flossie! Of course she'd want to be here. He won't be wanting her travelling on her own.'

'She could have come with that other woman, May – what's her name? She managed to get on a train and turn up here, with a little 'un in tow. She came to no harm.' Mavis looked put out. 'It's a puzzle to me why Zeph should send a friend at a time like this,' Flossie continued.

'She's not a friend. She works for our Dolly.' Mavis's large body inflated with pride.

'What's your Dolly need someone for?'

'Her cleaning, that's what.'

'She what?' Flossie could hardly believe her ears. 'Had an accident, has she?'

'Wouldn't you like to have someone to do your chores?' Mavis jumped to her daughter's defence.

'No, I would not. They wouldn't do them right for me.'

'Got standards have ee?'

'I have.' Flossie ploughed on unaware of the irony in Mavis's voice. 'And in any case, I've enough daughters. They help me.'

'Doubt if them's too happy with *that* ...' Mavis muttered.

'What you say?'

'Nothing.'

Mavis folded her arms across her ample bosom and, though still seated, looked truculent.

'Well, if you ask me it's all very odd.'

'But no one *is* asking you, are they?' Mavis said, with a snap.

Fortunately for both of them the conversation, which was rapidly deteriorating into an argument, ceased as the door opened.

'Rowan? What on earth are you doing here?'

'I couldn't stay away, Mum. How is she?'

'Sleeping,' her mother said, though she feared that 'comatose' might be closer to the truth. 'Nice of them to let you come.'

'Oh, they didn't. The housekeeper said I couldn't, that it was too late, and I said I was going and she shouted at me and I shouted back. I just walked out.'

'Good heavens, girl, what were you thinking? You'll be getting the sack.'

'I don't care. There are some things more important than work, Mum, and Mrs Joynston's one of them. And if they do give me the push I can always get a job at that blanket factory.'

'Hard work, that is. I doubt you'd be up to it. Noisy too, my Dolly says.'

'Anything to eat?' Rowan chose to ignore Mavis who, she knew, saw the darker side of everything.

Flossie smiled for the first time that day. 'You and your appetite! You'll get as big as a house.'

'She never will, Flossie. She's one of them can eat whatever she wants and never get fat, just like my Dolly. Not like us.' Mavis patted her ample hips and laughed, then remembered why she was there and stopped.

'Has Dr Bunting been?'

'He came this morning and we've sent for him again.'

'What did he say it was?'

'Pneumonia, brought on by exhaustion. And I'm not surprised, the hours she puts into this place. Scant thanks she gets for it too.'

'What about her parents?'

'Her father's been in but he was so upset he had to leave. She got too agitated when her mother was here and Zeph asked her to go – Melanie and her mum have never got on. I think old man Beasley should have pulled himself together, selfish old bugger. There's no point in thinking of yourself when it's them as is about to leave us needs all our attention.'

'She's not going to …' Rowan could not bring herself to say *that* word.

'It's in God's hands. Now don't take on,' Flossie snapped at her. 'If you can't control yourself you're no good to me either. We want no caterwauling here.' She was an odd mixture of kindness, understanding and abrupt intolerance; her daughter, aware of this, was not offended by her reaction.

'Sorry, Mum.' Rowan sniffed loudly.

'Yes?' Flossie said to a tentative tap on the door. May Snodland entered the darkened room, which was over-hot with the windows tight shut.

'My Charlie's settled and I wondered if I could do anything for you.'

Flossie appraised the slim young woman who stood in front of her. In these parts people from the next village were eyed with suspicion, let alone someone who came from far away and didn't speak the same as them. 'You could help out in the bar. Most of the customers have gone home, not wanting to be a nuisance, but there'll be some still there.'

'I've never worked in a bar, but I'll do my best.' She looked doubtful.

'Rowan here will show you the ropes. If anyone wants food tell them we're not serving tonight.'

Rowan accompanied her from the room.

'She don't look as if she's the strength to do anything for anyone, her's all skin and bone.' Flossie sniffed.

A sigh came from the bed.

'Yes, my lovely? What is it you want?' Melanie's hand was waving weakly in the air. She was mouthing something. Flossie leant over her, the better to hear. 'Yes? What you trying to say, my maid?' She stood up straight and looked across the bed at Mavis, who shrugged her shoulders.

'I didn't catch it.'

'I think she said "Xenia".'

'Surely not. Why would she want that troublesome minx here?'

'To make her peace, I expect.'

Rowan found only a few customers in the bar. There were the Robertson brothers and John Fuller, one of the cattlemen, but the rest had left out of respect. Richard Joynston was slumped in the corner, snoring loudly.

'You'd have thought he could have stayed awake, wouldn't you?' said Rowan, as she found a clean overall for May in a drawer the other side of the bar.

'With the skinful he's had he couldn't. Useless beggar.' Robert Robertson spat his contempt. 'Wonder how much he's had off her.'

'Doubt if he ever stayed sober long enough to know how to steal anything,' was his brother Fred's opinion. 'Still, if owt happens …' He nodded towards the bedrooms above. 'That'll put paid to his games.'

'But he's her husband – won't he cop the lot?'

'I don't see Melanie leaving her Zeph out in the cold.'

'True.' Robert looked thoughtfully at his pipe. 'Mind, I can't see him as much of a landlord. Miserable bugger and no mistake.'

'Perhaps he'll sell up. And then who would we get?'

The matter of who their landlord would be was of much importance to them. May Snodland stood awkwardly, not sure what she should be doing. She wished she had the courage to defend Zeph.

The matter apparently closed, the men stood and stared at May, much to her discomfort.

'Sorry, everyone, I forgot. This is May. She's come from Barlton to help,' Rowan explained.

'How do you do?' May said.

The men shuffled. 'You'm not from round here, then, not the way you talk?'

'No, I come from Kent.'

'And how you liking these parts?' Robert asked.

'Very much, particularly the people.'

'That's nice.' He beamed.

'You could die of thirst in this place. Call it an inn?' Fred grumbled, but jokingly.

'Sorry, what would you like?' May was flustered.

'Pint of ale – if it's not too much trouble.'

May glanced about her, even more agitated. 'That pump there.' Rowan pointed to it.

'Likes it here more than Kent?' Robert persisted.

'Well, Kent is my home …'

The men looked disapproving.

'That's not fair, Rob, as well you know. Stands to reason that home's best.' Rowan had stepped in. 'No matter where in the world I went I'd still love Cresswell best. Watch it, May!' Beer was gushing everywhere.

'Thinking of leaving us then, Rowan? Off to see the world?'

'One day, perhaps, John. But not yet. See, May, when you turn that tap it's best to have the glass under before you do.' She mopped up the spilt ale.

'How you settled up at the big house, Rowan?'

'I like the company but not the work – starts too early in the morning for me.'

'You want to aim at being a lady's maid. That's the best – travel, see the sights.'

'Not me. Looking after some spoilt woman like Lady Penelope? No, I'd like a position in a hotel. Regular hours, better pay.'

'How is the old bat?'

'I reckon she's putting it on, and so do lots of the others. She's too lazy, lying in bed, waited on hand and foot. She won't get better. I heard Miss Lettice say much the same to her brother.'

'His nibs, he still there?'

81

'No, they've gone. There's talk they'll be back for Christmas. But they say Miss Hannah's home from prison.'

'A Cresswell in prison, I never thought to see the day.' Robert sucked harder on his pipe.

'It's all wrong, ain't it? That huge house, all them maids and footmen for that old woman.'

'Here, Rob, have you thought how big the coffin'll have to be to get her in when she coughs it? Big as a house, I hear she is.'

'Fred, what a thing to say!'

'It's the truth, though, Rowan, and it's been bothering me for some time now. For a start, how do we get her down the stairs?'

'Slide her out the window,' Fred spluttered.

'Chop her up!' John slapped his thigh.

'Stop it, all of you,' Rowan ordered. 'You're scaring poor May. And so long as you don't have to pay the wages, Rob, what's it to do with us?'

'Waste of money, that's what it is.'

'It gives people work. If the estate wasn't there, what would we all be doing?' Rowan asked. 'If they closed the place down I'd be all right, but where would the likes of old people like the butler and cook go?'

Robert, Fred and John all burst out laughing. 'Don't tell 'em you think they're old! They'd have your guts for garters, specially that Eve Gilroy,' Robert gasped.

'Shows the advantage of working outside. After all, the gardens have to be kept up. We're all right, Rob. Pints all round, Rowan, if you don't mind,' Fred said.

'You hope you're all right,' Rowan poured the ale this time. 'May, you might as well go to bed. I'll manage here.'

'I thought I should wait for Mr Topsham – and Mrs Topsham too, of course.'

'I'll let them know you're here. You look tired.'

May removed her apron, said goodnight and left.

'Did I hear the back door go?' Rowan poked her head round the bar door in time to see a strained-looking Zeph and Dolly scuttling along the corridor, followed by the doctor. 'That was Zeph with the doctor.'

'Then it really is bad if he's turned out at this time of night. Should we wake him?' John nodded to the still sleeping Richard.

Rowan called his name, but when he told her, impolitely, to leave him alone, she gave up. 'I reckon it's time you all went home to your beds.'

'Getting a bit above yourself, aren't you, Rowan?'

'I don't think you should be here at a time like this – it isn't right.'

She spoke firmly for one so young and, as one, the men downed their pints, muttered goodnight and sheepishly shuffled out.

3

'Zeph, what are you doing here?' Melanie smiled wanly at her son. 'I thought you'd left for home.'

'I went to get Dolly and the children. I wanted to be with you.'

'How kind.'

'Shall I get them?'

'I'm so tired … Perhaps later …'

'Then you sleep. Like the doctor said.' Zeph leant forward, kissed her forehead, pulled the covers over her and tiptoed from the room.

Everyone had congregated in the kitchen and he walked into an uneasy silence. 'She seems better, Flossie. And the doctor isn't so worried.'

Flossie turned from the range where she had been heating milk. 'A miracle, that's what it is, Zeph. Flat out, her was. I think it was your voice rallied her. Calling for your sister her was. To tell you the truth, Zeph, that really worried me.'

'I understand.' He smiled at Flossie's indiscretion. 'I'd already sent her a telegram. I hope she'll be here in the morning.'

'I didn't know you knew where she was.' Dolly felt affronted at something else he had kept from her.

'I don't. But I know how to get a message to her.'

'She'll not be too happy when she turns up on a wild-goose chase,' Mavis said.

'She'll just have to put up with it.' Flossie had never had much time for Xenia. 'We really thought her was a goner. Didn't we, Mavis?'

'No, I never. You did.'

'So she's much better?' Dolly asked, in a controlled manner.

'Yes, she is. But the doctor says it happens. There's a crisis and then … Of course, she's tired but she already looks better than she did this morning.' Flossie sounded almost defensive.

'So we need not have rushed here like we did. I thought she must be on the way out.' Dolly's expression was one of intense irritation.

'The doctor said she was in a deep sleep, exhausted from the high temperature she's had,' Zeph explained.

'Asleep?' Dolly stood, hands on hip.

'We thought it was worse than that,' Flossie said anxiously, as if she had done something wrong.

'I didn't,' Mavis chipped in.

'Why've you changed your tune, Mavis?'

'Why didn't you speak up sooner, then, Mum? In future, Flossie, you should check with the doctor before you get into a panic,' Dolly declared.

'I beg your pardon?' Carefully Flossie placed the pan of boiling milk on the table. 'It were Dr Bunting suggested we call Zeph this morning. And why are you so angry? You should be pleased she's better, not getting at me.'

'It's not just Flossie!' Zeph put in. 'I was worried too – it's why I came to get you. And she's not out of danger yet. The doctor's concerned about her heart.'

'But we could have been told this tomorrow. It's all been so unnecessary, frightening us out of our skins.'

'Dolly, it's not Flossie's fault. You should apologise.'

'Me? What have I done wrong? I have to tear my children out of their beds and drive through the night, yet you think I'm in the wrong?' Dolly's voice had risen dangerously.

'What I would like to know, Dolly, is what would you be saying to us now if she'd got worse and we hadn't called you? No doubt you'd be shrieking at us that *that* was wrong!' Flossie said.

'I'm not shrieking. I just think people jumped to conclusions when there was no need for this upset.'

'You can leave me out of this. I didn't summon no one,' Mavis huffed.

'Well, thank you, Mavis. If anyone panicked it was you,' Flossie retorted.

'I'm not putting up with this.' Mavis stood up and stormed from the room, slamming the door behind her. Meanwhile, Rowan poured the milk into mugs. She looked upset, with all the anger swirling around her.

Flossie turned to Dolly. 'You should think before you open your trap, Dolly. For weeks Melanie hasn't been right. For weeks I've shouldered more than normal – not just the cooking but in the bar, the bedrooms. Her husband's done nothing. Nor had you, Zeph, until today. Melanie's my friend and I'm happy to do anything to help her, but I won't be spoken to like this.' She whipped off her apron. 'Rowan, you're coming with me.'

Rowan stood, then sat down, then stood again, indecision written all over her face. 'I have to go back to the big house, Mum.'

'Then make sure you do.' Flossie strode to the door, went out, slammed it, then opened it again and poked her head through. 'And my Alf won't be reporting for work tomorrow neither.' This time she slammed the door even louder so that the mirror beside it slid sideways and crashed to the floor, shattering into a hundred pieces.

There was a stunned silence.

'Now see what you've done!' Zeph turned on his wife.

'Don't you blame me! I've done nothing! Nothing!' She kept repeating it as if to reassure herself.

'It's often difficult to gauge how ill someone is. The body is an amazing thing,' May Snodland ventured.

'You keep your nose out of this. You're nothing to do with this family.'

'I'm sorry to upset you, Mrs Topsham, but I would remind you I was asked to come and help.'

'Not by me, you weren't. And there's nothing for you to do here. You're dismissed.'

'Mrs Topsham, please! No!' May begged.

'Dolly, that's enough we're all overwrought. Don't worry, May. We need you,' Zeph said.

Dolly glared at her husband.

'What's all the noise about?' Richard Joynston stumbled into the kitchen, dishevelled and blinking in the light as if he had just woken up. There was a crunching noise as he walked across the broken mirror but he didn't notice it.

'Woken up, then?' Zeph said sarcastically.

'Only the dead could sleep through this racket.' He swayed towards the dresser, took up a bottle of port and poured himself a mugful.

'Don't you think you've had enough?'

'I'll decide that, not you,' Richard slurred. 'Dolly, you here too?' He lunged towards her as if for a kiss. Dolly shrank away in disgust. Richard shrugged and slumped on to a chair. To Rowan's astonishment, he leant forward, put his head on his arms and, within seconds, he was snoring loudly.

There was a tap on the door and Hannah Cresswell entered. 'Zeph, I'm sorry I'm so late but I've only just heard about your mother. Despite the hour, I came immediately Alf told me. How is she?'

'She's much better, Miss Hannah. But you shouldn't have disturbed yourself.'

'Not like some of us,' Dolly muttered, but Zeph ignored her.

'I wondered if these might be of use to you.' Hannah placed a wicker basket on the kitchen table as Alf entered with another, heavier one. 'Such joyous tidings, Alf,' she went on. 'Mrs Joynston is much better. The time is irrelevant, Zeph, I would come willingly to your mother's aid. And, Dolly, how lovely to see you, and dear little Rowan.' Rowan bobbed, but Dolly didn't. 'Yes, well,' Hannah had seen Richard lolling on the wooden chair at the table. 'I shan't be a further bother to you. Goodnight, everyone.' She left the kitchen.

'Bah! Lady Bountiful!' Dolly sneered.

'Look, Dolly, you're cross with me but you need not be with everyone else. It was kind of her to turn out when she's only just out of prison. No doubt the last thing she wanted to do was come here on a cold night like this.' He lifted the check cloth that covered the basket.

'Would you like me to get you a knife and fork?'

'Thank you, Rowan.'

'If you'll excuse me, I really will go to bed this time.' May left the room.

Rowan thought the woman, tearful and upset, was about to cry, and she couldn't blame her if she did. What had got into Dolly? She was usually so easygoing. 'And I should be getting back to the big house,' she said, 'if I can get in at this hour.'

'No, Rowan, you'd best stay here. The house will be locked up for sure,' Dolly said.

But Rowan had sensed the antagonism between them all. 'I'd better go. I know a secret way in.' She began to put on her coat. 'I don't know, first Lady Cresswell and now your mum, both suddenly getting better. Night.'

Zeph took a game pie out of the basket, cut a slice and placed it on the plate Rowan had fetched for him. He picked it up.

'Where you going?' Dolly demanded.

'To sit with my mother. I don't think she should be left alone.'

'Always thinking of others and never of me.'

'That's not fair, Dolly, and you know it. But I don't want to argue with you because I'm tired. It's been a dreadful day.'

'I shan't be here in the morning, I'm going to my work.'

'You must do as you see fit. But perhaps instead of accusing me of thinking only of others you should examine yourself. All you care about is your business.'

'That's not true. I work as I do because of all of you. I want us to have a better life, and our children to have an education.'

'That's not the whole truth. You do it for yourself, too, because you enjoy it. You do it because you want things I cannot afford to buy for you. Don't try to make me feel guilty for what you want to do.'

He turned to leave but Dolly was on her feet and pushing past him out of the room, tears streaming down her face.

4

Hannah had been out of prison for nearly a month but she could not get the stench of the place out of her nostrils. As soon as she returned home she had burned all of the clothes she had worn there, right down to her chemise and stockings. She bathed twice a day, washed her hands incessantly, frequently scrubbed her nails, brushed her teeth and lost count of the times she had her hair washed. Her maid, Lavender, despaired. 'But your hair smells as sweet as it always does, Miss Cress-well.'

'Please, Lavender, I insist.'

The poor, patient woman had washed it, rinsed it and dressed it yet again. Hannah had said it was better, but she was not confident that it was.

When she had been incarcerated, she had longed with every fibre of her body to be at home, but once she was there, she developed a dreadful restlessness and could not settle to anything. Yet she did not want to be with other people or go out, lest she met someone she knew. She had had to force herself to visit Melanie when she heard she was ill.

She dealt with the restiveness by taking long walks in the park and woods. She went so often that even Cariad tired of them. Now when she called her the little Westie would scurry away and hide.

She knew what the problem was: her shame over the disgrace of her sentence and what it had done to her family, and at the failure to defy the authorities and keep to her hunger strike. She had given in and let everyone down – most of all herself.

Normally a reasonably content person, she was unprepared for the bleakness of the depression that gripped her. She did not know how best to deal with it since it was new to her. She would wake in the morning and find herself still in yesterday's black hole with no idea of how to climb out.

Agnes had been of no help. It was as if she took pleasure in Hannah's failure. 'How long did Fanny hold out?' she asked, innocently enough, but Hannah knew from the supercilious smile that she meant, *compared to you.*

Already Agnes was planning other campaigns and marches, reading pamphlets, contacting other chapters of the movement. 'There is only one way. The militant sisters are right. Action. We shall never succeed in our mission without it. At the next demonstration we must not weaken,' she proclaimed. Since she had taken no part in their activities, her constant use of the first person plural irritated Hannah beyond measure. To listen to her, one would have thought she had taken on the might of the government alone, that she was the heroine of the day.

'I shall do no more,' Hannah said quietly.

'Oh, come, Hannah. You are so admired.' Again the condescending smile.

'I don't think I am. By whom?' This question was met by an ominous silence. 'I don't like violence of any description. It loses us support. And I couldn't face another term in jail. I was frightened all the time.'

'Oh, Hannah, it wasn't as if they were going to hang you.' A hollow laugh followed, as Agnes wound the skein of wool Hannah was holding for her into a ball.

'You have no idea what it was like.'

'I do. You tell me often enough.'

Hannah was dismayed. How could anyone be so unfeeling? It was as if Agnes had no respect for her, as if she cared not a jot about her. 'Then I'm sorry I'm so tedious to you.'

'Not at all, my dear. You obviously need to talk about your experiences and who better than I to listen?'

'I should have chosen someone with more understanding and compassion.'

'That wasn't very kind.'

'You criticise me from morning till night.'

'Really, Hannah, your imagination is running riot. You're not in prison now. There is no need to be so over-sensitive, believing everyone is against you.'

'Aren't you?'

'Of course not. I'm your friend. Constantly concerned for you.'

'You have the strangest way of showing it. You goad me and don't like it when I respond. I'm tired of it.'

'Really, Hannah. What on earth has induced this little temper?'

'You are belittling me again.'

'Hannah, I feel I should call the doctor. Your voice is becoming shrill. Perhaps you are in need of a sedative.'

Hannah threw the skein of wool on to the floor.

'Hannah, dear, calm down.'

The infuriatingly smug smile galvanised her. Hannah stood up abruptly. 'I have had enough, Agnes. I would rather you were gone from my house.'

As if in slow motion, Agnes put down the ball of wool. 'Have a care, Hannah.'

'And what does that mean? Do you *really* think you can hurt me now? Am I not shamed enough as it is?'

'You know very well that I could make difficulties for you. I could tell of our little liaison.'

'Do as you wish.' Hannah felt a great swell of anger. 'People already gossip about us, so you will only be telling them what they already think they know.'

'And your poor family?'

'What difference will it make to them after the shame I have already inflicted on them?'

'As always, you think only of yourself. You seem to have forgotten there are others.'

Suddenly Hannah's face was ashen. She knew to what Agnes had referred. 'I confided in you because you were my friend. You promised you would never betray my confidences.'

'Did I?'

'You know you did. You made a vow.'

'Oh, really, Hannah, you sound like a schoolgirl. It is hardly my fault if you were so profligate with your family scandals. A secret once told is a secret no more.' Hannah wanted to shake her, make her promise not to tell. How could she have been so mistaken about her? How could she have been so stupid as to ignore the warnings of others, particularly Oliver?

'I see I have given you pause for thought,' Agnes said.

'You have.' She noticed Agnes relax, evidently thinking she was safe. 'If you do as I think you are planning to do, then you will hear from our family lawyer and you will be sued through every court in the land.' Hannah's anger was giving her courage now.

'Would your family agree with that? I think not. Lady Cresswell, I'm sure, will resist everyone knowing that she induced her own miscarriage.

And would she want the world to know it was not her husband's child?'

'She would deny everything and say you lie.'

'But then there's the unfortunate business of the missing silver and the sapphire ring. Your stepmother would be most interested to know that Coral stole it, wouldn't she?'

'Who would believe you?'

'You forget, the servants knew that objects were stolen – why did you not initially blame them?'

'And you consider that they would put their positions at risk by denying their employers? We are good to our staff.'

'And do you know what they really think of you?' She gave an unpleasant laugh. 'Undoubtedly they hate you all, but you have never known what it is to be dependent, to wait on others, have you? All you know is privilege.'

'I had no idea you hated me so.'

'I don't hate you. I pity you.'

'Not nearly as much as I have you, in the past, but no more. If you are right and the staff would not stand by us, I shall say I took them and thus protect my family.'

'You never would!'

'Oh, but yes. Agnes, I find your attitude towards me painful – and unforgivable. I wish you to leave my premises now.'

'I have no money!' Her voice had changed – she was wheedling now.

'Then you should have thought of that before you made your threats of blackmail. A criminal offence, as I'm sure you are aware. Perhaps I should report you to the authorities. Then we can see how much *you* like being in prison. Come, Cariad.' This time the dog, sensing the animosity in the room, followed her mistress at a run.

That had been a week ago, and once Agnes had gone Hannah wondered why she hadn't stood up to her years ago, instead of letting guilt and shame induce her to put up with the woman. Of course she hadn't thrown her out into the cold, so to speak – in any case, the weather was mild for December: she had given her a handsome cheque and a glowing reference.

Then one day, sitting at her desk, her account books laid out in front of her, she wished she hadn't been so generous. Agnes had always checked invoices for her and Hannah had merely handed over the money for which Agnes asked to settle them. Agnes had evidently thought Hannah didn't bother to keep track of her money. But Hannah did. She had a little notebook in which she had recorded the sums she had handed over, with the dates, a habit instilled in her by her grandmother: *If you don't know how much money you've spent, you might wake one day and discover it all gone.* Consequently she had known what she was spending but hadn't bothered to check where it had gone.

Now, looking at her books once again, she was having to face the reality that for years Agnes had been helping herself to money. Not large sums but small amounts that would go unnoticed. It was her own fault. Hannah was quite capable of doing her books and had done so for years. Idleness had made her hand over the task to her friend. Still, she thought, that was not strictly true: she had thought it was something constructive and important for Agnes to do, to give her some pride. What a betrayal.

When she had told Oliver what had happened he had wanted Agnes arrested there and then, but she stopped him. 'I do not wish to press charges, Oliver. I am partly to blame for being so weak with her.'

This had exasperated him even more, but he did not know of Hannah's quandary. How was she to explain to him her indiscretion in confiding in the woman?

It was against Hannah's nature to gossip and she preferred not to listen to it – she knew that once she heard someone begin, she needed all her willpower to move away. Even then she often failed. To instigate gossip was anathema to her. But what was gossip and what was information that should be passed on? She was afraid of Agnes and the damage she could cause. 'You see, Oliver, I've learnt that Agnes is a vicious woman. There are things I stupidly confided in her and which she will use against us.' She took a deep breath and finally told her brother what she knew about Coral and the miscarriage, the items stolen to pay her dressmaker's bills, all of which had happened years ago.

'Why did you tell her?' he asked.

'I needed to confide in someone. And it showed I trusted her,' she added lamely.

'Was the baby Mortie's?'

'I fear not. Or so she implied.' That poor baby. Hannah had long ago forgiven Coral for stealing the baubles and causing such mayhem in the house, but she could not countenance the destruction of the baby. She had always longed for a child, and even now she would think often of that poor little soul and wonder what she would have been like. She always thought of it as a girl. From Coral's demeanour, it was obvious that she had forgotten about it.

'We were right not to like our sister-in-law from the start.'

'I don't want Mortie told, Oliver, not ever.'

'I wouldn't dream of it. Though I doubt he'd be too upset. From what he says, they lead fairly separate lives.'

'Oh, how awful.' Hannah covered her face with her hands at the implication in his words.

'It's normal in their circle. No one is faithful.'

'I find that very sad.'

'That is life, Hannah, my love. Marriage is for a long time, people stray.'

She hoped this was not so with him and Esmeralda. She sometimes glimpsed sadness in her brother but had never asked him about it. 'I don't wish to know about such matters,' she said.

'I apologise. But back to Miss Beatty. I think you handled her in the best possible way. She won't do anything, I'm sure. But if she does, deny everything and sue her.'

How simple he had made it sound.

Now she was still bowed down with worry. For there was another matter. Was Esmeralda the reason for her brother's sadness? On the day of her arrest she had seen her at Dulcie's hotel with a man. Normally she would have thought there was an innocent explanation. But Dulcie's denial that Esmeralda was there worried her. It had been a blatant lie. Had Dulcie lied to protect Esmeralda's secret? It would be typical of her, however, to protect a client – was that the explanation?

Of her two brothers she loved Oliver most, and could not bear to see him betrayed and hurt. If she told him, would the hurt be too much for him? Would he hate her for telling him something he did not wish to hear? She loved Esmeralda too, but if she was being unfaithful to Oliver then Hannah wished never to set eyes on her again.

She decided she had to tell him.

5

Eve Gilroy was walking rapidly across the park dressed in her Sunday best even though it was Monday. She pulled the serge coat closer to her – winter was in the air – and clutched her umbrella, with its duck-head handle. She knew the maids laughed because she never went anywhere without her gamp, but today clouds were banking up to the east and she knew there'd be rain before long.

'Welcome, my dearest friend.' Gussie Fuller held the door wide for her.

'It'll soon be pouring.' Eve didn't react to the salutation – Gussie had always been prone to drama and exaggeration.

'All well at Cresswell?' Gussie asked, as she ushered Eve into her sitting-room, which was close to the kitchens at Lees Court. Eve took off her coat, smoothed her skirt and adjusted her belt with the big silver buckle, a present from Miss Cresswell. She crossed to the window and pulled back the somewhat worn curtain. The view was of the stables.

'Do you ever get smells from the horses?' It was a question she asked regularly because she knew it annoyed her friend.

'Not at all. They are kept immaculate. Mr Oliver sees to that. And I find it rather comforting to hear the animals snuffling through the night.'

'Of course you'd hear them with your bedroom next door.' She was adjusting her hat in front of the rather plain mirror that hung over the small fireplace; she preferred the ornate gilt one in the housekeeper's room at Cresswell.

'I find it most convenient having my rooms side by side in this manner.'

'You'll be expecting a bathroom next!' Eve laughed at the ridiculous notion.

'I shall probably be having one.' Gussie tossed her head with pride. 'Mrs Oliver is looking into it. She said it must be so inconvenient for me, having to go upstairs all the time.'

'She's more money than sense, that one,' Eve muttered, beneath her breath.

'You said?' Gussie was pouring the tea.

'How handy,' Eve answered. Gussie might be getting a bathroom but Eve thought, as she did every time she came here, that the room was not nearly as comfortably furnished as the one she had enjoyed when she worked for Sir Mortimer.

'What a to-do at Cresswell. I haven't seen you since poor Miss Cresswell was locked up.'

'If you ask me it should have been that Miss Beatty in the clink, not our dear Miss Cresswell. Thin as a rake, she is.'

'You've seen her?'

'Yes.'

'In the prison!' This was more an astonished statement than a question.

'No. They've let her out.'

'But I thought she was sentenced to three months?'

'There's not much point in being one of the most prominent families in the area if you can't pull strings here and there.'

'It isn't right, is it? One law for them and another for us.'

'Hasn't it always been that way? You'll never get that changed.'

'And she visited the manor? When was the last time she did that? I thought she'd never set foot there again.'

'She came to see Lady Penelope on her sick bed. Sick? My eye! And you'll never guess what happened when she did?'

'Her ladyship scolded her?'

'On the contrary, she was very understanding.'

'Good heavens above! She must be seriously ill.' Gussie laughed.

'She won't die – we're doomed to have her go on for ever. Only the good get taken before their time.' Eve looked with suspicion at the cheese and onion tartlet Gussie had placed before her.

'They're very nice, Eve. Honest. Not up to your standard, of course, but no one can cook like you. Your food's the thing I miss most from Cresswell, even after all this time.'

Eve glowed.

'I still wish you'd moved here with me. Mr Oliver would have you like a shot, even now.'

'Too late. Another five years and I'm retiring.'

'You! I'll believe it when I see it.'

'I don't want to die in harness, that's for sure. Sir Mortie's told me there'll be a cottage for me when I do decide. I promised I'd still turn out for special occasions. He was very grateful. What about you?'

'I haven't given it a thought, but I'm younger than you.'

Eve scowled. By a year, if that, she thought. 'Will Mr Oliver give you a cottage?' It was a sly question since she knew the answer, Gussie had not worked for him long enough for such a reward – you had to have put in twenty-five years to get a cottage. *She* would die in harness.

Gussie looked uncomfortable, frowning. 'Oh, I wouldn't want to stay, pensioned off like an old carthorse. Always beholden to them. Having to paint your front door their colour, not your own choice. And, in any case, I couldn't see someone else doing my duties. I shall move away.'

'Live where and on what?'

'I've my savings.'

'They won't last long. Edward's talking of leaving now.'

'Never! Where will he go?'

'He says Hilda owns a house at Whitby.'

'No!'

'They kept that dark, didn't they?'

'Has she been left it in a will?' There was a wistfulness in Gussie's voice, for this was one of her fondest dreams: that one day a letter would appear from a firm of lawyers telling her of a fine inheritance from a relative she never knew she had.

'No, she's always owned it.'

'Well, at least we now know why he married her. It's always been a mystery to me.'

'That's true.' Eve was not aware that she sighed. 'Thinking of turning it into a guesthouse, they are.'

'Bit of a come-down for Edward, wouldn't you say?'

'If you ask me, he doesn't want to do it. It's her. Says she wants to see more of her family.'

'Selfish bitch. He's a fine butler. He'll miss the manor and the lifestyle that goes with his position.'

'Could kill him, that could.' Eve nodded her head sagely. 'And how's poor Mrs Oliver?'

'She's all right, empty-headed as always. Not a sensible thought in her head. She's not much idea how to run a house, mind you. She'd be lost without me. She's off to Buxton.'

'What for?'

'To take the waters. She says it's for some aches and pains she's got.'

'She's young for rheumatism.'

'I reckon she hopes it'll help her have a baby. I think she thought this month she was going to but it came to nowt. Her maid, Bridget, told me.'

'Perhaps it's him at fault.'

'Mr Oliver? Don't be silly, Eve. He's a fine virile figure of a man. No, it's the von Ehrlichs, that's for sure – foreign blood.'

'Edward thinks he should change his name. Too Germanic, he said it was.'

'Oh, that's rubbish.'

'He says feelings are running high in the cities. It's not good to be German.'

'There won't be a war. The Kaiser's the king's cousin. Families don't fight each other.'

'Don't they? I've never met one that didn't.'

6

Esmeralda was constantly confused by her housekeeper, Mrs Fuller. One day she was respectful, the next far from it. She could be helpful in the extreme or downright obstructive. Esmeralda was aware that much of this was her own fault. It had been up to her to set the boundaries within the household at the beginning. But she hadn't. When she had married at eighteen she had had no desire to run her domain and been happy to rely on Gussie Fuller. It was, therefore, inevitable that the housekeeper had little respect for her. And, since that was so, it was not surprising that when Esmeralda tried to wrest back some control, Mrs Fuller resented it.

No doubt Esmeralda confused her too. She would go for weeks showing no interest in domestic arrangements, then suddenly would want to know everything that was going on, querying the ordering, combing the bills, inspecting the house. Why she swung from one extreme to the other she was not sure, although she had observed that her interest was always at its height when she felt restless.

Today Mrs Fuller's hands were folded in front of her rather old-fashioned full black skirt, as if she was controlling herself. She wore a supercilious smile – or so Esmeralda thought. It made her feel like a little girl again, rather than the mistress of this fine house.

'What is that fearful banging, Mrs Fuller?'

'The builders have begun on the new library, madam, as your husband instructed.'

'Of course, I'd quite forgotten.' She giggled nervously. There was no response from Mrs Fuller.

They were in the large sitting-room, which had once been two rooms and which Oliver had made into one. Esmeralda had preferred it as it was, when the proportions were perfect: the enlargement had ruined them. There were days when she felt quite sorry for the house – her husband was forever changing it, adding to it and pulling parts of it down. He had even changed its name from Lees Coppice, which he said sounded like a cottage, to Lees Court. She had felt it was unlucky to change it, rather as sailors never changed a ship's name. But he had thought her silly – she probably was. It was now more than three times the size it had been originally.

'This was such a sweet little house. I can't think why my husband wants to keep adding to it,' she said, thinking aloud. She did know: the grander he made it, the more he proved to her father how well he could look after her. What neither man understood was that she had never wanted a grand house. And sometimes, at night when she could not sleep, she would find herself wondering if his constant building was a sign that he was restless too.

'He thinks no doubt that it was not a suitable residence for someone in his position and of *his standing*.'

But evidently quite adequate for me, she thought wryly. When Esmeralda had been young and confident the housekeeper's attitude might have amused her but lately it had cowed her. She supposed that if she could find the courage she should admonish the woman – she was aware that she was being rude. It was so unfair. One of the reasons Esmeralda had employed her was that she had felt sorry for her – Mrs Fuller had been heartbroken at leaving Cresswell Manor. It had seemed so beneficial for them both: to the newly wed and inexperienced Esmeralda, Gussie Fuller was a godsend. Sometimes she wondered if the plain, spinsterish housekeeper was jealous of her.

Oliver was of no help. 'She's your servant and it's up to you to control her. If you feel she doesn't show you sufficient respect then dismiss her, but don't come whining to me about it.' She sighed. And how could she dismiss her when she was *so* old, fifty at least? Where would she go?

'Is there anything else? Madam?' There it was again, the barely controlled impatience.

'Oh, yes. I shall not be going to Buxton just yet after all.' There was no response from the housekeeper. 'My husband has made other plans … He will need me here.' Now, why had she explained herself? There was no need to do so. 'There's nothing else I can think of – at the moment.'

Mrs Fuller made to leave the room. 'A moment … Have you made the arrangements for my sister-in-law's visit for luncheon?'

'Of course.' Mrs Fuller turned away.

'I haven't finished, Mrs Fuller.' She was pleased with the sharpness of her tone – she should adopt it more often. But then she had to rack her brains for something to say. 'I shall be going instead in the New Year for a week.'

'Very well, Madam.'

'I shall give you the dates when I have finalised my plans. That will be all.'

Once the housekeeper had left, Esmeralda put her head into her hands. She never used to be like this. She had once had confidence in herself. Some had thought her forward – cocky, even. Was it just that she was getting older? Her thirtieth birthday was two years away, and already she felt sad at the prospect. She knew her beauty would fade and she dreaded becoming unnoticed, unimportant. Still, wasn't she unimportant already? Apart from her face, her dress sense and her ability to furnish a room, there was nothing to recommend her to anyone.

No doubt Hannah regarded her as a frivolous creature. Esmeralda admired her: Hannah did so much good and she did so little. While she did not agree with or approve of the suffragettes, she admired her sister-in-law's courage. If she were ever locked up in prison she knew she would die of fear in a matter of days. Then there was Hannah's support for the Temperance Movement. She knew she could never sign the pledge – she enjoyed champagne too much. Hannah helped Dulcie Prestwick with funds for her waifs' and strays' home, and she had heard Oliver complain frequently at the amount of money his sister had donated to Dulcie's library for the poor. To top it all, she was a successful businesswoman with her garden designing – not that Oliver would ever allow Esmeralda to have a career, even if there had been something she could do well enough. Such a paragon of a sister-in-law was enough to depress even the most stout-hearted.

How did she fill her own days? Esmeralda asked herself. Aimlessly, she answered. She read a lot, but Oliver never approved of the books she chose: he labelled them rubbish. She read of romance, dashing heroes and beautiful maidens. She liked happy endings because the heroes stayed in love with the heroines and were never annoyed by them. That was the root of her problem: she wanted to be like one of the women she read about.

A large part of her day was spent on grooming – but she did that as much for Oliver as for herself: it was her duty to look the best she could for her husband. And she always arranged the flowers that filled the house, which took much skill and hours of concentration – they were frequently admired. She decided the menus, and made her husband's life as comfortable as she could. She tried to be a good wife. But for all that she knew she bored Oliver and this knowledge made her nervous and tongue-tied in his company.

Of course, there was her interest in the estate school, but she had only become involved because her other sister-in-law, Coral, was so infrequently at the manor. She loved being with the little ones, reading to them, encouraging them, giving them prizes when they had done well. But a visit always left her low because she longed for a child of her own.

It was an agony that would not go away. And with Oliver's interest in her waning, it was hardly likely to happen.

'Come in,' she said, to a knock on her door.

'Miss Beatty to see you, madam. Are you receiving?'

'Oh dear.' Her husband loathed Agnes. The butler was holding out a silver salver on which lay Agnes's card. 'Shall I say that Madam is not at home?'

It would be best, but perhaps it would offend Hannah if she did not invite the woman in. 'No, Milner, show her in, please.'

'As you wish, madam.' He bowed. Strange … the butler was such an upright, sober man but she never felt flustered with him.

She prepared to meet her old companion, nervousness returning. 'Miss Beatty.' She approached her, hands held out in welcome.

'Dear Esmeralda.' Agnes thrust forward her cheek for Esmeralda to kiss. Esmeralda wondered why one had to kiss people one did not like. Surely kisses should be reserved for those one loved.

'What a lovely surprise.' She compounded the hypocrisy. 'Do sit down. Tea?' She crossed to the fireplace and the bell pull.

'No, thank you. I am glad to find you alone, Esmeralda. I need your help.' Agnes sank on to a chair in the well-remembered elegant, fluid motion that had always impressed her.

'*My* help?' Esmeralda was surprised.

'There is no easy way, and it shames me to tell you, but I fear I am destitute. I have nothing.' At which, from her small beaded bag, she took a handkerchief and dabbed her eyes. Esmeralda was transfixed with astonishment. This was one person she had never expected to see in tears.

'Oh dear. Good gracious. What can I do? Oh dear,' she repeated.

'I have lost everything. Hannah has requested that I leave her establishment and I have.'

'Have you disagreed?'

Agnes gave a short, bitter laugh and returned to dabbing her eyes. But Esmeralda had moved closer and saw, with mounting suspicion, that the woman's eyes were dry. As if she had become aware of this, Agnes lowered her head and began to sob, her shoulders heaving.

'Don't distress yourself, Miss Beatty. Please.' Esmeralda was embarrassed to see her like this: Miss Beatty had always been the one in control. She crossed to a tray of decanters and poured a small amount of brandy. 'Drink this. It will make you feel better.'

Agnes looked at her and then at the glass with an expression of horror.

'Esmeralda, how could you? You know I signed the pledge years ago.'

'I'm so sorry. I had quite forgotten.'

Agnes shook herself, evidently trying to pull herself together. 'Forgive me, Esmeralda, you are so kind and I am ungracious. My apologies,' she said hurriedly. Now Esmeralda could see that there really were tears in her eyes and felt ashamed of herself for thinking otherwise.

Esmeralda put the glass back. 'How can I help?' She was anxious: her husband and Hannah were due to come here – if they had fallen out with Miss Beatty they would not take kindly to finding her here.

'I was wondering if I could help you in some way in your home. Just like in the old days.' She smiled at her.

Esmeralda's mind was whirling. It was bad enough having to deal with Gussie Fuller but Agnes Beatty would undoubtedly make her feel even more inadequate. And there was Oliver. 'I'm afraid that is out of the question.'

'Not for old times' sake? I was a good friend to you.'

You did all you could to undermine my confidence, Esmeralda thought. 'You were,' she lied, 'but times have changed, and it would be so difficult for me. Hannah,' she said, in simple explanation.

'Has she spoken to you?'

'No, but she's coming to luncheon today.' She looked anxiously at her watch.

'Whatever she tells you is untrue. I have done nothing but help that woman. I have been a support to her in extreme times when her family sorely neglected her.'

'I don't think you can say that of my husband. He cares deeply for his sister.'

'She doesn't think so.'

'I don't believe that.'

'Then you accuse me of lying?'

'Of course not, but … ' Esmeralda was steeped in confusion, just as she had been in the past. 'He is my husband. I know him well.'

'As well as he knows you?' Agnes sat upright.

'I don't understand.' Which she didn't, but she knew she was being threatened.

'Don't you? You should take care, Esmeralda. You don't want him to know everything, do you?'

To her horror Esmeralda felt herself blush.

'As I thought.' Agnes nodded sagely.

'You don't understand.'

'Oh, but, my dear, I do.' She stood up.

'You put me in a difficult position, Miss Beatty. It is not that I don't wish to help you but for you to stay here is impossible – for you as well as me. However ... If you wouldn't mind waiting ...' She ran from the room to her study. From the secret drawer of her desk she removed the latest envelope her father had given her. As she skimmed back across the hall the front door opened and Oliver strode in.

'You're in a hurry,' he remarked.

'I have to change. Hannah will be here shortly.'

'You're going the wrong way.' He smiled at her indulgently.

She kissed his lips. 'I forgot something.'

'You'd better be quick. I just want to check the work on the library.' To her relief he walked away from the sitting-room.

Esmeralda went in. 'Perhaps this will help.' Agitated now, she handed Miss Beatty the envelope. 'My husband has returned. You must leave through the garden.' She raced across the room to open the french window. 'Quickly.'

Annoyingly Agnes walked slowly towards her. 'It is not in my nature to skulk.'

'I beg you, Miss Beatty. If you don't you will make things difficult for me.'

'Thank you for your help, even if it is not what I wished.' She tucked the envelope into her bag.

Esmeralda sagged with relief against the door as she watched her leave. She was not to know that her husband also observed Miss Beatty's departure.

7

Oliver was alerted by a chugging, banging, rattling noise from the driveway and abandoned his inspection of the new library. He moved ahead of the butler and was at the front door first just in time to see a well-wrapped-up Hannah clinging for dear life to the door of a large automobile, which juddered to a halt.

'That was such fun.' Hannah was glowing. 'Just what I needed.' This new interest had lifted her spirits.

'I'm so sorry, Miss Cresswell.' Her chauffeur was opening the door for her to step down.

'Nonsense, Alf. You've nothing to apologise for. You'll learn the ropes before you can say—' She paused as she thought. 'Rolls-Royce.' That was the make of her new car.

'Is this a new adventure?' Oliver asked, as he walked round the vehicle admiring the gleaming bodywork.

'It is. Alf and I took delivery this week and we're both very excited. It's much more comfortable than any motor I've ever ridden in.'

'How do you find it, Alf?'

'We didn't do so well today, Mr Oliver. It's them gears, they take some getting used to.'

'Horses are easier, then.'

'You could say that.' Alf grinned.

'Nonsense, Alf,' Hannah said. 'You did splendidly. We must move with the times. I am going to learn to drive.'

'I trust you will give us all plenty of warning so we can stay safe in our houses that day.'

'Beast!' Hannah pushed her brother playfully. 'It's so exhilarating. You should get one.'

'I've been thinking about it.' They were climbing the steps. 'Mind my sheep on the way out,' Oliver said to Alf over his shoulder, as he ushered his sister into the house.

'Good morning, Milner. How's Mrs Fuller?' Hannah enquired.

'The better for seeing you, Miss Cresswell.' The housekeeper had stepped forward, bobbing respectfully. 'And looking so well.' She beamed as Milner took Hannah's cape and muff.

'One of these days I shall steal dear Mrs Fuller from you, Oliver. You have been warned.'

The housekeeper blushed with pleasure.

'Do you want to see my new library?'

'More building work. When will it end, Oliver?'

'I want to build an orangery, the tennis courts need renewing and we need more bathrooms.'

'Perhaps you should have been an architect. Nice,' she said, as they looked at the large room, which still needed much imagination to see it as a library. 'Very large, isn't it?'

'Let's go into the morning-room, shall we? Esmeralda is late as usual.'

'That is the privilege of a beautiful woman. Plain Janes such as I must always arrive on time.'

Settled in the room, she looked about her. 'Esmeralda has such exquisite taste. I'd never have thought to put mauve and silver together. Oh,

I'm sorry, Oliver, I didn't notice what you were doing. I'd rather have a sherry.' She rejected the lemonade Oliver had poured for her.

'More changes?'

'I signed the pledge willingly – Agnes did not bully me into it – but I missed the odd sherry and glass of wine. I can assure you I've no intention of becoming a drunkard, though.' She smiled at her brother as she took the glass.

'I'm pleased to hear it.'

'I'm glad Esmeralda's late. I need to speak with you confidentially.'

'That sounds intriguing – but I've news for you too. I've just seen Agnes Beatty scuttling across the garden, like a burglar fearful of being caught.' Oliver laughed.

'Agnes? Here? Oh, really, how could she? What did she want?'

'I've no idea. I was not privy to the meeting. All very secretive.'

'She's a devious woman. She will have been here for a reason. And before you say it, I know I should have listened to your warning but I didn't and that's that.'

'It's always been a mystery to me as to why you took her in.'

'Loneliness can be a fearful thing. Anyway she was good company once and I was fond of her. But she presumed too much. Hence the motor-car – she never approved of them and I've always wanted one. Dear Papa always had such joy with his. So, you see, the motor and the sherry symbolise that I am my own person again.'

'I'm pleased to hear that too. But now it's your turn. What did you want to see me about?'

'It's so difficult and I have fought and argued with myself as to what I should do. I don't want to interfere and yet, on the other hand, you are my brother. You see—'

Esmeralda erupted into the room, swooped across in a flurry of primrose silk and kissed her sister-in-law. 'My dear Hannah, you look so much better than you did last week. There's more colour in your cheeks. And is that your motor? How dashing you are!' As she spoke she fluttered about the room. 'I had thought you would be in the drawing-room and silly me was sitting there all on my own waiting for you.' Nervously she rearranged a hyacinth, turning the Delft bowl so that the bloom was better seen.

'Why was Agnes Beatty here, Esmeralda?'

'Who, darling?'

'Don't play silly games, Esmeralda. I saw her leaving. Did you invite her?'

'Oliver, stop using that hectoring tone. You're frightening poor Esmeralda,' Hannah reprimanded him.

'I'm sorry, darling. I know how you feel about her. I didn't invite her, she just arrived,' Esmeralda said.

'Why did you receive her?'

'I thought …'

'What did you think, Esmeralda?'

'I thought it would be rude not to. After all, she was my companion for many years and she's never done me any harm.' She sounded almost defiant.

'You know how much I dislike her and I would have thought that was enough for you not to have been at home to her.'

'Truly, Oliver, I didn't know what to do for the best.'

'What did she want?'

'A position.'

There was a snort of derision from Oliver.

'Really!' Hannah tutted.

'Of course I told her it was out of the question.'

'Good. But then what did you do?'

'I told her she must leave.'

'I think you did something else, Esmeralda.'

She looked at Hannah as if for support. 'I gave her some money.'

'And where did you get it from? You have not asked me for any.'

'It was some I had left over from a shopping trip I made last week.' She could feel the heat of her blush and cursed it inwardly. But she was afraid: if Oliver found out about the money her father gave her he would never forgive her.

'That was very kind of you, Esmeralda, but I had already given her a large sum of money,' Hannah said.

'She told me she was destitute.'

'Then she lied. I have learnt that she's a dishonest woman. Oliver, please, don't be cross. Esmeralda was only being kind. You're making a mountain out of a molehill.'

'I don't like it. In future when you have money left over I suggest you return it to me.'

'Yes, Oliver.' She felt so humiliated. He'd never expected that of her before. And how could he speak to her so in front of another?'

'Oh, Oliver. You sound like her father. A woman needs money of her own, some independence,' Hannah said.

'Is that what the suffragettes teach you?' Oliver snapped.

Hannah gave Esmeralda an encouraging smile. 'Brother, when I listen to you quibbling over a little change from the shopping, I'm glad I never married.'

At that moment Milner came in to announce that luncheon was served.

Esmeralda did her best over the meal, but it was hard, especially with Milner and the footman in attendance. She knew that Oliver was furious with her, and perhaps that Hannah's defence of her had made matters worse. She wanted to throw down her napkin and race from the room. Even more, she wished she could run out into the fields as she had done when she was a girl.

'Was prison too awful, Hannah?'

'Esmeralda, that is hardly a topic for conversation for luncheon.'

'I'm sorry.' Again the blush.

'It was awful, an experience I'd rather forget, Esmeralda.' At least Hannah gave her a sympathetic smile.

'Of course. Silly of me.' She leant forward to pick up her wine-glass and knocked it over. Milner rushed to help her but she waved him away and patted the stain with her napkin.

'Put salt on it,' Hannah advised.

Abruptly Oliver dismissed the servants. 'You seem agitated today, Esmeralda. What is the matter?'

'I don't know.'

'If something is worrying you, you will feel better if you tell us,' Hannah added.

Esmeralda looked from one to the other. 'It was Miss Beatty. It will sound silly to you but I think she was threatening me and I couldn't understand why. She frightened me.'

'Oh dear.' Hannah leant back in her chair, suddenly very pale.

'Are you all right, Hannah?' Oliver asked.

'She is a dangerous woman. I fear she means to do this family great mischief.'

'How did she threaten you?' Oliver persisted.

'She didn't. Not baldly. I can't remember exactly what she said. But she was hinting at something and I don't know what it was. I've done nothing wrong or bad.' Except lie to you about how often I see my father.

'People like her seize on the smallest matter and blow it up out of all proportion,' he responded.

'I'm sorry I saw her, Oliver, I wish I hadn't. I really thought it was for the best.' Esmeralda felt close to tears. Her head began to pound and suddenly she felt sick. 'I wonder if you would excuse me. I feel unwell.' Hurriedly she got to her feet. 'I'm sorry, Hannah …' Without looking at her husband, she ran from the room.

'She should have been on the stage, always so dramatic,' Oliver remarked.

'She strikes me as a sad little thing.'

'What has she got to be sad about?'

'You?'

Oliver laughed. 'She has everything she wants and needs. She has more clothes than she can ever hope to wear, this lovely house. We went to Italy this year and we shall go to France next.'

'Perhaps she feels she no longer has you.'

'Of course she has me.'

'But not as she dreamt she would. She's a sweet child and no doubt has her dreams.'

'I married her, didn't I?'

'You did. And you were once much kinder to her than I have witnessed today. She's afraid of offending you, Oliver.'

Oliver poured himself another glass of wine. 'Oh, I know. You're not telling me anything I haven't thought of. Things are not right and I admit that I am often too sharp with her. But … it's so difficult. I mean … You see, we have nothing in common.'

'You had nothing when you wed. That has not changed. You must have known it then.'

'I had to marry her because I had compromised her honour.'

'Then why should she be punished for your mistakes? For that is what you are doing.'

'I sometimes think things would improve if only we had a child.'

'No doubt it would help. But what is the point of dwelling on it? I know all about that.'

'But living with it year in and year out …' He gazed out of the window. 'I get lonely. You said yourself that loneliness could be a fearful thing.'

'And I sympathise. But no doubt she suffers too.'

He stared into his glass, then lifted his head abruptly. 'Are you over your incarceration?'

'I still have nightmares and feel guilty about the other women, but I have no intention of returning. I do not have the courage to be a rebel. In that Agnes was right.'

'You were very brave. No,' he upheld his hand, 'I won't let you deny it.'

106

'You're very kind.' She managed to laugh.

'Earlier you said there was something you wished to discuss with me.'

Hannah studied her brother. 'It was nothing.' She smiled.

'They've only themselves to blame,' she said aloud, as she sped along the Devon lanes in her hired trap, impervious to the cold and the light rain that threatened to turn to snow.

She was driving at breakneck speed up the long, winding drive towards the enormous house. 'What else am I to do?' The words were whipped away by the stiff breeze. Seconds later she saw a smart carriage on the drive. He was entertaining. Should she persist?

The choice was taken out of her hands as the front door swung open and a footman appeared, followed by a boy to take her pony and trap. 'Miss Beatty to see Mr von Ehrlich,' she announced, handing over her card.

She stood in the cavernous hall with its many banners. It was such a long time since she had been here, and her departure had been ignominious. Would he agree to see her? She thought so: if she had the measure of the man, his curiosity would get the better of him.

The footman reappeared and she was led up the stairs to the drawing-room. Long ago she had recognised in Stanislas someone similar to herself and had once hoped they would have a liaison that led to marriage. However, she had regretfully concluded that he was a little afraid of her. Her strength had been that she had known of a fraudulent business deal he had done, and, by judicious hints had secured herself instead a position of luxury in his employ. Her power had ended, though, with the death of the victim. Sad.

'Miss Beatty, what a surprise. To what do I owe the pleasure of your visit after such a long time?'

'I am hoping you might see your way to helping me.'

'And why should I?'

'I have information that may interest you … pertaining to the Cresswell family.'

'Take a seat, Miss Beatty. You always were a clever woman.' He bowed her into a chair.

Chapter Four

Christmas 1913–New Year 1914

1

23 December

'I don't want you to feel you have to. And of *course* it depends on your own plans. And of *course* the decision is yours.' Esmeralda smiled sweetly at Mrs Fuller, who stood silently before her. 'If you need time to think about it, I shall quite understand.' She shuffled her notebook and the menu cards on her desk. 'So?'

'It might help, Mrs Oliver, if I was given some idea of what I must make a decision about.'

'Didn't I say? Oh dear.' She laughed. 'My mind is all over the place. I've arranged with Lady Cresswell that, should you wish, you will be most welcome in the servants' hall at the manor for the festivities unless, of course you'd prefer to take a little holiday away from us.'

'I don't know what to say, madam. I'm touched at your thoughtfulness.' The housekeeper seemed stunned, as if this was not what she had been expecting to hear.

'We shall, of course, be there for ten days, so if you have friends or family …'

'Well, I had intended …' Mrs Fuller fingered her face. 'But in the light of such generosity, I shall be most happy to come to the manor.'

'Milner and Cook, do you know if they have plans?'

'They've been talking of going to Torquay, madam. Apparently Mr Milner's aunt has a …' she paused, as if about to impart important information '… a *boarding-house.*'

'How sensible of them. And how splendid, Mrs Fuller, that you will accompany my husband and me. We shall all have a grand time.'

Except *she* wouldn't be having a grand time, Esmeralda thought, when finally she was alone. Her heart was filled with dread at the prospect of Christmas with Oliver's family. She already knew what it would be like. Oliver and his brother would snipe at each other. Morts would be sad – since his wife's death she hadn't seen him smile once. If Lettice was there, and it was not confirmed that she would be, she would be on tenterhooks all the time. Esmeralda was convinced that Lettice was afraid of Hugo. She had no idea why. He had always been charming to her, but who could tell what went on in a marriage? And Coral would try to put her down at every turn – she would have invited some of her grand friends who always intimidated Esmeralda. At least Hannah was coming this year. And Esmeralda would have to dance attendance on Lady Penelope, a terrifying prospect because the woman despised her and had no compunction in telling her how unsuitable a wife she was for her son. At least the old woman would still be bedridden. Esmeralda was truly shocked by her unfeeling attitude.

In previous years Oliver, who didn't enjoy his family's company at Christmas either, had always arranged for them to travel, usually to a fine *auberge* they liked in Bavaria. But this year, because everyone was convinced it would be Penelope's last Christmas, it had been decided that they should remain here.

'I remember my grandmother managed six *last* Christmases before she died,' she had said to Oliver, in a vain attempt to get him to change his plans. Instead, he had reprimanded her for insensitivity. Once upon a time he would have laughed.

Once upon a time ... The loveliest words in the English language after *I love you*. They conjured up happiness and living happily ever after. From a pigeon-hole in her desk she took some writing-paper and wrote once more to the manager of the Palace Hotel in Buxton to arrange another date. Twice she had had to cancel her booking because Oliver had made alternative plans without consulting her. Surely other wives were asked about arrangements that concerned them – but Lettice had assured her that Hugo never discussed anything with her. It really was unreasonable. After all, she never invited anyone to the house without checking, first, that Oliver would be available and, second, that they were guests he was happy to receive.

Yet another friend who had taken the waters at Buxton was with child. She had been wondering if she should mention it to Oliver but knew he would pooh-pooh such an idea. She was also afraid that he might construe it as criticism of himself for the lack of loving in their marriage.

All in all it was much easier to be a man, she decided. But then, she thought, as she smoothed a sheet of tissue paper, it would be dreadful to have to worry about money and politics. With all the drawbacks it was nicer to be a woman but, best of all, a woman who felt truly loved.

She pressed a knot in the wood, which released the spring of a secret compartment. From it she took the two miniatures she had had painted by Dulcie Prestwick's son. She studied them, making up her mind which to choose. It had been such fun in his studio down by the harbour. She had sat in the window watching the comings and goings, stiff at first, but then he had relaxed her with his banter. He had flirted with her quite outrageously, which had been thrilling and *so* dangerous.

'This one,' she said, and wrapped it in the paper. Her father would like it. The more serious one would suit Oliver. She would wrap his later. Now she was off to Barlton for some last-minute shopping and to give her father his present.

Although she was only a few miles from her home Rowan frequently felt homesick. If she stood on tiptoe to look out of the window in her bedroom high in the eaves of Cresswell Manor, she could just see the chimney of her parents' house – at least, she liked to think it was but there were so many chimneys all huddled together at Cresswell-by-the-Sea. On her half day off each week she rarely went home. The 'half day' was a misnomer. She could leave the manor but had to be back by five. So, by the time she had washed and changed and walked across the park, there was just an hour before she had to leave to be back in time to change into her uniform for work in the evening.

Despite this she was happy. She was in awe of the senior staff, who were so grand they rarely spoke to her, but the rest were young and there was always someone to chatter or play cards with. They were to have their own dance this Christmas, which was causing quite a flutter among the maids as to what they would wear. She had listened to how some of the others talked and was learning to speak nicely, as they did.

The footmen had to be watched, and the last thing she wanted was to get involved with any of them. She might lose her job or, worse, be dismissed with no character reference.

It struck her that this was unfair. When it happened, as it did with depressing regularity, it was always the maids who were punished, rarely the men. If the latter were disciplined it was merely a demotion, or a docking of wages, yet they were just as guilty.

The work itself was dull. As soon as she had cleaned one room she had to do the same in another. No one ever noticed and complimented her. But if she missed something Mrs Herbert shouted at her, and Jane, the head housemaid, was a real Tartar. If she ever became a housekeeper she would never shout at anyone, Rowan thought, because she would remember how awful it was. Still, she was better off than Willow, who worked in the kitchens. The cook yelled at her all day, every day. She claimed it didn't bother her but Rowan wasn't so sure.

Rowan, Willow and Mary frequently talked of getting jobs at the blanket factory in Barlton, where the hours were regular, the evenings free and the money was better. Rowan would be able to live at home with her family and never feel homesick again. But the work there was backbreaking, she'd have to give her parents the money she earned to cover her keep and she'd be back to sharing a bed with her sisters again. She liked having her own little room at the manor.

This afternoon she was going home. She was carrying a hessian bag she had borrowed from the cook with presents for her family.

'And you crocheted this yourself?' Her mother held up the lacy-looking collar Rowan had made for her.

'Mary showed me how. There's a couple of mistakes,' she said apologetically.

'It's the most beautiful thing I've ever seen.'

She'd made dolls' furniture for her younger sisters, from matchboxes she'd saved up, bought a wooden sword from one of the footmen for Oak, her brother, and she'd embroidered her older sister's initials on a handkerchief. Everyone oohed and aahed at her cleverness, and she reciprocated when they produced a salmon-pink sateen nightdress case for her.

'Open it,' said Maple.

'How lovely.' She smiled as she removed a clumsily sewn lavender sachet. 'And you made it yourself, Holly? How clever you are with your fingers!' She planted a kiss on the child's cheek. Bought presents, like her nightdress case, were the most prized, and she felt ashamed now of her efforts – even more so when her mother produced a fine cotton blouse with fashionable leg-o'-mutton sleeves and rows of broderie anglaise down the front. There and then in the cramped sitting-room she took off her old blouse and put on the new one.

'Fits you perfect, it does.' Flossie glowed with pride.

'I can wear it to the servants' ball. But it must have been expensive – you shouldn't have, Mum.'

'Get on with you! We're doing all right, me and your dad, thanks to Melanie. The days of poverty are long gone.'

'How is she?'

'Better, but not herself. No one's saying but they're worried about her ticker.'

'Poor lady.'

'Her memory's a bit wobbly and she gets tired ever so fast, poor soul. And her's not walking right. I've been wondering if she's had a little stroke. But you're not to breathe a word of this. Zeph wouldn't like it.'

'Oh, I won't, Mum.'

'It's hard for her. She was always so busy and it's a trial for her to have to sit and watch others.'

'Why are they being secretive about it?'

'You know what people are like round here – they're ashamed. I'm surprised at Zeph, though, I'd have thought he'd have more sense, but when I asked him, sympathetic like, he near bit my head off. But I'm glad he's come home to run the business for her. That don't suit Dolly, though. Real cross sticks, she's been.'

'What about her business in Barlton?'

'Makes a lot of money, so I'm told. But she's changed, not nearly the little sunbeam she used to be.'

'And to think she started as a scullerymaid up at the big house.' Rowan was astonished that such a thing could be possible.

'Falling for a baby was her good fortune. A proper gentleman is Zeph, did the right thing by her and all. But they're not happy.'

'No?'

'You can see it in Zeph's eyes.'

'Did that Xenia come?'

'Did her hell! But no one told Melanie she'd been sent for so she hasn't been disappointed. Though why they'd want a mischievous baggage like her around beats me. Different as chalk and cheese, her and Zeph. You'd never think they was twins … Why didn't Willow come?'

'She couldn't get off,' Rowan lied. In fact Willow was probably canoodling with Freddie, one of the under-footmen. Rowan thought she was stupid. Putting herself at risk, she was. She'd tried to stop her but Willow had told her to shut up. She couldn't say anything to her mother or she'd have Willow out of there before you could say Jack Robinson, and Willow had a fiery temper.

'Big party expected for Christmas?'

'You can say that again. Mrs Herbert's in a rare old tizzy. The whole family's coming, and some friends of Lady Cresswell, and Mr Morts is bringing someone. Cook says we should be about twenty-five and then you have to add in all the staff that'll come with the guests. We're having extra help in the kitchens. And we could do with a few more pairs of hands. Think of all those breakfast trays not to mention the pots. I don't know why they can't empty their own piss.'

'Privilege of being rich, that is. So, you won't get over at all, either of you?'

'No hope of that. But they've been training me to wait at table. I'm terrified. What if I pour soup down Lady Coral's front?'

Everyone thought this a fine joke.

Eve Gilroy was a flurry of movement. She was barking orders like a regimental sergeant major. Her kitchen- and scullerymaids, including help from the village, were rushing about, faces creased with anxiety. In fact, Eve was enjoying herself immensely, not that she would say so. But those who knew her well recognised the signs: she sang hymns loudly all the time.

An endless stream of people came to the back door. More game arrived and Willow had to hang it in the game larder, standing precariously on a stool. Since the birds had been dead for a week already she had to pinch her nose. So far she'd plucked fifteen brace of pheasant, a basketful of partridge and pigeons, and ten geese, with another five to go. She was constantly sneezing from the down that filled the room with a fine feathery mist.

The gardeners were arriving with trugs of vegetables, fruit from the vast heated greenhouse, armfuls of flowers, holly and mistletoe.

Whitaker was supervising the transfer of the greenery to the flower-room. 'Not so fast, Edward. A nice bunch of mistletoe in my kitchen won't go amiss.' Eve smiled coquettishly.

The farmer brought in ten fillets of beef, and the dairymaids produced cream, cheese and butter.

Hilda appeared from the cold room with a cake: she had modelled angels with wings of spun sugar, holly and berries from marzipan to decorate it. 'What do you think?' she asked the kitchen staff proudly.

'Oh, it's lovely, Mrs Whitaker!' Willow clapped.

'Stop that racket, Willow. Very nice,' said Eve, with a sniff.

Lettice was lurking within earshot of the front door waiting for Morts to arrive. He was late, which added to her impatience. If only he knew how she longed to see him he would have hurried. But he did not for she had felt she should not confide her problems to anyone. It would be too disloyal to the husband she loathed.

When she heard a motor, she had the door open and was rushing out long before the footman and Whitaker had appeared. She jumped up and down with joy as a fine, noisy motor, with Morts' grinning face behind the wheel, drew up.

'You're here!' There was a high-pitched squeal behind her as her two daughters, Charlotte and Georgina, with their harassed nanny in hot pursuit, tumbled out of the house.

'Uncle! You've come. Have you brought me a present!'

'Charlotte, how rude!' But Lettice was laughing.

'Younkle! Present?' Three-year-old Georgina was twirling round, a mass of fine white cotton, lace-trimmed petticoat and flashing red shoes.

Both girls had long blonde hair swept back in ringlets and their father's blue eyes. But theirs were full of laughter, Hugo's with spite.

'Chrisymas.' Georgina pointed at the pile of gaily wrapped parcels piled on the back seat of the car.

Morts leant down and swept her into his arms. Charlotte clung to his trousers. 'And how are my two favourite young ladies? Ramsey, come and meet this pair of mischiefs.'

From the other side of the car a tall, hefty man, in a vast leather driving coat, deer-stalker on his head and goggles covering half of his face, strode around the front of the car. He clutched at his heart and staggered back to lean on the motor. 'Lawks, Mort, you told me they were stunners but you didn't prepare me for quite such beauties!'

The girls stood silent until he whisked off his goggles and leant down. 'Boo!' he bellowed, and they jumped with cries of delicious fright and collapsed in giggles on to the ground. 'Ramsey, my sister Mrs Hamilton. Lettice, this rogue is my friend Ramsey Poldown.'

He took Lettice's hand and bowed over it. Then he looked up and she was gazing into the kindest eyes imaginable. Large, dark and full of compassion, as if he knew she was troubled. 'It is so kind of your family to allow me to join you.'

'It is our pleasure, Mr Poldown.' Lettice's heart was racing and she felt suddenly hot in the chilly December weather.

2

Christmas Eve

Lettice was not an idle person, but she permitted herself a luxurious stretch and snuggled down under the blankets instead of ringing for her maid. Yesterday evening had been wonderful. She lay on her back looking up at the pleated silk on the canopy above her and the porcelain plaque of cupids kissing. She laughed to herself. She doubted she would ever forget the sight of her daughters, one on her brother's back, the other on Ramsey's, racing down the centre of the drawing-room. They had all collapsed into a shrieking heap at the end. As the race marshal she had declared it a dead heat. Her little girls had never been so happy. When it was time for them to go to bed, Lettice had felt quite guilty at handing them over to the nanny when they were so overexcited. First, Charlotte had been sick and then Georgina, but Ramsey had apologised to the nanny, declaring it was all his fault. Lettice had been stunned. Hugo would have had an hysterical rant – and he wouldn't have been playing with them in the first place.

Ramsey. She placed her hands behind her head and smiled dreamily. Never in her whole life had she met anyone she had liked so instantly. He was so easy to be with. He saw everything as a joke and had lifted her spirits until she too was happy; it had been a long time since she had felt like that. After one evening she felt as if she had known him all her life. No wonder he was Morts' favourite friend.

'Why have I not had the pleasure of meeting you before, Ramsey? I thought I'd met all of Morts' friends.'

'I've been in Argentine for the past four years.' He grinned.

'How interesting.' But her spirits dropped. 'Shall you return?'

'Unfortunately not, for the foreseeable future, although I should like to eventually. I liked the life there and the people are most hospitable.'

She would like to ask him what would keep him in Britain but she lacked the temerity. 'Your friends will be made happy by that,' she said shyly.

'Most likely they would be glad to see the back of me.'

'Why did you go?'

'The fate of the second son, I fear, Lettice. My elder brother is an insufferable prig and I felt the further away from him I could be when he came into his inheritance the better. I am ashamed to say that I don't like him very much.'

'I can't imagine you disliking anyone.'

'You don't know my brother.'

She blushed now to remember that she had asked him to call her Lettice. So unlike her, and what would Hugo think when he arrived? She was glad that Ramsey was not returning immediately to the Argentine. She found him attractive – not in a physical way, of course – although he was not handsome. She liked his eyes and the dimple that appeared when he smiled, but it was his personality that set him apart.

Last night he had listened to her as if he was really interested in what she had to say, and had laughed at her jokes. He had made her feel important.

'Heady stuff,' she said to herself, as she rang for her maid. Five minutes later, she was engulfed by her squealing, giggling little girls and the time for thinking was over.

With the bustle of the day it was as if the house was coming to life and enjoying itself. Now that the decorations were in place, even the gloomiest corners shone. A fifteen-foot tree had been placed in the entrance hall and Whitaker, still maintaining his dignity, was perilously high on a ladder adjusting the angel. 'I like things shipshape,' he explained, liking to use his seafaring father's expressions. 'It was crooked,' he said to the startled footman, who held the ladder. Whitaker replaced his frock-coat just as the sound of arrivals penetrated the large hall. He did not so much walk as glide towards the front door. There he paused, waiting for the optimum moment to open the door with a flourish, as a carriage and a motor-car arrived together at the steps.

'Nearly beat you. Hope I didn't frighten your horses too much, Mortie dear?' Hannah was laughing as she jumped from the driving seat of her Rolls, closely followed by Cariad, who added to the confusion by chasing her tail in frenzied circles, yapping with excitement. Hannah adjusted her beret and tugged at her tweed knickerbockers.

'Hannah, you look more like a boy each time I see you.' Coral kissed the air by her sister-in-law's cheek. 'No more prison, I hope,' she added, then swept up the stone steps. 'Good morning, Whitaker. No problems, I trust?'

'None whatsoever, my lady.' The butler held the door wide for her.

Mortie gave his sister a bear-hug. 'Ignore her, Hannah. She got out of bed the wrong side this morning.'

'I've forgotten already,' she said, but she hadn't. Coral always upset her, which seemed unfair. Hannah had done so much for her in the past.

'Tell me, do you drive this monster?'

'I most certainly do, and very well too. Isn't that so, Alf?'

''Tis, sir. Miss Cresswell's a natural.' He stood to attention in his new smart grey uniform with shiny black boots.

'Alf is a wonderful teacher. Very patient. Do you want a go?'

'I don't need a teacher,' Mortie boasted, as he climbed behind the wheel.

Hannah hastened to the other side. 'You can go, Alf. I'll keep the car here.'

'Thank you, Miss.' He doffed his chauffeur's cap.

'See to Cariad, Whitaker,' Hannah called, as Mortie kangarooed the car across the forecourt, the exhaust banging. The carriage ponies whinnied with terror.

Alf made his way to the back of the house and knocked on the kitchen door.

'Alf, this is a pleasure. Willow, make your father a cup of tea and give him some of my seed cake.' Eve Gilroy was flushed from her exertions. 'And, Edward, you take the weight off your pins, too.'

Alf sipped gratefully at the sweet tea. 'I needed this. Miss Cresswell's new motor's very cold when you're driving along.'

'What did she want to get a big thing like that for?' Whitaker asked. 'Nasty, noisy things.'

'She likes to keep abreast of the times, does Miss Cresswell. You should see the new cleaner she's bought the maids, works on electricity. It frightens that poor dog, though – it makes such a noise, sucking up the dirt. Her maid says it's faster to do it by hand, only she don't dare.' He laughed. 'I enjoy driving the Rolls, though, even if it is a bit cold. When we get home I just put it in the garage, no feeding or watering, no rubbing down, no new straw. Much easier.'

'I like your uniform, Dad. Makes you look ever so smart.'

'I told our Flossie she'll have to keep an eye on me. Ladies like a uniform, don't they, Mr Whitaker?'

'I couldn't say, I'm sure. I trust you weren't seen?' Whitaker enquired. 'Her ladyship doesn't like the servants to be seen in the grounds.'

Eve snorted as she rammed stuffing into yet another goose.

'Now, Eve! It's how it is.'

'You'd think we all had the plague.'

'Don't worry, Mr Whitaker. I walked down as far as the ha-ha. No one saw me.'

'Dad!' Rowan was skidding across the kitchen towards her father and hugged him hard. 'What a lovely surprise! I couldn't believe it when Mary said you was here.'

'I've come over with Miss Cresswell. She drove!' He rolled his eyes. 'It's a miracle we got here in one piece. Now she's gone off with Sir Mortie so I've got to walk back. I thought I'd have a cuppa first.'

'I don't know! Miss Cresswell's a mystery to me. She can be so thoughtful yet so inconsiderate too. She's always been the same,' Eve said crossly.

'Still, it's her motor.'

'If she can drive the dratted thing she needn't have brought you with her. Selfish, that's how I see it.'

'Eve …' Whitaker warned.

'I speaks my mind, Edward, as you well know.'

'Busy, are you?' Alf changed the subject. He agreed with the cook but couldn't see the point in anyone falling out over it, and he knew these servants of old. You had to watch what you said for fear they might repeat it to the wrong ears.

'Thirty – the numbers keep going up. All the Christmas specialities make it hard. Still, fortunately for me, young Lettice has been in charge and she told me to get in extra helpers. Her mother wouldn't have let me. There'll be hell to pay when she finds out.' She laughed.

Rowan was sitting as close to her father as she could get. 'It's very exciting, Dad. We're to get presents tonight. The carol singers are coming and we'll have punch.'

'Then make sure you don't get squiffy. I must say, Rowan, you look a picture in your uniform.'

'Oh, this is nothing. You should see me in my evening uniform. I've the loveliest lacy cap with ribbons that go right down to my waist.'

'Bet that cost a pretty penny.'

'I don't have to pay for it – not like the rest of my uniform. We're loaned them but we have to starch them ourselves.'

The kitchen door burst open and Coral Cresswell swept in, still in her hat and fur. Everyone scrabbled to their feet, Whitaker trying to pull on his jacket. 'Who arranged this menu?' she demanded.

Eve put down her spoon. 'Miss Lettice and me did.' She adjusted the starched bib of her overall.

'How could you? We cannot possibly have chicken fricassée for luncheon. People will think I'm serving leftovers.'

'There's nothing left over in my fricassée. It's all fresh.'

'It's a glorified stew.' At this criticism Eve sucked in her cheeks. 'And there's no game tonight. And only five courses. What were you thinking, Mrs Gilroy?'

Eve wiped her hands on a tea-towel with a slow deliberation that made the kitchen staff hold their breath. She adjusted her belt. 'I was thinking, *my lady*, that with such a *large* dinner tonight you would *appreciate* a lighter meal at luncheon. And since no one can give me numbers, the fricassée was ideal since I can stretch it if more arrive. That's what I was thinking.' She spoke in a measured tone.

'It will have to be changed.'

Pointedly Eve looked at the clock on the wall. 'There isn't time to change *anything*, begging your pardon, your ladyship.'

'What about one of them?' She pointed at the row of geese on the long pine table.

'They're for tomorrow and there's no time to cook one now. And, in any case, if we have them today your guests will find it rum that we repeat the same dish two days running.'

'Well, think of something else.' Coral waved the offending menu agitatedly. 'It's too bad of you. What will the Comte de Ceneuil think? and him a Frenchman.'

This was a mistake. 'Them as eat snails and frogs are hardly in a position to criticise *my* menus!'

Rowan gasped.

'It's too bad.' Coral was getting more flustered by the minute. 'Lettice should have known better. And as for you, Mrs Gilroy, with all your experience—'

'You could have written.'

'I beg your pardon?'

'If you was so fussed by what was to be served you could have written or telegraphed your wishes to me. I can read, you know.'

'Don't be impertinent, Mrs Gilroy.'

'I'm not, my lady. I'm just pointing out the facts to you. That, or you should have been here to make the arrangements yourself.'

'You are insufferably rude, woman.'

'I'm nobody's *woman*!' Eve bellowed. She removed her apron, threw it among the geese and stalked out of the kitchen along the corridor to the butler's pantry where she knew she would find a bottle of brandy.

'She will have to go!' Coral swept into the hall, Whitaker hurrying behind her, divesting herself of her coat and fighting with the fur tippet she wore round her neck.

'Who?' asked Mortie, shrugging off his astrakhan coat with Whitaker's help.

'Mrs Gilroy!' The fur, a fox with his tail firmly clenched in his mouth, was proving recalcitrant.

'Oh, is she leaving? Can I have her?' Esmeralda, newly arrived with Oliver, asked excitedly. 'She's the most divine cook.'

'Mrs Gilroy leaving at Christmas?' Mortie's expression was pained.

'This time she's gone too far with her impertinence.' Coral plopped herself down on an intricately carved oak chair and tried to see where the tippet's catch was.

'Coral, let me.' Hannah stepped forward and released it from the large Cairngorm brooch it had become entwined with. 'Where's Felix?'

'Don't talk to me about that wretched boy!'

'Why? What has happened?'

'He telegraphed that he had gone to my parents, that he didn't want to come here. He did not even have the courtesy to tell me to my face.'

'How strange. That's not like Felix. I wonder why. Still, it will be nice for your parents to have him with them, won't it?'

'For goodness' sake, Hannah. Stop asking such stupid questions – I have so much to put up with. And now Mrs Gilroy is ruining Christmas for me.'

'You must not let her upset you so. She's always been the same.'

'She's a servant, Hannah! How dare she speak to me in that tone?'

'Coral, with so many guests due this is hardly the best time to dismiss her.'

Mortie's expression was one of terminal misery.

'She can go afterwards.' Coral was fanning herself.

'God knows what she would do to the food,' Mortie said dolefully. 'What if she spat in it?'

'Oh, Mortie, don't be so very stupid.'

Whitaker coughed in a discreet manner.

'You see, Whitaker agrees with me.'

'He didn't say a word.'

'He didn't have to.'

'Shall I see if I can resolve the situation?' Hannah asked.

Coral's 'No,' and Mortie's 'Yes,' rang out in unison. But the sudden arrival of three sets of guests had distracted Coral, who changed from ruffled mistress to charming hostess as she swooped across the hall to greet them.

Hannah slipped through a door at the back of the hall, hidden behind a large tapestry screen, and into an ill-lit chilly area. There were no carpets on the floor, no pictures on the walls. She had always hated it as a child, and in her house the servants' quarters, if not as lovely as her own, were much pleasanter.

There was chaos in the kitchen. The kitchenmaids were staring at the staggering amounts of food on the table and the scullerymaid was in tears. Hilda was trying to calm everyone.

'Miss Cresswell, how nice to see you.' Mrs Herbert stood up. 'We've such a problem and I should be upstairs settling the guests.'

'What has happened? My sister-in-law is very upset.'

'As we all are, Miss Cresswell. Her ladyship did not approve of the menus and wanted them changed. Mrs Gilroy became … well, not herself. She said it could not be done.'

'Probably not at this late hour. You go and see to the guests, Mrs Herbert, and I'll see what I can do here.'

There was a banging at the back door. 'Cooee!' someone called. To everyone's amazement Mrs Fuller leapt into the kitchen, waving her umbrella. 'Oh, Miss Cresswell! I'm sorry.'

'Mrs Fuller, the very person – come with me. Mrs Herbert, you get along upstairs. With Mrs Fuller here, all will be resolved in the kitchen.'

'Thrown one of her tantrums, has she?' Mrs Fuller asked as they hurried along the service corridor to the butler's pantry. They found Eve Gilroy sobbing into a brandy glass.

'What are you doing here?' she asked, at the sight of her friend.

'Been invited for Christmas with you. Isn't that nice? I'm supposed to be a surprise for you.'

'Invited by whom?'

'Well, her ladyship, but we both know it was Mrs Oliver what arranged it.'

The cook continued to weep. Suddenly she saw Hannah and attempted to stand up, but had to sit down again quickly.

'I'm so sorry you're upset, Mrs Gilroy,' Hannah said.

'Upset!'

Hannah and Gussie Fuller were left in no doubt as to the extent of her misery.

'I'm not surprised you're perturbed, Mrs Gilroy. Menus are not to be treated lightly.' Hannah was putting the top back on the brandy decanter. 'And with so many meals to cook, it would be difficult to change.' She placed the decanter on a high shelf.

'Why can't her ladyship understand that?'

'She has had a long journey and no doubt her nerves are frayed—'

'Not as frayed as mine. And I'm not apologising when I've done nothing wrong.'

'Quite so, Mrs Gilroy. Did I notice some quail in the kitchen?'

'You did, Miss Cresswell.'

'And, no doubt, we have some fish. If it wasn't too much bother you might consider making some quenelles, perhaps with a chaudfroid sauce – no one makes quenelles as light as you do – and that would be another course.'

'I could. But what about my fricassée? Stew, she said it was, leftovers. My fricassée's never that.'

'Do you remember those wonderful crêpes you used to make for my father? I should love some. Are they too difficult to prepare at such short notice?'

'I could stuff them with my fricassée, cover them with a cheese sauce.'

'What a joy!' Hannah clapped her hands. 'And Lady Penelope will enjoy them too.' She glanced at her watch. 'Good heavens, look at the time. I've so much to do.'

'Me too, Miss Cresswell. Come along, Gussie. We've work to do.' And they followed Hannah out of the pantry.

On her way back to the front of the house Hannah met Lettice, who was very distressed. 'Mama is furious with me. It's all my fault.'

'It's all resolved now, Lettice darling.'

'Thank you, Aunt – what would we do without you? Mrs Gilroy has so much to do over the next few days that I decided on a light luncheon. That was all.'

'And very considerate it was of you.' Hannah linked her arm through Lettice's. 'Dear girl, there's nothing of you,' she said anxiously. 'Do you eat enough?'

'All the time, Aunt. I just don't put on weight.'

'Are you happy?'

'Of course.' She laughed – falsely, Hannah thought.

Lettice pushed open the door and they stepped into the hall. As they did so, Hannah felt her niece freeze.

'There you are! Where the devil were you?'

'And good morning to you too, Hugo. Merry Christmas,' Hannah said pointedly.

'Aunt Hannah. I didn't see you in the shadows.'

'Evidently not.' She sounded uncustomarily waspish.

3

Although Rowan had watched the tree in the hall being decorated nothing had prepared her for the sight of it now lit. Candlelight flickered on the brightly coloured baubles and the wings of the angel at the top fluttered in the heat. It was the most beautiful thing she had ever seen she confided to Mary, who, having been at the manor for three years, was less impressed.

The servants stood in a long line that snaked round the hall. Although Whitaker had told them they were to wait in silence, no one took much notice: the whispering became chattering that grew louder the longer they stood there.

'They always do this to us,' Mary complained. 'Rude, I call it.'

Eventually there was a flurry at the top of the stairs and the family appeared with their guests, led by Coral in flaming crimson. The dinner gowns of silk and satin, in all the colours of the rainbow, swished as the women sashayed down. Rowan was entranced at the way they moved, their heads held high on slender necks, hair piled up with jewels and flowers that made them seem taller than they were. Diamonds, rubies, emeralds and sapphires glistened in the light. Rowan felt as if she was watching angels.

'I reckon her ladyship's put on weight. Hardly surprising, is it?' Mary whispered.

'Don't spoil it. I think they all look lovely.'

Mary sniffed.

Then Rowan saw him, resplendent in white tie, with diamond studs sparkling on the front of his dress shirt. He walked as proudly as the women, dark hair smoothed sleek. Rowan had never seen Morts in white tie and tails before and held her breath at the sight of his beauty.

The family arranged themselves in front of the great stone fireplace with a pile of presents on a table to the side. Whitaker held a long list in his hand and, at a nod from Coral, began to read out names in order of seniority.

Rowan did not mind that it took so long because she could watch Morts. How gracious he was, how courteous. He had a smile for every-one. And then it was her turn.

'Rowan Marshall,' Whitaker called, and she felt sick with nerves as she stepped forward, crossed in front of the fireplace, saw Mrs Herbert hand a small parcel and envelope to Coral. The gloved hand was extended to her and she remembered to bob as she accepted her gift. She was nervous of looking her employer in the eye but she did not know why. 'Thank you, my lady.' She bobbed again.

Then it was over and she was accepting a small glass of punch. They waited, sipping the drink, as the gardeners and outside servants shuffled past.

'This warms your cockles, doesn't it?' She had been joined by Willow. 'When can we open these?'

'Not till us is finished in here. You'll get in trouble if you do,' Mary whispered.

'You thought any more about the factory, Rowan?' asked Willow.

'No.' She had decided to enjoy Christmas here, then give notice but that had been before she had seen Morts looking so romantic and splendid.

'Well, I'm going,' Willow stated.

'You never are?' Mary murmured.

'I'm fed up with being screamed at by that old cow Gilroy. Why should I put up with it? I do my work but she's always finding fault.'

'And you think they won't shout at you in the blanket factory?'

'Perhaps, but at least I can go home at night.'

'I changed my mind when I found out he's a German. I'm not going to work for one of them, that's for sure.'

'Who's a German?' Rowan asked. Rumours were racing around the manor, these days, about how bad the Germans were. She had heard that a poor German sausage dog had been hanged somewhere.

'The owner, of course. In league with the Kaiser, he is.'

There was a banging at the door and in marched the church choir, resplendent in their red cassocks. Rowan recognised most of them, but she almost burst with pride when she saw Oak bringing up the rear, holding a huge candle. What a fine figure of a boy he was, even though he was only twelve. The singing brought tears to her eyes, especially when everyone joined in, and their voices soared to the rafters of the ancient hall.

Poor Willow missed it all. She had been called away by the cook who had slipped out just as the choir was getting into its stride. It must always have been like this, Rowan thought. Her own ancestors had probably stood in this spot listening to the same music with the Cresswell's forebears. She blushed when she saw that Morts was staring at her.

'I thought it was never going to end, gets longer every year. And the choir was off key,' Eve Gilroy complained.

'Were they?' Gussie Fuller enquired.

'Of course, you haven't got my ear. I've perfect pitch.'

Eve flew about her kitchen, a picture of perpetual motion. She might make a fuss, she might shout and throw saucepans, but she was always on time and everything would be perfect as usual.

'I'm surprised you chose the Royal Worcester, Mrs Herbert. Old Lady Cresswell always preferred the Crown Derby.'

'It wasn't my choice, Mrs Fuller.'

'Really? I *am* surprised. I was always consulted on the table setting, the flowers, the silverware. It was a duty I enjoyed.' She picked up the guest list, which was lying on the table. 'I see you put Miss Cresswell in the Childer bedroom. She'll be upset by that, she always used to stay in her old suite.'

'At her request, Mrs Fuller. She said as how she did not want the old memories coming back.' Mrs Herbert looked quietly triumphant. 'Now, if you'll excuse me, I've duties to attend to.'

Mrs Herbert's chatelaine clinked as she hurried up the back stairs to the main bedroom corridor. There, she checked that the maids had tidied the bedrooms to her exacting standards. She insisted that the sheets were turned back and folded to an exact three-foot triangle and liked the nightwear laid out with all ribbons and laces undone. She fussed over the curtains, demanded that the fire irons be laid just so. At the dressing-tables, she checked each hairbrush for cleanliness and ran a finger over the surface to see if a dusting of powder remained. In the bathrooms she counted the number of towels folded over the wooden rails, and was only satisfied if she could see her face in the brass taps. All bottles of oil, bath salts and cologne had to be full, with the tops loosened for ease of opening. In the dressing-rooms, she examined clothes to make sure they had been correctly brushed, mended and hung; that boots and shoes had trees in them, that the washing had been bagged for the laundrymaids to collect.

While all this was going on, the maids waited anxiously. Her inspection over, she clapped her hands and lined them up. 'Now you may open your presents.' As always there were no congratulations on work well done. Rowan had a theory that the housekeeper was always disappointed to find nothing wrong so she could not bring herself to praise them.

Rowan tore at the envelope. Inside she found a Christmas card with a shiny half-crown. She squealed with excitement.

'Mean, I calls it,' said Mary, who, being more senior, had two.

'Mary, *five shillings*! What will you spend it on?'

'I've a fancy for a new bonnet. You?'

'I'll probably give it to my mother.'

'Goody Two Shoes, that's what you are.'

Then, with fumbling fingers, Rowan opened the small parcel, wrapped in lovely paper. 'Soap.' She sniffed it. 'Geranium!'

'That's 'cause her ladyship don't like geranium. Probably someone gave it to her and she's hiving it off on you.'

'Oh, Mary, don't spoil it, please.'

Mrs Herbert bustled along the line telling them all how lucky they were. 'Now, the four of you who are helping in the dining-room, go and find Mr Whitaker for instructions.'

Half of Rowan was terrified but the other half was thrilled to be seeing Morts again.

Coral seated her guests graciously. The men had been instructed before-hand as to whom they would escort into dinner. She was vexed that one party's vehicle had broken down near Basingstoke and they would not arrive before tomorrow. 'It's so vexing of them. Horses are so much more reliable than those infernal machines, which only fools are seduced into buying,' she snapped.

Hannah smiled to herself.

'No one ever gives a thought to my seating plans,' Coral fretted. She was particularly put out because the missing group included two young women, whom she had been keen for Morts to meet – it was time, with his future responsibilities, that he thought of marrying again. 'It's too bad of them,' she continued.

Lettice was glad they had not arrived for, in consequence, she was seated between her brother and Ramsey. She could not have wished for a better place, and was only sorry that Hugo was directly opposite her. His proximity made her nervous.

Rowan was behind the footman who stood at Hugo's chair. Lettice smiled at her reassuringly. At least she wasn't the only nervous person here, she thought. Further down the table she saw the Prestwicks, such a dear couple, old but so in love. If only …

'Don't you think that girl is the most beautiful creature you've ever set eyes on, Lettice?'

'She's lovely, Morts. And sweet with it. Don't you harm her!' She tapped his hand with her fan.

'Would I?'

'No, of course not. I was only teasing.' And it was true, but when Morts looked at the young housemaid his expression worried her.

Three courses had been served without mishap and Rowan was almost enjoying herself. Her task was simple: the footman removed the plates, and gave them to her. She took them to the small room at the side of the dining-room and placed them in the trolley, which one of the kitchenmaids rolled back to the kitchen, having left another trolley full of clean warm china. She took the required number of plates back to the footman. She need not worry about spilling anything since she was not allowed near the food.

Morts had smiled at her a dozen times. She knew she had stared at him and that she shouldn't, but she couldn't help it. She was in love for sure. Why else did her stomach feel full of butterflies, and her pulse race?

The conversation had moved to the possibility of war. Coral did her best to stop it, declaring that there wouldn't be one. 'I met the Kaiser once, a charming man, devoted to his grandmother, the dear Queen Victoria. He respected his uncle too. The king told me so himself.' She looked nostalgic as she spoke of that other time when Edward VII had been on the throne, and Coral and Mortie had been at the centre of things.

But the men wished to discuss the subject. To Lettice they all sounded as if they were looking forward to war.

'I've been wondering if we should not perhaps begin to train some of the men. Purely as a defensive measure ... just in case,' Oliver suggested.

'I'm not having troops drilling outside my windows!'

'But you're hardly ever here, Coral. They won't bother you.'

'I don't think we should encourage violence in the lower orders.'

'You are mistaken. We should be prepared.'

'But Germany is hundreds of miles away. You don't mean you imagine that marauding troops will come here?' Coral laughed.

'Of course not, but we should be prepared to fight. Sometimes it is better to be ready and hope one will not be called upon.'

There was a mutter of agreement from the other men.

'Whack 'em when they least expect it. Never liked 'em myself.' Mortie had offered his pennyworth, undeterred by his wife's furious frown.

'That's not true, Mortie,' she said. 'You adored the Kaiser.'

'I did not,' he protested, as conversation swung to the character of the German ruler.

'And what do you think, Mrs Hamilton?' Ramsey asked.

Lettice smiled at him with relief. At the beginning of the evening she had made herself avoid him, hard though that was: she had been afraid he might use her Christian name and that Hugo would hear. She need not have worried, of course, because he was a gentleman. 'I hate all this talk of fighting,' she said. 'Look at all the young lives wasted in the Boer War. It still gives me nightmares just thinking about them. Surely what problems there are can be resolved by talking.'

'It's not always that simple, Mrs Hamilton.'

'Talk gets us nowhere. The Hun need to be taught a short, sharp lesson!'

Lettice was alarmed: she had not been aware that Hugo was listening to them and he had sounded drunk, which was unusual – in company his manners were always impeccable. He reserved excessive drinking, spite and malice for when they were alone.

'But your wife was saying—'

'Take no notice of what she says. She hasn't an intelligent thought in her whole body.' Hugo had spoken loudly and Lettice heard a sharp intake of breath from the other diners. A stunned silence enveloped them, then noisy chattering erupted as they endeavoured to disguise the embarrassing episode. She was upset to be humiliated in front of everyone but her husband's opinion no longer hurt her. He said it too often for that.

'I find your wife has a fine, interesting mind,' Ramsey told him.

Hugo snorted.

'Good gracious, that's the first time anyone has ever said that about my daughter! I've failed!' Coral slapped her forehead daintily. 'I told her it was best to hide any intelligence she has inherited – from me, of course, not dear Mortie.' Several laughed tentatively, others looked as if they wished they were elsewhere.

Lettice was mortified. Hugo looked supercilious.

'Why are you being so impolite to my niece, Hugo? Her opinion was perfectly valid,' Oliver asked quietly.

'I wasn't aware that I was,' Hugo responded.

'Then that makes it worse. Lettice is a sweet, gentle person. She deserves better.'

'She has all she needs.'

'Except happiness.'

Hugo jumped to his feet and threw down his napkin. 'How dare you!'

'She's my niece.'

Lettice was aware of everyone at the table leaning forward the better to see and hear.

'Shall we ladies retire?' Coral swept to her feet. 'Now, you naughty boys, behave yourselves.' She gave them the arch smile she thought attractive and tapped Hugo with her fan. 'Charades in the drawing-room when you've finished, gentlemen.'

Lettice did not ask her mother to excuse her but ran up the stairs two at a time to her room. There she threw herself on to the bed and cried. To be so humiliated in front of so many people – in front of Ramsey! She was so unhappy ...

She was woken by Hugo crashing into the room. She had no idea how much later it was. 'You bitch!' he shouted at her. 'Want Ramsey, do you? Well, you'll have me – you're mine!' He took her roughly, as he always did. At least it was all over quickly.

Lettice waited until his breathing indicated that he was asleep, then crept out of bed and into the bathroom. There, high on a cupboard, she felt for a small box. It contained a douche she had bought in Paris. The last thing she wanted was another of his children growing inside her.

4

Christmas Day, 1913

Dolly opened the windows wide in the bar and popped her head out to take deep breaths of fresh air. The crisp breeze from the sea was a tonic and she needed it. She was exhausted. Heavens, she felt as if she had drunk a whole bottle of wine rather than the one glass of sherry she had had last night.

From the next room she could hear Apollo and Cordelia bickering, which they did constantly, she didn't know why. They had everything they wanted, she saw to that, and their stockings had been bulging this morning. Why could they not be more content? Perhaps it wasn't surprising that they were like this. They were only aping their elders – everyone was cross at the moment. The problems seemed insoluble. Whoever gave way, she or Zeph, one would be the loser, and what effect would that have on their future? Work, she told herself, was the best solution.

From the cupboard she took a broom. Then she scattered sawdust over the floor and swept it up. She moved swiftly about the bar, picking up the ashtrays and tipping the contents into a bucket. She collected the tankards and put them to soak. It should all have been done last night, but everyone had been too tired. From the scullery she fetched a bucket of soapy water and began to scrub the tables.

This place was filthy. Neglected. It smelt – a horrible combination of tobacco, cabbage and old men's sweat. How could Melanie have let it get like this? Next she found some newspaper and attacked the window-panes, which were so dirty from smoke fumes she could barely see out.

'Didn't you hear the children? They're fighting,' was Zeph's greeting as he came in. He looked tired too and more dishevelled than usual.

'I thought I'd make matters worse if I interfered.' She tried to smile but Zeph's face remained impassive. They had gone to bed angry and not speaking, had lain facing away from each other, spines rigid with unspoken hurts.

'Do you want some breakfast?' Perhaps she could use food to ease the atmosphere.

'I made myself some toast.'

'Where's Flossie got to?' She was mopping the pine tables with an old towel, soaking up the water. 'She's never late.'

'I told her not to come in, to spend Christmas Day with her family.'

'That was nice of you. When are we opening?'

'We're not. It's a family day.'

'Oh, Zeph, that's so thoughtful. I would have hated us all to work to-day, of all days. But what will your mother say?'

'I haven't told her. She's a bit low.'

'She's all right, though?'

'Yes. Each day she's a little better and stronger.'

'Perhaps she hoped your sister would come and is disappointed she didn't. Still, she's got Timmy.' Everyone had been worried that Timmy, Zeph's younger brother by a good seven years, had not turned up when he'd been expected. Melanie had been looking forward to seeing him. Eventually he had arrived yesterday evening, with a long, involved tale of missed trains. When he had caught one, he had fallen asleep and woken up miles away in Plymouth, where he had had to beg a lift back to Cresswell on a horse-drawn cart.

'Why didn't you tell me she'd been so ill?' Timmy had turned on his brother when, with his mother settled for the night, they had congre-gated in the kitchen for a nightcap.

'I told you a couple of weeks ago when I found out. It's hardly *my* fault if you turn up when the crisis is over.'

'I can't just take leave, you know. There has to be a good reason.'

'I'd have thought your mother's illness was reason enough.'

'You didn't tell me how bad it was.'

'I did. You couldn't be bothered.'

'You bastard!'

Dolly had stepped in. 'You two falling out isn't going to help. Pull yourselves together. Your mother's much better, Timmy, and we should be grateful for that.'

Her intervention had calmed Zeph. 'Whisky?' he asked his brother.

'Thanks. So, you've taken over, Zeph?'

Dolly placed a platter of cheese, pickles and a fresh loaf of bread on the table.

'Yes.' Zeph hacked off a piece of bread.

'Did Mum ask you to?'

'No, but someone had to help out and Richard's worse than useless. He's always drunk.'

'Bit uppity of you, wasn't it?'

'I don't know what you mean.' Zeph stared at his brother.

'It's quite simple. This is a successful pub. I know Mum's done well with the hotel, and she's bought God knows how many cottages. She's a wealthy woman, wouldn't you say?'

'What are you implying?'

'I'd like to know how much you're making out of this.'

'Timmy!' Dolly was aghast.

'It's a fair question,' Timmy said, 'and certainly I've a right to ask it.'

'You think I'm stealing from Mum?'

'I didn't say that.'

'No, but that's what you mean, isn't it?'

Dolly sat upright in her chair. 'Zeph gave up a good position to come here, I'll have you know. *And* against my advice.'

'Good position? When was he last promoted? And I'm not alone in wondering what's going on – Richard says he hasn't seen a penny in the week or so you've been here, Zeph.'

'He hasn't seen a penny because I've made sure he didn't. Don't you understand that *he's* been robbing Mother blind?'

'How, if he's always drunk?'

'I reckon he's had his hand in the till. And he buys things and says they cost more than they did. So I've put a stop to it.'

'I've only your word for that.'

'For goodness' sake, Timmy. This is your brother you're insulting. If anyone's out of pocket because of this it's us. We still have the rent to pay on our house in Barlton and I'm personally losing money by having to be here. I have my own business.' She tossed her head proudly. 'It can't run itself so I'm having to leave here at five in the morning to attend to it, then get back for the children's tea. Don't you lecture us.'

'Put the missus out to work, then, have you, Zeph? Call yourself a man?'

'Why, you bastard—'

'But I'm not the bastard around here, am I?'

At this, Zeph was on his feet, lunging at his brother.

Dolly manoeuvred herself between them. 'Stop it, both of you. Melanie might hear. Do you want to make her ill again?'

Zeph sat down. 'I've only been trying to help.'

'Is it helpful to bring that Snodland woman and her brat with you? Two more mouths to feed? Or is there more to that than meets the eye?'

Dolly was back on her feet. 'How dare you speak to my husband like that? May works for me and she's here to help.' Even though I need her more in Barlton, she thought.

'I don't know what the army's done to you, Timmy, but it hasn't improved you.' Zeph seemed sad and defeated.

'I see what's what, these days. No one can pull the wool over my eyes. I'm twenty-one, so I don't need you to tell me what I should and shouldn't do.' He stood up. 'I'm off to bed.' They watched him leave.

'That was horrible.' Dolly said. 'And calling you a bastard? That was unkind.' That Zeph and his sister were illegitimate was a subject he and Dolly did not discuss. She knew how it upset him. 'What a horrible man he's become saying those awful things.' She began to clear the table.

'Did you have to boast?'

'What do you mean?' Dolly turned from the sink where she had begun to wash the dishes.

'You made me look a fool – more or less told him I can't support my own family!'

'I'm not going to listen to this. You've had too much ale.' She began to remove her pinafore.

'But you will listen. Sit.' There was something in his tone that made her do as he bade her. 'I've let you keep your business so far, but it's got to stop now. I need you here – it's obvious.'

'And I told you I'm not coming back to Cress. I'm happy where we are.' Her heart began to pound. 'We've already discussed this and there's nothing more to be said.' She began to rise.

'Sit down! It's your duty to be here.'

'I am here as much as I can be, but I see my duty as being to my children. I work for them and you.'

'As I said, you have your business because you love it – more than you love me.'

'That's a stupid thing to say. The children need educating. They're happy at their school in Barlton. They can't be moved – they're both doing well with their lessons.'

'One school is much like another. They'll settle here at the village school.'

'You can say that because you've had your posh education. You've no idea what's best for them. Since we can't afford for them to go private – though not for want of my trying – they'll stay where they are in Barlton.'

'You don't seem to be listening to me. I said we're moving here permanently.'

'You don't need me. You've got May here. Although I must say your brother's made me think. We're short of money and you insisted she came here with us. She was supposed to be helping me, not you.' She put her hands on the table. 'I've so many dreams, and if I don't do anything about them no one else will.'

'Back to that, are we? You're accusing me of being a bad provider.'

'Well, aren't you?'

'I suited well enough at the beginning. I was a good enough catch when—'

'When you *had* to marry me? I'd like to remind you that you loved me then and I didn't make the baby all on my own.' She stood up. 'I'm going to bed. I don't want to hear any more of this rubbish.' She had rushed from the room, determined that he would not see her crying.

Now it was the morning and last night's bitterness would not leave her. Matters had to be faced. 'Zeph …' she said.

'We have to talk, Dolly.'

'I know.' She sat down opposite him at one of the bar tables. She was relieved that he wanted to sort everything out. She hated there to be bad feeling between them.

'I'd like you to give up the business,' he said.

Dolly half rose.

'No, let me finish. I would like you to give it up, but I understand what it means to you. And I respect your determination to continue.'

Dolly sat down again.

'I have to stay here. You do see that, don't you?'

'Yes. But it wasn't what I had imagined. If I'd wanted to run a pub I'd have suggested we do it a long time ago.'

'Is it Melanie? Is that why you don't want to live here?'

'Of course not. I like her, and she's only ever been kind to me. But she's married to Richard and I don't like living with them. It's not right. And with him always drunk, it's not good for the children.'

'Has he fondled you?'

'I wasn't going to say but, yes, he did. Nothing serious, he was too drunk for that.' She gave a wry smile.

'He did it to May, too.'

'Why did she tell you and not me?'

'Because I was there, I suppose. Oh, Dolly, don't let us be distracted. I've got a plan. I'm going to see Sir Mortie and to ask him if I can buy one of his cottages with a few acres of land. We'll make our home here, a proper home. You've always wanted us to have a house of our own.'

'That's true,' she said, but not in the countryside, she thought. 'And how will you pay for it?' She tried not to sound sharp.

'I shall ask him for a loan. I've plans for this place. I've studied the books, and I can take a reasonable salary.'

'That will upset Timmy even more. You're going to have to square it with him, Melanie and Richard.'

'Damn Timmy and Richard. What do they do for her? Nothing. Anyway, I've already discussed it with her and she's happy with the arrangement.'

'I'm sure she is.'

'What does that mean?'

'I'm sure she'll be pleased to have you help her. For goodness' sake, Zeph, don't imagine things that aren't there.' Which was not strictly true: she liked her mother-in-law, with distance between them, and didn't know how it would be if they all lived on top of each other.

'I've worked it out. I'll spread the repayments, ask for a low-interest rate … After all, they owe me …' Whenever he spoke of his father, Sir Mortie Cresswell, it was with bitterness in his voice.

'Why not rent from him?'

'Because it's your dream to have your own house, and for once I would be doing something to make you happy.'

'Oh, Zeph, I don't know what to say. It would be lovely. But, house or no house, I'm not giving up the business.'

'I've been thinking what best to do about that. Perhaps you could just work in the mornings. There's several men who live here and work in Barlton.'

'But the expense of travelling back and forth?'

'You keep telling me how well you're doing.' He grinned at her.

'But … You know I've started advertising for nurses? I've had so many enquiries.' She smiled. 'It would be a long day for the children, though.'

'That's the one thing I insist on – they go to school here. I'm not backing down on that. May will look after them while you're away. I've asked her already.'

'Do you know what annoys me more than anything else, Zeph? It's the way you discuss things with her before you talk to me. I am your wife, you know, or have you forgotten?' Although she was laughing there was a distinct edge to her voice.

'Where's my sodding breakfast?' Richard had appeared in the doorway.

'Ask for it like that and you can bloody starve!' Dolly snapped.

5

Christmas Day, 1913

'Morts tells me you have a wishing tree here.' Ramsey and Lettice were in the drawing-room where everyone was meeting before lunch.

'Why, yes, at the top of Childer's Hill. It's a lovely spot.'

'I should love to go and make a wish.'

'You believe in magic?'

'I rely on it.' Ramsey laughed. Lettice loved his laugh, such a genuine, joyous sound.

'We could go after luncheon. A walk will do us good. And I promised the girls that we should do something exciting this afternoon. They have been so good.' And I can be with you, which will make me very happy, she thought, shocking herself with her boldness.

'Your grandmother continues to improve, I trust?'

'Oh, yes, she's much better, thank you.' Unfortunately she was *very* much better – she was even more difficult and strident. Esmeralda had taken over from Lettice, who had been sitting with her since they had returned from church, so she was surprised now when her aunt joined them with Hugo.

'Who's with Grandmama? Should I return?' She had begun to get to her feet.

'One of the maids. She's sleeping. When I read to her she always nods off. Perhaps I bore her.'

'I thought that was Lettice's prerogative,' Hugo said.

'What? Her going to sleep?'

'No, reading to her,' Hugo said, with a charming smile, but there was no smile in his eyes when they met Lettice's.

'We're planning to climb Childer's Hill this afternoon. Anyone coming?' Lettice asked, glad to change the subject.

'I shall be resting. I can't think of anything worse than climbing the hill,' Esmeralda said.

'I remember when you did – on a lovely summer's day when we first met you.'

'Gracious, Lettice! What a memory you have. I'd forgotten that.'

But Lettice didn't believe her. She was sure that she had watched Esmeralda fall in love with Oliver that day, exuding such happiness and confidence.

'I was young then,' Esmeralda added, 'Now I'm an old woman.'

'My dear Esmeralda, you will never be old.' Hugo bowed, took her hand and brushed it with a kiss.

Esmeralda giggled with embarrassment. 'You are as gallant as a Frenchman, Hugo. I wish Oliver was more like you.'

You don't know my husband, Lettice thought. You don't know how cruel he can be. And how could you criticise Oliver? He's the kindest man I know. But, then, some people liked Hugo – was Oliver like Hugo when he and Esmeralda were alone and no charade had to be played out for the benefit of others?

'Luncheon is served, my lady,' Whitaker announced, and, with a flurry, everyone paired up.

Rowan was tired. They had not got to bed until gone two last night and she'd still had to be up at six. Worse, her feet were killing her – she must get some new shoes. She wondered how many miles she had already walked today. To her disappointment she was not asked to help serve luncheon. She'd been looking forward to that and the chance to see *him*. Instead she was racing from kitchen to dining-room carrying heavy trays, terrified she was going to drop one. In the odd lull she had raced upstairs to check the five bedrooms she had been allocated. She had picked up the clothes that the women, who had not brought their maids, had left scattered about. While she folded and put them away she wondered why they treated such lovely things so carelessly. If she had silk stockings with lace tops she would guard them with her life.

She always enjoyed tidying the dressing-tables. She loved sniffing the bottles, smearing a little of the expensive creams on her face. She was fascinated by the rouge. She couldn't imagine using it and wasn't sure she would want it plastered on her skin. Best of all she liked the perfumes and wished she had the courage to spray a little on. She never did – the housekeeper might smell it and then she'd be in trouble.

Once the rooms were done, she raced back to Mr Whitaker for further instructions.

'You're not needed here. Mrs Herbert wants to see you.' He did not look at her as he spoke, which was strange.

'After dinner?'

'How many times, girl? It's not dinner, it's luncheon. Now, away with you.'

'But—'

'Now.' When Mr Whitaker spoke in that way everyone jumped to his order. She raced along the corridor. A summons to the housekeeper's room invariably meant trouble and she'd seen others emerge in tears or angry. She went over in her mind anything she might have done wrong, but couldn't think of anything. She got on with everyone and she wasn't lazy.

'Ah, Rowan, come in.' Mrs Herbert smiled without looking at her directly, and Rowan tensed. 'I fear I have bad news for you.'

'My mother? Has something happened to one of my sisters? My brother?'

'No, nothing like that. I fear I have to tell you that you are no longer required here.'

'What?'

'You will vacate your room in one hour.'

'But why? What have I done?'

'I'm not at liberty to say. You will not be given a character reference either.'

'What about my wages?'

'You will be paid for the days you have worked this month.'

'That's not fair.'

'I don't think you are in any position to say that.' Mrs Herbert looked uncomfortable, but Rowan was too upset to notice.

'I work hard. Who has complained about me? I've a right to know.'

'Her ladyship wishes you to be gone. Now, kindly go and pack. Leave your uniform on your bed.'

'But what about the amount I've already paid towards it?'

'You will be reimbursed some of it but the rest will be deducted for usage.'

'But—'

Mrs Herbert held up her hand. 'There is nothing further to be said. Thank you, Rowan, that will be all.'

From the drawing-room window, Esmeralda watched as the party set off to climb Childer's Hill. She had lied to Lettice: she would have loved to go with them – and she remembered that first meeting as if it were yesterday. That day had been the happiest of her life. It had been the day she told Oliver she loved him, and had said, 'I wish you would learn to love me as I love you!' That had been her wish at the wishing tree and she had said it aloud, to Oliver, as bold as brass. The woman she was now would never have the courage to say such a thing; the girl she had been had not thought twice before she spoke.

It was bad luck to tell your wish, they had warned her, but she had taken no heed. And in a way her wish had been granted. She had married him, but she was soon aware that he did not love her as she loved him. She could never go back to the wishing tree: it would remind her of happier times, which would be too much to bear. She sighed.

'Such a deep sigh, Esmeralda.'

'You made me jump. I didn't see you there when I came in.' She laughed as Hugo stood up. 'I came to watch them leave.'

'And I thought you had come to find me.'

'Why should I do such a thing?' She smiled, enjoying the mild flirtation – he was a handsome man.

'Because you are attracted to me.'

'Hugo! What gives you such an idea?'

'The way you look at me.'

'I was not aware that I looked at you any differently from anyone else.'

'Then you fib.'

He came close to her and she was suddenly aware of his masculinity. She stepped back sharply. 'Then I must change my manner.' She laughed.

'You look at me with the expression of a woman searching for love …' He took a step closer.

'Really! How impertinent.' She laughed again, nervously now.

'How can the truth be impertinence?'

She could smell his cologne. 'I beg you, Hugo. Stop this nonsense. You are frightening me.'

'How delicious.'

'I am married!'

'Not happily. I'm an expert on unhappy marriages. I see it in your eyes. You long for me. You long for excitement. You long to get away from your stuffed shirt of a husband.'

That brought Esmeralda to her senses. 'I'm sorry, Hugo, I must insist you stop. How dare you insult the man I love? Now, if you will excuse me …' With as much dignity as she could muster, Esmeralda left the room as quickly as she could.

'It's steep.' Ramsey was clutching at his heart playfully and staggering up the hill, making Charlotte and Georgina laugh.

'It's worth it for the view. Look, Morts is up there already. Come on, slowcoach.' She put out her hand to pull him up the slope and felt a tingle as their hands touched.

Morts was explaining the view to the other guests who had climbed with them, pointing out various parts of the estate.

'It's like being a bird,' said one of the women.

'So, what do we do, Lettice?' Ramsey asked her.

'You have to walk round the tree three times, wishing three times for whatever it is you want.'

'Oh, how lovely,' another woman trilled. Laughing and joking, the party began to walk round the gnarled old tree in a crocodile.

Lettice longed for them to be quiet: wishing was a serious business.

She closed her eyes. *I wish that somehow, somewhere, I can find happiness with Ramsey.* Stupid, she knew, but she repeated it the requisite three times.

'I wonder how many of your ancestors have done this,' Ramsey said as, with his arm beneath her elbow, he assisted Lettice.

'And how many have stood on this spot and looked proudly at their possessions. I know Morts often comes up here.'

'What did you wish?' he asked.

'Oh, you must never tell. If you do it will never come true.'

'Then wild horses will not drag my wish from me.' He looked at her intently and she allowed herself to hope that perhaps she had featured in it. 'I sense you are unhappy, Lettice, which pains me.'

'Really, Ramsey!' Her heart sang that he had noticed, that he cared.

'Tell me, please, it matters to me.'

'I'm not unhappy – at this moment.' She allowed herself to look at him as she said this. 'And who has the right to expect always to be happy?' She pointed towards her little girls. 'They are, but it will not last …'

'I do. I expect to be happy all my life.'

'If you achieve it you will be a fortunate man. For me, I am content with the odd moments …' She looked down at her hands. 'When I'm unhappy I can always unwrap the happy memories and savour them.' She was having such an intimate conversation with him. 'You're very easy to talk to.'

'Then I'm glad.'

'Lettice, who do you think that is?' Morts handed her the binoculars he had brought with him.

Lettice focused on a small figure scurrying across the garden. 'It's one of the maids.'

'Rowan?'

'Perhaps. Whoever it is, she's crying. I wonder—'

Lettice did not finish the sentence because Morts was hurling himself down the hill. 'Oh dear,' she said.

'Where's the fire?' a man called.

'Morts!' Lettice called. 'Stop! Don't be a fool!' But the wind whisked away her words and she knew he could not have heard her.

'Let him go. He needs to feel differently. He's had enough sadness.' Ramsey laid a restraining hand on her arm.

'But a maid? It's wrong.'

'It isn't to him.'

'Has he talked to you about her?'

'No, he's said nothing.' Lettice thought he was not telling her the whole truth, but liked him for protecting Morts. 'He's had a lot to bear for one so young,' he added.

Lettice laughed. 'You talk as if you were an old man.'

'I'm twenty-eight.'

'You don't look a day over twenty-seven,' she teased. Then they stood in silence, watching Morts' breakneck progress down the hill.

'Do these wishes ever come true?' Ramsey wondered.

'It has been known.' She smiled shyly at him.

Rowan could not see where she was going for the tears that filled her eyes. She knew she had done nothing wrong. Had someone lied about her? She had not even been given any money in lieu of notice. 'Mean!' she said. 'If that's what being rich does to a body then they can keep it.'

She was crossing the garden in front of the house. When she had set out, she had taken the back way as usual. Then she had decided to go across the front, which was forbidden to the servants. 'As if we were rubbish! As if we were spoiling the view.'

She could hear her name being called. She turned round to see the housekeeper hanging out of a window, calling at her and waving her round to the back. Rowan stuck out her tongue. She saw several maids in other windows, laughing, and waved to them as if she hadn't a care in the world. 'I don't need you,' she shouted at the house.

Her bag was heavy, not that she had much in it – a small print of an angel, a book of poems she was reading one by one. She was not aware of the incongruous picture she made as she strode: her fine pheasant-feathered hat was jammed on the wrong way round – it had been a parting present from Mary.

She wondered what her mother would say. She'd be cross – but she could hardly be cross with Rowan when she'd done nothing wrong.

'Rowan, wait!'

She ducked her head. The last person she wanted to see when she looked like this was Mr Morts.

'Where are you going? What's happened? Why are you crying?'

'I'm not crying. It's the wind – I got something in my eye.'

'You have your bag. Are you going away?'

She stopped and swung round to face him. 'I've been sacked, given my marching orders.' She started walking again.

'Who dismissed you?'

'The housekeeper, on your mother's order. She made Mrs Herbert do her dirty work for her.' She wondered why she had imagined she liked him when he was just another Cresswell.

'There has to be a reason.'

'I was not given one. Just told I had an hour to get out – as if I was a criminal.' She was about to cry again and sniffed loudly.

'I'm so sorry. Is there anything I can do?'

'Unlikely.'

'I don't know what to say.'

'Your sort never do.'

He grabbed her arm. 'Rowan, don't be like this with me. I'm sorry and I want to help you … You see … I think I'm falling in love with you.'

Rowan stopped dead in her tracks. 'Oh, really, sir, don't be so bloody ridiculous. Now, I'd appreciate it if you'd leave me alone. I've a long walk ahead of me.' With that, she tossed her head and walked away without a backward glance. Her heart was breaking.

6

Christmas Night, 1913

Rowan went straight to her parents' cottage. As soon as she walked through the door and saw her parents, sisters and Oak, she burst into tears again.

'Rowan, what on earth—' Her mother was immediately at her side, scooping her into her arms.

'I've been dismissed,' she sobbed. 'Without a character.'

Flossie stepped back and held her daughter at arm's length. 'What did you do wrong?'

Rowan stopped sobbing. 'Nothing!'

'You must have done something.'

'I didn't, Mum, honest.'

'You been playing about with one of them footmen?'

How could her mother think she was lying? Rowan already felt angry with the Cresswells for their treatment of her, and now she was angry with her mother for not accepting her word. She felt alone in the world.

'I beg your pardon? How dare you?' she said. She was shaking now, with a mixture of fury and nerves.

'Don't you speak to me like that, young woman, or I'll give you a clip round the ear!'

'I thought the one place I would be listened to and trusted would be here, with my family. And what do I get? Accusations and suspicion.'

'You don't get dismissed with no notice for nothing so you'd best come clean. Then I'll see as how I can help you.'

'Mum. I just said—'

'Now, look here.' Alf had stood up from his chair by the fire where he had been enjoying a pipe. 'All these words flying around aren't going to help no one. If the girl says she's done nothing then that's an end to it.'

'But—'

'I'll have none of your buts, Flossie. She's our daughter and she needs us. Why should she lie to us?'

'But—'

'I want no more of it,' Alf said, with a sternness no one had heard before. His entire family were open-mouthed with astonishment. Their mother was the one who was always in control and it was to her they looked for guidance. Their easygoing father agreed with whatever his beloved wife said.

'Whatever you say, Alf.' Flossie gazed at him adoringly.

'First thing we must do is find out what's what – I shall ask Miss Cresswell the next time I see her. But now we'll ask our little girl here what her wants to do.'

'I don't want no one getting into trouble over me.'

'Miss Cresswell's a fair-minded woman. They's every right to employ who they want, but to withhold a character, that's not right.'

'Do you think I'll need one if I go for a job in Barlton?'

'You're not going to Barlton,' her mother said.

'I've got to work, Mum. I can't be a burden on you for ever. The hotel might take me. Or there's the factory.'

'He's taking on staff like there's no tomorrow. Got a big contract to fill. It's hard work but the wages are fairer than most. There's no flies on that von Ehrlich chappie – pay enough and people stay.' Alf was methodically filling his pipe and pressing down the tobacco with his new tamper, a Christmas gift from his wife.

'Where would she stay? I'm not having my daughter lodging with any Tom, Dick or Harry.'

'There's always Dolly and Zeph. Perhaps she could rent a room from them. Help Dolly a bit,' Alf suggested.

'We couldn't rely on them. They're in a right state as it is. He wants to stay here with his mother and she wants to go back to Barlton. It's tearing poor Melanie apart, just when her needs some peace and quiet.'

'You don't mean they argue in front of her?' Rowan was shocked.

'No, but she hears them.'

'What do you think they'll do, Flossie?'

'I reckon as they'll go back. That Dolly Pepper's a forceful woman. Always seems to get her way.'

'Just like another maid as I knows.' Alf pinched Flossie's bottom, which made their children laugh.

'We shall see.' Flossie looked at her downcast daughter. 'I'm sorry, maid. Of course I believe you. I was shocked, that was all, and I never stop worrying about you – can't help myself. And I want to wring those Cresswells' necks.'

Christmas lunch in the servants' hall, consumed long after the family had finished theirs, had been a muted affair. It always was; it was one of the few occasions when the table was graced with the presence of the most senior staff. With the butler at one end of the table and the cook at the other, everyone had to mind their Ps and Qs. The moment they left, the noise rose and threatened to take off the rafters. They were not offended by the evident relief at their departure; they paused in the passageway and listened, smiling at each other. They could remember the stilted festive meals of their own youth.

'I just hope none of them gets too drunk – we've a busy day tomorrow, what with the meet.' Eve settled into her favourite chair in the housekeeper's sitting-room where they had retired for coffee and brandy. Lavender sat on the pouffe and Hilda was on the overstuffed sofa, Gussie Fuller beside her. Gussie glared at Eve, who was in the seat she favoured when she had worked there.

'Still, it was kind of the family to order cold cuts for tonight and serve themselves,' Philomel Herbert pointed out, as she sat down on a hard chair.

'Someone's still got to prepare it and lay it all out,' Eve countered. 'And who will *that* be?'

'This Christmas has been one of the best ever. It was such a pleasure to find you were to join us, Gussie.' Whitaker skilfully manoeuvred the conversation to another tack. 'I took the liberty of chilling champagne.' He drew their attention to the wine-coolers where three bottles nestled in ice.

'How kind of you, Edward,' they chorused, blithely ignoring the fact that the bottles had come from their master's cellar and not from any generosity on the butler's part.

'Well, it's strange to be back in my old haunt. It's changed from my time.' Gussie looked about her old room.

'It was a little too cluttered for my taste,' Philomel explained.

'I would hardly call it cluttered. Tasteful, more like.' Gussie bridled. 'I prefer a more modern look.'

'Sparse, you mean.'

'As always, Eve, a superb luncheon. Our thanks.' Whitaker, knowing Gussie of old, diplomatically changed the subject again. He had poured their drinks and they raised their glasses to the cook.

'It was nothing,' she said, but glowed with pride at their acknowledgement of her skill. 'It's always the same, though, isn't it? Who thanked us today? Miss Hannah and Miss Lettice. We never see sight nor sound of her ladyship, do we? No manners, that one, for all her fine breeding.'

'I thought it was good of Mrs Oliver to pop in,' Hilda added.

'Probably only did it because the others came.' Gussie Fuller sniffed disapprovingly.

'I've never understood why you're so down on her. She's always struck me as a nice woman, and so happy.'

'It's all false, Hilda. She's not a bit happy.'

'Then she's to be admired because she doesn't inflict her misery on others,' Hilda said, quite sharply.

'Tell us, Philomel, what is this we hear about Rowan?' The butler, having topped up everyone's glass, finally settled into the semicircle round the fire. 'I was shocked.'

'I felt for the poor child, having to tell her on Christmas Day. She's a good worker too.'

'So, what had she done?' Gussie leant forward.

'Over-familiarity, her ladyship said.'

'With whom? She seemed polite enough to me,' Hilda said.

'She did not elaborate, though I can guess. The truth is, Edward, I think a certain young man has taken a shine to her and her ladyship thought to nip it in the bud.'

'Very wise.' Gussie nodded.

'Unfair, though. The girl can't help her looks,' Hilda countered.

'What did I say when she came here? She's too pretty for her own good.' Eve looked almost pleased that her warning had proved right.

'She can't help that! What's she supposed to do? Cover her face?' Hilda was incensed.

'I suppose it could be said that in a way her ladyship is protecting her. What if the young master had persisted and pursued her, what would she have done? It's a rare girl who wouldn't let it go to her head. How long before there was real trouble?'

'I take your point, Eve, but to not give her a character when, as far as anyone knows, she's done nothing – that's not fair,' Whitaker said.

'I fear it will lead to unrest. Several of the maids have been talking about leaving. Rowan was popular and some of them have been in tears. I overheard them discussing her dismissal and I didn't like their tone,' said the housekeeper.

'Didn't you put a stop to it, Philomel?'

'I did, Edward. But this sort of thing might just tip them into going.' Philomel sipped her champagne and giggled. 'Oh, the bubbles!'

145

'I suppose they'll be off to the factory in Barlton?' Whitaker asked.

'He pays well.'

'While he's recruiting. You mark my words, as soon as he has the numbers he needs they'll see a dramatic fall in their wages. That's how men like him get rich,' Whitaker said seriously.

'Mr Oliver still won't have him in the house,' Gussie told them.

'Why is he taking on so many new workers, Edward? The *Barlton Gazette* had a large advertisement last week.'

'I'm told he's *acquired* a contract from the government.' Whitaker's emphasis was masterly, implying all manner of shenanigans. 'Blankets. Thousands of them.'

'What do they want so many for?'

'War, Gussie. It'll be uniforms next.'

'Uniforms? I've not seen any soldiers running around in their birthday suits.' She thought this was funny, and so did Eve, but Whitaker was not impressed.

'There will be recruitment of men, you mark my words.' This caused a rustle of apprehension. 'The khaki dye the army uses is German and we'll have to find an alternative. It'll be Kitchener blue until then.' He began to stuff his pipe, a new acquisition, with tobacco. 'We can't be using German dye, can we?'

'I don't fancy the soldiery in blue. It wouldn't seem right.'

'A temporary measure, I'm sure.'

'Get on with you, Edward. There's not going to be a war.' Eve laughed.

'I wish I had your confidence. But when the balance of power shifts there's trouble.'

All the women were impressed by the assurance with which he spoke. But then they laughed at him for scaring them. No one believed him.

7

Boxing Day, 1913

The forecourt of Cresswell Manor was bustling with people, horses and hounds. The riders, enjoying their stirrup cup, were bantering, and the horses pawed the ground, eager to be off, the air was heavy with their earthy smell. The hounds were snuffling about, baying hysterically and whining.

For once, Coral was up early to play the attentive hostess – which she was doing admirably. Mortie, never fond of horses and never known to ride, shouted at those who were mounted rather than get too close to the unreliable brutes. Oliver, on a particularly fine dark bay, was resplendent in sage green – the members of the Cresswell Hunt eschewed pink. Morts was similarly attired. Uncharacteristically, his mother was fussing over him, begging him to take care, which he regarded with a fair degree of cynicism – but it was embarrassing all the same.

Esmeralda, her hair tucked into a lacy snood, top hat at a rakish angle, was looking her best. Many were the admiring glances she received but, like many beautiful women, she seemed unaware of them.

From an upstairs window Lettice watched her husband, surrounded by a group of admiring women. He cut a fine figure on horseback. She looked everywhere but could not spot the man she really wanted to see.

Whitaker moved imperturbably among the horses, keeping an eye on the footmen who were carrying trays of drinks and choice morsels to eat. There had been occasions in the past when footmen had become insensible after a hastily drunk tankard of the alcoholic cup.

The butler was greeted on all sides since everyone knew him. He had a special word for Prinny Rosemount who, at ninety, was the oldest member of the field and had never been known to miss a day's hunting. With her was her cousin, younger by two years, Rupert Westmacott. He was a large, noisy soul, who always rode with his peg leg strapped to his back – the real one had been shot off in India. If he fell off, he had to lie where he was, like an upside-down beetle, until someone came to right him and help him with his leg. He roared good-naturedly at the jokes about wooden legs and beetles, all of which he'd heard a thousand times before.

At last the hounds were gathered together by the whipper-in. The horn echoed off the hill, the horses began to move and hounds sang. Then they were streaming down the drive and out over the meadows.

'Such a pretty sight,' Coral said.

'Good turnout, wouldn't you say? Why, there you are, Hannah. You missed them.'

She wasn't sorry. This Christmas had been her first venture out after the shame of her incarceration and she had purposely held back, not wishing to see old family friends. The house party had been bad enough, with Coral and Mortie's friends' snide remarks. 'I was worried Cariad might get kicked. She's not as agile as she used to be.' She clutched her dog close to her.

'That dog smells. It should be shot,' Coral said.

'Of course it smells – of dog. What would you expect it to smell of? Elephant?' Mortie laughed at his own joke.

'It's a good job your mother doesn't know the animal's here. You know she longs for it to be returned to her. After all, it is her dog.'

'She's not, she's mine. Father asked me to look after her.' Hannah held Cariad even closer. She would not relinquish her to anyone. The little dog was her last link with her beloved father. She changed the subject. 'Well, dear brother and Coral, thank you so much for a delightful Christmas. I'm glad I took notice of you and came.'

'Couldn't have my little sister all on her own, could I? Why, this is the first Christmas you've spent here since …' Mortie's good-natured face creased with the effort of remembering.

'Father's last Christmas but one, eleven years ago.'

'So silly of you.'

'I don't think so, Coral. As you know, I was told I was not welcome.'

'But you know what Penelope's like. You shouldn't have taken any notice of her.'

'Bit difficult not to, hey?' Mortie guffawed.

'I sensed it wasn't only my stepmother who objected.'

'Your friendship with that unspeakable Beatty woman put everyone in an impossible position,' Coral told her.

'Shall we see you before we leave?' Mortie interrupted.

'When are you going to Derbyshire?'

'Tomorrow.'

'What about your mother?' she asked. She herself had no intention of looking after Penelope, who had caused her so much unhappiness as a child. She had only agreed to come here this year after she had been assured that her stepmother was bedridden.

'Lettice is staying.'

'And Hugo has not objected?'

'No, he's coming with us.' Mortie winked at her, and Hannah hoped that that did not mean what she thought it might. Poor Lettice.

They all looked up as, from the rear of the house, they heard an engine. Whitaker and a footman appeared with Hannah's cases as Alf rolled to a halt. Hannah climbed into the car and blew kisses to her brother. She hoped Coral would not think any were intended for her.

She had not lied to them – it had been fun, she thought, as they motored down the drive. She had particularly enjoyed the charades and it had been pleasant to be with her family again. She had avoided her stepmother, of course, and hardened herself against Coral's spite. Best of all, though, was spending time with Lettice and Morts. Such dear children. If only they were happier.

And now things had to change, Hannah told herself. She could not become a recluse. She had to be more active. First, she would search out the women who had gone to prison with her. She had been avoiding them, which was cowardly, and they needed her help.

Her life was blessed and, what was more, she enjoyed good health and copious energy. She must harness that, fill her days so that loneliness was kept at bay. She had to stop *thinking* about doing things and get on with them.

As they approached her house, she leant forward. It was so beautiful and now she had it just as she wanted it. Only one thing was missing: someone to share it with. 'Stop that!' she admonished herself.

'Miss Hannah?'

'Nothing, Alf. Just talking to myself.' She allowed him to help her down.

'If I might have a quick word, Miss?'

'Yes, Alf. What is it?'

She stood patiently while Alf relayed his daughter's dilemma. 'I'm not sure what I can do to help, Alf. You should have come to me sooner. My sister-in-law leaves tomorrow.'

'It's not knowing what she's done wrong. It's just not fair, Miss. And no testimonial!'

'I have to agree with that, Alf. Leave it with me and I'll see what I can do. Come, Cariad.' She swept into the comfort of her home.

She took off her hat and went straight to the telephone. She knew that if she didn't act immediately she would find reasons not to. The operator connected her to the manor and Hannah asked to speak to her sister-in-law.

'I won't beat about the bush, Coral. Alf has just told me about his daughter, Rowan.'

'Little slut!' She heard Coral say.

'Rowan?'

'I'm not taking her back.'

'I don't think they expect that. She needs a reference to get further employment.'

'I'm not prepared to give one.'

'What has she done wrong?'

'Ogling.'

149

'I'm sorry?'

'*Ogling.* I said it plainly enough.'

'Who?'

'Why, Morts, of course. Ogling him at dinner, at church! I'm not having it, Hannah. The boy needs protecting.'

'He's hardly a boy, and it's normally the young woman who needs protection,' Hannah said, with irony.

'Not in this case. She's like a vulture. She had to go. Most unsuitable.' And with that she replaced the receiver, leaving Hannah with a puzzled frown.

'Such manners!' she expostulated. She summoned Alf. 'I'm afraid I could get no sense as to why she was dismissed. I'm sorry, Alf. However, it sounds to me as if she has been treated most unfairly. The vicar is in need of a maid. I shall suggest he speaks to Rowan, which I hope will help.'

Alf's gratitude embarrassed her as she hated lying to anyone. *Ogling!* From what she had observed, Morts had done his fair share of that.

Lettice had checked on her grandmother. As always when she found her asleep she was relieved, then felt ashamed of it. She could not settle to anything and found herself wandering aimlessly about the house. Finally she went to the library in search of a book. The only good thing about Coral being mistress of the house was that there was more light reading than there had been in her grandfather's day.

'Oh, you made me jump!' she exclaimed, as a figure stood up from one of the wing chairs.

'I'm sorry.' Ramsey grinned at her.

'You didn't go hunting?'

'Not my favourite sport. The best thing about it, I've always thought, is the long hot bath at the end of the day.'

'What are you reading?'

'Edgar Allan Poe. I like to frighten myself. And you?'

'I came to find something, but nothing improving.'

'You sound like a woman after my own heart.' As he said this, he looked at her with such intensity that she found herself holding her breath.

'Where do you live, Ramsey?' she asked, to cover her confusion.

'I have a farm near Widecombe.'

'How strange that we've not met before.'

'I only purchased it a couple of months ago.'

'Do you like it?'

'I love it. On the moor when night falls, the world recedes and you feel you are alone in the universe. At times like that I feel I'm back on the pampas.'

'Do you like being alone?' She supposed she was flirting.

'Rather than being with just anyone – yes. But if I were with my soul-mate, I would never wish to be alone.'

'And have you found your soulmate?' Her pulse fluttered with fear as she waited for his answer.

'I begin to think I have.'

Now she was unsure. Perhaps he was speaking of someone else, another woman he had found and loved. She contemplated this prospect bleakly.

'But she belongs to another.' There was no mistaking his expression as he stared intently at her.

'Is your farm large?' She was flustered.

'No. I have little money.'

'I've never thought money of any great importance.'

'Only people who have an abundance of it say that.' She was afraid that he was admonishing her, but he was smiling kindly.

'I have to confess that it's not something I've ever had to think about.' She laughed.

'I fear my lack of it is what makes your mother disapprove of me as a companion for her son.'

'It wouldn't bother Morts.'

'I know. It doesn't.' He picked up a book from a side table and studied the binding. 'Shall you be here long?'

'I hope so. My mother is leaving and I shall stay because of my grand-mother.'

'So you don't want to go home?'

'This is my home.'

'And your husband?'

'He is going away too. I don't think he cares if I'm here or not.'

'Excellent.' Ramsey did a jig and clapped. He looked so adorable and funny that she could not help laughing.

Gussie Fuller had gone to bed early but, unable to sleep, she put on her dressing-gown and made her way down to the kitchen to heat some milk. She knew why she was awake: she had enjoyed being here but it had made her long to be back permanently. And seeing so much of Edward had unsettled her. He was the most attractive man she had ever met – so manly and knowledgeable.

'Why, Edward, up so late?' Her spirits lifted at the sight of the butler at the pine table with a bottle of port and a glass in front of him.

'I couldn't sleep.'

'Neither could I. No doubt you won't want any milk?'

'Not really. Might I entice you to a glass of port?'

'I don't mind if I do.' She sat down beside him, suddenly aware that she was in her nightclothes. She felt quite dizzy.

'Why could you not sleep, Gussie?'

There! At last! He's used her christian name! 'I found it quite hard to come back here and be with you … all.' She sighed. 'It's hard to see Philomel in my place.'

'She's not a patch on you, Gussie.'

'Why, Edward, how kind.'

'It's the truth. So, you're not happy at Mr Oliver's establishment?'

'It's not that, Edward. It's just not what I am used to. I've only ever worked for people of standing and, not to put too fine a point on it, Mrs Oliver is not what you would call top-drawer.'

'No, but she seems pleasant enough. And Mr Oliver chose her.'

'Oh, she is, but … It's difficult to put into words.'

'You have your standards.'

'Exactly. You always were the one to come up with the right words. I suppose, too, that I get lonely. It's a much smaller staff and I can't get along with Bridget, Mrs Oliver's maid.' She leant forward. 'She's Irish.'

'I've never had anything against the Irish.'

'Nor me,' she said hurriedly, 'but her ways aren't mine.' She sipped her port, wishing she hadn't mentioned the maid. 'And you, Edward, are you still happy?'

Slowly he poured himself another glass. 'No, Gussie, I'm not.'

She was taken aback. It had not been the answer she was expecting. 'Might I enquire why, Edward, dear?' How forward!

'I don't want to give all this up. It's my life.' He spoke quite loudly.

Gussie was astonished to see tears in his eyes. 'Of course it is. And a better butler doesn't exist. But has anyone said you've got to leave? I should think Sir Mortie would be quite at sea without your guiding hand.'

'Oh, no. They have offered me inducements to stay. It's Hilda. She's adamant.'

'About what?' she asked, although she knew.

'Moving to Whitby to run a guesthouse.'

Gussie laughed. 'I've never heard anything so silly in all my life. *You?*

In a guesthouse? You're far too skilled for that.'

'Thank you, Gussie.' He topped up their glasses.

'And what sort of person would frequent such a place? You might all be murdered in your beds!'

'It will be a respectable establishment.'

'I'm sure it is,' she said soothingly, afraid she might have gone too far. 'Then don't go. It's quite simple.'

'But it isn't.' He had to blow his nose rather loudly. 'An elderly aunt lives in Hilda's house there and Hilda worries about her. She says she's going with or without me.'

Gussie was transfixed. Half a dozen responses skidded across her mind. She said, 'Not a very dutiful wife, is she?' He did not respond. 'I should tell her to go, if I were you, and you can stay here where you belong.' She was shocked by her boldness but what had she to lose? This might be her last chance with Edward. 'Stay with those who appreciate you,' she added, for good measure.

'I'll fetch us another bottle,' he said, but when he stood up he swayed alarmingly. Gussie settled back in her chair with a satisfied smile.

The bar was full, even though it was nearly midnight. Many of the local farmers had been on the hunt and all had come in to slake their thirst, and stayed. The noise was deafening. It was the first time Melanie had ventured into the bar since her illness. The welcome she received lifted her spirits.

'Mum, you shouldn't be here. We can manage.'

'I'll wash some glasses.'

'I don't think you should.'

'Zeph, I feel better to be in here. I'll fret otherwise.' She had been riddled with guilt ever since she had heard the influx of drinkers arrive.

She worked contentedly, sitting on a stool, washing the glasses, listening to the odd snippets of conversation, laughing at the least rude jokes.

Everyone looked up as the door burst open. In a flurry and a swirl of cold air, a woman appeared, her black and scarlet cloak whirling about her. The men stood back, rather like the parting of the Red Sea, and she strode through them.

'Xenia?' Melanie had to hold on to the bar to stop herself falling off the stool.

'I thought if I waited until today you'd either be dead or better,' she said. The patrons' eyebrows shot into their hairlines. 'Champagne, Zeph. If you have any in this God-forsaken hole.'

Chapter Five

January to April 1914

1

Melanie, on her hands and knees with only her rear visible, was delving into the back of a cupboard on the landing. On one side of her lay a pile of neatly folded linen, on the other a stack of discarded sheets.

'What on earth are you doing? Here, let me.'

She inched out of the cupboard and sat back on her haunches. 'I'm sorting this. It's long overdue. Look, we can tear these up and use them as dusters. Those have got a few more years in them.' She patted the neater pile. 'I've found things in there that I'd forgotten I had.'

'You shouldn't be doing that. You're not up to it.'

'Flossie, it does me good to keep busy.'

'What did Dr Bunting say? What about your heart?'

'There's nothing wrong with it. The man exaggerates. And he said I could do things if I wanted. Stop fussing, Flossie. You're as bad as Zeph.'

'You don't seem to realise the fright you gave us. I thought you were dying.' At the memory of Melanie's illness tears welled in her eyes.

Melanie hauled herself upright. 'There's a lot more life in me yet, I promise.' She put her arms about her friend and hugged her. 'You're too good to me.'

'And why not? Who's saved my bacon more times than I can remember?'

'I need to keep occupied, Flossie. It takes my mind off things.'

'Why don't you just sit in an easy chair and read a book?'

'Because I'm tired of reading. I can't relax.'

'Then come and have a cuppa with me in the kitchen. I can find you something to do sitting down. It'll make me a lot happier.' She led the way down the stairs, chattering, followed by a regretful Melanie, who had been enjoying herself.

'Now, what's the problem this time? Xenia?' Flossie put a cup of tea in front of her.

'I don't understand my own daughter, Flossie, and it makes me so sad.

154

Just look at her – the expensive clothes, the jewellery, even the perfume she wears. You don't have to be clever to see that she's up to no good.'

'She told me she was on the stage.'

'That's what she tells everyone.'

'Maybe she is.'

'Then why, when I ask her what plays she'd been in, was she so vague?'

'Perhaps she's forgotten.'

'I wish I could believe it.'

'Still, you can't just presume she's lying.'

'Can't I?' Melanie gave a sad smile. 'Flossie, I fear she has a rich protector.'

'That's my dream!' Flossie grinned. 'Sorry, it's not funny, is it?'

'You are, but the situation isn't. I worry what the future holds for her when her looks have gone, when she's old.'

'I'd have thought she was bright enough to take care of herself.' Flossie had no time for Xenia, as Melanie knew, and thought her a stuck-up minx. 'What does Zeph say?'

'They barely speak.'

'I can't imagine any of mine doing that.'

'But they were never close, even as children. And with Zeph away at boarding-school so early, they drifted even further apart.'

'They've had such chances in life, haven't they?'

'And look at them! Zeph insisted on helping me! I always hoped he would enter a profession and become a gentleman.'

'He doesn't need a profession to be that. He's one of nature's gents, he is.'

'What a lovely thing to say.' Melanie smiled at her dearest friend, the only person she ever confided in. 'Xenia is so bitter towards me, yet Zeph has forgiven me.' She paused. 'At least, I think he has. It seems that my punishment will never end.'

'You shouldn't talk like that. Heavens, how old were you when that Sir Mortie had his way with you? Fifteen, sixteen?'

'I thought he loved me. I was so innocent.'

'It must be hard on Zeph to look at all they've got and know that it should all have been his one day, instead of that Morts'. After all, he's really Sir M's first-born, isn't he?'

'Oh, I don't think Zeph gives it a thought.'

'Doesn't he?'

'He never mentions it.'

'That doesn't mean he don't think about it. 'Twould be human nature, after all, to wonder about what might have been.'

'He's too intelligent for that.'

'Sir Mortie might have married you.'

Melanie laughed at the idea. 'That's a housemaid's dream and it doesn't happen in real life. No, I was the fool and I had to pay for it. But they've been good to us. Look at this place. Old Sir Mortimer didn't have to leave it to me, did he?'

'The gossip it caused!'

'I've never understood why people think they have the right to know one's business. When I inherited this place the viciousness ruined any chance of a reconciliation with my mother.'

'Did you want one?'

'Not particularly.' This amused them enormously. 'We'd never got on well, but not seeing Father for so long hurt me.'

'How's Rowan?' she asked, wanting to change the subject.

'I put my foot down. She went to that there factory and took a job, but I'd heard things about the girls who work there – smoking and fast with the boys – so, with Miss Cresswell's help, I found her a job with the vicar instead. He was a bit difficult about it – her having no references from the big house. He hinted that the one Miss Cresswell gave her might even be a forgery. I nearly hit him, but instead I gave him a little chat about Christian forgiveness and eventually he saw it my way.'

'Oh, Flossie!' Melanie was laughing. 'She could have come here to work.'

'I didn't want that.'

'Why not?'

'Nothing.' Flossie stood up abruptly and moved away from the table. Melanie wondered why. 'Anyway, I've got to get on,' Flossie continued. 'I thought I'd put a stew on today – it's cold enough to freeze the balls off a brass monkey. Now, if you take my advice, you'll go and have a lay down. No doubt you'll be helping out tonight again.'

To get away from Flossie's well-meant nagging, Melanie did as she had been told. She tried to read but found she couldn't. Her own life made any novel seem ridiculous. Here she was, in her mid-forties, with no great worries about money and her future, a woman who had wanted love all her life and never found it. She was a mother of three who saw only one of her children regularly and feared that he was the only one who respected her. She supposed that to the world she was a success but she felt an abject failure. She should never have married her first husband and only did so because her mother had made her, to give the twins a name. She had married Richard out of loneliness, which was almost as bad.

If only Xenia had not come – she had only stirred up problems. She had heard Zeph and her daughter arguing several times about money, and things had been said that should not have been. Worse, Xenia had teamed up with Timmy against poor Zeph. She wondered whether, if she hadn't the money and this property, they would be arguing like this. Why did money change people?

She had begged Xenia to stay at the Cresswell Arms in the hope that they could all find some resolution, but she had gone to Courtney Lacey to stay with the von Ehrlich man, just as she had when she had run away in 1902. He was dangerous but he and Xenia were well matched. Now, having caused all this trouble, Xenia had returned to London. Melanie only knew this because one of the coachmen had told her. It had hurt that her daughter had not said goodbye.

She understood Xenia's bitterness – the hardest thing Melanie had ever done was to tell the girl that the young man she had set her cap at, Morts Cresswell, was her half-brother. While Melanie could understand that she would hate her for, as she saw it, destroying her happiness, she could not understand why she should turn her spite on her brother too – after all, he was in a similar position.

And now Henry was threatening to come home from Canada. She did not want her brother here. She did not want to be reminded of the dreadful night when he had killed her first husband in the bar even though it had been in her defence. For over ten years she had lived in fear that either Robert or Fred Robertson, who had witnessed it, would get drunk one night and spill the beans. She was tired of putting up with their familiarity, the way they seemed to think it was their right to drink here for as long as they wanted because they had done her brother a favour in lying to the constable.

It had cost her dear too: she had lost count of the money she had handed over to them. Not that they ever threatened her, but if they were in debt or trouble, hers was the first purse they turned to.

When she was poor she had dreamt of having money and had not known of the problems it could bring. But now she did. It spawned trouble. And she would be haunted by her deeds for the rest of her life.

Thinking was a dangerous occupation, she told herself, and idleness was not in her nature. She slid across her bed and stood up. If she was very quiet Flossie need never know she was back in the linen cupboard.

Zeph had to wait impatiently until February before Sir Mortie re-turned to his estate and he could arrange to see him. It had not been an easy few weeks. Dolly was unhappy but, in her stubborn way, would not admit that travelling each day to her office and working as hard as she did was too much for her. She was permanently tired, which made her irritable. In his equally stubborn way, Zeph would not sympathise since he considered it her own fault. The tension between them affected everyone who lived and worked at the Cresswell Arms.

With Dolly catching the early-morning train to Barlton, him serving in the bar until long past midnight and Dolly going to bed early, days passed without them speaking to each other. There were many nights when he lay beside her and would have liked to touch her, but always decided against it. In consequence he was becoming bad-tempered too.

Without May's help, Dolly's regime could never have been possible, yet he felt that Dolly did not appreciate the efforts the woman made. She was always willing. The children were immaculately dressed. When they returned from school there was always a meal waiting for them, which May made so that Flossie wasn't put out. She washed and ironed all the family's laundry, kept their rooms spick and span, and helped Zeph in the bar. She was always good-natured and nothing was too much trouble for her. He found himself searching out her company more and more. They enjoyed the same books, they were both interested in politics and he could talk to her in a way he could not to Dolly.

At last Sir Mortie returned. Zeph spruced himself up, brushed his hair and put pomade on it to keep it flat. He decided to wear his best suit and his almost new boots. On the walk to the manor he rehearsed in his mind what he would say to the man he knew was his father, although no one acknowledged the relationship.

Whitaker showed him into the library where Mortie was sitting at a long table surrounded by papers. He did not look up so Zeph was forced to stand awkwardly and wait for his attention. He watched the man, short, fat, red-faced. Apart from their dark colouring, Zeph could see no similarity between them, for he was tall and slim. It was difficult now to see what had attracted his mother to the man.

He looked round the room. Adam bookcases lined three walls and large casement windows the fourth. There was the warm, comforting smell of old leather bindings, and a fire crackled in the stone fireplace, which was embossed with the Cresswell arms – which might have been his.

'So, what can I do for you, Zeph?' Sir Mortie said eventually. 'You'll have to be quick. I'm only here for the day.' As he spoke he was removing papers from an attaché case, flicking through them, then putting them back again in a disordered way.

Zeph was annoyed by his distraction. 'I would like to buy a cottage from you, sir. Briar Cottage is empty and would suit me.'

'Would it? Not backward in coming forward, are you?' Mortie laughed.

'I've discovered that you get nowhere if you don't ask for what you want.'

'Could be true. Buy, you say. How are you intending to pay?'

Zeph convinced himself that the other man was sneering at him. 'I've eight pounds saved, sir. I trust you would loan me the rest and I would pay you back over a five-year term with interest at one and a half per cent.'

'One and a half?' Mortie slapped his thigh and laughed, so loudly that Zeph could see his nostrils. 'I'm not going to get rich on that, am I? Government securities will pay me more than that.' He spoke as one who understood the world of finance and was in control of his own affairs, but Zeph knew that that was not so.

'I've studied my figures and it's all I can afford.'

'I thought you worked for our solicitor, Battle, in Barlton. Why would you want a cottage here when you work there?'

'I am no longer in his employ. My mother has been unwell and I felt it my duty to come home and help her.'

'Duty, eh?' Mortie looked perplexed. Duty had never over-exercised his mind.

'Yes, sir.'

'Why can't you live with her? Place is big enough.'

'Because I want a home of my own.'

'Just because you want something doesn't mean you can have it.' Mortie smiled somewhat smugly.

Zeph balled his hands with frustration and wished he'd gone to Oliver instead.

'Why should I help you?'

'I would have thought that was evident, sir.'

'Really! How – what?' he blustered.

'Because you are my father,' Zeph said quietly.

'So your mother said.'

His hands were fists now. 'I've no reason to doubt her word. Have you, sir?' He longed to smash in Mortie's face.

'Quite so.' Mortie was shamefaced. 'I shouldn't have said that.'

'No, sir.'

'We were both so young …'

'I have never asked for anything, sir, in all the years I have known.'

'Has my family not done enough for your mother?'

'For my mother, yes. I am asking this for myself.'

'How am I to know you won't keep asking me for money?'

'You don't.'

'You could give your word.'

'I could. But what guarantee have you that I wouldn't break it?'

'A gentleman never breaks his word.'

'And that's the crux of it, sir. Due to the circumstances of my birth I am not and never will be regarded as a gentleman.'

'And if I don't agree?' Mortie was fiddling with his papers again.

'Any consequences would be yours, sir.'

'Do I detect a hint of blackmail here?'

'That may be so.' Zeph felt uneasy. 'I believe there are members of your family who are not aware of mine and my sister's relationship to you.'

'If I remember, your sister was at one time prancing around calling herself Cresswell?'

He was not going to get his wish. It was all going wrong, Zeph thought. 'She did so as a joke, and for a few days only. She then left the district.' He could have killed Xenia when he had heard what she had done, no doubt put up to it by that von Ehrlich man. 'It was a one day wonder … sir.' He deliberately inserted a pause. Mortie looked at him long and hard.

'Bright, aren't you?'

'I am told so.'

'I don't want my children to know – ever. You are obviously not a gentleman but if you give me your word, I will regard you as one.'

'I would never knowingly hurt either of your children, sir. I have nothing but admiration for both of them.' Which was true. He felt his response was evasive enough – how was he to know what the future might hold for them all?♣

'I'll see what can be done.' Mortie looked flustered as does one who knows he is being outwitted. 'It's not that easy. I shall have to consult with my brother. A courtesy, you understand.'

'Yes, sir.' As he took his leave he congratulated himself on managing to keep his temper. He was content with the way the interview had gone, even if there had been moments when he thought he wasn't going to get his way. He was not surprised to be told that Sir Mortie would consult his brother. It had nothing to do with courtesy, as he claimed: he had to. When Zeph had been working for Mr Battle, he had written up the terms of old Sir Mortimer's will. He knew that the old man, recognising that his son was incompetent, had set up a trust to protect the land for his grandson. He knew, too, that the trustees were Oliver and Hannah Cresswell. He was aware that there was an entail on the house and pleasure grounds, and had painstakingly made a copy of the will, which now rested in a secret place. If Mr Battle had been aware of Zeph's parentage, he probably wouldn't have let him anywhere near the Cresswell business.

Today, the logical person to have seen was Oliver but Zeph wanted to deal with his father.

As he left, making a point of using the front door, which was banned to the likes of him, he met Oliver, who paused, as if surprised to find him there, then merely exchanged a greeting.

He was a few yards down the drive when Hannah Cresswell's Rolls appeared. She pulled up and leant out of the window. 'We don't often see you here, Zeph. How's your mother?'

'Very well, thank you, Miss Cresswell. Doing too much, of course.'

'And Dolly? I hear she has an employment agency providing servants.'

'She does, in Barlton.'

'You must be proud of her success.'

'Yes,' he said bleakly.

'You were never very good at hiding your feelings, Zeph, were you? Don't you approve?'

'I wish she spent more time at home with her family.'

'But if she is a woman blessed with ambition she would be most unhappy if she was unable to pursue it.' Zeph decided not to argue: knowing the truth of this did not help him. 'Did you come to see anyone specifically?'

'Sir Mortie.'

'Oh, I see.'

'I came to ask if I might buy a cottage.'

'Really? Did he agree?'

'He's to discuss it with you.'

161

'Are you not happy at the Cresswell Arms? Such a fine place your mother has made of it.'

'Dolly would be happier with a home of her own.'

'I expect she would.' With a grinding of gears that made Zeph wince, she set off again.

Mortie was waiting in the library. He greeted his brother in an off-hand manner. Whitaker poured them both whisky and soda. On hearing Hannah's car, he instructed the butler to pour her some barley water.

'She's drinking wine again, and sherry,' Oliver informed his brother.

'Glad to hear it. Non-drinkers always make me nervous, as if they're standing in judgement. Pour her some sherry, Whitaker.'

'Didn't you notice at Christmas?' Oliver asked.

'Of course I did. I forgot.'

'Everything all right?'

'Why do you ask?'

'You seem a bit fidgety.'

'Just want to get back to town and have this infernal meeting over with. I hate meetings,' he said petulantly.

'Sometimes they're necessary.'

There was a flurry of greetings. Hannah removed her gloves and thanked the butler as she accepted the sherry.

Once Whitaker had withdrawn and they were alone, Oliver laid out several ledgers, then he opened a notepad, which he placed in front of him. 'I'm grateful you could both come to this meeting, and I realise it was at great inconvenience to you, Mortie. However, there are several serious issues to discuss.'

'Oh, Lawks,' said Mortie.

'Not to beat about the bush, the income from the estate is falling far short of the outgoings.'

'Well, that's your job to sort out, not mine. You're the trustee.'

'I am, but I'm not spending it. *You* are.'

'Before we move on to whatever gloom you have to impart, there's a couple of things I want to mention.' Mortie looked quite belligerent.

'Can't you do that when I've finished?'

'No.'

'Very well.' Oliver sat back with a resigned expression. Hannah fiddled with the cuff of her blouse. She had a sense of foreboding.

'I've just had young Zeph here. He wants to buy Briar Cottage. I said

I'd have to discuss it with you two. You can tell him it's not possible – I don't want to.'

'Why?'

'Don't you think we've done enough for that family? He's had opportunities put his way – he had a good position with Battle – and if he chooses to throw it all up and work in a public house that's not my affair.'

'I don't think Zeph can ever be paid his due. And he's a good man,' Oliver said.

'What is this about?' Hannah asked.

'It's a long story.'

'Since I am a trustee, I have a right to know, if it is relevant to the estate, Oliver. Please don't treat me in such an offhand manner.'

'I'm sorry, Hannah, but it's Mortie's business, not mine.'

Hannah looked questioningly at Mortie, who appeared sulky and trapped. 'Is it that you're Zeph's father?' she asked.

'How did you know that?' Mortie spluttered, and choked on his whisky. Oliver had to bang him on the back.

'It's a rumour that has swirled around for years. I know everyone thinks that Papa was Zeph's father, but I worked out long ago that it was you. If that's so, then you should help him. I agree with Oliver that nothing can compensate him entirely, and it must have taken courage to approach you.' Mortie managed to look ashamed and petulant at the same time.

'What's he offering?' Oliver asked.

'Eight pounds as a deposit and the rest over five years at one and a half per cent. Bloody cheek.'

'We should accept it.'

'We should *what*?' Mortie almost knocked over his drink.

'Briar Cottage is in need of repair. It will cost a lot to put it right,' said Oliver.

'Is Zeph aware of that?' Hannah asked.

'He's no fool.'

'I still think we should point it out to him,' she said.

'As you wish.' Oliver was making pencilled notes on his pad.

'Does that include land with it? We *must* keep the land,' Mortie expostulated.

'I disagree, Mortie. I suggest we include three acres with the property. Zeph will need some land to keep a few animals and grow vegetables,' said Oliver.

163

'But Father always said—'

'Father is no longer here but if he was I'm sure he would agree with me.' Oliver frowned at his brother but the fight had gone out of Mortie. 'Is that all? Might I now proceed?'

'No. There's another problem. Sorry, Oliver, but this is a big one. I'm in a bit of a stew. You see, well … I'm in debt.'

Oliver laughed. 'When aren't you? How much did you borrow?' He picked up his pencil again.

'Two thousand pounds.'

'How much?' Oliver dropped his pencil with a clatter. It rolled across the table.

'Oh, Mortie. How could you be so silly?' Hannah exclaimed.

'I knew you'd both be cross with me. It's not my fault.'

'Then whose fault is it?'

'I don't have enough income for my needs. It's all right for you, Oliver, you're rich. And Father left Hannah enough to look after herself. I've obligations and I had to borrow.'

'Might I ask the terms?'

'Six per cent.'

'*Mortie!*'

'No one respectable charges that. It's usury. Who has loaned it to you?' Oliver growled.

'I went to a respectable firm in the City, Eldridge and Buchan. Charming coves. But I've not always paid on time, you know how it is, so I now owe them …' He scrabbled among his papers. 'Two thousand five hundred pounds, five shillings and sevenpence. I don't understand that or what the sevenpence is for.'

'Because you haven't paid on time the interest has compounded. You're a fool, Mortie.'

'As you frequently tell me.' Mortie assumed an expression of boredom.

'If we don't act, the debt will increase relentlessly.'

'I knew you'd understand, Oliver.'

'I don't understand at all, Mortie. How you could have been so stupid? Why didn't you come to me?'

'Because you'd have said no. You always do.'

'Brothers, there's no point in us arguing. What's done is done. We should concentrate on solving the problem.'

'We shall have to sell some land. The trouble with that is that word will get round and, no doubt, add to the complications,' Oliver answered.

'What do you mean "complications"?' Hannah asked.

'We are frequently late in paying our bills. If it was rumoured that we were in difficulty our lines of credit might close.'

'Rubbish! I haven't paid my tailor for a good five years,' Mortie stated.

'If he got wind of this I can assure you the account would appear overnight. You had better make a list of all that you owe, Mortie, and we'll see what we can do to settle as much as we can.'

'Less of the *we* if you don't mind, Oliver You are my younger brother. The money is *mine*. You just look after it for me.'

'Mortie!' Hannah cried. 'You should not speak to Oliver in such a manner.'

'If you feel like that I can always retire from the trusteeship,' Oliver added. 'As it is it takes up too much of my time. I would—'

'Oliver, *please*. You know Mortie says things without thinking. He doesn't mean it.'

'Do you mean it or not, Mortie?'

For a moment it looked as if he was about to say he did. 'Of course not. Sorry, Oliver.'

'Really, you two, it's as if we were back in the nursery.'

'I might be able to help with the gossip. This chap, Cooper, Scottish, I think, is quite interested in buying some land to cover the debt. I said … Well, I said I'd arrange it. In fact,' Mortie yawned, 'he's been down and had a dekko. I told him to have a look at the old Chessman land.' He stood up, poured himself some more whisky and began to prowl round the room, as if he was distancing himself from them.

'How sad,' said Hannah. 'We used to picnic there, with the brook running through.'

'Why on earth would a Scotsman be interested in buying land in Devon? It seems strange to me.' Oliver looked puzzled.

'I never asked him.'

'He's nothing to do with von Ehrlich, is he? The Chessman land marches close to his.'

'As if I would deal with him! I know what you think of your father-in-law, Oliver, and I'd never compromise your principles.'

'I'm glad to hear it.'

'Poor Esmeralda. Wouldn't it be simpler to make peace with him?' Hannah asked.

Oliver gave his sister such a dismissive look that she said no more. 'At least this makes the matters I wished to discuss with you even more pertinent. Kindly sit down and listen.'

Mortie took his seat. 'Will it take long?'

'As long as is required. As I said, the income is falling far too short of the outgoings. We have to – or rather, Mortie since you so dislike me saying *we*, you are going to have to pull in your horns. For a start, the number of staff employed here when you are so rarely in residence is ridiculous. There's not much we can do about the outside staff, who are needed for maintenance, but the indoor staff must be halved. I'd prefer a token number to remain here, and when you come you'll bring the rest with you.'

'We can't do that. What about Mother?'

'Perhaps I could help out,' Hannah suggested.

'No, Hannah. Father wanted you to have that allowance.'

'Why don't you mind your own business, Oliver? If Hannah wants to help me that's up to her, not you. She's got money from her mother as well as Father. Hardly seems fair,' Mortie complained.

'If Hannah helped you out, with the amount you need, her financial position would be at risk. No. Mother, bedridden as she is, does not need a full complement of footmen, ten maids and two cooks.'

'But Hilda is a pastry cook, not like Mrs Gilroy,' Hannah interrupted.

'I still say it's an extravagance we can ill afford. If Mortie and Coral curtailed their spending it would help, but I can't see Coral economising on her wardrobe.'

At this Mortie blanched.

'To be fair to you, Mortie, Father did not leave the estate in good heart. He made that disastrous investment with my father-in-law just before his death, which left us with no alternative but to sell some land – unfortunately to Stanislas. I want him to have no more.'

'I agree. A beastly man.'

'Thanks, Hannah. But the upshot is that, whatever we do, the glory days of this estate are gone. Times have changed and we must change too or we shall sink.'

'You will find that there isn't a full complement of staff here, anyway, Oliver. It gets harder and harder to replace people when they leave. That wretched factory in Barlton – another of your father-in-law's ventures – is too attractive to them. I wish von Ehrlich had never come here. But if he hadn't you would not be married to dear Esmeralda, would you?' To Hannah's dismay, her remark had displeased him. She hurried on: 'And, Oliver, if you release staff, will that not make tongues wag?'

'Probably, but it's a rare house now that is fully staffed. The sale of land would be much more significant.'

'I never thought I'd say it but I'm almost glad Papa isn't here to see all of this.'

3

Whitaker tripped over the linoleum as he skimmed towards the kitchen. A footman gaped: normally the butler's sedate walk never varied.

'Eve! Hilda! You'll never guess what I've just heard,' he said, as he skidded to a halt.

'Judging by your speed, it must be serious,' Eve commented.

'It's that all right! We're to be dismissed!'

Eve and Hilda both let out a high-pitched shriek, and Eve sat down abruptly. 'Well I never.' She fanned herself with the oven cloth. 'I've come over all funny.'

'Dismissed? What on earth for? We've done nothing wrong.' Hilda pulled out a chair for her husband to sit down. 'You're ashen, Edward.'

'I'm shocked, Hilda. It's a sorry state of affairs. I feel as if I've been scuttled amidships.'

'Let's get this straight.' Hilda joined them at the table.

'I'll make us a cuppa.' Eve stood up.

'But what about luncheon, Eve?'

'If they're going to give me the push they can damned well wait – if you'll pardon my French.' As always, a large kettle was boiling on the hob. 'You lot, out!' she shouted at the kitchen and scullerymaid, who had popped in to see what the fuss was about. They scurried off but stationed themselves outside the door, the better to hear. The tea made, Eve took the precaution of fetching a bottle of whisky from the dresser to fortify it.

When she had sat down and poured them each a cup, Whitaker elaborated. 'Money – or, rather, in their case, lack of it – is the problem. It sounds to me as if they're heading for Queer Street. They're going to sell off some land and cut down the staff.'

'Sell *land*? Gawd! Sir Mortimer must be spinning in his grave.' Eve was wielding the whisky liberally.

'Capital and land should never be touched, my old father used to say.'

'Your father had land, Edward? My, my.'

'Of course, Eve, he owned no land himself, but the family he served had far more than the Cresswells. They were a *ducal* family.' He straightened, underlining his pride at the remote association. 'My father learnt the principle from them. It's a maxim we can all live by. If your incomings don't cover your outgoings, something is seriously wrong.'

'Never a borrower nor a lender be.'

'Exactly, Hilda. Mind you,' he took a sip of his heavily laced tea, 'I've been expecting something like this – you've only got to look at the state of the land, the woods. And you can always tell how things are by the state of the retainers' cottages.'

'Everyone's complaining about the roofs and the water supply. I said to Gussie only the other day that there'd be an outbreak of illness if something wasn't done. Now, Mr Oliver's building lovely cottages for his workers,' said Eve.

'And look at the fine house Miss Cresswell built for her gardening assistant down by the kitchen gardens.'

'Once you know the signs it all adds up. I've thought for some time that keeping this house fully staffed when they're hardly ever here is an extravagance.' Whitaker shook his head despondently.

'Mind you, we're all needed. I've never noticed idle hands when the family's away. In a place this size there's always something to do. I'm sure I'll be safe – I'm always busy.'

'Because you have the staff to feed. No staff ...' Whitaker shrugged his shoulders eloquently.

'But there's her ladyship. The amount she eats, I'm sure I'm safe for as long as she's alive.'

This made everyone laugh.

'But what's brought this on?' Hilda asked.

'Profligacy, Hilda. And we all suffer.'

'Well, it won't matter much to us, Edward,' Hilda averred.

The look that Eve gave her would have shrivelled anyone else, but Hilda was used to her and ignored it.

'No doubt you'll be regretting listening at doors, Edward,' Eve said waspishly.

'I most certainly did no such thing. I overheard their raised voices.'

Eve raised one eyebrow cynically. Then she squealed, 'Oh!' and clapped a hand over her mouth. 'What about the cottage I was expecting? I was promised one for my retirement. Will they take that away from me?'

'Seems they're selling cottages. Young Zeph's buying one.'

'Him? Why, the cheek of it!'

'And what's more we've all been mistaken about his parentage. It wasn't old Sir Mortimer sired him but Sir Mortie.' Whitaker was delighted to be first with this piece of news.

'Well I never.'

A bell rang outside in the passage. 'That's them wanting their luncheon, no doubt.' Whitaker got to his feet and brushed down his morning coat, which had acquired a sprinkling of flour.

Eve stood and snatched up the salt box and scattered a large handful over the vegetables. 'I'll show them! Where's that dratted Willow got to? Willow!' she screeched. But Willow was long gone to share the news with the lads in the stables.

Half-way through luncheon Hannah wished she had not stayed. The atmosphere was heavy with Mortie's resentment and, when the situation had been explained to Coral, she had fainted – or pretended to. Hannah had had to fetch the sal volatile. Mortie, of course, was in a mighty sulk. She felt sorry for him: he was not the most intelligent of people and was childlike in his view of the world, so it was inevitable that he would behave as if his favourite toy had been taken from him. 'I don't know how I shall bring myself to tell Morts. He will be horrified,' he said mournfully.

'I've discussed the problems with him when he was last here,' Oliver said.

'You did what? When? He hasn't been here.' Coral's voice was shrill.

'He was here about three weeks ago,' Hannah told her.

'What for?'

'I didn't ask him.'

'If that slut's been after him again I shall have her banned from the estate. How dare she? And how dare you speak to our son before Mortie?'

'I'm sorry, Coral. I tried to contact Mortie but he did not answer any of my numerous letters. He was always out when I telephoned. I have lost count of the number of times I have asked him for this meeting. I felt it my duty to speak to Morts, since he is the remainderman of this trust.'

'And I suppose Hannah knew too.'

'Not the details, Coral,' Hannah reassured her, 'just that the situation was serious.'

'Well, I hope you can keep it to yourself this time,' Coral said, with a significant glare.

'Of course.' Hannah was puzzled, and a little troubled too.

'This food is disgusting! What on earth has happened? Whitaker, tell Mrs Gilroy that this is inedible.' Coral threw her napkin on to the table.

'Yes, my lady.' Witaker bowed his way out.

'She's probably learnt what's afoot and this is her revenge.' Oliver could not help smiling.

'And how would she have managed that?'

'No doubt Whitaker listened at the door.'

'Whitaker would do no such thing.'

'All butlers listen at doors.'

'I can't stand any more of this nonsense! I need to speak to you, Hannah, on another matter.' Coral swept from the room without a backward glance, certain that Hannah would follow her. Hannah excused herself and left her brothers alone.

Coral went up the stairs and to her sitting-room. 'You are a serpent in the breast of this family,' she began. Then she crept up to the door and swung it open dramatically to check that no one was eavesdropping. She closed it again and twirled round to face Hannah, eyes blazing with fury. 'How could you when we have been so good to you? After all we have done for you!'

Hannah couldn't think of one thing that Coral had done for her but forbore to say so. 'I don't understand,' she said instead.

'Are you aware that Felix has run away from Eton? He is refusing to return.'

'I had no idea.'

'For the same reason that he would not come here at Christmas.'

'I was sorry he didn't come. I missed him.'

'Don't lie to me. You hate us. You're a barren, miserable spinster who relies on other women for comfort. You are despicable.'

Hannah, who had not been invited to sit, promptly did so. Her legs would no longer support her. 'Perhaps you would explain. I would never do anything to harm Felix.' She was perplexed by all of this venom.

'You have ruined his life – and he's barely fifteen. You are evil.'

Coral loomed over her, and for a minute Hannah thought she was about to hit her. She got to her feet again – she felt too vulnerable sitting down. 'If you would explain yourself, Coral – and calm down or you will injure yourself.'

In answer Coral thrust a letter at her.

WHAT'S IT LIKE TO HAVE AN ABORTIONIST AND

A THIEF FOR A MOTHER, FELIX?
A WELL-WISHER

'How awful.' Despite the risk Hannah sat down again.
'Isn't it?' Coral thrust another sheet of paper at her.

INTERESTING, ISN'T IT? FELIX
CRESSWELL'S MOTHER IS AN
ABORTIONIST AND A THIEF

'That one was sent to several of his friends and to a beak. The boy is beside himself with shame. Worse, he refuses to speak to me. He is threatening to show his father unless …' At this she burst into tears and had to sit down too.

'The poor boy. But why are you blaming me?'

'Only two people knew of my problems. You and I. Am I likely to do anything like this to my son?'

'Really, Coral, I can't imagine why you would think I had anything to do with such despicable behaviour.'

'No, but you have confided my secret to someone. And who springs to mind? Agnes Beatty! This is her revenge on you, you nincompoop. I wish you were dead!' Coral screamed, with hatred in her eyes. Then she began to sob, a loud, gulping, ugly noise.

Hannah was stunned. She had no defence. She had confided in Agnes in the days when she had loved and trusted her. That she could do this to an innocent boy! 'I'm sorry, Coral. I did tell her.'

'And who gave you that right?'

'No one. I should never have done so. But this is wicked. Should we call the police?'

'Oh, don't be so stupid, Hannah. That would only make matters worse. No. You have forfeited your position in this family. This is your doing, and your responsibility. I wish never to set eyes on you again. I hate you.' She turned her back and left the room.

That night Hannah could not sleep. Coral was right: she was to blame. She should never have shared a confidence. Certainly not with someone outside the family, who would have no loyalty to them. And what sort of loyalty had she exhibited? None. It would sadden her to be excluded from family events but she had been partially excluded for some time; it was only since Agnes had departed that she had been invited back.

It was true that Agnes was spiteful, but she did not understand why she would harm a young boy like this. The more she thought about it the less she believed that Agnes was responsible. But if it hadn't been Agnes, who was it?

Of course. This was the work of Stanislas von Ehrlich. He hated them all enough to have done this.

3

As she packed up her house in Barlton Dolly was disconsolate. She knelt on the sitting-room floor, carefully wrapping in newspaper her best china tea set.

'This house was all I ever wanted,' she sobbed, 'and now I don't want to leave it.' She hiccuped. 'To give all this up for a cottage in Cresswell is too much to bear.' She fumbled in the pocket of her pinny for a handkerchief but could not find one.

'Here you are, Mrs Topsham. Take this one. It's clean.' May, who was helping her, handed over hers. Dolly smiled through her tears. Then, pink-eyed, she looked about her. The pictures were stacked and the larger pieces of furniture had already gone. 'I've lived on the estate all my life – I was born there. It's a step back, not forward.'

'It must be hard for you.' May clucked in sympathy.

'I can just hear them mocking me for trying to get away.' More tears threatened but a trumpet into the handkerchief stemmed them. 'Zeph didn't even discuss it with me. He just went off and bought the cottage. He might have told me, let me see it too.' She was folding the hankie into neat little squares.

Just then they heard the children squabbling.

'I'll see to them.' May jumped up and was soon reasoning with them. She was good with them, Dolly thought, which secretly annoyed her. Dolly knew that she herself would probably have shouted at them by now, if not clipped them round the ear.

They would be leaving their school – she had fought Zeph tooth and nail over that, determined to persuade him to change his mind. They'd have to make new friends, and the village school would never give them the education that the one they'd been attending in Barlton could offer. They wouldn't even speak like the children they'd be with in Cress – she'd seen to that with the elocution lessons she'd paid for. Now they

172

sounded more like their father than her, and the estate children would tease them for it.

She had padded the teapot spout with napkins and put it into the box with the rest of the china. Nearly done now.

'They'd fallen out over a book,' May explained, as she came back into the room. 'Now, where were we? Oh, Mrs Topsham, don't take on so. Would you like me to make you some camomile and catnip tea? It can be very soothing.'

'No, thank you. I'd best be getting on.'

'That's the spirit. It's a lovely cottage and I'm sure you'll be happy there, once you're settled. Moving is always such an upheaval. But some would give their eye-teeth for such a pretty house. I know I would.'

'It's too dark and poky.'

'A coat of whitewash will soon put that right.'

'I like living in the town, though, with all the bustle, the carriages and motors, the trams. There's life here. That estate, why, we might as well all be dead.'

'I expect you'll get used to it,' May said briskly. Dolly looked up sharply. She'd never heard her speak so incisively before, as if she was annoyed with her. 'In time …' May added, almost as an afterthought. 'Now, these tablecloths, shall I put them in this box or that one?'

'That one. Have you seen the kitchen? It's disgusting.'

'Mr Topsham told me an old couple had lived there.'

'Yes, my grandfather's brother – I can still smell them.' She wrinkled her nose.

'It must be wonderful to live where your family has always been, where your roots are. It must make you feel so safe.'

'Trapped, more like.'

'Poor you. But don't worry about the cottage. I'll soon sort that out for you, Mrs Topsham. A good scrub and it'll be fine.'

'What would I do without you, May?' Dolly, who was still sitting on the floor, leant back against the wall, the picture of dejection.

'Cheer up, Mrs Topsham. You've a wonderful man, and now your own home too, which no one can take away from you.'

'It's as if he doesn't care what I think.' For a second she wondered if she should be talking to May like this but misery got the better of her. 'I don't think he's even aware of what I've achieved.'

'But he is. He's so proud of you. He tells everyone – even when they don't want to know.' She laughed, but Dolly didn't join in.

'Why can't he tell me. Why tell everyone else?'

'I expect because he thinks you already know. Right. That's this room done. Where next?'

'I've done enough for today. I'm tired.'

'I've been thinking, Mrs Topsham. Of course, it's none of my business but that journey from Cress each day on the train must be tiring you out.'

'It's long hours.'

'I met a friend the other day. She told me that close to the office there's a woman, recently widowed, about to take in lodgers. A clean and respectable house,' she added. 'I've been thinking ... Those days when you're so tired you could sleep there.'

'But the cost.'

'For someone regular she'd make a special price.'

'You seem to know a lot about it.'

'My friend thought of me – in case things didn't work out for me at Cress.'

'But I couldn't do that. What would people think? I mean, leaving my family ...'

'It wouldn't be like that if it was just Wednesday and Thursday nights. They needn't even know, what with the cottage being a bit distant from the rest.'

'I'd be seen at Cress Halt.'

'I hadn't thought of that.'

'It was very kind of you to think of me and suggest it, May. Some nights I can barely put one foot in front of the other.'

'I know, Mrs Topsham, I've seen you. I've thought often that you'd make yourself ill with overwork.' May stood with a bag of linen in her hand.

'A special rate for a regular. I mean, I wouldn't like to think of some-one else sleeping in my bed.' Dolly shuddered.

'I could give you her address. You could have a chat with her.'

'But what about the children and Zeph? How would they manage?'

'I could cook and clean for them.'

'But Zeph finishes so late at night you couldn't stay ... But perhaps ...' Plans were tumbling over in her head. 'What if you moved into the cottage? You and Charlie could have the attic room and you could look after the children while Zeph's at work.'

'I don't know.'

'It's not easy for you living at the inn, with all that noise of a night time.'

'But ... I would love to do this but—'

'That's settled, then.'

'Mrs Topsham, you should discuss it with your husband first. I feel guilty telling you about the woman now. Is it the best thing for your family?'

'Yes – for them and me. I'm so grateful to you, May. I owe you a big debt.' She stood up and picked up a box. 'I'll talk to Zeph tomorrow, after the move,' she said decisively, happy again.

Dolly had been practising all day what she would say to Zeph and still had not decided which was the best explanation of the many she had come up with.

Alf Marshall had been helping them move the contents of the Barlton house. He had brought along his son Oak to give them a hand. The boy was so big now he could do as much as any man. She and May had not stopped arranging furniture and unpacking boxes since six this morning. True to her word, last night May had scoured the kitchen until it gleamed and the smell of mildew had been banished. Now Dolly was happy to place her precious china and utensils in the cupboards.

'I think it's lovely.' May was looking about the front parlour, where she had just finished hanging a pair of curtains that Melanie had found for her daughter-in-law. The windows were wide open and a spring breeze was lifting them. 'You've a lovely view.' This side of the cottage overlooked the garden, and beyond, the Cresswell Manor park, with the house just visible. 'You'll see its lights from here at night. That'll be nice when you're alone and Mr Topsham's at work.'

Dolly had to acknowledge that her furniture and ornaments fitted in nicely, but she was still not happy with the purchase. She did not even know how much the cottage had cost. She had asked but all Zeph said was 'Enough.'

There was a rap on the door, which May answered. 'Look what Flossie's sent over from the inn.' She was carrying a pan of stew. 'You see? That's one advantage of being here. No one would do that for you in Barlton, would they?' Dolly knew she was right, but decided not to answer. 'I must be going.' May picked up her shawl, and called Charlie from the garden. 'Look at the pickle you're in,' she said to her scruffy son as she put on his cardigan. 'Happy new home, Mrs Topsham. And remember what they say – new house, new baby!' She was laughing as she left.

If she was going to talk to Zeph uninterrupted she had better put the children to bed first, Dolly decided. As it was, the move had overexcited them and they were making so much noise she had a bad headache. She snapped at them several times as she gave them their supper. 'Bed now,' she ordered. They slipped from the table and obediently climbed the stairs. She had expected them to be difficult about it but they trotted off happily to their new rooms. They did not settle immediately but raced about squealing, and she had to shout at them several times. She wished she could be as calm and controlled with them as May.

What a stroke of luck it had been to find May. She was a treasure. If she moved in with them it would make things so much easier.

Alone, she wandered round the downstairs room. Now that it was cleaned, and her own bits and bobs were in place, it wasn't so bad. The kitchen was much larger than the one in the house at Barlton. The range, which she had approached with suspicion – she had had problems with the one in her last kitchen – had been easy to light. She washed the children's plates in the small scullery that led off it – she needed a few more shelves for the saucepans, she thought. That done, she returned to the parlour. The inglenook was old-fashioned but it brought back memories of her own childhood, evenings in winter when they had huddled together on the settle warming their toes at the fire.

There was another room off the small hall, which was empty. She had no idea what they would use it for and, in any case, they did not have enough furniture for it. All the more reason for her to carry on with her business. It was the only way they would have money for extras like that.

She went upstairs to check that the children were in bed – she did not trust the sudden silence. But Apollo was fast asleep, collapsed on his bed with his slippers on. She pulled them off and covered him with a blanket, then crossed the landing to Cordelia's room. She was sleeping neat in her bed, her clothes folded on the chair. In her own and Zeph's room, Dolly turned down the bed, making it look more inviting, and laid their nightclothes ready. She patted a little of her precious perfume behind her ears, then crept up the stairs to the attic. May and her little boy would be comfortable up here and she would have the satisfaction of knowing she was helping the woman as well as herself. If only Zeph would agree ...

It had been sensible to insist that he stayed at work while she got on with the move. That way he would walk into a settled house, and not be irritable from the chaos that today had been.

With the lamps lit, it looked so cosy. About ten, which was early for him, she heard the gate creak. She ran out to meet him, kissed his cheek and led him into the house, insisting he keep his eyes closed. In the parlour the oil lamp was burning, and although it was still warm, she had lit a fire. 'Open your eyes. What do you think?'

Zeph stood in the room transfixed. She was not sure but she thought there were tears in his eyes. 'It's better than I ever dreamt possible. Are you happier about it now?'

'Much. I couldn't see what it would be like. You were right and I was wrong.'

He bent down and kissed her full on the mouth. 'We shall be happy here.'

'I hope so.'

'It's up to us, Dolly. We can make what we will of our lives.' He prowled round the room, inspecting all the familiar objects. 'I've never really studied that picture before. It looks different.'

'A new setting makes you see things differently. You look even more handsome here.'

He crossed the room and hugged her tight.

'Careful, Zeph. We don't want a new baby, now, do we?' She was smiling. 'Did you eat?'

'No. I wanted us to have our first meal here together.'

'Then come with me.' She had laid the table with their best china and three candles and had asked Melanie for a bottle of wine.

'That looks romantic.'

'We're celebrating.'

'And you're truly glad to be living here?'

'It's lovely. I've realised how lucky we are to have our own home and not be renting. I've been so silly.' This was half true. 'It's ours, no one else's.' She ladled out Flossie's stew.

'I knew you'd see things the same way as me. You've made me happy, Dolly.'

'You're a good man, Zeph. I know how fortunate I am.'

'So will you give up the business?'

There was a long pause. Carefully she placed the plate in front of him. This was the moment. She was aware that she was holding her breath, then realised he was too. She sat down.

'I can't do that, Zeph.'

He put down his knife and fork, frowning.

'But hear me out – please. I've been thinking a lot. If I work for another year or two we can pay off the debt to Sir Mortie so much faster.' He did not respond. 'I know I get too tired and then I'm ratty, but I've come up with a plan to solve that.' She began to tell him about the room in Barlton, her idea that May should move in with them. He was no longer frowning but listening intently. 'So, what do you think?'

'You must do as you wish, Dolly,' she heard him say, to her astonishment and joy.

5

Rowan had been working at the vicar's for four months and had hated every minute of it. She remembered her days at the manor with longing. She had thought she worked hard there, but it had been nothing compared to what she had to do in this household. She began work at six, as she had with the Cresswells, but she woke in a dark, damp basement room, which only had room for her bed and a small chest of drawers. Her pretty attic bedroom now seemed a dream.

There was no one to chat to as she lit the range – there was no kitchen-maid – and it was always a battle to get the monster going before the bad-tempered, unfriendly cook appeared. Rowan had concluded that she would prefer to be shouted at by the likes of Mrs Gilroy rather than put up with this woman's sullenness – and Mrs Painter's food was disgusting. Rowan had lost weight since she had been here for she could not eat it. Gravy, mashed potatoes, and custard were lumpy, meat was grey and tough, while chicken ended up the consistency of cardboard. Vegetables were cooked to mush and the smell of boiled cabbage pervaded the house. Why the vicar put up with it was a mystery. 'I think he sees it as a penance,' she had told her mother. Used as she was to Flossie's and Mrs Gilroy's delicious meals, it was a particular trial.

The house was small, compared with Cresswell Manor; there, she had had five bedrooms and bathrooms as her responsibility, and had worked in the team when the drawing-room, ballroom and dining-room were cleaned. Here she did the whole house with no help: four attic rooms, six bedrooms, the stairs, reception rooms, hall, porch, front steps and kitchen.

'Mum, I can't go on. The work's too much and no one says thank you for anything.'

'You do look tired, but you needn't think you're going to work in that factory. The stories I've heard would make your hair stand on end.'

'Tell me!'

'You're too young to hear.'

'Mum,' Rowan laughed, 'you can't say something like that and not finish. I'm over sixteen now.'

'I suppose I can't protect you for ever. Well … I've heard three girls are in the family way.' She pursed her lips.

'Who?'

'One worked with you – Mary's her name.'

'Oh, no! She was so good to me. I must see her.'

'She's gone back to Bodmin in shame. Let that be a lesson to you, Rowan.'

'Oh, Mum, as if I ever would!'

'I hope you mean that. And as to please and thank you, well, you can't expect it when people are paying you.'

'I don't see why not. Melanie's always thanking you.'

'That's different. She's one of us. The vicar isn't.'

'He's a miserable old thing. He smells all musty because he doesn't wash.'

'He's better than the one we had before. Sacked, he was. Sir Mortimer insisted. He tried to have his way with Miss Cresswell.'

'That can't be true. She's so *old*.'

'She hasn't always been. Now, the last vicar was truly miserable but he had a tragic life, what with his wife killing herself.'

'Did she?'

'Big scandal, it was. She was in love with Mr Oliver and broke her vows, she did. When he got engaged she jumped into the sea. Zeph tried to save her – very brave, he was.'

'No! And her a vicar's wife!' Rowan's eyed widened with shock. 'Mr Oliver must have been so upset.'

'Not that you'd notice,' Flossie said, with a sniff. 'A cold fish he is.'

'The poor vicar. So what's happened to this one? He's a widower too. Seems dangerous to be married to a parson.'

'Rowan, you are a one! I heard she died in childbirth, having young Simon.'

'I feel sorry for him – he's not allowed to have anything to do with other boys. Alone in his room, he is, when he's home from school. I've never heard him and his dad have a chat like we all do.'

'Yes, but we're a proper family,' Flossie said, with a measure of pride.

Now Rowan was facing another day of drudgery. Her mother did not understand how miserable she was. She'd give it another month and, if things didn't improve, she would leave. In fact, she thought, as she scrubbed the front step, why wait a month. She already knew that nothing would improve.

Over the last week her work had been harder because Simon, the vicar's son, had been sent home from school. Mr Fogget had implied that he was ill, but he seemed well to Rowan. No doubt he'd done something wrong and been expelled. She could respect him for that, especially if he'd done it because he was unhappy. She wished she had the courage to do something mischievous.

In her eyes Simon was a sad creature. He was podgy – she wondered how he had become so fat with the awful food served in his house – his face was the colour of suet pudding and covered with red spots, his dark hair was lank and overlong, and he lumbered about the house, permanently bored. He seemed to have no interests, no hobbies. He rarely went out, and although he had a horse she had never seen him on it. In consequence, the animal was as fat as its owner.

'Why don't you read a book?' she asked, finding him in the front parlour, which she had to dust.

'I don't like reading.'

'Don't you? I love it. You can get lost in a book. Cheers you up.' He didn't look convinced. 'Can you play that?' She pointed to the harmonium in the corner.

'No.'

'I'd like to learn. It must be lovely to be able to sit down and make music, don't you think?'

'I don't like music.'

She turned to face him, duster in one hand, and pushed the hair out of her eyes. 'You don't like much, do you?'

He did not answer.

'You must get lonely here.' There was no reply. 'I've a brother of your age, thirteen or thereabouts. How old are you?'

'Sixteen.'

'Well, Oak is big for his age. Would you like to meet him?'

'He's got a stupid name.'

'I think it's lovely. It suits him too – he's so strong. He loves going in the woods. He's got a camp up at Maiden's Wood. You could go with him.'

'I doubt my father would approve of me associating with him.' He got to his feet.

'Suit yourself.' She returned to the dusting.

What a miserable person he was. She was sure that if she persevered she

180

could help him. Each day she sought him out and tried to get him interested in doing something. If he carried on like this he'd be as big as a house before long. Nothing she said or suggested met with his pleasure, but Rowan could be stubborn and she had decided to change him.

A week later she was still trying. 'I've got to go to Mrs Winters, the old lady in Rose Cottage. She's ill and I'm taking her a cake my mother made for her. Would you like to come?' She asked Simon, who, although it was ten o'clock, was still at breakfast in the dining-room.

'No, but I'd like to kiss you.'

'Oh, Master Fogget, whatever next?' She laughed, thinking it was a joke.

'Don't laugh at me.'

'I'm not. It was the thought of you kissing me. Your father would have my guts for garters, if you did.' She bent down to pick up the thread from the carpet. The force with which he leapt on her sent her sprawling on the rug, scraping her face on the rough weave. 'Get off me!'

'You like me, you know you do.'

'I don't.' She was wriggling beneath him as she spoke, trying to unseat him, but his weight pressed her into the carpet. She feared he was about to break her back.

'You follow me everywhere,' he said.

'I don't! I have work to do!' She spoke with difficulty now, as the breath was squeezed out of her. He shifted and then, to her horror, she felt his hands lifting her skirt, inching their way up her thigh. She lay still for a second, her heart pumping as if it would burst. 'A moment, Simon dear,' she said, controlling her voice so that it emerged soft and silky. 'I'm so uncomfortable. Get off me, there's a dear. Let me …' She felt his weight ease.

She turned round to see him crouching over her. With one swift movement she lifted her booted foot and kicked him as hard as she could in the crotch. 'You dirty little beast, how dare you?' And with that she was racing from the room. She opened the front door and jumped down the front steps and bumped straight into the vicar.

'Rowan, what is amiss?'

'Your son!' Without a backward glance she ran as fast as she could down the drive, and made for the safety of home.

Two hundred yards later she screeched to a halt. 'Bugger them. My hat!' she said aloud. 'I've done nothing wrong.' She turned and hurried back. She went in at the back door and flew down the servants' staircase to her room. Rapidly she packed her few possessions, put on her precious hat and rammed in a hatpin.

As quietly as she could she crept back up the stairs. She'd reached the top when the cook, her apron streaked with blood, grabbed her. 'Not so fast. The Reverend wants to see you.'

'I don't want to see him.'

'You're coming with me.' Mrs Painter was taller and double Rowan's weight so she hauled her easily along the corridor, through the door and into the hall. There stood the vicar and his son, who was crying and rubbing his face.

'How dare you attack my son?' the vicar shouted.

'He attacked me first.'

'You lie.'

At that Rowan dropped her bag on the floor and took a step forward. 'No one accuses me of lying. He grabbed me, pushed my face to the floor. Look.' She stuck her cheek forward and pointed at the carpet burn, which was now livid.

'She fell over and blamed me,' Simon whined.

'You pushed me! And, what's more, he put his filthy fingers up my skirt. No one does that to me.'

The vicar took a step forward, his hand raised as if he intended to strike her. Rowan stood her ground. 'I wouldn't, if I were you. I'll go to Sir Mortie and tell him and he'll sack you, just like the one before you.'

The vicar lowered his hand. 'I don't believe you. I believe my son.'

'Then you're a fool. You should punish him.'

'She's been following me everywhere. She loves me. It's her fault.'

The vicar paused. Even the cook snorted.

'And you believe that? Do you really think that someone like me would look twice at a fat ugly toad like him? I felt sorry for him because he's lonely, but I shan't bother in future.'

'Just a minute, young woman. I wish to search your bag. How do I know you haven't stolen from me?'

Rowan was shocked into silence but picked up her bag and clutched it to her. 'Over my dead body. How dare you?'

A knock on the front door diverted everyone. Mrs Painter stepped forward to open it. 'Vicar. I wondered …' At the sight of Rowan, Morts Cresswell was rendered speechless.

'Thank goodness you're here, sir,' Rowan cried out. 'I have been molested by Simon here, accused of stealing and prevented from leaving. Would you save me, please?'

'This is shocking, Vicar. How could you accuse Rowan, of all people? And as for you, Simon …' But the boy had disappeared. 'Come, Rowan. I shall listen to Rowan's side of the story and then I shall judge whether or not to speak to my father.'

'But you wanted to see me, Mr Cresswell?'

'Not any longer. Come, Rowan, I'll escort you home.'

6

'It was very kind of you to bring Rowan home, Mr Morts, but you shouldn't have put yourself out.'

'It was no trouble, Mrs Marshall.'

'What you must be thinking of her I hate to imagine.' Flossie turned to Rowan. 'You've got to stop upsetting people like this, my girl.'

'Excuse me! I was the one who was upset!' Rowan said indignantly, which made Morts smile.

'I was happy to be of assistance, Mrs Marshall. It was fortunate I arrived at the vicarage when I did. I assure you, Rowan was in the right.'

'Um,' said Flossie.

'Mum!'

'As I say, it's very kind.' Flossie stood in the kitchen of the Cresswell Arms, wishing he would go, but Morts apparently had no intention of doing so. 'Well, as I said …' She trailed off. She had no idea how to get rid of the gentry.

'I asked Mr Morts in for a bite,' Rowan said, still fuming.

'It was most kind of her, Mrs Marshall. And I am peckish – I arrived this morning from Exeter and had little breakfast.'

'You'll never guess what Mr Morts is here for, Mum. We saw them in the park. Ever so funny it was. All the gardeners, carpenters, the farm men – oh everybody – they were marching. All out of step they were.'

'Fighting! It's all you men want to talk about. That Mr Asquith said as there was no need for him to order men to go as soldiers. I agree with him there won't be a war.'

'I hope you're right, Mrs Marshall. No sane person wants to go and fight, does he?'

'You should hear them in the bar of a night when they've had a bit too much – "*Kill the Germans!*" they shout. Disgusting, it is. And your family, Mr Morts, I trust they're well.'

'There's little change with my grandmother, but my sister has returned to care for her and I shall keep her company.'

'We've heard you're getting rid of staff. Is that so?'

'Mum!' Rowan was appalled at her mother's forwardness.

'Not that I'm aware of, Mrs Marshall.'

'Odd how rumours start, isn't it, Mr Morts?'

'Most odd, Mrs Marshall.' He was hiding something, Rowan thought. 'Still,' he rubbed his hands together, 'I would be most obliged if I might eat here. I've heard much about your wonderful food, Mrs Marshall.'

'It was quite right and proper of you, Rowan, to invite the gentleman.' Flossie was looking pleased with the compliment and Rowan was marvelling at how beautifully he spoke. 'But the likes of you can't eat in my kitchen, Mr Morts. 'Twouldn't do. Show him to the dining-room, Rowan. There's a good girl.'

'I'm quite content to eat here.'

'Dining-room, Rowan,' Flossie said, so sharply that even Morts obeyed. 'And you come straight back here, my girl. I want a word with you.'

Morts did not know Flossie so he failed to pick up on her ominous tone. 'I was rather hoping that Rowan might eat with me. She's hungry too – she told me …'

''Twouldn't be right, to be sure.'

'I can't agree, Mrs Marshall. In fact, I would be honoured if you would join me, Rowan?' He said this in a rush on his way to the door.

Without daring to look at her mother, Rowan followed, giggling at Flossie's explosion of anger as she shut the door – 'And take that hat off!' was the last thing she heard.

'The dining-room is along here,' she said, suddenly shy with him, which she hadn't been on the walk to the Cresswell Arms. Now she was unsure that she wanted to eat with him.

'I think your hat's lovely,' Morts said. He was equally shy, but she was not to know that.

There were only a handful of customers and Melanie was serving lunch. 'A table for one, Mr Morts?'

'No, thank you, for two. Rowan is with me.'

Melanie gave Rowan a questioning look, then showed them to a table tucked out of sight and handed them the menu.

'A bottle of champagne, please, Mrs Joynston.'

'I can't drink. My mother would kill me,' Rowan told him.

'Not just one little glass? I'll look after you.'

Melanie returned with the champagne, poured it, and rammed the bottle noisily into a bucket of ice.

'She's cross – her cook's daughter playing lah-di-dah.' Rowan giggled.

'You couldn't be lah-di-dah if you tried. You're a natural lady.' He smiled at her tenderly.

Rowan felt a strange warmth in her stomach. When she looked at him it intensified. She took a tentative sip of her champagne. Her mother was so cross with her already that she might as well try it. 'It's lovely,' she pronounced.

'I want to give you the best.'

'Mr Morts, please don't or I'll have to leave. You embarrass me when you talk like that.'

'Then I apologise. Ah, Mrs Joynston. What would you like to eat, Rowan?'

'You decide for me.'

'We'll have whitebait and the steak pie I've heard so much about.'

Rowan waited for Melanie to leave them. 'She's really cross with me.'

'Would you like to go elsewhere?' He began to stand up.

'No, it's all right. I'll weather the storm. If not, I'll just have to run away.' She tried to laugh but in fact she was quite scared.

'I keep wanting to call her Mrs Topsham – her old name. That's how I knew her when I was young.'

'Lots of people forget, especially now Zeph's working here.'

'Do you get on with him?'

'He's very nice and fair, but a bit miserable.'

'You'd make anyone appear a misery – you've such *joie de vivre*.'

'What's that?'

'It's French and it means you love life.'

'Well, when you think of the opposite there's nothing to be but cheerful.'

'You've forgiven my family, then?'

'I've forgiven *you*. You had nothing to do with it. But the rest can all jump in the fire, as far as I'm concerned – well, not Miss Hannah. She's nice. Did you ever find out why I was dismissed?'

'No.'

'You're fibbing.' She grinned at him.

'I didn't want you getting all cross with me again, just as we've made friends.'

'So, what was it? What had I done wrong?'

'You're too pretty.'

Rowan blushed to the roots of her hair. 'What's that got to do with me being a maid?'

'My mother realised I was taken with you, and thought that by getting rid of you I would forget. But you're always in my thoughts. I want to take care of you, help you, teach you. I meant what I said to you that day. I feel I love you.'

Rowan stopped smiling. 'Please don't say such things to me.'

'What do I have to do to conquer the citadel of your heart?' He looked so serious.

'Don't spoil it, Mr Morts. Not now. You know it can't be.' She said the words that were expected of her, but in her heart she longed that it *could* be, and when his hand touched hers she did not move it.

Flossie was making bread. As she entered the kitchen Rowan wondered if her mother was thinking of her as she kneaded the dough violently – she looked cross enough.

'I hear you was drinking.'

'I had half a glass of champagne and very nice it was too,' Rowan said, defiant.

'You shouldn't have gone in there with him. It's not right.'

'He thought it was. What did we do wrong?'

'He is who he is and you are who you are. The two don't mix. You're here to serve his sort, not eat with them!' Thwack! The dough was thrown on the table and flour rose in a cloud above it.

'We were talking, that's all. It's not as if we were doing anything wrong. There were others in the room – we could hardly have got up to any-thing. Although I can't say I wouldn't have liked to.'

The slap took her unawares and knocked her sideways. Her mother had never hit her before and Rowan burst into tears, more from hurt dignity than pain.

'Sit there and listen to me.' Flossie pointed at one of the chairs.

'I don't want to.'

'You'll do as I say. Sit.' And, like an obedient dog, Rowan did as she was told.

'What's wrong with you? First the Cresswells and now the vicar's son. Are you one of those loose women?'

Rowan was on her feet again. 'I did nothing in either house. It's hardly my fault if people like me in the wrong way. I can't help it.' She was sobbing now.

Flossie put the bread to one side, sat down beside her daughter and took her hand. 'Oh, Rowan, you're so innocent. You don't see yourself as others do. You're a great beauty and men will always bother you. I fear for you.' To Rowan's horror, it was her mother's turn to cry – she'd never cried in front of Rowan before – and she did not know what to do.

At that point, Melanie entered the kitchen. 'Oh dear,' she said, about to retreat.

'Melanie, please. Speak to Rowan! She doesn't understand what danger she's in. Perhaps she'll listen to you. She won't to me.' And Flossie howled into an oven cloth.

'What's happened, Rowan?'

'It was awful, Mrs Topsham. I was dusting, talking to the vicar's son, and he jumped on me, tried to have his way with me and Mother blames me. I did nothing. What's more, she thinks I did wrong in running away. What was I supposed to do? Stay there and let him?'

'I'm sure she doesn't think it's your fault. She's trying to tell you that, with your lovely face, men will always want you, and that you should be on your guard.'

'I felt sorry for him. I was only talking to him to cheer him up.'

'If a man is stupid he will misinterpret your intentions. And, no doubt, your mother has been wondering what you were doing with Morts Cresswell.'

'He saved me from the vicar and walked me home. Then he asked me to eat with him and I don't see anything wrong with that.'

'And you're right, Rowan if that was all it was. But look in that mirror. That was what he wanted sitting opposite him. And that's wrong.'

'He's not like that. He talks to me. He's interested in *me*, not just my face.'

'And why do you think that is? Don't be stupid, girl. He's after your body, that's what,' her mother interjected.

'He's not! He's kind and honourable. How dare you talk about him like that?'

'And don't you speak to me in that tone, Miss!'

Melanie held up her hand. 'Shouting at each other isn't going to solve this, is it?' Shamefaced, the pair agreed. 'Rowan, listen a moment. I want to tell you my story. I worked at the manor just like you. I was young, silly and pretty. I caught the eye of Sir Mortie. He was handsome, in those days. He told me he loved me and wanted to marry me, and I believed him. Like a fool I went to his bed …' She paused. Rowan did not know where to look: she had never felt so embarrassed in her life.

But it was not over. 'Once I found I was with child, his interest in me disappeared. He even questioned whether he was the father. I was shamed and humiliated. My parents disowned me. And I married a man whom I grew to hate. Do you want that to happen to you?'

Rowan's face was suffused with blood. She looked at her hands rather than at Melanie. 'Of course not. But I'm not you.' Her heart was pumping hard. What did they think she was like? How dare they? She stood up. 'I didn't get into his bed. I've more respect for myself than that.'

'Rowan!' Flossie shouted. 'You will apologise.'

'No, Flossie. There's no need. I understand her anger. And Rowan is far too intelligent not to think about what I've said to her.'

'I know what you're saying, and it's just not necessary.' As quickly as her anger had flared it died down. 'Can I go now?' she asked, like the child they had made her feel.

Released, Rowan ran home to her parents' cottage. In her sisters' bedroom she flung herself on to the bed, looked at the ceiling and hugged herself. How could Melanie compare Morts with his gross, ugly father? 'He loves me,' she said aloud, to the empty room, and hugged herself tighter.

7

Lettice had only been in residence at Cresswell Manor for two days but she was already tired. Her grandmother was ever more demanding. Physically Lady Penelope appeared better but she would have none of it. 'I never get any sympathy. I'm ill. Why does no one believe me?' she whined.

'But the doctor says you're much better.' Lettice tried to placate her.

'I'll say if I'm better! No one else can judge. The doctor isn't inside my body so how can he know how I feel?'

'He has much experience in these matters, and he says you should be trying to get up more.'

'How can I, racked with pain as I am?'

Lettice was concerned that she was about to cry. She hated it when her grandmother did that – it wasn't real crying for there were never any tears, but she made such an ugly noise and her complexion always became alarmingly mottled. Instead the old woman rootled on her cluttered bedside table for a chocolate.

'And get the maid to sort this muddle out.' She managed to imply it was the maid's fault she was in a pickle, not her own.

'I'll do it.' Lettice stepped towards the cabinet.

'I don't want you touching my things. You might steal something.'

'Oh, Grandmama, really!' Lettice was used to the insults.

'Where's your brother?'

'He's gone riding on Childer's Hill.' She wondered if he was going there to wish, as they all did. He was mooning about the place at the moment. Perhaps he had fallen in love. It would be most satisfactory if he had.

'What's he doing here?'

'He's come to help Uncle Oliver instruct the men on soldiering.'

'Waste of time. And don't let them do any of their infernal drilling within my earshot.'

'No, Grandmama.'

'And your parents, where are they?'

'They've gone to Norway.'

'They always were selfish, and I lavished so much love on that boy.' She required another chocolate to console her. 'I'm tired. Call my maid, I need to sleep.'

As always, Lettice left the sickroom as quickly as decency allowed. She had some letters to write before she had luncheon with her brother. In the afternoon she wanted to call on Aunt Hannah, but she had learnt from bitter experience not to count on anything when her grandmother was involved.

'You look happy,' she said to Morts, as they took their places at the table. As there were just the two of them she had ordered their meal to be served in the breakfast room. 'I thought this was cosier.'

'It's such a glorious day.'

'It's been raining.' She laughed at him. 'What's more, this is by far the wettest March anyone can remember.'

'Well, yes, I suppose it is.' He looked abashed, then grinned at her.

'I shall think you're in love if you carry on like this,' she whispered, so that the servants would not hear.

He looked even more discomfited. 'I stood on the top of Childer's Hill and thought there was not a finer view in the whole kingdom.' He coughed and made a fuss of opening his napkin.

'I'd agree. And did you wish?'

'But of course. One can't go there and not wish.'

'Then you are.'

'I am what?'

'You know.' She made a play of pursing her lips and clutching at her heart.

'Have you lost your senses?' he said gruffly, turning to see if Whitaker had noticed.

'No, have you?' She grinned at him.

'I've been wondering if we could invite Ramsey over for a couple of days. That's if you don't mind.' It was his turn to tease her.

'Of course you can invite your friend.' Her heart was racing. How perfect, she thought. Ever since Morts had arrived she had been waiting for an opportunity to mention Ramsey and think of an excuse to see him.

After she had returned to her husband's house she had thought of him all the time. Best of all, she had even dreamt of him, which had been wonderful, even if waking up had been cruel. Just by meeting him her life had changed. Although there could never be anything between them, just knowing that he was a mere two hundred miles away had lightened her spirits. To her surprise it had even made life with Hugo tolerable.

This would be Esmeralda's second visit to Buxton. She had come in February and had enjoyed the break, even though her father had been unable to join her as they had planned. She had found she did not mind. In fact, she had discovered she liked having only herself to think about. But no baby had resulted from the visit. Though disappointed, she had not been surprised. She had decided now that she would never conceive, and with that acceptance she had become calmer.

'Mrs Cresswell, welcome back to the Palace.' The hotel manager bowed.

'I so enjoyed my last stay, Mr Bolter, that I could not keep away.'

'I hope the weather will improve for you. It has been so inclement. However, the sun is doing its best today.'

'I've never minded rain.'

'I wish all my clients could be so phlegmatic.'

He clicked his fingers at the porter, who loaded Esmeralda's case on to a trolley and disappeared with them into the nether regions of the vast hotel. She rejected the lift and climbed the sweeping staircase. She always walked whenever she could since she was determined to keep her trim figure. If she could not give Oliver the longed-for child, at least he would have a wife he could be proud of.

She stood at the window of her suite and looked across the gardens to the town. In February, the dark colour of the millstone grit buildings had given the town a somewhat dour look. Today, in April with a glimmer of sun, it no longer looked so forbidding.

The management had kindly laid out some leaflets about the local attractions in her room. She would go to a concert in the Octagon, and perhaps to the relatively new opera house. If the weather improved she would take one of the many recommended walks and even inspect a cave or two. Last time, with the rain, she had spent most of her time sheltering in the Colonnades.

The people had been so friendly, and lacked the suspicion of strangers for which Devonians were famous. She wondered if she would meet anyone congenial to talk with. She liked making acquaintances in a hotel – one could be friendly for a few days, without the need to meet again. She could treat these people with a degree of detachment: she knew little of them and they knew nothing of her. And she could pretend to be anything – a woman of mystery, a widow, a mother of six. She smiled at her silliness.

While she had learnt to enjoy being on her own, it did not stop her wishing that Oliver was here – the old Oliver, the man she had had fun with, the man who had spoilt her. The man she had laughed and loved with.

She leant her forehead on the window. He had not seemed in the least bit put out when she had told him she was coming here for another week. Probably he had not even noticed she had gone. He worked too hard; as if their own estate was not enough, he toiled for his brother's too. She sighed. 'Oh, Oliver.' There were days when she wondered if she would ever be happy again.

Bridget, her maid, helped her change out of her travelling clothes. Then, refreshed and with her maid as chaperone, she headed once more down the long staircase in search of tea.

When they had been seated for a short time a pair of hands was placed over her eyes, and she jumped with fright.

'Who is it?' she demanded, and relaxed on hearing Bridget giggle. It must be someone she knew. 'Let me see.' She turned to her chair. 'Papa, what are you doing here? You're a monster.'

He hugged her, smiling at her pleasure. She dismissed her maid.

'I wanted to surprise you, Esmeralda, my darling. My plans changed and I thought, Shall I tell her or not?'

'But how did you know I was here? I only decided to come two days ago.'

Stanislas placed a finger over his lips. 'Spies,' he said softly.

'Oh, how funny you are. All you needed to do was telephone me. But this is delightful. I have such plans, depending on the weather.'

'Travelling north is always a gamble, but we shall explore the town together.'

'I particularly wanted to see the wild flowers. I've read that there is an abundance of them here.'

The manager approached. 'Mr Eldridge, a telegram.' He held out the salver containing the buff envelope.

'Thank you.' He ripped it open and read it. 'There will be no reply.'

'Eldridge? Why did he call you that? Surely that was my grandmother's maiden name? What mischief are you up to, Papa?'

'Nothing, I promise.' He held up his hands. 'It is not wise, my dear, in these troubled times to have a name that sounds too Germanic.'

'But that is silly.'

'I assure you it isn't. I have friends who have been attacked.'

'Papa!'

'I have lost business already.'

Her eyes filled with tears.

'Sweet daughter, you must not fear. Now I am plain Stanley Eldridge, English to the core.'

'Oliver is convinced that war is inevitable. They are training the estate workers to fight.'

'That sounds somewhat extreme.' His smile was supercilious.

'Oh, he's having a lovely time playing soldiers. It was the reason I could get away for a few days. I shall not be missed since, no doubt, my generals, Oliver and Morts, are planning their own battle of Waterloo.'

'What about Felix?'

'He hasn't been to the house since before Christmas. He's run away from school and is staying with Coral's parents. I don't know why.'

'Is he?' A small smile flitted about his mouth.

'What do you know, Papa? What have you been doing?'

'Me? I've done nothing. And I know nothing – no one ever tells me anything. And who wants tea? Champagne for my daughter and myself,' he said, with a flourish.

'Oh, Papa, we shall have such fun. I'm so happy you're here to look after me.'

Lettice had gone for a walk in the park. After the rain the air was fresh and everywhere she looked daffodils were nodding in the breeze. She paused. Dogs were barking in the distance, the horses were snuffling in the stables and footsteps were crunching on the gravel path.

Ahead was the small thatched summerhouse that had been such a favourite of her grandfather – he had often sat there during the last year of his life. She had liked to join him and had fond memories of their chats. Now she went in and sat on the bench, hoping that whoever it was would pass by. She wanted to be alone to think of the one subject that occupied so much of her time these days.

'Lettice?' A figure had appeared in the opening.

'Ramsey?' She jumped up and, to her undying shame, hurled herself into his arms. 'I was just thinking of you,' she said ingenuously.

8

'I'm not sure what came over me. You must forgive me.' Lettice was blushing. What a ridiculous way to have behaved!'

'I shan't forgive you,' Ramsey said seriously.

'Oh.' Lettice was downcast and her colour deepened.

'Because I found your welcome delightful and would like you always to greet me so.' He picked her up and twirled her round so that she squealed with delight and felt a young woman again, instead of a respectable matron with two children. 'It's a great honour that you were thinking about me. But what in particular?'

'I was thinking …' Would he find her confession too forward? Still, if she didn't tell him he'd never know '… of how much time I spend wishing you were here. And, hey presto, there you were. It was such a surprise that you caught me unawares.' The blush had subsided and she was laughing with sheer joy.

He sat beside her on the wooden bench. 'Then I am content. And I have a confession to make too. I spend much time thinking of you and wanting to see you. I know I shouldn't but I can't help it.'

'It's difficult not to, isn't it? It's as if my mind has been taken over.'

'That it has been kidnapped by some mysterious force.'

'Exactly.'

'Then there is nothing we can do about it, is there? And I asked myself what was wrong with dreams.'

'Oh, yes.' She clapped her hands. 'I shall remember that when I next feel guilty.'

'Then it's a good thing I came, isn't it?'

They sat for a moment in contented silence. Just being beside him was enough for her, she realised.

'This summerhouse is delightful.'

'Isn't it?' She looked about her at the shell-encrusted walls. 'My grandfather built it. He'd seen a grotto in Rome and wanted one here. As children we saved any shells we found and he would buy them from us.'

'How much did he pay?'

'A penny for a small shell and twopence for the big ones. Those are mine.' She pointed at a group of cockle shells arranged as a medallion. 'It was such fun working out the patterns. Grandfather found the more exotic ones on his travels or had them sent to him. But I always thought buying them was cheating.'

'I like the simpler decorations best, the oyster and mussel shells, and your cockles.'

'And the winkles. I loved eating them so we ended up with rather a lot, I'm afraid.' She pointed to the frieze of dark shells that marched round the small room. 'Happy memories, all of them. I wish you had met my grandfather. He was fun – we always seemed to be laughing when he was here. Not …' She was about to say 'not like now', but decided it would be disloyal.

'A place can be perfect, can't it, until one person dies and it is changed.'

'When he died it was as if the sun went in for ever.'

'Did you spend much time here?'

'Yes, I did. Poor Morts was sent away to school, of course. At the time I resented it and thought it wasn't fair, but now, looking back, it means I have so many more memories of Grandpapa than I might otherwise. Aunt Hannah took care of us. In fact, she brought us up. Mama and Papa were always travelling.'

'I like her. She's a courageous woman to stand up for her principles in such a way.'

'I'm glad you feel like that about her. My mother says she's a disgrace to the family, but I'm proud of her. I shiver just thinking about prison. She's not one of the militant suffragettes, you know. She disapproves of breaking windows and that sort of thing. She just got caught up in a mêlée.'

'Morts said something about her being banned from the manor.'

'That's my mother's doing. It isn't the same without her popping in, but I go to her. She and my mother argued, but I don't know what about. She still comes when Mother is away – Oliver insisted.'

'He seems a sad man. Do you know why?'

'I fear he and Esmeralda are unhappy, but I don't like to pry and ask her why. It makes me sad since I love them both.'

'She is very lonely. Perhaps they are not companionable.'

'What do you mean?'

'Perhaps they have too little in common. Many people find that out after they marry, more's the pity. What I'm saying, I suppose, is that perhaps they bore each other.'

'I've never thought of that. I find both of them such delightful company. She is always so alive and happy.'

'Have you not noticed that people who are *always* happy are hiding something? They don't want people to know they are unhappy.'

'I've never thought of that either. In just a few minutes, you've given me so much to think about.' How extraordinary he was, so perceptive. 'Now you mention it, I've sometimes seen a sad look on her face, but it's always gone in a trice and I think I imagined it.'

'I've seen you do that.'

'But I don't claim to be happy. Morts is always saying what a misery I've turned into.' She was smiling as she spoke.

'Is it your husband makes you so?'

'I …' She looked down at her hands, holding them still on her lap. 'Yes,' she answered simply. 'But I shouldn't say it.'

'Yet you are saying it to me?'

'Even worse. But I know you are to be trusted. I've never spoken of him to anyone else.'

'Then perhaps you should. Talking may make it better.'

'I don't want you to think … He's not cruel to me in the accepted sense. He sees that I have all I want and need. He has never beaten me.'

'But?' He took her hand, as if to give her courage.

'I sometimes think he might one day. I irritate him so much. I can never do anything right. He makes me feel stupid and then I get nervous and become clumsy and make mistakes, which annoys him even more. I feel I am on a roundabout with him and I don't know how to get off.'

'But you are not stupid. You are bright and intelligent and good company.'

'It's kind of you to say so.'

'I'm not being kind, it is how I regard you.'

'But I can't be like that with him. He frightens me. He makes me feel ugly and gauche when we are in company. There are days when I feel he has made the old me disappear.'

'He is cruel, then. There are different ways to be vicious. I've heard him be unconscionably rude to you.'

'That was a mistake. He is never normally like that when others are around. I think he was intoxicated.' She looked out to the gardens, a riot of colour with the spring flowers blooming. Suddenly she jumped up. 'Please, forget everything I've just said. I should not have confided in you. I now feel guilty for talking to you in this manner. It was so disloyal of me.'

'My dear Lettice, I couldn't forget and neither will I forgive him. I am honoured that you have chosen to confide in me. It is not your fault that you feel like this. He has made you. Morts worries about you, you know. No one has the right to make another feel less than they are.'

'But why is Hugo like this? What have I done? When we married I thought he loved me but within days I knew he didn't. Why wed me in the first place?'

'There are men who change when they possess someone. And there are others whose feelings are only intensified by that intimacy.'

'Some days when I look to the future, I fear it. The thought of living like this ... But why are we wasting precious time in talking about unhappiness? Today I'm filled with joy.'

He pulled her down on to the bench beside him. 'Something has happened between us, Lettice, hasn't it?' She nodded. 'It's as if you have bewitched me.'

'You have captivated me too. Delicious, isn't it? I know I should think of other things but I have decided not even to try to stop thinking of you.'

'Oh, Lettice. I love you so much.'

'And I love you.'

He kissed her, and she felt as if she had never been so happy. She had no past, no future, simply this precious moment.

Esmeralda had taken the waters and been to the baths, and was convinced she felt better already.

'You look well, madam,' Bridget said, as she dressed Esmeralda's hair for dinner with her father.

'I feel it too.' And she knew why – she was away from Oliver, released from having to worry that she was annoying him. Away from having to think of amusing things to say, away from having to pretend that she was as happy as a lark. Perhaps going away on her own had been a good idea. The last time, on her return, he had seemed genuinely pleased to see her and they had been loving to each other for several weeks. But then his irritation had returned and her misery with it.

'I think I'll wear yellow. My father likes me in it.' Oliver preferred her in blue. She stepped into the duchess satin gown by Worth. Though styles were simpler than they had been a few years ago, the front panel of this dress was still ornately embroidered; often she hankered for the more elaborate gowns of ten years ago.

Bridget buttoned her in, then fetched her the matching shoes and bag. 'You look a picture, madam.'

'The topaz and diamond choker, don't you think, Bridget?'

'Perfect, madam.'

'I might be late – you know my papa – but I can manage this dress so if you want to go to bed, please do so.'

'Thank you, madam. I've been feeling a bit off colour.'

'I thought so.' She picked up her gloves and began to put them on. She hadn't thought any such thing – she hadn't even noticed. Selfish creature, she told herself, and decided to buy her maid a gift in the morning.

As arranged, her father was waiting for her in the lobby. 'You never know who's lurking in these public places,' he had once said to her, which had made her laugh, and he insisted on being with her whenever she was in public rooms. 'Shall we?' He gave her his arm. She was aware of people staring at them, for they made a handsome couple. She knew, to her amusement, that there was always much speculation as to their relationship.

Once they were seated a waiter appeared with their champagne. Her father had such a presence that they never waited long for anything. 'Not my presence, my wallet,' he had explained to her, when once she had complimented him.

Now he said, 'I had good news, today. I've acquired more land.'

'Why do you want more?'

'Because it's an irreplaceable asset. The good Lord isn't making more of it.'

'Where is it?'

'At Cresswell.' He sat back, with a self-satisfied expression.

'But how? Oliver has sworn ...'

'For the simple reason he does not know that I have bought it. I'd like to be in the vicinity when he finds out.' He laughed loudly.

Esmeralda's happiness was dissipating rapidly. 'Why do you put me in such a difficult position, Papa? It's not funny!'

He was grinning at her. 'I'm sorry.' He coughed, but he could not stop smiling.

'You don't seem to understand that it's not fair to me. Oliver will think I knew, that I deceived him. He will be furious.'

'Of course he won't. Why should he think that? Anyway, I thought you had a sense of humour. There's your husband protecting his brother's land from the likes of me and there I am buying it at his brother's instigation.'

'Mortie knows?'

'He approached my company and, through his stupidity, I was able to step in.'

'I hate to lie.'

'Then I won't tell Mortie that I am behind the purchase.'

'But he will find out, and then Oliver will know!'

'If he does, you can say you had no idea of my intentions. That you are not privy to my business. But you lie to him all the time.'

'I never do.'

'So you told him I would be here, then?'

'No, because I didn't know you would be, did I?'

'You will tell him when you return?'

'Yes,' she replied, although she was not sure that she would.

'Ha, Petroc!' To her relief the conversation ended there for her father was waving at a young man who had entered the room. 'Esmeralda, my darling, let me introduce a friend of mine, Petroc Cornish. Petroc, my daughter Mrs Cresswell.'

The man bowed deeply, took her hand and brushed the air above it with his lips. 'At last. I'm honoured to meet you. I've heard so much about you from your father.' He spoke in a low, husky voice that she found peculiarly attractive.

'With Mrs Cresswell's permission, would you care to dine with us, Petroc? That is, if you are alone.'

'I'd be most honoured, if Mrs Cresswell agrees.'

'It would please me very much, Mr Cornish.' Normally she would have resented anyone else intruding on her precious time with her father, but not tonight.

'I am alone and I had feared being lonely.' He smiled at her.

Esmeralda always enjoyed being with her father but that evening was special. She had never been so much amused. Petroc was a fund of stories, each funnier than the next. He had charm, too, and made her feel that she was the one person in the world he wanted to talk to that night. And he laughed at her little stories and jokes.

When they moved from the dining-room her father invited him to accompany them for coffee and a brandy. She found she was glad that he agreed.

He loved dogs. 'I've found all my life that if people like dogs I like them,' she said.

'Then I am relieved.' He gave her one of his crooked, but attractive smiles.

'But it's true. All the people I don't like dislike them.'

'Mention one.' Her father looked at her benignly.

'I can do better. I'll give you two. Miss Beatty and my mother-in-law. Gorgons, both of them.'

'She's right,' her father said. 'They're both difficult women.'

'I thought you liked Agnes, Papa.'

'Only as long as I have to,' he replied.

'You have a dog here, Mrs Cresswell?'

'Sadly, no. I had a Pekinese but he died last year at a great age. Somehow ...' As she spoke of her beloved Mr Woo, her eyes filled with tears '... I haven't been able to think of having another. It seems so disloyal.'

'But, my dear Mrs Cresswell, you can't be without a dog.'

'One day I shall find another Mr Woo, I'm sure.'

Just as she was about to leave them, her father was called to the telephone. 'You stay with Petroc, my dear, until I get back. We can't neglect a guest, can we?'

Esmeralda found she was glad to be left alone with him – and her father must like and trust him to leave her with him unchaperoned.

'If you like flowers, I insist on accompanying you to see the wild ones that grow here so profusely. It's caused by the escarpment ...' As he explained the local flora she studied him. With his blond hair, which was thick and straight, his clear blue eyes and fine bones, he reminded her of Oliver. He was tall and lean, not thin but muscular, also like her husband. And he had a melodious voice, as Oliver did.

'You are so like my husband,' she said suddenly, then clapped a hand over her mouth. 'Oh, forgive me, please. I was so rude to interrupt you.'

'Not at all. I take it as a compliment to be compared with him for he is a lucky man.' As he said this, he looked at her intently, which made her blush and lower her eyes. He doesn't make me laugh as you do, she thought.

Her father reappeared and she felt quite sorry that he had. 'Mr Cornish has suggested we go for a walk tomorrow, Papa.'

'Splendid. Shall we meet here at ten?'

She felt happier than she had in weeks as she kissed him goodnight and formally shook Petroc's hand.

9

Esmeralda dressed with particular care. The day was glorious, almost like summer. She chose a cream linen suit, a high-necked white blouse, and brand new cream kid boots with tiny pearl buttons. She had tiny feet and liked her shoes to match what she was wearing. Bridget was still unwell and Esmeralda had insisted she remained in bed. She had had to dress her hair herself, not entirely successfully, so she was glad she had a hat large enough to cover it. Parasol in hand, she tripped down the long staircase eager to join her father and excited that Petroc would be there too.

She was in for a disappointment – her father was not waiting for her. He had left a note that he had been called away on business and would meet her for dinner. He entreated her to enjoy her day with Petroc – underlining the sentence twice.

The absence of her father put her in a quandary. Should she go with Petroc on her own? With no chaperone she should not – she had to pro-tect her honour. But her father had said she should *enjoy* the day. Had he known Bridget was ill and would be unable to accompany them? And what would Oliver think if he knew? But, then, how would he find out? She was twisting the note in her hands. Perhaps it would be for the best if she went back to her room. She was about to climb the stairs when she heard her name called. It was Petroc.

'Mrs Cresswell, I am so sorry that your father is not to be with us, but I trust our little expedition is still to take place?' Resplendent in a well-cut light-coloured suit, a gold-topped stick in his hand, his moustache neatly waxed and an intoxicating smell of sandalwood about him, Petroc stood before her, hat in hand, bowing. 'It's such a glorious day.'

'It would be such a shame not to go, but I wonder ...'

'I realise the difficult position you find yourself in. I trust your maid is improved?'

'She is much the same.' She must have mentioned it last night even though she could not recall having done so.

'With your maid indisposed, I have taken the liberty of asking Miss Muller, a respectable woman who is staying here, to accompany us – she is alone and wants to see the flowers. That is, of course, if you are in agreement?'

'How sensitive of you. Thank you. I shall be delighted to meet her.'

Bessie Muller was not quite what Esmeralda had expected. She was far younger than she had envisaged – she always associated the name Bessie with someone middle-aged. She was refreshingly merry but Esmeralda felt her choice of clothes was not entirely successful. They were a mish-mash of colour and style; her coat was far too tight and her skirt a little too short – but skirts were shortening every year. Her hair was a riot of blonde curls, which Esmeralda envied. She was almost certain that Bessie had powder on her cheeks. Still, there were days when, feeling a little off-colour, she herself resorted to help. Times were changing. 'How delightful to meet you, Miss Muller.'

'Charmed, I'm sure,' was the unexpected answer. Was that a London accent? Esmeralda thought that she shouldn't judge people by their speech. She prided herself on being egalitarian.

'We shall have such fun, the three of us. Ladies.' With a bow, a flurry and much laughter, Petroc linked arms with the young women and they marched out of the hotel. In the bright sunshine, Esmeralda and Bessie immediately put up their parasols with a sharp click.

They started out at a good pace, but as the sun beat down, Bessie began to lag behind. 'Perhaps the walk is too much for her,' Esmeralda said.

'I'm sure she is stronger than she seems.'

Despite his reassurance, Esmeralda retraced her steps. Petroc remained where he was.

'It's my ankle.' Bessie sat down on a bench, rubbing it.

'Have you hurt it?' Esmeralda asked, concerned.

'Weeks ago. It's why I'm here. A friend said the waters might help.'

'You poor dear. Did you trip?'

'Dancing.'

'You like dancing?'

'Sometimes. I'm a dancer, you see.'

'How exciting,' Esmeralda said. 'I've never met a dancer before. You must tell me all about it.' She recovered herself quickly. Her father would be most put out at her having met such a person, but she was glad she had not known before since she had come to like Bessie – she was such a cheerful person, just what she needed. Her occupation explained the clothes.

'Don't wait for me,' Bessie said. 'You two go on without me.'

Esmeralda returned to Petroc.

'Perhaps Miss Muller has had too many late nights and the hill is too steep for her after all,' he said.

'She tells me she's a dancer.'

Petroc stopped walking. 'I did not know she was. I must apologise, Mrs Cresswell, I had no idea. I would never have introduced you to such a person.'

'Please don't apologise. I don't mind. She's very sweet.'

'But a professional person – what will your father say?'

'We will not tell him.' Esmeralda turned and waved to Bessie, who raised her hand in return. 'She's a jolly soul.'

'Isn't she? She has such a capacity for enjoyment. A real free spirit – but now we understand why. Are you one such, Mrs Cresswell?'

'A free spirit? Within myself, and in my dreams, I am.'

'I should love to be in your dreams.'

Esmeralda twirled her parasol to hide her confusion. 'But convention restricts all of us, doesn't it?' It was safer to ignore what he had said.

'Your father is restricted by nothing.'

'You are right. But, then, he is a man and it is easier for him.'

'I should hate it if you were a man.' There it was again, the low, husky voice that made her feel foolishly elated.

'Nothing ever stands in the way of Papa. Sometimes I wish it did.' She would speak only of him and pretend that Petroc hadn't said what he had.

'He tells me that he and your husband are not the best of friends.'

'He said that?' She hadn't expected him to confide that to anyone and was not sure that she liked it. 'I don't think he should have discussed my family matters with you.'

'He meant no harm. It saddens him, he told me. Of course, I would never repeat it to a living soul.'

'I am glad.' She paused to look down at the town spread below them. 'It is a great sadness to me that they are not friends.'

'If I were your husband I would feel shame that I caused you any unhappiness. I would strive to give you nothing but joy.'

'Oh, he does. Well ... I think he tries ...' And then, to her astonishment, she found herself confiding in Petroc, telling him things about her life that she had never told anyone else, her thoughts and fears. Although she knew she shouldn't, she seemed unable to stop. Perhaps this was what had happened to her father, she thought, which made her feel better about it. 'You are truly one of the easiest people to talk to I have ever met,' she said, 'but I trust ...'

'Your confidence is sacred to me, Mrs Cresswell. I am honoured that you should choose me even if it pains me to hear of your sadness. If there's anything I can do you have only to ask.'

'Really, Mr Cornish, you have already helped me by being here on this walk ... with me ...' She smiled shyly. 'It has been such a pleasure and I feel infinitely better already. Ha, here comes Miss Muller.' She felt quite disappointed to see their companion toiling up the hill towards them.

Back at the hotel the three enjoyed luncheon together. Esmeralda knew she was flirting with him, but so was Bessie, which made it seem innocent. To her surprise, she found it easy to flirt. Once or twice she thought she should not be doing so, but it was such fun that she dismissed her reservations. Eventually, with regret, she rose to her feet. 'You must excuse me. I must visit my poor maid.' She left them reluctantly but was cheered by the arrangements they had made to meet for champagne before dinner.

Bridget was worse. 'It's just a cold, Mrs Cresswell.'

'But you have such a fever. I shall call the doctor for you.'

'How will you manage without me?'

'I can always get one of the hotel maids to assist me. I shall feel happier if you stay where you are.'

The doctor attended, and ordered Bridget to remain in bed for at least two days. Esmeralda arranged for a nurse to look after her and give her the medicines the doctor had left. 'Enough for a hospital,' she had joked, before she returned to her suite.

She changed into a muslin and lace peignoir, opened the window on to the balcony and settled down with her new novel. She was more tired than she had realised for she nodded off. She woke with a start at a knock on the door.

'Enter,' she called, but no one came in. There was another tap on the door. She opened it cautiously, aware of the state of her dress. 'Oh!' she exclaimed. A Pekinese puppy sat in a wicker basket lined with pink. 'Oh, you dear sweet creature. Who are you?' She bent down. Then she saw a pair of men's shoes and looked up. 'Mr Cornish?' She stood up with the puppy in her arms. 'For me?'

'Who else? Your sorrow over Mr Woo moved me. I hope you don't mind?'

'Mind? I'm deliriously happy.' She buried her head in the dog's white coat and inhaled the lovely biscuity smell. 'Is it a he or a she?'

'A lady for a lady. And here.' He picked up a basket. 'All for her.'

Esmeralda looked at it, at another one on the floor and the dog in her arms. 'Perhaps you could help me?' She indicated her room and he followed her in. She put the puppy on the floor and clapped as the little animal scurried about, her black nose sniffing this way and that, the fine white pelt blooming round her, making her look twice her size. 'Oh, the dear! Has she a name? Then we must choose one. Have you any preference?'

'I suggest Esmeralda,' he said, in that husky voice.

'Mr Cornish, how can I give her my own name?'

'It is the most beautiful name in the world.'

'Mr Cornish, if I didn't know better I would think you were flirting with me.'

'I am.'

She blushed and fluttered about the room after the puppy. 'Blossom! That is what I shall call her. A Chinese name would be so *passé*. Oh, how I love her.' She picked up the puppy and it licked her cheek. She kissed it.

'I wish I was Blossom,' he said.

'It really is the loveliest gift I have ever received, Mr Cornish.' She chose to ignore his remark, which she thought rather silly. Who had ever heard of a man called Blossom?

'I wish you would call me Petroc.'

'Then Petroc it is.' Laughing, she stood on tiptoe and kissed his cheek.

He grabbed the puppy from her and flung it across the room. It handed with a thump and yelped. 'Petroc!' But that was all she had time to say before his mouth was clamped on hers. She tasted whisky and cigars, which made her shudder. 'Please.' But he held her tighter. 'No. Please, no!' He was ripping at her peignoir, and she tried to cry out, but he clamped his hand over her mouth, hooked his leg round hers and she fell to the floor with a bang. She struggled to stand but he put a foot on her as he unbuttoned his trousers rapidly.

'Please, Petroc! No!'

'How prettily you protest. But I know you want me – that you are longing for me.' He prised apart her legs, flicked up her torn gown and pushed into her, riding her roughly, tearing at her breasts with his teeth. She cried out in agony, but he took no notice of her and lunged into her so that she screamed. 'Shut up or I'll kill you.' He slapped her face so hard that her head jolted and she saw stars. Then, as suddenly as the attack had begun, it ended and he was lifting himself off her, adjusting his trousers.

She began to cry. Afraid to move yet afraid to stay there. Slowly she sat up, pulling the remains of her peignoir about her. 'How could you?'

'Oh, come, Esmeralda, you've been wanting me all day. You've flirted with me, led me on. You invited me in – I didn't ask to be here. Until dinner.' He bowed and was gone.

The minute the door had slammed she tried to stand but could not. But the dog was whimpering so she crawled across the floor to her. 'Blossom, I'm so sorry. Forgive me.' And she sobbed into the puppy's soft coat.

It was evening. Esmeralda had sat for a long time in the same place, comforting the puppy who had been more frightened than hurt. She had then got up, put the dog into her basket and gone into the bathroom. She was afraid to look in the mirror, certain that her face was damaged. When she plucked up the courage to do so, she saw a bruise where he had hit her but, to her relief, no other injury. She stripped and began to run her bath. As it filled she looked at herself in the long mirror. She was bruised all over. She shuddered at the memory and put her hands over her face. She turned off the taps, got into the water, sank back and wept. How stupid she had been. What should she do?

She could not tell her father – he would kill the man. Then she would risk losing him to the hangman. She could not tell Bridget. Petroc had been right: she had invited him in so she was to blame. How could she have been so wrong about him? Anyone who could treat a dog as he had done was evil.

She would tell no one and she would leave tonight.

Bridget was too ill to come with her so she arranged with the manager for someone to pack her clothes and for her trunks to be stored until Bridget was well enough to travel.

'I've left money for the doctor and I'm sorry to leave you, Bridget, but I have to go.'

'What's happened, madam? You've a bruise—'

'So silly. I slipped on my walk today. You know me, I'm such a baby …' She patted her eyes with her handkerchief to explain their puffed and red appearance to her maid.

'I'll come with you.' Bridget made to get out of her bed.

'No. I insist. Not until you are better.' She swept from the room and began to descend the stairs, carrying the little dog. Then, from the mezzanine, she saw her father in deep conversation with Petroc and felt sick with apprehension. She almost cried out when she saw her father hand him an envelope. She knew what it meant. She waited until both men had left the hall, then ran down the stairs as quickly as she could.

At the station she waited impatiently for her train to arrive. She wanted to put as many miles as possible between herself and the scene of her torment.

A couple on the platform opposite attracted her attention just as a train pulled in. Petroc and Bessie! They were laughing together. They must have known each other for some time. He was a complete sham.

How much did her father know? She could not bring herself to contemplate that and hugged the puppy to her.

Petroc and Bessie climbed on to the train and settled themselves. She wanted to hide but was rooted to the spot. Then Petroc glanced out of the window, saw her and bowed.

Alone on the platform, Esmeralda burst into tears.

Chapter Six

July–August 1914

1

There was uproar at the Cresswell Arms. The public bar was full to bursting and men outside were trying to push in.

Zeph jumped on to the bar. 'Gentlemen, please!' Everyone roared with laughter – it was the first and only time they had been referred to as *gentlemen*. 'Please be quieter. We cannot proceed if you don't calm down.' Some complied, but many hadn't heard what he had said.

Oliver Cresswell joined him. He rapped on the bar sharply with a metal spirit measure, then leapt on to it. 'May I have your attention, please?' The room quietened. 'First, let me say how proud I am that so many of you have stepped forward at this critical time. Thank you.' This went down well. 'Now, I suggest that all those under the age of eighteen leave.' There was grumbling as several youths, disappointment etched on their faces, made their way through the press to the door.

'Oi, Oak, you're not even fourteen. Out.' Robert Robertson hooked his thumb. Oak Marshall blushed a deep red, put his head down and butted his way out. 'Flossie would have a fit if she knew he'd been in here.'

'Now, all those over thirty-five, please do the same,' Oliver ordered. There was a shuffling of feet and a marked increase in the whispering.

'I'm not moving,' Robert declared, and several others, who were obviously nearer fifty than forty, concurred.

'What about those outside, Robert?'

'Too bloody bad. They should have got their arses down here sooner. We can tell them whatever's said.'

'I haven't finished. There will be space for them. Anyone under five foot six will be excluded.'

'So tall?' someone shouted from the back.

'It's not my decision. Blame the authorities.'

'You can be brave at five foot four.'

'I know, Jim, but it's probably something to do with the uniforms, which have already been made.' Oliver spoke kindly for it was obvious that Jim Beaton, a shepherd, was nowhere near five foot four. 'I've had a measure mark put by the door for any of you who aren't sure how tall you are.' Or short, he thought. 'Zeph will help you. There's just one more thing …' He checked a paper in his hand. 'Chests must be at least thirty-four inches.'

This caused much mirth, and some crude remarks were batted about, pertaining mainly to wives and sweethearts.

The room was less full now. Oliver could see several men who did not meet the requirements but hadn't the heart to make them go. Size had never crossed his mind before, but now he could see that many were of short slight build. The spaces were soon filled up with those from outside and he had to go through the whole rigmarole again.

'I knew we'd have a good turnout, that we could rely on you.' There was a good-natured cheer. 'As you know, we've already got a small group, who signed up in March. I'm proud of them and how well they've shaped up, but there aren't enough of us and some are too old so we need more. Also, and I hope you agree, we should be better organised. It's all been rather amateur. So, this is a preliminary meeting to look into the forma-tion of the Cresswell Territorials. My brother and I thought it best to be prepared.' This was not strictly true. Mortie had shown no interest in the group.

'Here! Why are you organising us? You're over forty,' a voice at the back yelled, and everyone laughed.

'Yes, but he's officer class,' someone retorted, which made them laugh even louder.

Oliver grinned. Then he went on, 'After last month's tragic shooting of the archduke in Sarajevo, the situation is grave.' There was silence. Most men were still puzzled as to why the death of someone they'd never heard of in a far-away country they hadn't known existed should affect them. 'Of course,' Oliver continued, 'we can still hope but war seems inevitable.'

'Smash the Hun!' The cheer was deafening.

'Some of us, according to people I have spoken to, will be needed. As I understand it, the standing army will go to fight and we will defend this country. We volunteers will be called Territorials.' They repeated the word as if getting used to the sound of it. 'We shall be attached to the Barlton Fusiliers.' This was greeted with a loud boo.

'Why do us need they?' Robert shouted.

'Numbers. We have to join with them. That's how battalions are created, small groups joining together. We will then be part of the Devonshires, who, as some of you know, were the Eleventh Regiment of

Foot.' There was no objection. No doubt they liked the idea of being associated with such a famous regiment. 'If you like, we shall be in charge while they are away. Now, I want no ill feeling towards the Barlton lads – we've all got to get on together. Since none of us can be sure what is to happen, what training will be offered, I'm not having anyone from this estate being put into the firing line without them learning one or two basics.'

'But you just said we'd be used for defence.'

'I did. But what if we were invaded?'

This led to a stunned silence. It was evident that it had occurred to no one that their land might be overrun by Germans. 'As a precaution I've taken it upon myself to ask Sergeant Miller here to whip us into shape. I know nearly all of you shoot game but in the army you'll use a rifle so the sergeant will be giving us instruction in arms and arms care.' This was met with disapproval, and several men muttered, 'Insult!' Oliver chose to ignore them. 'My brother and I are making a contribution to this. All able-bodied men registering with Sergeant Miller will be given a bonus to their wages at the conclusion of our training time.'

Horses outside on the quay reared in their shafts at the yelling and cheering that emanated from the inn.

What Oliver had said was not strictly true. The money would come out of his own pocket. The estate could afford no extras.

'What happens after it's all over, sir?'

'When we've *won*?' Another raucous cheer. 'All your jobs are secured on our word of honour. During any absences your families will be cared for, I promise.'

When he had finished he climbed down. He smiled as the sergeant and his assistant disappeared into the stampede to take names. 'Nothing wrong with our men, is there, Zeph?'

'No, sir, but I hope they know what they're doing.'

'You don't feel inclined to join?'

'I don't have time, sir.'

'I understand. Good luck, then.'

'Did Mr Oliver say anything about getting rid of any staff?' Eve Gilroy asked Whitaker, as soon as he entered the kitchen.

Gussie, who was visiting, straightened her back, patted her hair and moistened her lips. 'A worrying time for you all,' she said, satisfied that nothing like that would happen to her.

'Not a word. And I think the worry might be over, Eve. I doubt they'll want to rid themselves of us now. With the younger men off to war, how would they manage without us?'

'I can't believe this is happening. But we shouldn't give up hope, should we?'

'I regret that the days of hope are over, Eve. I fear for the young.'

'You wouldn't enlist, Edward?' Gussie Fuller asked.

'If my king and country needed me, of course I would.'

'But we've already got an army, isn't that enough? What do they want all the young men for?'

'I read that the Germans can mobilise an army of over three million. If that is so, our army will be annihilated. They'll be recruiting many, to be sure. A most upsetting day, Eve, and a restorative is in order.'

'I wouldn't say no.' She giggled, as was her wont when drink was in the offing. 'I've been wondering if I should get in extra stores. What do you think, Edward?'

'I've already placed an order with the wine merchant – just in case.' Once the whisky was poured, he settled back in his favourite chair. 'And how is life with you, Gussie? All well?'

'We muddle along, Edward. Of course, there's nothing like the smooth running of this house, and I doubt there ever will be.'

'Mr Oliver was most impressive this afternoon. Inspiring. The men were enthused by him. We shall have a fine group, that's for sure.'

'Mrs Oliver is all over the place. I should think he'd be quite glad to go off to war just to be away from her.'

'Gussie! That's a dreadful thing to say. Wicked,' Eve admonished her.

'You don't live with her, Eve. Edgy she is, a right bundle of nerves, our Esmeralda, and I find myself getting twitchy too. It's catching.'

'She's always seemed a happy, equable woman to me,' Whitaker pronounced.

'She's not been herself since she came back from taking the waters. I said to Cook, "Maybe they made her ill instead of better."'

'Poor soul. Such a nice person, despite her background.' Whitaker set great store by breeding.

'Of course, he goes away quite a bit – more than he used to. To London. He says it's to do with the war, or so the butler tells me. But I think sudden absences are always suspicious. It's not as if there's a war on yet and he isn't in the army.' Gussie accepted more whisky.

'You mean he's got a fancy woman? I can't believe that of him. An honourable man is Mr Oliver.' Eve was frowning.

'The aristocracy behave differently from the rest of us,' said Whitaker.

'It's a pity Mr and Mr Oliver have no children. I always feel little ones cement a marriage.'

'You say the most beautiful things, Edward,' Eve told him, and Gussie scowled.

Then the flattery and flirting ceased. Hilda had joined them.

'Did you know your Oak was in there with the men, Flossie?' Melanie had gone through to the kitchen.

'Never! You rascal.' Although she laughed, she looked shocked as she swung round to her son, who was eating a bowl of apple pie and clotted cream. 'What was you doing in there?'

'I wanted to know what were going on.'

'Don't you get any ideas, will you?'

'Oh, Mum, of course I won't.' He stood up and slouched out of the kitchen. Flossie sat down hard. 'He's up to something – he could lie, and no one would know how old he is because he's so big.'

'He certainly looks seventeen. But he wouldn't, would he? Oh, Flossie, try not to worry.' Even as she said it Melanie thought how silly it sounded. She put the kettle on. 'Perhaps you should let him join in with the men when they do their drill and marching. He'd enjoy that, a boy of his age.'

'It would lead to trouble.'

'But don't you see? He couldn't do anything. They would all keep an eye on him. He couldn't enlist because they'd tell the officer how old he is.'

'You might be right. But what if Mr Oliver agreed? Then all the other lads would be jealous and cause no end of problems.'

'I'll suggest a cadet force to him and they can all join in. There! Does that make you feel better?'

'It does. You're an angel to me and mine, Melanie. I don't know what we'd do without you. When you was ill I was that frightened – for you as well as us, of course.'

Melanie leant forward and patted her hand. 'What's the news of your Rowan?'

'She sits at home moping. I don't know what's wrong with her. She used to be such a bright spark.'

'Perhaps she's in love.'

Flossie snorted.

'You mean she does nothing?'

'She tidies for me – she's not idle – but she's not herself. I'm at my wits' end.'

'Children! They're nothing but a worry and it seems to get worse as they get older. I've given up on Xenia. I know now there's nothing I can do about her. She'll take her own road to perdition,' she said sadly. 'But now there's Zeph to worry about. He and Dolly – I don't know what they're up to but it's no way to conduct a marriage.'

'I don't trust that May.'

'Why not? She seems pleasant enough.'

'Oh, she is – too pleasant. I never trust people who are too nice.'

'You're nice.'

'But I've a wicked temper on me.'

'That's true.' They both laughed.

'No, she's after something, and I hope for your Dolly's sake it ain't Zeph.'

'You're being a bit harsh. She's got a child to care for and no man – she must be frightened all the time, afraid she might offend.'

'I hope you're right,' Dolly said.

'But if not, there's nothing we can do. We just have to watch and wait, be there for them when we're needed. I blame myself with my two – I let them down and they'll never forgive me. If only I hadn't had to tell them who their father is. It's made them both so bitter. I worry for the future, Flossie.'

Later that night, Melanie was waiting for Zeph to close the bar. When she heard the door to the passage shut, she called, 'May I have a word, Zeph?'

'Of course.' He followed her into the snug.

'I want to talk to you about May. I'm worried.'

'I don't know what I'd do without her here.'

'That's not what I meant. It's difficult to know how to say this but I think it's wrong that you live under the same roof with her when Dolly's away. It's not proper.'

'She works for us.'

'I know. And she's wonderful with the children. But when Dolly stays in Barlton the two of you shouldn't sleep under the same roof.'

'What would I do with the children? I have to be here by six. They don't go to school until a couple of hours later. May cares for them and she's good with them, never a cross word.'

'I know all that. But can't you sleep here when Dolly is away?'

'I don't always know what her plans are. You should be talking to Dolly, rather than me. She's the one who's taken that room in Barlton.' He got to his feet.

'I can't help worrying – and people talk.'

'Do you think I care what people say about me? There's enough for them to gossip about anyway, as you well know.'

'Zeph, please. I'm sorry I said anything but I felt I should. Of course, you think it's none of my business.'

'I appreciate your concern for me and my family. But you have nothing to fear.' He bent and kissed the top of his mother's head.

'Sleep tight,' she said, as she always did.

It was a clear night as Zeph hurried home. He paused to look up at the sky, the stars shining like crystals. He could not believe that war was imminent. Would he fight? He didn't know. He didn't want to, not like some of the fools at this morning's meeting.

He pushed open the front door.

She was waiting for him. 'Zeph,' she said softly, as she slipped into his arms.

'Oh, May, my darling,' he whispered.

2

Esmeralda studied herself in the mirror on her dressing-table. It was over two months since her return from Buxton and she still looked dreadful. She had dark rings under her eyes from lack of sleep. Her hair had lost its shine, and her complexion, normally fair and perfect, looked grey and blotchy. Once when she had been unhappy she could make herself appear otherwise. Not now. Just looking at the bedraggled creature she had become made her want to cry, but she had cried too much already.

'You must have caught that horrible fever I had.' Bridget fussed over her, massaging oil into her hair, which she covered with a hot towel in an effort to bring back the sheen.

'Do you think so?' Esmeralda clutched at this suggestion. 'But you were so ill – I haven't been as bad as that.'

'Takes different people different ways. Illness is funny that way. Like when some get better and others die.'

'Please don't talk about dying.' If only you knew, she thought. 'But I've had no fever and you did. I just feel so tired and with no interest in anything.'

'We could get some wool and start knitting, in case this horrible war begins.'

'I can't knit. I never learnt.'

'I could teach you or you could organise a knitting circle.'

'Me?' She sounded listless, she knew. It was a mystery why Bridget was so patient with her.

'Yes. If you arranged to have some knitters meet here it might be fun.'

'But who?'

'There's Miss Cresswell, the doctor's wife – I know a lot on the estate would like to be doing something to help, just in case. The men have their marching so we could have our knitting. You could give them tea and biscuits, make it an outing for everyone.'

'I could …' It was a good idea, Esmeralda thought, and she *should* do something. She'd heard that the doctor's wife had begun to give lessons in first aid. 'Where's my purse? Perhaps you could go into Cress this after-noon and get whatever we need. It's a good idea, Bridget. And if I can't do it – I'm sure I'd be all fingers and thumbs – you can do it for me.' The towel was finally wound round her head to Bridget's satisfaction. 'Go now, Bridget. I need to lie down.'

'But your hair?'

'I'll wait until you come home. I promise not to touch it.' She wanted peace and quiet.

Alone, she took off the towel. She felt it would do no good – the shine had to come from within her. She'd agreed to do it because Bridget was so keen to try, and she was fond of the girl and her enthusiasm. She wished she could catch some of her maid's energy.

She had been impossible to live with since she had returned from Buxton. She had been so nervous when she entered the house but for-tunately Oliver had been delayed in London. She had two days to try to recover and for the bruises to subside – two days to repair the damage that that monster had inflicted upon her. But Oliver had noticed the bruise on her face, which she had hoped to disguise with cream and powder. She said she had fallen and hurt herself. 'So silly of me, I wore my new boots on a walk. My own fault.'

'Women! You need old shoes for country walking,' was all he had said. They had heard a scratch at the door. 'What the devil?' He opened it and Blossom swept past him without a sideways glance and leapt straight on to her mistress's lap. 'Yours?' he asked.

'I couldn't resist her.' She nuzzled the dog.

'You bought her?'

'A woman I met at the spa introduced me to the breeder.' Yet another lie. She could not look at him. 'I fell in love with Blossom immediately.'

'A shame. I was going to buy you one.' .

'How kind. Of course you still could. Perhaps in a little while. Two would be lovely.' That was an idea that, even in the circumstances, made her smile.

She remembered how frightened she had been when he had turned to her that first night back. Normally she went eagerly into his arms. That night she had been afraid he would notice the bite on her breast, the bruises. Petroc had made her fear her own husband, that he had destroyed her joy in making love with Oliver. She was filled with hatred, had wanted to curl up alone with Blossom.

'Are you unwell?'

'No, that light is hurting my eyes.' She sank back with relief when he turned it off and somehow, she would never know how, she pretended eagerness for him to love her. The worst lie of all.

Just thinking about it brought tears to her eyes and trickling down her cheeks. Then there was her father. She could not banish the image of him passing that foul creature the envelope. It was what he did when he needed to bribe someone. The money was handed over in brown envelopes, not the heavy white ones he used for correspondence.

He was quite capable of asking Petroc to court her, to make her want to leave Oliver. Oh, yes, she could believe that of him. And Bessie's presence as a chaperone was too neat. Her father would make certain she was not compromised.

He loved her too much to order Petroc rape her, though. No father would do that, surely. But she, better than most, knew how ruthless her father was.

From her bedside table she took the latest of several letters he had sent her, asking her to meet him in Barlton – each more pathetic than the last. She had ignored them. She was afraid that if she saw him he would know immediately what had happened to her. And she wanted no one to know what she had endured. Her shameful secret had to remain hers alone.

It was inevitable, though, that she would face him sooner or later. If she didn't, he might make problems for her with Oliver. But, apart from that, she herself had to know the truth. Not yet, though.

'Here you are! Are you tired? It's not like you to rest at this time of day.' Oliver had entered the room.

'I didn't hear you.' Surreptitiously she wiped away the tears. 'How was the meeting?'

'Poor souls, they're happy at the prospect of war. They have no idea how bad it might be. Still, if we can train them, they may survive.'

'My darling, please don't talk in that way. You frighten me. Please say there will be no war.'

'I wish I could, my dear, but it would be a lie.'

'But you will be safe? Please say you will. You can't be a soldier, you're too old.'

Oliver laughed. 'Not a compliment, Esmeralda.'

His laughter made her laugh too. 'I didn't mean it like that.'

'I understand. If I'm needed, of course I will have to enlist, but the professionals, I hope, will have put an end to this nonsense within a few weeks. But people I have spoken to in London think it will last longer than that, that it will be only a matter of time before the volunteers are called upon.' He crossed the room and stood by the bed. 'You don't look at all well. You should see the doctor.'

'There's no need.' She sat up in alarm.

'I met Bridget. She's concerned too. I'll go and call him.'

'No, please …' But he had left the room.

The doctor's examination had been trying. She had convinced herself that somehow he would realise what had happened to her. Mysteriously he seemed most interested in how much of the waters she had drunk at Buxton. 'Sometimes it isn't as pure as it should be.'

'Oh, no, it was nothing like that. I haven't been sick. But my maid had a fever.'

'Your husband said you had had a fall, bruised your face and hurt your leg.'

'So silly, yes.' She felt herself blush. 'The hills are quite steep and I had on the silliest shoes.'

'You ladies.' He smiled benignly at her. 'You must be more careful in future, Mrs Cresswell. Wear only sensible shoes.'

Esmeralda's face showed her horror at that idea, which amused the doctor. 'You don't want any harm to come to your baby, do you?' he said.

Esmeralda sat bolt upright. 'Baby?'

'It's early days and I cannot be a hundred per cent certain, but most likely you are with child. It would explain your fatigue. Some ladies blossom and others are pulled down in the early days. We should know for certain in a few more weeks. Meanwhile you must take great care of yourself. Rest as much as possible. Eat light but nutritious food. I shall mix you a tonic and have it sent over.' As he spoke he was packing his medical bag. Then he bade her farewell and was gone.

Oliver! He mustn't tell him, not yet. She slipped off the bed and raced after him. From the stairs, she saw him in the hall talking to her husband. 'Doctor!' she called. 'Doctor, a moment!'

'Now, Mrs Cresswell, what did I say? You must take care of yourself in your condition.'

'What condition?' Oliver asked.

And Esmeralda fainted.

3

Rowan found living at home irksome after her short period of freedom. It wasn't that she didn't love her family, but in her time away she had grown used to privacy and space, and she missed it. Pretty as their cottage was, and as grateful as they were to Melanie for allowing them to live there, it was small and cramped with two adults and six children still at home, and arguments broke out with depressing regularity.

Rowan put on her best blouse and skirt, and set off for Hannah Cresswell's house. She had known Miss Cresswell all her life, respected and liked her. Of all the family she was the most approachable. If anyone would understand that what had happened to her at the manor and the vicarage was unfair, it was her. Rowan needed to find work. She couldn't depend indefinitely on her parents for support. And daydreams wouldn't feed her.

Daydreams! As she walked along in the summer heat she smiled to herself. They took up a large part of her day. Silly dreams, too, because she hadn't seen Morts since they had had their lunch together. He'd sent a note with Oak, who was working in the stables, and fortunately her brother had had the sense not to give it to her until they were alone. She hadn't answered it: she couldn't see the point. She had listened to Melanie, whom she knew had told her the truth. But it didn't stop her longing and wishing.

At the back door she knocked and waited. 'Yes?' A bad-tempered parlourmaid had appeared.

'I wondered if I might see Miss Cresswell.'

'She expecting you?'

'No.'

'Then you can't. I'm not going to bother her.'

'But if you would just ask her if Rowan Marshall might have a word …' The maid began to shut the door. 'Here, you!' Rowan's temper flared. 'Wait a minute!' She pushed at the door and managed to get it open again.

'Didn't you hear what I said?' The maid blustered, but looked scared.

'Who do you think you are, telling me if I can or can't see her? Just go and ask her. Now!' And to make sure she wasn't shut out this time she stepped smartly into the back hall.

The girl disappeared slamming a door behind her. A minute later she was back. 'This way,' she said, with ill grace.

'Rowan, to what do I owe this pleasure? Grace, tea for us both, please.' The girl glowered. 'Sit down, Rowan dear. Tell me what has been happening to you.'

'Miss Cresswell, it's been dreadful …' And she launched into her tale of woe.

'Such a dreadful boy, the vicar's son,' said Hannah, as soon as she had finished. Rowan smiled. At least Miss Cresswell believed her.

'Simon's lonely and miserable and if you want to find him you know he'll be in the kitchen – he's always eating. I hated what he tried to do to me, but it doesn't stop me feeling sorry for him.'

'You were always a kind girl, Rowan. It is most unfair that Mr Fogget refused you a testimonial. Was there anything else?'

'Nothing.' She wouldn't tell Miss Cresswell about the way she'd been treated by Lady Cresswell.

'My family didn't treat you well either, did they?' Hannah said, to Rowan's astonishment.

'How did you know?'

'Your father told me. I telephoned to Lady Cresswell but she was not co-operative. I admire you for being discreet about them and trying to shield me from the information.'

'That's all right,' Rowan said ingenuously. 'Do you know what I did wrong?'

'You did nothing wrong. You were too pretty, and you can't help that, can you?'

'That's what Mr Morts told me but I didn't believe him.'

Hannah frowned. 'Your modesty does you credit. But I have to ask. Do you have a romantic interest in my nephew?' She hated to ask: it seemed so intrusive.

Rowan smiled. 'What would be the point, with him being a toff and me being me?'

'So, how can I help you?'

'I need work, Miss Cresswell My mother won't let me go to Barlton – even though Lady Prestwick had said I could work for her. She won't let me work in the factory either.'

'She's right about the factory, but you would have been safe with Lady Prestwick. However, your mother's wishes must be respected.'

'I wondered if you needed more staff. I'd work hard and you understand why I've got no character. I thought with a lady like you, no man living here, that I'd be safe.'

This amused Hannah. 'Unfortunately I don't need any help in the house.' She saw Rowan's disappointment. 'For the moment,' she added.

'You could do with a politer maid,' Rowan said, with spirit, and regretted it. 'I should not have said that.'

'Perhaps not.' But Hannah was smiling. 'Tell me, you read and write, don't you? Do you know anything about gardening?'

'I'm good at reading and writing, and I like gardens. I don't know anything about them, though. My dad does all the gardening, you see, and he wouldn't let anyone near his vegetables.'

'I might have a position for you in my horticultural business. You would have to learn the names of all the plants in the greenhouses, how to propagate and how to keep files and records.'

'I could do that.' Rowan said, without the least idea of what propagating was.

'Are you sure you know what I mean?'

'Oh, yes.'

'Rowan?' Hannah smiled at her.

'All right, Miss Cresswell, I don't. But I could learn. I'm bright.'

Hannah laughed. 'I'm sure you are. You would, of course, be working with the gardeners, and Miss Sprite, my head gardener, will look after you and teach you.'

'A lady gardener?'

'Yes. She is a talented plantswoman and I am lucky to have her.'

Rowan thought it was a strange arrangement, women gardening, but if it meant work she didn't mind. 'There is one problem, though. What if Lady Cresswell sees me?'

'It's unlikely. She never goes near the greenhouses and, in any case, the business is mine. You would live with Miss Sprite in the new cottage close to the walled garden. It's most comfortable. What do you think?'

'I feel like the cat what's had the cream.'

'The cat *that's* had the cream, Rowan!' But she was laughing.

Flossie was closeted with Melanie. 'Gardening, I ask you! For a girl! It doesn't seem right. Have you ever heard of such a thing?'

'Of course. Why, women are doing many things these days. I heard of a lady doctor recently.'

'Never! I wouldn't like that. Stands to reason a man doctor would know more, doesn't it?'

'I'm not so sure. If women were properly trained, I wouldn't mind.'

'I suppose it takes all sorts.' But Flossie did not seem persuaded.

'I know some women who are cleverer than their husbands.' Myself among them, Melanie thought. 'And look at all the things you can do that Alf can't.'

'That's true. But, then, I could never drive that monster of Miss Hannah's and my Alf can. It's just that I think women should stay in the kitchen where they belong.'

Melanie decided not to comment. She knew that when Flossie had made up her mind there was no changing it. But she could try. 'Still, about Rowan, you have no cause to worry. Miss Hannah, I gather, is well thought of as a landscape gardener – I think that's what it's called. Zeph was telling me that her business is successful and expanding all the time.'

'It might be but that's not all … I'm not too happy our Rowan being with … Well, you know, women like *that*.' Unusually Flossie looked embarrassed. 'I don't want anyone interfering with our Rowan …'

'Flossie, it's not like you to listen to tittle-tattle. In any case I never believed the gossip that went about at the time. What could be more sensible than two lonely women living together? If you and I were left alone and you chose to move in here, would people talk?'

'They'd better not! I'd give 'em what for.'

'Exactly!'

'You've made me feel stupid now.'

'I didn't mean to.'

'Do you know this Miss Sprite?'

'I've never met her but I hear she's pleasant enough.'

'It's just I live in fear for our girl. She's so pretty and she doesn't seem to be aware of it.'

'That's because you've brought her up so well. There's not an ounce of conceit in her.'

There was no one at the cottage so Rowan left her bag and went to the walled garden to find Miss Sprite. The gate creaked as she opened it. She loved this place – she always had. The two acres were surrounded by red-brick walls that trapped the heat and it smelt of summer. The air was full of the drone of the bees, crickets were chirping, butterflies were everywhere and there seemed more birds here than outside – it was as if they knew no dogs or cats were allowed.

A noisy clatter and a tuneless hum came from one of the long greenhouses. 'Hello,' Rowan called. 'Is anyone here?'

From behind a swathe of greenery a face appeared. 'You must be Rowan.' Emily Sprite was about thirty, pretty with a winning smile. She wore a strange mélange of clothes: dark green linen knickerbockers, tucked into canvas boots, with a loose, flowing chiffon blouse in swirling blues, and a long scarf in yellows and greens. A large broad-brimmed cotton hat, from which dangled a sunflower, sat on her head and under it her curly red hair battled to be free.

'Oh, you look lovely.' Rowan clapped her hands with pleasure. 'Like a bird from a foreign country.'

'What an adorable description. And you are ravishing, my dear. I'm so sorry I wasn't at the cottage but I got so involved with this *Silybum marianum*. She's being such a nuisance. Normally they're no trouble but this one's always wanting attention.'

'It looks like milk thistle.'

'You know your plants? That's wonderful!'

'Only some. What did you call it?'

'*Silybum marianum*. It's the Latin name – you'll learn them all in time.'

'But what's Miss Cresswell growing them for?'

'For the herb gardens. She's famous for them. It's not all flowers, you know. We've a fine line in trees too. Now, where was I? You'll want to see your room. I'm so glad Hannah sent you. There's so much to do. And I shall teach you. Soon you will be expert too …' She moved so quickly that Rowan had almost to run to keep up with her. Before she had even seen her room she had decided she was going to be happy here.

4

Lettice lay on her back in the long grass of Upper Meadow and watched the skylarks swooping and diving in the clear blue skies. It was, she decided, almost too hot to breathe. She had been here a good half-hour, waiting. She knew he would come. He always did.

She had never been so happy. Without doubt Ramsey was her other half, the one poets wrote about and, until now, she had only dreamt of. It wasn't just that their interests were so similar or that they had the same sense of humour, it was as if each knew what the other was thinking. Sometimes they finished each other's sentences, like an old married couple who had been together for decades.

To be in a room crowded with other people, and know that he would look across and give her the smile he reserved for her made her even happier. To brush against him, as if by accident, bestowed on her such joy that it was as if she had been touched by lightning.

At night she dreamt of him and suppressed passion flooded her. In the morning when she woke it was always with a sense of loss, but she was helped by the conviction that his dreams had been the same so his mind, at least, had taken her.

Their inability to cement their love had made her feelings stronger, more precious. While she longed for his body, she knew, deep within her, that even without it their feelings would deepen. There was a bittersweetness to their abstinence.

And yet ... She sat up and looked about her in the summer haze. Far below her, she could see men cutting the hay with scythes, arms wielding the sharp blades forward, bodies moving in rhythm. They reminded her of ballet dancers. That was what love had done to her. It had changed the world so that she saw beauty everywhere. It had opened her eyes and made her aware in a way nothing else ever had.

And yet ... Happy as she was, she did not want to go on in this way. With war coming, everything had changed. While he had assured her he would not enlist to fight, she feared that, as a former soldier, he would be given no choice. He had joked that he was too old to fight, but she knew he was protecting her. If he went, and if he died, her life would be over too. And if he went, and if he died, and they had not consummated their love that, she was sure, would be a wickedness. A love such as theirs should be celebrated and confirmed.

She had written to her husband and asked if she might stay another month with her grandmother. He had not replied. That lack of a response had helped her to a significant conclusion. She was not part of his life, so why should she pretend that he was part of hers?

'Without doubt this is the most glorious summer ever.' Ramsey flung himself on to the grass beside her. 'And, what is more, this is the happiest, most glorious summer of my life.' He kissed her cheek.

'Mine too. Though it rained yesterday.' She grinned at him.

'Who noticed?'

She raised her arms above her head and stretched as languorously as a cat. 'Do you really love me?'

'How can you ask? Do I have to go and fight battles to prove my love?'

She put her finger over his lips. 'No talk of battles.'

He laughed. 'I told you, I have no intention of enlisting. I meant more an Arthurial joust.'

'How much do you love me?'

Alerted by the seriousness of her tone, he sat up and faced her. 'More than I ever dreamt possible. My only regret is that we did not meet years ago.'

'Would you be with me through all strife?'

'Of course. But why all these questions?'

'I have decided to ask my husband for a divorce.' She said these momentous words so quietly that he had to ask her to repeat them, convinced he had not heard her properly.

'On what grounds?'

'My adultery with you. Then I can be with you.'

Ramsey was rendered speechless. He took her into his arms and held her tightly, the heat of their bodies intermingling. Now he could not speak as tears tumbled down his cheeks and spattered on to her face.

'Oh, my darling, please don't cry.' Lettice was alarmed.

'I can't help it. That you would put yourself through such shame for me.'

'No, my darling. I'd do it for *us*.' She was laughing now, with delight at his reaction, and joy that the decision was made.

He wiped his tears. 'What must you think of me, a grown man, weeping?'

'It makes me love you more. It takes a courageous man to weep.'

Then his face became serious. 'Have you thought of the consequences? You would be ostracised by society, a disgraced woman.'

'What do I care about society? And how can loving you disgrace me?'

He took her hand. 'My love, the sacrifice you would make is too great. You would lose your children.'

'I don't think so. He never notices them – they aren't boys. It's one of the reasons he's always so cross with me. I never gave him an heir. He won't want them.'

'I fear you're mistaken. He may not be interested in them now, but if he thinks he's losing you, his interest will grow overnight. He will take them to punish you. And I cannot have that on my conscience. It would destroy you, them and, eventually, us.'

'We could run away with them to the Argentine. We could make our life there.'

'And never come home. You would never see your brother again. Or this place. No, my darling, it is out of the question.'

'But my longing for you is so great. I need you …' She began to blush. 'There is no easy way to say this, but I want you to make love to me. Please,' she added, in her innocence.

Ramsey groaned and put his head into his hands. 'My sweet one, there is nothing I want more. But you ask how much I love you. Well, I have not made love to you because I want to protect you. That shows the extent of my love for you.'

'Then what am I do to? I can no longer live with him and he doesn't want me. How can I live this charade for the rest of my life?'

'Many do.'

'And, no doubt, I would have, but I met you. Even then perhaps I would have continued as everyone expects me to, but now, with all this talk of war, I can't and I won't. If I can't be with you, I will not be with him.'

'We need advice from a lawyer. Perhaps you and Hugo could separate and the children stay with you. I could remain in the shadows.'

'But that makes it seem that our love is something to be ashamed of and it isn't. I don't want to skulk and hide. I don't want something lovely to be tarnished.'

'I can't think what I have done for the gods to bless me with you. But there is something …' He appeared to be weighing it up.

'Yes?' She felt suddenly afraid, as if he was about to tell her something bad.

'I don't know if I should tell you. But …'

'You have to, now you've begun. Is it something horrible?'

'No, far from it – to me. It might even be a solution. When did you last see Hugo?'

'A couple of months ago.'

'And do you know if he has financial problems?'

'I'm not sure. He doesn't behave as if he does, but he always objects to every penny I spend.' She did not say bitterly but in a tone of resignation.

'He has a lover.'

She broke out in a wide smile. 'So, it's true. I thought as much. I don't mind – in fact, I'm rather pleased.'

'She's American, and very rich.'

'How nice for her.'

'But don't you see? If he is short of money and she is as rich as everyone says, perhaps you asking for a divorce might be for him a blessing in disguise. If so, he can be the gentleman he thinks he is and do the decent thing by you and his new lady, and you will keep the girls.'

'Oh, Ramsey, if only it's true! How can we find out?'

'We take a lawyer's advice and employ a detective.'

'How exciting. And you and me?'

'Together for ever.' And then he really kissed her.

5

Despite the dreadful circumstances, her fear of being found out, that her father might create mischief, that Petroc might reappear, and despite her burden of guilt, Esmeralda could not remember when she had felt so happy. It was not just that a life was growing within her, it was because she had become important to Oliver. He lavished attention on her. He fussed over her. He was aware of her. She almost allowed herself to believe he loved her.

Under this avalanche of concern she blossomed. Her skin had a special glow, her hair shone and, physically, she had never felt better. She was so happy that there were times when she could persuade herself that nothing had gone wrong in her life. That she had never been to Buxton or met Petroc.

But, without warning, the horror would flood back to her. When that happened bleakness overwhelmed her and she was sure she was the wickedest woman on earth.

Even then Oliver was solicitous, excusing her, understanding her. Those were the dark times when she felt she had to tell him she had no right to this comfort, to this care, to this baby. That she must tell him she could not know who was the father of her child.

As always, when she went to see her father she dressed with meticulous care. She was confident that he would not be aware of her condition: her stomach was only slightly larger and she had always been full-breasted. In any case she could dress to disguise her shape, she told herself. She put on a blouse that was on the big side and, despite the heat, a loose-fitting linen coat. She did not wish to see him but she knew she had to. It would be dangerous not to: when he was angry, her father was capable of anything.

When she stepped into the Victoria Hotel he was waiting for her, in the usual private sitting room. 'This must be the first time I've arrived before you,' he said, and kissed her cheek. 'Is something wrong? I usually receive a much more effusive welcome.'

'I'm sorry, Papa. It's the heat.' She put her arms about him, smelt the familiar pomade, but for the first time she did not feel safe with him. 'How are you getting on with your new name? I find it difficult to remember.'

'I am used to it now. Anyway, your grandmother always called me Stan. But it was a wise decision – anti-German feeling is running high.'

'But we aren't German.'

'No, but our name makes it seem that we are.'

'Grandmama once told me you had made it up. Is that true?'

'Yes.' It was not the answer she had expected.

'Why?'

'Because it sounded mysterious and important – all the things I wasn't when I first went into business.'

'Then you must be sad to lose it.' Suddenly she felt sorry for him and longed to be free of doubts about him. She wanted their relationship to be as it had been in the past – when she had trusted him.

'In a way, I am. What an intuitive soul you are, Esmeralda. Ah, here is our champagne.'

'Not for me, Papa. Just some water.'

'Are you unwell?'

'No. It's the heat.'

'You look remarkably beautiful today.'

'Thank you.' She covered her eyes demurely. 'And tell me, your scar, how did you get it? Was it in a duel, as everyone says?'

He laughed. 'So many questions. You've never been interested before. Why now?'

'I don't know. I suppose I'm just curious.' She wanted to know everything so that one day she could explain to her child.

'As a child I fell out of my perambulator and crashed into some iron railings. I've never lied about it – people just presume it's something more exotic. Are you disappointed?' He smiled at her with all of that old charm.

'No, I find it endearing.' Surely her fears about him could not be grounded in reality. 'How is the business? You make yourself most unpopular with all the big houses in the district. No one can keep any staff – they all go to Barlton to work for you. Even I've lost two maids.'

'They have more dignity working for me. We live through a period of change, Esmeralda. In a short time our large houses will be white elephants and we won't get staff for love nor money. But, still, that is of no interest to you, I'm sure. But, thank you for asking. Business at the factory goes well. This war is a great help to me.'

'Tell me it won't come to that. Surely Mr Asquith will make the Germans see sense.'

'I most sincerely hope he doesn't.'

'Papa, that is a dreadful thing to say.'

'It's the truth. A war is the best thing that could happen to me. I've already got orders I'd never have dreamt of. I'm opening another factory nearer London and then I shall cut back on my transport costs.'

'But what about the people working for you here?'

'I shall keep it open but with a smaller staff. They can move to the new factory or go back to being servants.'

'But that is so unfair.'

'What's unfair about it? They came because they wanted more money. I didn't force them. I'm not a charity.'

'But surely you have some responsibility to them.' All her doubts were rushing back.

'None whatsoever. But you are not interested in matters of business. Why haven't I seen you for so long? Why did you ignore my letters?'

She looked everywhere in the room but at him. Her heart was pounding so loudly that she could hear it. 'Did you know Petroc before we went to Buxton?'

'Yes – we met there by chance.'

'Did you?'

'Yes.'

'Papa, I think you lie.'

He choked on his champagne. 'I beg your pardon? You accuse your father of lying?'

'Yes. I do.'

'On what grounds?'

'I saw you handing him an envelope and when you do that it usually means there is money in it.'

'There was. He had done a little job for me.'

'Was meeting me, and trying to seduce me, the job?'

She had never seen her father flush before, but he did so now. He sat upright in his chair. 'He did? Why, I will kill him—'

'No, you won't. I'm sure you planned it. I was meant to fall in love with him, wasn't I? But why, Papa?'

From his pocket he took a large handkerchief and trumpeted into it. If she was supposed to think he was overcome with emotion it did not work. 'You know why. My relationship with your husband means that I never see you. When you have children ...'

At this Esmeralda knocked her glass of water flying. She patted ineffectually at the water on the table with a napkin.

He caught her hand. 'Tell me, are you?'

'With child? No, Papa, I'm not.' But she reddened. He let go of her hand but continued to stare at her in the penetrating way that always unnerved her.

'And if you were, how would I know the child? Your husband would make sure I never did.'

'Then the solution is in your hands, Papa. If you could be friends I would be so much happier.'

'I wish him dead. You'd be better off with a man like Petroc. A good friend of mine.'

'And someone you can control. Him and his mistress, too. Yes, I met her. Was that part of your plan?' She stood up to go. 'I'm angry with you, Papa. You put me in danger. You thought only of yourself and not of me. It is best if we do not meet for a while.'

'Esmeralda, don't go. Listen to me.' It was the first time she had ever heard her father plead.

'I had better not. I might say things I would regret later. Goodbye, Papa.'

She left the room, and walked straight into Dulcie Prestwick.

'Esmeralda, are you unwell? You look so pale.'

'I need to get home.'

'Let me find a room for you so that you can lie down.'

The door to the sitting room burst open. 'Esmeralda, come here. I demand you return!' her father bellowed.

'Please, Lady Prestwick, don't let him anywhere near me!' She ran down the stairs, determined to get away from him as swiftly as possible.

6

'You are looking so well, dear *Aunt* Esmeralda.' Lettice kissed her and they giggled. With only four years between them, their relationship amused them.

'As do you, my dear niece.' There was more giggling.

'And this is the new Mr Woo?' Lettice bent down to pat the Pekinese.

'No, this is Miss Blossom.' Lettice shook the puppy's paw. 'And how is your grandmother?'

'Just the same, but it's kind of you to come to see her.'

'I only came because Oliver was visiting. He feels guilty that he doesn't come more often.'

'I don't see why he should. My father is rarely here and he was always the favoured one.'

'I've never understood why. Oliver is the conscientious, caring one of the two. You don't favour one of your daughters, do you?'

'I couldn't imagine doing any such thing. They have different strengths and weaknesses but I love them both the same. You will, too, when you have children.'

Should she tell her now? Esmeralda wondered. It was a golden opportunity. No, she decided, not yet. She stood up. 'We'd better get it over with and see your grandmother.' She had not told anyone that she was going to have a baby, but now it was only a matter of time before Oliver was telling the world – he was so proud.

'You look peaky,' was her mother-in-law's greeting.

'And you look well.'

'Don't be stupid. I'm seriously ill. How my son tolerates living with someone as silly as you, I've never been able to fathom.'

'Yes, Lady Cresswell. Of course you are right.' She had wanted to sound ironic but failed because she tended to agree with her mother-in-law. She leant forward to give her the customary kiss. How she hated to do so for Penelope Cresswell was an unattractive lump who smelt.

'Are you with child yet?'

Esmeralda chose not to answer.

'Why not? It's about time, isn't it?'

'I think that is my husband's and my business, no one else's,' she heard herself say. Lettice was looking at her with what could only be admiration.

'I beg your pardon? How dare you speak to me in such a manner?'

'Then don't be so rude.' She couldn't back down now.

'Then why do you look *enceinte*?'

Esmeralda could not speak French, so she did not know what she was being asked.

Lettice stepped in to rescue her. 'Esmeralda looks the same as ever to me, Grandmama.'

'You can't fool me. It's around the eyes – I can always tell. So why are you denying it. Is it not Oliver's?'

'Grandmama!' Lettice exclaimed.

'I really don't know what pleasure you get out of being so intolerably rude, Lady Cresswell, but I have no intention of staying here to listen to you.' Esmeralda turned on her heel and, shaking with nerves as well as rage, swept from the room. On the landing, she leant against the wall and tears tumbled down her face.

'Esmeralda, that was truly dreadful! She goes too far.' Lettice had joined her. 'Don't let her upset you. She's just a wicked, bitter old woman. Come with me.' Lettice held out her hand and led Esmeralda, as if she were a child, along the corridor to her own rooms. There, she sent her maid to get them some tea.

'Poor darling,' she said soothingly.

'I don't know why she hates me so.'

'Esmeralda, she's horrible to all of us. It was your turn today. She's always telling me that she feels sorry for Hugo having to live with someone as stupid as me. The trouble is, we all think it is only ourselves she is dreadful to since she rarely does it in front of anyone else, and never in front of our husbands – not that Hugo would care. But I've learnt. Try to ignore her. I know it's difficult but why should she make you unhappy?'

Still clutching her handkerchief, Esmeralda stopped crying. 'Are you telling me the truth or simply trying to make me feel better?'

'It's the truth. And I can promise you it's only a matter of time before she will be concentrating all her venom on me.' The tea arrived and Lettice was occupied in pouring it. Then she sat beside Esmeralda. 'If I tell you something will you promise not to repeat it to a living soul?'

'Of course.'

'I need to tell someone or I think I shall go mad.'

'I swear not to tell anyone – not even Oliver.'

'I'm in love,' Lettice said baldly.

'With Hugo?' But even as Esmeralda asked she knew it was a stupid question.

'No. With the kindest, sweetest man. He has changed my life.'

'Oh, Lettice, do be careful.' Esmeralda sat forward. 'If Hugo finds out, what will happen?' She had lowered her voice for fear that one of the maids might be listening.

'I'm going to ask him for a separation.'

Esmeralda's hand shot to her mouth to stifle a shocked exclamation. 'But how? Your life will be ruined.'

'No, it won't. I shall be happier then I've ever been. I can't continue to live as I am. I have to be careful but I hope I can persuade him, and not lose my darling girls.'

'Is Hugo violent to you?'

'No, but he makes me feel stupid, he has sapped all my confidence and he denigrates me at every turn. He has not abused my body yet, but he is destroying my soul.'

'Poor Lettice. I am so sorry. I had no idea.' He propositions other women too, she thought, but decided to keep that to herself.

'You need not feel sorry for me. I have never been so much in love or so loved.'

'But you must be afraid?'

'No – with Ramsey beside me, what have I to fear?'

'Ramsey, you say. He's a nice man. I'd noticed nothing between you.'

'We've been very discreet. But you do promise you won't tell any-one?'

'I promise.' She felt enormously honoured that Lettice had confided in her – it must have taken great courage on Lettice's part. And she under-stood her need to tell. 'Lettice, I can prove to you that I will never divulge your secret if I tell you mine. Will you vow to keep my confidence? Then we shall be in the same position, needing to rely on each other.'

'You can trust me.'

Esmeralda sat for a moment, collecting her thoughts. 'Your grand-mother was right. I am going to have a baby.'

'Oh, Esmeralda, that's the most wonderful news! But why the secret?'

'Oliver does not want anyone to know until we are quite sure the baby is safe.'

'But he is wise not to tell, and it shows how much he cares about you.'

'My dreadful secret, which haunts me, is that I cannot be sure that it is his.' There! The awful words were in the open and immediately she felt a weight lift off her. Someone was sharing her problem.

It was Lettice's turn to clasp a hand over her mouth. For a distressing moment Esmeralda saw shock, anger and disgust flit over her face. Then she stood up, moved to the door and opened it abruptly to check that no one was listening. 'You can never be sure in this house,' she said. Then she returned to Esmeralda's side. 'I thought you were happy with Oliver.' Her voice was strained, and Esmeralda knew how appalled she was by this news.

'I was. I am. I love him more than life.'

'Then I don't understand what you are telling me. Why take a lover if you feel like that about my uncle?'

'There was no affair, no lover. I was attacked. There was a man who had his way with me ...' And, slowly at first, for it was painful to recount, she told Lettice the whole sorry tale.

'My poor dear friend.' Lettice was immediately holding her tight. 'How could I have doubted you for a second? Forgive me.'

'But it's all my fault. And I am haunted by the horror of it.' She began to sob.

'Esmeralda, don't cry – you'll make yourself ill.' She fussed about her, getting water, handing her a dry handkerchief when her own became soaked. 'The first thing you must do is stop blaming yourself. It was not your fault. You did nothing wrong.'

'But I did. You don't understand. I flirted with him in an unseemly manner. He presumed—'

'You must not make excuses for him. He had no right to do such a thing to you. If every woman who flirted was attacked like that it would happen to nearly every female in the kingdom. He is despicable! He should be horsewhipped within an inch of his life.'

'I'm so afraid. Your grandmother knows – she has just said so. She read my guilt.'

'Nonsense! She is a malicious, bad-tempered old woman who insults everyone.'

'What if she says the same to Oliver?'

'He knows his mother – he will ignore her.'

'But I'm so scared.'

'Then you must stop being so. You will damage your baby, and whatever has happened, it is not the child's fault.'

'But, Lettice, what do I do?'

'Nothing. There isn't anything you can do. You will be happy, your baby will be born. You must put this misery behind you, and try to forget.'

'But how can I? How can I forget the horror and my part in it? If only I could clear my conscience.'

'Esmeralda, you can't. You mustn't! If you are thinking of telling Oliver then don't. What good will it do? As it is, he is overjoyed no doubt at the prospect of being a father.'

'But he has a right to know.'

'And do you have the right to destroy his happiness for ever? Dear friend, don't think of it, I beg you. Promise me.'

'I promise …'

7

'Do you like your new position?'

Rowan was bending over a pot of bergamot, which she now knew were called *Monarda didyma*, and she was proud of the knowledge she was accumulating. She had been searching for parasites, but the familiar voice made her jump and bang her head on a large bamboo that was overhanging the bench she was working on. 'Mr Morts! You took me by surprise.' She straightened, pushing a wisp of hair off her face. He leant forward and brushed back another curl. It was a light touch but such an intimate action. 'When did you get back here?' she asked.

'Last night. You didn't answer my letters.'

'No.'

'Are you going to explain why?'

'I couldn't see any point to it. I like you very much, but when you talk all silly with me, well, it's just plain nonsense and I don't want to be hearing it.' She bent down so that he could not see her face and guess she was lying.

'I see. Well, I had best warn you I will not give up. I know how I feel and I can't change that.' He stepped smartly out of the way while she moved the pot she had been tending and collected another containing evening primrose.

'They're called *Oenothera biennis*,' she said.

'Changing the subject, are you?' He smiled. 'Very well. I'll do the same.

I heard from my aunt you were working for her. Are you happy doing so?' he asked formally, but he was grinning.

'Very, thank you,' she replied. 'You'll never get me back in a house as a maid again. I'm in the fresh air, your aunt leaves me alone, and have you met Miss Sprite? She's a bit batty but ever so nice and she teaches me so much and she—'

'I'm sorry, Rowan – I can't keep it up. I've got to say that I'm so happy to be seeing you again.' He stepped forward as if he was about to touch her but she moved back. 'I hated being in London. I wanted to get back here so that I could see you.'

'I know about Xenia,' she said suddenly.

He looked surprised at the turn the conversation had taken. 'That was a long time ago.'

'But she's a warning to the likes of me.'

'What on earth do you mean?'

'About Xenia.'

He looked at her, puzzled. 'One day she was here and then she just left. I never heard from her again. She made me feel a failure and I lost my confidence for some time, but I was only a boy. Later I decided that learning how to deal with disappointments was part of growing up. But what of her? I'd forgotten about her.'

'Oh, it's nothing.' So he did not know that Xenia was his half-sister, and she was not going to be the one to tell him.

'Go on, tell me.'

She put on her sunhat. 'I've got to take these begonias over to the gate – Ferdie's bringing the wagon round. They're to go to a garden later this afternoon.'

'Let me help you.' He lifted the box.

'Thank you. And you could help me with the tubs of lavender and the hydrangea.' She would have liked to show off her knowledge of their proper names but she was so excited at seeing him that they had gone clean out of her mind.

'Do you think my aunt will pay me too?'

'No, but she might dock it from my wages.' Out in the sunshine they walked down the pathways between the bedding plants to the long trolleys by the gate.

'What is your job?'

'At the moment it's sorting out the plants for three new gardens. I have to count them and put them in the book so that when Miss Cresswell does her bills she knows who has had what. Then there's the inventory, you see. That has to be kept up to date so that we know how many plants we have. And don't forget the weeding.' Rowan pulled a face.

'And does my aunt grow all these?'

'Yes, and she's going to start selling the seeds of some of the plants.'

'And what does Miss Sprite do?'

'She's ever so clever. She knows so much about the plants, and when they're sick she tells us how to make them better. And she does the propagating. They want to grow a blue rose.'

'How do you do that?'

'Don't ask me!' She laughed.

'I love it when you laugh. Are you living at home?'

'No, with Miss Sprite. We have a lovely cottage. Your aunt had it built. It's so modern. We've a bathroom and a pantry and the kitchen is a room of its own. It's Paradise! Your mother did me a favour by getting rid of me,' she announced airily.

'Might I visit you there?'

'I'd rather you didn't. I don't want ...'

'People knowing?'

'Sort of.' Suddenly she felt shy. 'Still, what do I mean? There's nothing to know and never will be. There, that's them sorted.' She stood, hands on hips, counting the boxes.

'I was wondering if you would care to come to the picture-house in Barlton with me.'

'Have you not listened to a word I've said? We have to forget each other and how we might have once felt. Least, you did, I didn't.'

'That's not true, Rowan, and you know it. I promise not to talk silly, as you call it. We're friends, we like each other – what harm can there be in going to the pictures together?' He looked out across the garden. 'Unless, of course, you have to ask your parents' permission.'

'Not much point in my doing that. You know what the answer would be.' She considered the notion of doing something her parents would not approve of. She liked him, and being with him, very much ... and what harm could it possibly do? 'Yes, please, I'll come. On my afternoon off.' She decided there and then not to tell anyone what they were up to, and immediately began to plan what to wear from her rather scant collection of clothes.

Rowan had thought it best to meet Morts out of sight of the house and the cottages. She hoped she looked all right. She'd never been to the picture-house and was not sure what she should wear. From her meagre wardrobe she chose a long cream linen skirt that had once been Miss Cresswell's and which she had 'rescued' from a parcel she had made up for the waifs' and strays' home in Barlton. With it she wore her best white blouse. Upon seeing her, Miss Sprite had been very excited.

'A young man?' she had asked, rather coyly.

'Yes.' As Rowan answered she wondered if there would ever be a day when she didn't blush. 'Just a friend.'

'But of course. Am I allowed to know his name?'

'I'd rather not.'

'Is he from here?'

'Yes.'

'Then you must look your prettiest. Stay there.' And Miss Sprite ran up the stairs. 'Here,' she was hurrying back, 'that blouse needs this.' She produced a cameo brooch and pinned it at the neck. 'And this hat is perfect for you.' From a box she took out a wonderful straw hat decorated with cherries, daisies and red ribbon that hung half-way down Rowan's back. 'It's far too young-looking for me, but I love it so,' she said. Rowan agreed, and was happy to put it on. 'And this.' From another bag, rather like a magician, she pulled out a long chiffon scarf that was also scattered with cherries. 'There! Now, don't we look a picture? And finally ...' Holding a perfume bottle and directing it at Rowan, she pressed the gold-tasselled ball and a squirt of the most delicious scent enveloped her. The smell made her smile. Miss Sprite looked at Rowan's feet. 'I'm afraid I can't help you there – yours are so small and mine so big.' Rowan had on the most decent pair of boots she owned.

'You're so kind. Thank you.' Rowan kissed her.

'He will bring you home, won't he? I don't want you out late alone.'

'He will.'

'And ... I'm not sure how to put this ... You'll be a good girl, won't you?'

'I will.' And Rowan ran off before Miss Sprite said something that might embarrass her. She held on to her hat as she sped out of the gate and down the lane. Ten minutes later she made herself slow down. She did not want to arrive out of breath – or early, appearing too keen.

Sitting in the darkness of the picture-house she felt closer to him than ever before. They laughed at the same moment, and when a sad bit came she was almost sure he wiped away a tear. The music helped, of course, for the pianist was talented. When Morts held her hand Rowan thought she would die of happiness there and then. She had felt so proud coming here in his motor-car, the first time she had ridden in anything so grand. She would have liked everyone she knew to see her, but on the other hand she hoped no one had for they would rush to tell her mother who she was with.

When they emerged into the sunshine they were both blinking. 'That was lovely. Such a pretty actress. And her face was so big.'

'Not as pretty as you, though. You could be an actress if you wanted.'

'No, I never could.'

'Shall we walk awhile?'

'That would be lovely,' she said, although she wished he had suggested a ride in his motor – she could walk any day. They strolled down to the quay and sat on the sea wall to watch the boats come in. 'I love it here. Some of the girls long to get away and go to London but I never want to live anywhere else in the whole world.'

'Then you're lucky. It's a rare person who is as content as you.'

'But I have everything I need. I love my work – now ...' She glanced slyly at him.

'I'd hate to wait on people, and I hated seeing you having to put up with my family.'

'But that's over. And I'm so happy with my lodgings. I could do with some more money, but that's all.' She laughed. Then, aware that her feet were visible, she covered them quickly with her skirt. 'Please don't look at my boots.'

'They're a bit scuffed.'

'I know.' She bristled.

'Would you allow me to buy you new ones?'

She jumped off the wall. 'No, I wouldn't.' She began to walk quickly along the cobbled quay, which hurt her feet through the thin soles.

'Rowan, don't be cross.'

'You were rude.'

'And insensitive. I apologise.'

'I accept. Your apology, not the boots.' But she longed for new boots. She pushed him playfully, knowing she could not stay cross with him.

'Are you hungry?'

'Starving.' This answer made Morts grin. 'What's funny?' she asked.

'Your honesty. Most ladies would deny they were hungry.'

Rowan was upset, and Morts grabbed her hand. 'Don't get upset again, please! That was meant as a compliment.'

'We've a lot to learn about each other, haven't we?' Rowan said seriously.

'Does that mean …'

'Yes, I think it does. But I'm afraid I'll get hurt.'

'I'd never knowingly hurt you. At least we know we have to learn. And if I hurt your feelings, you must say so.'

'I promise. And if I upset or embarrass you, you must say so too.'

In the middle of the street they stopped, solemnly shook hands and burst out laughing. He kissed her then, full on the lips, for all to see. For her the world stopped briefly and she was unaware of anything but him. Then she ducked her head. What had he been thinking of? He should know she would not do such a thing, not here for all to see!

'Sorry,' he said. 'I shouldn't have done that but your lips are irresistible.'

'What will people think?' She grinned at him. She longed to feel his lips on hers again. Shyly she gave him her hand and they ran up the hill.

'I can't go in there.' Rowan refused to climb the steps that led up to the front door of the Victoria.

'Why not? It's the best food in town.'

'It's too posh for the likes of me.'

'I don't think so.'

'But I do. I'd feel uncomfortable in there. Something for you to learn.'

'Very well. Instead …' he looked up and down the street … we'll go to the King William. They do a wonderful steak pie.'

'In this heat?' She was glad he had not argued with her.

A few minutes later they settled at a table tucked away to one side since she told him she would be more comfortable there. 'If I do something wrong, there's just you to see, and I don't mind if it's you.'

'You could never do anything wrong in my eyes.' He picked up her hand and kissed the back of her wrist. It was such an intimate action that she blushed and felt happier than she had thought possible. They ordered their meal – he chose the pie he had praised and she a ham salad. She felt at home there because it was like the Cresswell Arms. Soon they were talking about everything under the sun.

'Tell me about your wife?' she dared to ask after he had mentioned her.

'She was wonderful, sweet and kind. I thought I would never stop grieving for her. But one day I woke up and knew I had to. That she would have hated me to be so unhappy.'

Rowan put out her hand to touch his comfortingly. 'It seems cruel that you should lose both her and your child.'

'It was. I raged at God for a long time – I doubt he was too bothered by it.'

'I don't think there is a God.'

'Don't you?' He looked quite taken aback.

'If I was God I wouldn't be so unfair. Letting some be happy and some be so sad. And some so rich and others so poor.'

'I believe in Him.'

'It must be easier if you're rich.'

Morts exploded with an infectious laugh. 'Rowan, you're priceless.'

For a second she looked unsure, but when she realised he was not laughing at her she joined in. 'It's true, though.'

'You make me very happy. Ever since I met you I've felt better just knowing you were here.' He took her hand and squeezed it. 'You have nothing to fear from me.'

'Don't I?'

'No. I will care for you and protect you, always.'

'Everyone warns me, Melanie in particular. Her life was ruined by a rich man.'

'I didn't know that. But you're not her and I'm not the rich man in her life. And I promise you can trust me.'

'I did not mean this to happen.'

'How can we control our hearts?'

'What would your mother say about it?'

'She won't like it, but I can't help who I fall in love with. And it's my life, not hers.'

She sat in a daze – he had said he loved her again! 'It will be difficult – and other people will try to make it impossible,' she said.

'Do you know what my old nanny Wishart used to say to me? "Young Mortimer," she'd say, "nothing in this life is impossible if you try hard enough."'

Rowan looked at him, her eyes full of her love, and felt confident that he meant what he said. That she really would be safe with him. She had tried not to love him. She had tried not to see him. She had even tried not to be here. But it was as if there was a conspiracy against all her good intentions.

D olly had been in Barlton for five days, which she knew was too long
to be away from her family but she had been so busy. It wasn't that
she wanted to be absent but that she could not turn away business and
her responsibilities were growing. She was torn between her obligation
to her clients and guilt at neglecting her children and husband.

The nursing arm of her agency had built quickly, beyond her expecta-
tions. However, with people's health involved, and only a sketchy knowledge of medical matters, it was an increasing worry to her. She lived
in fear that one of her nurses might harm rather than help a patient
– trained nurses were impossible to find so she was employing women
with only their experience to offer. She had also discovered that some
had a tendency to drink too much – brought on by the suffering they
witnessed, Dolly reasoned. She didn't want to think badly of anyone. In
consequence, she felt she had to check for herself that all was well, which
she had never needed to do on the cleaning side.

Everything took so much time. When she checked up on the nurses
she was often delayed by the patients' relatives. They liked to talk to her
and, she presumed, were seeking reassurance. She was always at pains to
explain that she only found the staff for them, but then she discovered
that with a well-chosen word or two she could ease their anxiety. So, she
had given up being honest and often pretended she knew far more than
she did. Once, having been let down by a 'nurse' she had stayed beside
the sick bed of an old man who had died in the night, and had had to lay
him out, which she had not enjoyed.

Although she missed her family on the nights she stayed in Barlton,
she found consolation in her bank book. The amount of money she
was saving, despite the expense of the room, was most satisfactory. If
only Zeph would agree, a private school for the children was no longer
beyond her reach. But he would never allow it, so there was no point in
thinking about it.

She was beginning to wonder if she should rent a house in Barlton
so that the children could come and stay in the school holidays. But
what sort of marriage would that be? She had to do something with her
savings, though, something that would earn her more than the interest
the banks paid. Property, she had concluded, was the answer. She wanted
to use her savings as a deposit, then borrow some money from the bank
to buy a small house and become a landlady – the rent would pay the

bank. And having purchased one, what was to stop her buying a second and a third? But when she discussed this plan with the bank manager, she was most put out to discover that they would only consider her proposal if her husband approached them. Since it was her money, and she had earned it, she thought this most unfair. And Zeph, she knew, would not agree.

When she was lonely, she talked to her landlady. Lily Freeman was always welcoming and glad of her company. Over the months they had become friends.

'Your husband is most understanding, letting you sleep away from home so often,' Lily said as one evening, as she poured them some tea.

'He works long hours himself. He understands.'

'Many wouldn't.'

'I know I'm lucky. But he knows I'm doing what I do for all of us.'

'Who looks after the children when you're away?'

'A friend. She worked for me here in Barlton, moved to Cresswell with us and now she's a friend.'

'So she's lucky too.'

'She's aware of that. She has a little one and, unfortunately, no husband so she has to work.'

'Has she been widowed?'

'Well, in confidence, I'm not sure. I've never liked to pry.'

'Of course not, but if she hasn't told you, it would seem she isn't. There's no shame in being widowed.'

'She simply said there was no Mr Snodland, that he was long gone, and I presumed he was dead.'

'Of course, it's none of my business …' Lily settled into her chair with the expression of one who feels it is '… but it sounds to me as if you should be wary. Of course "gone" could mean he's dead, but it could also mean he's left her and perhaps you should be asking yourself why. And if she's not a widow, and wasn't married to this Mr Snodland, she can't have any morals, can she? She probably brought it all on herself.'

'I suppose so.' As Dolly had had a shotgun marriage, she felt she was in no position to stand in judgement on May.

'Have you not thought she might be after your husband?'

Dolly laughed merrily. 'Oh, I don't worry about that. Even if she was immoral my husband isn't. And May knows which side her bread's buttered. She's grateful to me and always will be.'

Lily Freeman gave a loud sniff.

Dolly, however, was not concerned. She prided herself on being a good judge of people. Even the drinkers among her nurses had had good reason to turn to the bottle: they were good women who had fallen on hard times. May, she was sure, would not risk her security, and Charlie's, for a man.

Apart from missing the children, Dolly was content with her life. In fact, she couldn't imagine now how she had thought herself content as a wife and mother. She would *never* go back to those days.

'This is the life,' she said, as she opened her window and looked out at the moonlit scene before she went to bed.

May woke up and felt in the bed beside her, but he was not there. It always gave her a start to find him gone. She had lost count of how many times in the past it had happened to her. Her great fear was that he had tired of her and gone for good.

In the moonlight she slipped from the bed. It was still so hot – no wonder she had woken. She had no need of a dressing-gown but, for modesty's sake, she slipped a shawl round her shoulders. The room smelt of their coupling and she smiled at the memory. She must change the sheets in the morning, in case Dolly came home.

Dolly was an enigma to May, how she could put all of this at risk in pursuit of money. The woman was insane. Although she was grateful to her, and always would be, for giving her a chance in life, she felt no guilt at what she did with Dolly's husband. Why should she? If Dolly chose to neglect him and their marriage, May felt the blame was Dolly's, not hers.

She was not surprised that Zeph was up: he had tossed and turned last night, unable to sleep. She feared that his conscience might make him send her away. He had told her of the argument he'd had with his mother about her. She'd warned him that May might have set her cap at him. 'I had to hide a smile,' Zeph had said. 'Neither of us did any such thing. It just happened, didn't it?'

'Yes – we were overwhelmed with love, weren't we?' Ominously he had not responded to that, but she had hidden her own smile. Astute Melanie. Of course May had set her cap at him, and why not?

'I once tried to explain to her that Dolly and I had nothing in common,' Zeph said. 'She was not receptive to the idea.'

'But you and I are as if we were joined.'

Zeph had laughed. 'She would say that was romantic nonsense.'

'But we know differently, don't we?' She had kissed him. 'Your mother sounds as if she has never loved.'

'I don't think she has.'

'So how can you expect her to understand what we have, Zeph?' In truth May feared Melanie and what she said to him: she wielded a great deal of influence over her son. However, May thought it was a bit rich for Melanie, with her past, to stand in judgement.

'Zeph, are you there? she whispered into the sitting-room, not wanting to wake the children – Zeph's constant fear. There was no reply. She tiptoed into the kitchen, newly decorated and gleaming. She had worked so hard on this house. She had painted and scrubbed, sewn curtains and bedcovers. She loved it. But it was not hers.

The times when Dolly came back were hard to bear. Then the cottage became Dolly's, but May knew it was really hers. She hardly slept when Dolly was at home: her great fear was that Zeph, as a man, had lied to her when he said he no longer took his wife. That he no longer wanted her. She would sit on her bed in her tiny room in the eaves and listen as hard as she could for any sounds from theirs. She did not know what she would do if she heard them – sometimes she thought she would rush in and claim him for her own. Sometimes she dreamt that Dolly became ill and died; sometimes she wished that the train to Barlton would crash, or that a coach would run her over. It amazed her that Dolly did not sense she was unwanted and in the way.

'There you are. I was wondering where you'd got to.' May had found him at the bottom of the garden, staring over the hedge, lost in his own world.

'I needed to think.'

There was something different about his expression. A lost look, as if he was not here with her. 'Is something wrong?'

'No more than usual. It's strange, May. I can go weeks without being bothered, then suddenly I'm twisted with longing and bitterness.'

She clutched at her nightdress, fear filling her. 'At what?' she asked but dreaded his reply.

'Seeing what should one day be mine and knowing it never can be.' He pointed at the estate in front of them, the old house looming in the speckled light of dawn. 'I am bitter about the injustice of life.'

'It must be hard for you.' She linked her arm in his. 'I don't think I could be as calm about it as you.'

'It comes and goes.'

'But it's hard for you. Have you never thought that you might be better far away from here?' It was the first time she had dared to put what was a frequent thought into words. But what a perfect solution it would be for them both.

243

'I don't think I could live anywhere but here. It would be like tearing my heart out to leave.'

Then you'll have to put up with it, she thought. 'Come indoors. Let me make you some tea.' She took his hand and led him back up the path. The garden they were planting was growing fast. Next year they would be able to grow all the vegetables they needed. They were getting a pig next week and shortly a goat. She had worked hard on the garden. Like the cottage, it was hers.

She lit the oil lamp and put the kettle on the range, which she'd banked up for the night. 'It's too hot in here – you go into the sitting-room. I'll bring the tea through.'

When she carried in the tray he was sitting at the table, his head in his hands. She poured the tea and cut him a slice of the cake she'd made the day before. That was where she and Dolly differed: Dolly often *bought* cake, which May regarded as an abomination. And half the time she didn't bother with a pretty milk jug but ladled it from the large kitchen jug.

'It's hard to stop the milk going off in this heat. I did as you suggested and put the jug in the soaked earthenware pot, but it only keeps a day or two at the most. And the butter's rancid again.' She was chattering inanely, fearful of his mood.

'We can't go on like this, May,' he said, without warning, yet somehow she had known he would say something like this.

'I know, my darling.' She thought it best to agree.

'We are not being fair to anyone. The children, Dolly, ourselves.'

'Do you want me to go?' He'd listened to his mother, just as she'd feared.

'No. I've been wicked and you should not suffer for my lack of control. I don't know what to do for the best.'

'We can go on as we are. What Dolly doesn't know can't hurt her, can it?'

'But it isn't right.'

'It's right for me. I don't mind how we live so long as I have you. I love you, Zeph.'

'But what to do for the best? I wonder if I shouldn't tell Dolly straight, then see what happens.'

'Oh, you mustn't do that. It would hurt her so much and she's been good to me. She would hate me. And what would happen to Charlie and me?'

'I will always look after you both, you know that.'

'Standing in the garden on your own in the middle of the night is a dangerous thing to do – my mother always said thinking too much was bad for you. You've upset yourself – and how could you when we've just made love?' She was leaning across the table, allowing the front of her nightdress to fall open suggestively.

He groaned. 'Oh, May.' He looked at her, and she was overjoyed to see the desire in his eyes. 'You're right. You always are.'

There was no time to return to bed so he took her there and then. Later, she lay beside him on the peg rug as he slipped into slumber. She could not risk losing him and all of this. Perhaps it *was* time that Dolly knew.

9

'Do you disapprove?' Rowan asked Miss Sprite, as they tied up the large white lilies ready for dispatch to the Victoria Hotel in Barlton. The supply of fresh-cut flowers was a new venture of Miss Cresswell's.

'Why should I?' Emily Sprite spoke clearly, despite the twine in her mouth.

'You know. One of my sort hobnobbing with one of his.'

Emily laid the twine on the bench between them. 'You've always struck me as a highly intelligent person – if uneducated.' Rowan grinned with pride. 'So, as such, you must have considered these problems and what the eventual outcome will probably be.'

'Well, I have and I haven't.'

'If you don't mind my saying so, that is a considerably muddled answer.'

'The trouble is that in here,' Rowan tapped her head, 'I know nothing can come of it, that Morts will never marry me, but this,' she struck at her heart, 'won't listen to me.'

'Ah, treacherous things, hearts. I can tell you all about them.'

'Can you really?' Rowan's voice brimmed with curiosity.

Emily laughed. 'I suppose you think I'm dreadfully old and know nothing of love.'

'Well, I don't want to sound rude but ...'

'When you're sixteen, anyone over the age of twenty must seem ancient. Look.' She undid the two top buttons of her shirt and withdrew

245

a chain on which hung a diamond ring. 'See? You didn't know that this aged woman has a fiancé, did you?'

'No! How exciting.' She raced round the bench the better to see the ring. 'Are they real diamonds?'

'They are.'

'But where is he?'

'He's in the army, stationed in Exeter with the Eleventh Foot, the Devonshires.'

'My, doesn't that sound grand? Is he an officer?'

'A captain. I see him as often as I can.'

'Does he look handsome in his uniform?'

'Oh, yes ...' A dreamy expression spread across Emily's face.

'And when are you to marry?'

'Next July.'

'Why are you waiting so long if you love each other and, well ...' She paused.

'Go on, say it.' Emily was smiling.

'Well, you don't want to wait too long at your age, do you?'

At this Emily laughed. 'Oh, Rowan, I like you so much and the way you always say what you're thinking. You're probably right and, left to our own devices, we would get married tomorrow. But my parents are abroad and won't get leave until next summer.'

'Are they in the army too?'

'No, my father is a diplomat. He works in an embassy in India, looking after England's business and citizens there.'

'Well I never. I learn a lot here. And do they approve of him?'

'Not really. My mother's a frightful snob and hoped for better for me. But my heart got in the way, just like yours, and I love my Cyril and always will. So, she'll have to put up with it.' She returned to bundling up the lilies. 'Still, that's one of the advantages of being so *old* – no one can stop me.'

'But isn't it sad that she's not happy for you? I'm not sure I could marry someone my mother didn't approve of. It's the other way round for you – your mother doesn't approve of him, and Morts' mother can't be doing with me.' She gave a dramatic shudder. 'But you work, and my mother says ladies never do. You're a lady, aren't you?'

'I like to think so. It's a secret. My mother doesn't know I work. She thinks I'm staying with Hannah – she knows her brother, Sir Mortie. But I hate doing nothing and the money goes towards my bottom drawer.'

'Does your Cyril think there will be a war? I went to see my mother and it was all anyone was talking about.'

'I fear it's inevitable, but Cyril thinks, as most people do, that it will all be over by Christmas.'

'Morts won't have to go and fight, will he?'

'Bless you, no. The standing army will go, and there will be some enlistment, I expect, but they will be volunteers. He won't want to leave you, will he?'

'I hope not.'

'The thing is, Rowan, if he loves you nothing will stop him being with you. If others can influence him, he does not love you enough. It's the same with you and your feelings for him.'

'I'll remember that.'

When Rowan had first come to live in the cottage she had not expected to make friends with Emily; but when Willow came unexpectedly to visit she had cause to remember their conversation, and to feel glad that someone understood.

'Mum's worried sick at you walking out with his nibs.'

'Who told her that?'

'Everyone's talking about it. You was seen in Barlton, holding hands, and once or twice in the lanes. Did he kiss you in the picture-house?' Willow giggled.

'No, he didn't, and if he had it wouldn't be any of your business.' Which was true. The kiss in the street would remain her secret, even from her sister.

'You're mad.'

'I'm no such thing.'

'He'll drop you once he's had his way. His sort always do.'

'That's Mum talking.'

'It's what everyone's saying.'

'I don't care what they say. He hasn't, I wouldn't let him, and I don't see why everyone wants to spoil it for us.'

'They don't. They don't want you made unhappy.' Willow sat down at the small table in the cottage and helped herself to a slice of cheese.

'Who's talking?' Despite herself Rowan wanted to know.

'Everyone. I heard Mr Whitaker telling Mrs Gilroy that he'd heard a huge row. Mr Morts was shouting, he said.'

'Who at?'

'His mother.'

'No!' Her stomach clenched with fear. 'But she's not here.'

'He was speaking on the telephone, silly. He was rowing so loud that Whitaker said he couldn't help overhearing. We had a laugh at that – listening at doors, more like.'

'What did he say?' Her pulse was racing, but she had to know.

'That it was his life and he'd walk out with who he wanted.'

'Oh, Willow, he said that?'

'Trouble is, Rowan, did he mean it or did he just know Mr Whitaker was listening? It won't come to aught, honest, you and him. I'm only telling you for your own good. It'll end in tears. And I don't want you broken-hearted because I love you.'

'It isn't like that. We love each other but we're friends too. He's not like the other boys. He cares about me, makes me feel like a princess, and no one else can do that.'

'But look at the differences between you. You've nothing in common.'

'How do you know? You're not with us when we're together. He teaches me. He lends me books to read. He tells me about other countries.'

'Is that why you're talking all posh, like?'

'I'm not.'

'You are.'

'Well, I don't mean to. And he never corrects me when I say anything silly. Miss Sprite does, though.'

'What – that old spinster woman? What can she teach you?'

'She's one of the cleverest people I know. She knows lots of things and she helps me. She teaches me manners too. So don't you say anything rotten about her.'

'What shall I tell Mum?'

'She sent you?'

'Of course she did. I'd hardly be snooping for myself, would I? She thought you might listen to me.' This information made Rowan splutter, then roll about with mirth. Willow, too, was laughing. 'If only she knew how many I've had in my knickers, she'd die.' And at that they both collapsed in helpless giggles.

For once, Dolly had left for Barlton after Zeph had gone to work and had missed the early-morning train.

'Heavens, I overslept! You should have woken me, May.'

'I didn't like to, Mrs Topsham. And your husband said to leave you to sleep. He said you work too hard.'

'Yes, but it's worth it, isn't it?'

'It must be. You give up so much.'

'I'm determined my children will have a better start in life than I did.'

'How commendable.' May knew that Dolly would not understand the word but would be too proud to ask what she meant. 'Will you be back tonight?'

'Yes, if you could tell my husband.'

All that day May cleaned and scoured. Not easy with the children on their summer holidays. She was not sure why she was devoting even more care and attention than usual to her tasks – perhaps to keep her nerves under control. She had plans to fulfil. The housework done, she began to prepare the evening meal. She made a bacon-and-egg tart and picked some salad. Then she took a bottle of home-made elderflower wine down to the river and tied it to a branch to cool in the water.

The children fed and safely tucked up in bed, she went to Zeph's room and put her own nightdress on the bed. For good measure, she placed a kirby-grip on the dressing-table.

When Dolly arrived at just past nine she pretended surprise. 'I wasn't expecting you this evening, Mrs Topsham.'

'I told you this morning I'd be back. Did you not tell my husband?'

'I forgot. I'm sorry.'

'Never mind. It wouldn't have made much difference, the hours he works. I'll go and surprise him at the inn. I'll eat when we get back, some of that delicious pie you made that I spied in the kitchen.'

May watched her as she walked towards the door, her mind racing. 'What was that?' She looked up at the ceiling. 'Was it one of the children? I'll go.' She stepped forward.

'No, I will.'

'Are you sure?' But as Dolly left the room she allowed herself a quiet smile.

She did not have long to wait, heart pounding.

'Could you explain this?' Dolly had appeared holding May's nightdress between finger and thumb.

'That's mine.'

'What was it doing on my bed?'

'Your bed? I've no idea. Perhaps the children …'

'You sly bitch!'

'Please, Dolly, I've no idea what it was doing there.'

'Then this?' She waved the kirby-grip, for dark hair.

'I promise you—'

'Get out of my sight.'

May ran up the stairs into her room, locked the door and sat on her bed. Dolly had looked so angry and she wasn't going to take any risks.

She had to wait until eleven for the shouting to start. Safe in the knowledge that Zeph was back, she crept down to the landing, clutching a pillow, sat comfortably at the top of the stairs and settled down to listen.

'How could you?' Dolly began, sounding amazingly calm.

'I was going to talk to you the next time I saw you.' Zeph sounded weary.

'So you don't deny what's been going on? That you've slept with that whore?' May didn't like being called that. Neither did she like the controlled way in which Dolly was behaving. They should have been screaming at each other by now.

'What would be the point?'

'And what did you intend to tell me?'

'That I had been unfaithful and that I was sorry. I was going to beg your forgiveness.'

May sat upright. That was not what he should have been saying.

'And you expected me to forgive you?'

'I had hopes, yes.'

Why weren't they shouting?

'What has happened to us, Zeph?' There was a catch in Dolly's voice.

May rolled her eyes with exasperation.

'I was lonely, Dolly.'

'Bah!'

May smiled. She could imagine the angry expression on Dolly's face.

'You'd destroy all we have because you're lonely? Zeph, that's a sorry thing to say.'

'But it's the truth. Had you been here I would have stayed faithful to you.'

'Then it's my fault that you chose to sleep with another woman?'

'I didn't say that. Only that I felt alone.'

'You'll be saying "abandoned" in a minute.' There was irony in her voice. That was better, thought May. 'All I've been doing is trying to make sure our children have a better chance in life than I did. Is that wrong?'

'No, but I don't think it's the truth. You work as you do for your own satisfaction. It has nothing to do with the children.'

'That's unfair, Zeph. I work all the hours because—'

'Because you enjoy it. Don't lie to me, and stop lying to yourself. Have you ever stopped to wonder how your behaviour makes me feel?'

'But we discussed this at the time.'

'No, we did not. I told you how I felt, that I had to return here and I wanted you with me. You chose to ignore what I wanted. I should not have done what I have but it has happened, and now we must decide how to go on.'

'I want that woman out of our lives. She's sly. I told her I'd be home tonight when I didn't see you this morning. She purposely left her night-dress on our bed. She wanted me to find out.'

'I can't believe she'd do such a thing. She's a kind, caring woman.'

'She's not. She's cold and selfish. And I hope you're listening to this, May,' Dolly shouted up the stairs. May sat quiet.

'Of course she isn't.'

'That only shows how little you know her.'

'You've had nothing but praise for her until now.'

'I was a fool.'

Suddenly the door was shut and May was forced to move down the stairs to listen outside it, ready at a moment to escape into the kitchen.

'So, what do we do? I feel an obligation to May. I can't just throw her out. I would have to continue to help her.'

'I don't want you to.'

'There's the child to consider.'

'You must never see her again.'

There was a long pause before Zeph spoke. 'Very well, but I must find her accommodation. She can't be put out on the streets.'

'She'd be quite at home there.'

'Dolly, please don't. Charlie has done nothing wrong.'

'Very well, but not here.'

'And you?'

'I don't know, Zeph. I feel betrayed and angry. I'm not sure I can for-give you. We shall have to see. Now all I want is to go to bed. I have a busy day tomorrow.'

'Then you have learnt nothing?'

'I wasn't aware you were teaching me a lesson. Though I have learnt that you're not to be trusted.'

May, tears falling silently down her cheeks, heard Dolly moving across the sitting-room and rapidly made her escape.

'Eve! Hilda! Such momentous news! It's happened. The waiting is over. Our beloved country is at war!' Whitaker had made the announcement in his most important voice. His words boomed round the kitchen and into the scullery whence, the door open against the August heat, it carried into the yard. Willow and the scullerymaid, who had been sitting on the back steps, squealed with excitement and rushed into the kitchen.

'Well, I never did!' Eve sat down abruptly, her wooden spoon clattering to the floor. 'War. Whoever would have thought it?'

'It's been on the cards long enough, Eve,' Hilda said.

'Oh, Hilda, don't go on – you know what I mean.'

'We must go to Whitby, Edward. Immediately.' Hilda sat down beside Eve.

'Whatever for? Surely our duty is to stay here.' Eve looked at her with surprise.

'I've an aged aunt to care for. She'll be afraid.'

'Well,' Eve responded sharply, 'we couldn't manage without *you*, Edward.' She hoped Hilda would realise that *she* was not regarded as indispensable.

'I shall remain here, of course, until Sir Mortie divulges his intentions.'

'I doubt they'll come. And our duty is to my family, not to those who employ us.' Hilda, normally pale-faced, had gone pink with indignation.

'I should think it's highly likely that the family will return. It won't be safe in London.'

'Won't be safe? Heavens above! What can you mean?' Eve fanned herself with her oven-cloth. 'Surely you're not suggesting the fiendish Hun will invade?'

'No, of course not. But until our troops have beaten them into the ground, there is always the possibility of bombardment from the air.'

'The air?' Eve was aware she sounded stupid, repeating things.

'Airships, Eve. Remember, they are well advanced with their aviation.'

'Whatever next? The wickedness of them!'

'We need to make plans, Eve. Order supplies. We need an inventory of all we have in stock and how long you think it will last.'

'I always keep a good store-cupboard, as you know, but there's no harm in stocking up with more. I shall go to Barlton and make my purchases.'

'The bank holiday has been extended, Eve.'

'What on earth for? We need the shops open at a time like this.'

'The shops will be open but the banks will be closed to stop a run on money. People will panic about their savings.'

The colour drained from Eve's face as she thought of her little nest egg. 'Will our money be safe?'

'Of course. The government will be acting to protect us all.'

'If you won't come with me to Whitby I shall have to go by myself, Edward,' Hilda asserted.

'Hilda dear, we must not do anything too hurriedly and regret it later. We should bide our time.'

Hilda rolled her eyes and sighed deeply.

'Your husband's right, Hilda. I hope you stay, Edward. I'll feel safer with you here.' If looks could kill, Eve thought, she'd have been dead from Hilda's poisonous glare, but she ignored it. She bustled across to the dresser. 'I've already got a list of my dry stores.' She returned with her notebook, which she put on the table. 'But we should think of matches, candles …'

'I've already arranged a delivery of coal and coke,' said Whitaker. 'I do wish Sir Mortie was here, but I expect Mr Oliver will be over shortly. Where are you going, Hilda?'

'To pack,' she said shortly.

Emily Sprite was in tears when she told Rowan.

'Don't cry, Emily.' Rowan was still getting used to calling her by her Christian name, but Emily had insisted that she did. It was such an honour.

'I'm worried about Cyril. If anything should happen to him I wouldn't want to carry on living.'

'Oh, Emily, you mustn't say wicked things like that. Of course you would – Cyril would expect it of you.' She had never met the man so it was presumptuous of her to guess what he would want, Rowan thought. But how would she feel if anything happened to Morts? He wasn't a soldier, though, so she needn't worry.

'He'd be shocked,' Emily agreed. 'You're right. But how would I continue, knowing he wasn't in this world …' Tears stopped her finishing the sentence.

'Still, I expect he's quite happy,' Rowan said brightly.

Emily looked puzzled. 'I mean, if you're a soldier it's what you want to do, isn't it, fight?' Her logic seemed to upset Emily even more. 'I'm sorry,' Rowan said, and passed her a clean handkerchief.

'No. You're right. It's silly of me. After all, we've known for months that this was likely to happen. What about Morts? Won't he enlist?'

'Why would he do that? He's not interested in being a soldier.'

'Many will see it as their duty to sign up.'

'You don't think so? Oh, no. But only the other day you said that the army would be enough.'

'And so I thought, until Cyril told me that recruiting stations are to be set up. He will be coming to Barlton. I shall have to go there. Immediately.' She fluttered out of the room, her scarves floating about her like ecto-plasm, activity stemming the tears far better than Rowan's sympathy.

Rowan slipped on her coat and was soon speeding across the park. She had to see Morts. She'd go to the stables, see if his motor was there and leave a note asking him to come and see her. Her heart was pound-ing, she felt sick and her thoughts were in turmoil.

As she raced past the two monkey-puzzle trees she heard her name called. She stopped and turned to see him hurrying towards her. She fled to him, sobbing at the sight of him. 'Oh, Morts.' She flung herself into his arms. 'Please don't be a soldier.'

'Dear Rowan.' He was holding her tight, caressing her hair, covering her face with the tiny tender kisses one uses to placate a child. 'Shush … Don't be afraid.' He let her cry in his arms. 'Come, let's go back to your cottage.' He took her hand. She thought he had suggested it to get her away from prying eyes because he did not want anyone to know about them. But as they walked he had his arm about her, and kept stopping to kiss her for all to see.

In the cottage parlour they sat on the small sofa, pressing close to each other, as if they could not be apart for a second.

'I know you'll go. When Emily told me what was happening, I knew. I just knew.'

'It's my duty, sweetheart. I have to. I should have joined Oliver's group ages ago, but I kept putting it off and hoping the situation would be resolved.'

'What shall I do without you?'

'You must pretend I'm just in London – you're used to that. And maybe they won't need me.'

'But they will. You're just the sort of man they'll need – strong and honourable – more's the pity.'

254

'If I go, we can write to each other. I'll write to you every day.'

'I can't believe it's come to this. For months I've heard the talk of war, but I took no notice. If I didn't think about it, it would all go away. I knew it was serious, but not so serious. And for us to find each other, then be parted …'

'It's cruel, I know.' He put his arm round her and pulled her even closer.

'I don't even know where Germany is.' She was trying not to cry.

'I shall buy you an atlas and show you.'

She stroked his face as if memorising it. 'Before you go – if you go – I want to spend the night with you. I want to be truly yours.'

'Oh, my darling, what a wonderful thing to say. But we can't. I love you for saying that but it wouldn't be right.'

'You don't understand.'

'Oh, my darling, I do …' He silenced her with a kiss.

It was Morts who had put his head round their grandmother's bedroom door to tell her and Lettice that the country was at war.

'Such silliness! The Germans are such dears. Why I remember when the Kaiser told me …' and Penelope was happily reminiscing about her own glory days.

Lettice sat on the chair beside the bed and did not hear her rambling. She was transfixed with shock. They had all been expecting it, but she had put it to the back of her mind, not wishing to face the truth or the terrible changes that would come.

There was a knock at the door and the maid opened it. She returned with a silver salver on which lay a telegram. Penelope automatically put out her hand to accept it.

'It's for Mrs Hamilton, your ladyship.'

'For me?' Lettice's heart sank. She knew who it was from even before she opened it. 'Return stop Hugo,' it said. That was all.

'What is it? Who is it from?' Penelope demanded. Lettice said nothing, a multitude of thoughts racing through her head. 'Is it your husband?'

Still Lettice said nothing. Then her mind cleared, as if fog had lifted. 'I have to go.'

'Quite proper. Give dear Hugo my love.'

Lettice ran to her room and packed a bag. She did not call for her maid. She scooped up some of her jewellery and crammed it in. Then she sat at her desk and scribbled a note, rushed to her daughters' room and, without summoning the nanny, stuffed clothes and toys into two bags. She was unused to carrying anything heavy and the luggage banged against her legs as she hauled it down the back stairs and out into the stableyard.

'Ferdie,' she called, to one of the grooms who was having a surreptitious cigarette. He cupped it behind his back. 'Please harness my pony to the yellow cart. I'll be back within ten minutes.'

Lettice ran back into the house and the nursery, where her daughters were playing with their dolls' house. The nanny was sitting in the corner, sewing. 'Come, my darlings.' She held out her hands to them, panting. The nanny got to her feet.

'But we're playing.'

'Come! Hurry!' she snapped. It was the first time she had spoken sharply to them and their bewilderment showed on their faces. They looked from Lettice to the nanny, and the youngest, Georgina, burst into tears. 'We've no time for that now!' Lettice grabbed her daughters' hands and pulled them towards the door.

'Mrs Hamilton!' The nanny began to follow.

'I'll send for you later,' Lettice said, with no intention of doing any such thing. For some time now she had suspected that the nanny spied on her for Hugo.

She was breathless when she got back to the governess cart and bundled in the children. 'Give this to Mr Morts the minute he returns.' She handed Ferdie the note. 'Give it to no one else.'

'Yes, Miss Lettice,' he said, touching his cap. 'Would you like me to take you wherever you're going?'

'No, thank you. I can manage.'

She took up the reins, cracked the whip and the smart little cart moved forward with a jolt. Ferdie jumped back as he released his hold on the pony's bridle.

Once they were off the estate, bowling along the narrow lanes, her turmoil subsided. Away from Cresswell, Hugo's influence on her lessened. Her daughters were holding on to the sides of the cart for grim death and she slowed the pony. She had made the decision! She was free! But was she? They reached a steep hill. She stopped, told the children to get out, and led the pony – to her shame, he was sweating – up the hill.

The turmoil she had felt was replaced with realisation of the enormity of what she had done. She was afraid and felt desperately alone. If she turned round and went back, no damage would have been done. But she would face years of loneliness. Then a greater fear entered her mind: what if Ramsey objected? What if she saw in his face that he did not want her? Well, thought Lettice, she had only her pride to lose.

Two hours later she turned the governess cart through the gateway and into the yard. Ramsey was scything the grass at the front of the Devon longhouse, his Dartmoor home. His face lit up with pleasure. 'Lettice, what a wonderful surprise! And the girls too.'

'You may not think it so when I tell you what I have done.' She was suddenly sick with apprehension.

Ramsey turned towards the house. 'Phyllis,' he called. A young girl appeared from the interior of the house. 'Some lemonade for these young ladies, please.' The girls giggled at being referred to thus, then jumped down from the cart. 'Bertie!' he shouted again. A boy appeared from a barn. 'See to this pony for me, there's a good chap.' He held out his hand to Lettice. 'Come, my love,' and led her to a bench under a beech tree, the sweep of the moor in front of them. 'What has happened?'

'You must tell me honestly what you feel. I acted without thinking, but on the way here I saw how selfish I was being. You see, I've run away.'

Ramsey gazed at her with a wide grin. 'To me?'

'Who else is there?'

'Then I'm honoured.' He picked up her hand and kissed it. 'My dream.'

'You aren't cross? You don't think me presumptuous?'

'Of course not. But what happened?'

From her pocket she took the telegram and handed it to him. 'Not one to waste words, is he?' He laughed. 'But why so suddenly?'

'Living in such a remote place, as you do, you may not be aware that war has been declared against Germany. Almost immediately after we heard at Cresswell I received this.'

The smile left his face. 'I feared as much.'

'And I wanted to be with you.'

'As I need to be with you.' He lifted her hand turned it over and kissed her palm.

'Everyone is saying it will be over by Christmas.'

'I hope they're right.'

'You don't think it will be?'

'Who am I to know?'

'Don't try to protect me. Tell me what you think.'

'The Germans are well armed and prepared. We are not. I fear it will last much longer than Christmas.'

'Will you go?'

'I'd hoped not to, and I'll bide my time ...' He shrugged. 'But my home is yours for as long as you want. If I have to go I shall return, and then we shall sort out all your problems.' He leant forward and kissed her full on the mouth.

The bar at the Cresswell Arms was packed.

'Bugger all work getting done today,' said Robert, sucking at his pipe.

'I reckon every man-jack and boy from the estate is here. Does you proud, don't it?' his brother said.

'Makes me sad I'm too old to go or I'd be with them.'

'What ages are they looking for then?'

'Eighteen to thirty-five, so I heard.'

'Then we'll still be quite well staffed. Load of old sods, we are.'

'Phil Greenaway says he's going to lie about his age. Says they won't check.'

'The slates some are running up, they'll have to join up to escape paying them.'

'Heard the latest about the manor? Truckloads are on their way.'

'Truckloads of what?'

'Army beds and blankets.'

'Whatever for? There's no Germans hereabouts.'

'God knows, but that's what I heard.'

'Bet the blankets came from that man von Ehrlich's factory. Filthy Kraut. Making money left, right and centre.'

'Calls hisself Eldridge now, he does.'

'He can call himself whatever he likes. It don't make him an Englishman, now, do it? He'll always be a Kraut, stands to reason.'

'Have you heard? They found some Germans disguised as nuns over Dawlish way – came in by sea, they did.'

'They Dawlish types always had too much imagination for their own good.' Robert laughed.

Suddenly they heard banging and young Sol Pepper jumped up on to the bar. 'All of you, them as hasn't joined the Territorials, we've organised four carts. They as want a lift into Barlton are all welcome.'

There was a whoop of joy from the assembled company, a rush for the door and, like water emptying out of a sink, everyone left.

Zeph stood alone behind the bar. He was tired and worried. As if he didn't have problems, now war had come. If all the men went to the army, as they were saying they would, how could the inn keep going? His life was in ruins, it seemed. Dolly had returned to Barlton, taking the children with her, and he missed them more than he had imagined possible. She had gone to think, she had said. What had bothered him most was that she was not angry with him but reasoned and calm when he had expected tears and tantrums. It was as if, in a strange way, she was glad it had happened. He had always known she was ambitious but not that she might prefer to be a single woman.

He had kept his side of the bargain and told May she must leave. She had not stopped crying since. Each sob, each wail deepened his guilt. He had reassured her that he would give her a small allowance – but he could not afford much.

This morning his stepfather had collapsed and everyone, including the doctor, at first feared he'd had a stroke. Dolly had been to see Melanie and had told her everything, so his mother was barely speaking to him. Even Flossie had ignored his request for some tea.

He began to clear the glasses. If he joined up, no one could get at him …

Hannah, while horrified that their fears were now reality, telephoned to Dulcie Prestwick to discuss the plans that, for several weeks, she had been mulling over. Dulcie, it transpired, had been about to telephone her.

Alf was summoned, and Hannah, with a large bag of notebooks and pencils, made notes as they drove along.

'Bit of excitement, isn't it, Miss Cresswell?'

'I'd call it a tragedy. You must be so thankful that your Oak's still a child.'

'We are that. Flossie was in tears when I left, tears of relief. There's a lot that are looking forward to it, mind. Must say I'm glad I'm too old. Not that I'd dare tell anyone but you, Miss Cresswell.'

'Quite, Alf. It shows how intelligent you are. This joy at the prospect of killing fills me with anxiety. Have they all forgotten the Boer War and our losses there, the poor wounded coming home?'

'I heard as Sir Mortie's turning the manor into a hospital. Is that so, Miss?'

'A convalescent home for officers. There will be much for his wife to organise.' If she deigns to, she thought.

'That's good of him.' Alf negotiated the bumpy crossing of the railway line at Bottoms Holt.

'Isn't it?' she said, and hoped there was not too much irony in her tone. She knew Mortie. It wasn't patriotism that had moved him – he had seen in the gesture a short-term solution to some of the estate's financial problems. Oliver had told her how proud Mortie had been of his acumen in being one of the first to volunteer his property. 'He is delighted at the amount he thinks the estate could charge the government for the privilege of using it and the inconvenience to Mortie and Coral. My fear is that they will regard it as generosity on his part, which will only make matters worse.'

'But surely the government will contribute something.'

'Undoubtedly, but not as much as he thinks.'

'I knew I could rely on you, Hannah, to be one of the first,' Dulcie said, as she showed her into her private sitting room at the hotel.

'I thought the same of you.'

Four other women were in the room, all of whom Hannah knew, though not well. Two were pleased to see her, and two diffident. Since her incarceration she had become used to this – some people did not want to associate with a former prisoner but longed to know someone of her standing. She would have felt sorry for them in their dilemma, had it not affected her personally.

Once tea was served Dulcie took command. An hour later Margaret Flatley was charged with organising a sewing and knitting circle, with Dulcie volunteering her women at the waifs' and strays' home. Sylvia Proctor was to investigate arranging soup kitchens for those families whose men had enlisted. Daphne Millstone, a quiet soul, had suggested perhaps they should found a group to write letters to men at the front whose wives and mothers were illiterate. Hannah volunteered to set up a first-aid group since it was always best to be prepared. She felt better to be doing something, she thought, as she climbed into her car for the journey home. She had felt helpless earlier, but now she was full of ideas and energy.

As the car swung out of the hotel entrance she shuddered as she passed the park, the scene of her downfall a mere year ago. So much had happened in that time. 'What's that noise, Alf?' She could hear a brass band and cheering.

'I took the liberty while you was with Lady Prestwick to have a look-see. They've not wasted any time. There's an army sergeant and an officer busy recruiting already. Crowds, there are.'

'Such patriotism is humbling,' she said, despite her reservations.

'More like the pay they're promising,' Alf said with a grin. 'A shilling a day don't sound much but then there's the boot allowance and there's talk of a bounty.'

The car progressed along Gold Street. 'Stop a moment, Alf. I see Miss

Sprite.' She stepped from the car and waved to attract her attention. 'My dear Emily, what is the matter?'

'Oh, Hannah, it's so awful! All these young men are hungry to go and fight. It breaks my heart to see them ...'

Oliver was dressing in his Territorial Army uniform. He'd been instructed at the start of hostilities to report to Barlton. The war was only a week old and already he was weary of it. During that time he'd ridden over to tell Whitaker the plans for the house and to put in hand the necessary conversions.

'A hospital, I heard, Mr Oliver – though one never knows what to believe. It's hardly suitable, is it?'

'More a convalescent home, Whitaker. Perhaps it will never be used, but as a precaution my brother wants it arranged now. The hospital in Barlton could never cope with an influx. Of course, it will be for officers only.'

'I'm glad to hear it, sir. We want no riffraff here.'

'Tell the men to help you move the furniture from the gallery and the drawing-room. We should remove all but the largest paintings, take down the tapestries if it's possible and store them in the attics.'

'And the silver, sir? The Sèvres? The Ming vases?'

'I leave you to decide what should be stored and where, Whitaker – after all you know this house and its contents better than most. An inventory and the whereabouts of everything might be a good idea. It will be a long task but I know it will be safe in your capable hands.'

'Most kind of you to say so, sir. It will be my privilege. Mrs Gilroy has been worrying, as we all have, as to what will become of us.'

'We shall need Mrs Gilroy, with so many extra mouths to feed. And Mrs Whitaker too, of course.'

'Unfortunately my wife felt it her duty to go to her aunt in Whitby, an aged lady of a highly nervous disposition.' Whitaker spoke so stiffly that Oliver realised he had been badly hurt.

'It must have been a hard decision for her.' He had thought it the most diplomatic thing to say. 'How many of the footmen have enlisted?'

'Four, sir. But there are one or two sixteen-year-olds I've been keeping my eye on and they might be suitable to train.'

'I fear we're going to be less in need of footmen than help of a more general nature.' This news obviously wounded Whitaker. 'The beds and bedding have been ordered and should arrive either today or tomorrow. Rather too soon. I'd hoped we'd have more time to prepare.'

'And will there be nursing staff? Only I was thinking of accommodation for them, sir.'

'Until the beds get here we shall not know how many we're to cater for. I asked but no one seemed to know – I hope the war will be a short one. My brother will ask our sister to run it. We did not wish to frighten her by mentioning it previously.'

'But do you expect many casualties, Mr Oliver?'

'I'm no soldier, Whitaker, but the powers-that-be don't have the same degree of confidence in our military abilities as the man in the street. But I would appreciate you keeping that to yourself.'

'But of course. And your mother?'

'It should not affect her. Her rooms are fairly isolated, are they not?'

'Will Sir Mortie be returning, sir?'

'I don't think he's made up his mind yet, Whitaker. He's relying on us.'

'And we shall not let him down.' Whitaker had stood as poker-straight as if he were on parade.

Now Oliver was sorting the papers he needed to take with him. 'Come in,' he said, to a tap on the door. 'Esmeralda, what a fuss it all is.'

'Do you have to go?'

'Just for an hour or two. I must show willing.'

'Will you go to fight?'

'I doubt it. I'm too old, and they need people like me to rally the others. If I can I shall – I'd feel guilty sending men to do something I won't do myself.'

'If you go I don't know what I'll do.'

'Then don't worry your sweet head about something that hasn't happened.'

'But if you go it will be my fault. It will be my punishment.'

'What on earth do you mean, my love? Punishment for what?'

'Well, it's hard but you see—' She began, and was interrupted by a knock. It was Hannah.

'What was it you wanted to say, Esmeralda?' he asked, once the greetings were over.

'It was nothing,' she said, and wondered if she would ever find the courage to tell him what she knew she must.

Chapter Seven

September–November 1914

1

Lettice awoke in her customary position: entwined in Ramsey's arms. It was as if, even when sleeping, they were drawn to each other like magnets. Every morning when she woke she was smiling, and would not have been surprised if she had smiled all night in her sleep.

When they had first consummated their love she had expected to feel wicked and wanton. Instead she had felt whole, wonderful and a woman. Their lovemaking was a revelation to her – she had not known that such gentleness, such joy were possible. While she had been afraid of her husband when she was in his bed, in Ramsey's there was only delight. While Hugo had assaulted her body, Ramsey worshipped it. She turned over. Why spoil the present with nightmares from the past?

Lying here in this modest farmhouse, in the plain bedroom with serviceable sheets on the bed, was better to her than the grandeur, the silks and satins of her husband's home. A frown chased away the smile momentarily – she didn't want to think of Hugo … She must banish the memories. Instead she would think of the day ahead and what she would do with their precious hours together.

Hugo, however, invaded her thoughts, looming large and threatening. She was worried that his silence was prolonged. She had expected many demands by now, orders for her to return, or if not her, their daughters. She had expected threats and lawyers' letters, but none had arrived. Waiting for them, she had decided, was worse than having received them. He was playing games with her, hoping she would make a mistake and let him know where she was. Then, no doubt, he would tear the children from her and all happiness would be lost to her for ever …

Ramsey stirred. 'Let's,' he said, and he, too, was smiling. Gently she removed herself from his embrace, propped herself up on one elbow, and allowed her love to flow from her into him.

How much longer did they have together? Rumours swept the country and she had tried without success to close her ears to them. Each one fuelled her worries for Ramsey – he had not yet enlisted, but she knew it was only a matter of time before he did. She had heard, most alarming of all, that some of the Territorial battalions, of which the Cresswell Territorials was one, were about to be sent to France instead of fulfilling their role as a local defence corps, which Ramsey had told her was the original plan. There was endless talk that the Germans had landed, that they were marching on Barlton – although logic told her that it was an unlikely place for them to invade first. There were rumours of German spies everywhere, in all manner of disguises. She was constantly afraid.

She brushed Ramsey's cheek with the gentlest kiss; she dared not disturb him for then he would put his arms round her, his passion would transfer to her and they would be lost in love, which would never do in the morning. She slipped quietly from the bed, opened the door and peered out to make sure the landing was clear, then tiptoed along to her own bedroom. There, she ruffled the sheets in the hope that, to the maid, the bed would appear to have been slept in. She didn't want the staff here, small as it was, to gossip – in these parts everyone was related, and someone might have family at Cresswell. And it would be disastrous if her daughters, young as they were, found out she slept with Ramsey.

She gazed into the mirror, placed in front of the window for the light. She looked different, she thought. Her face was fuller, gentler, content, and she smiled at the happy woman she saw. The complete woman, she thought, and hugged herself with glee. A new world had opened up to her with her new-found passion. She had dutifully allowed her husband to invade her body but found that she searched for her lover, and longed for him to be within her. She could blush at her fervour in coupling with him, at the way her thoughts, even in the middle of the day, would turn to the night ahead.

Those rare nights when he did not turn to her were bleak. She could not sleep but would lie, listening to his breathing, willing him to wake and take her. On those nights another fear entered her heart and mind – that he had tired of her, no longer loved her. The next time he made love to her the fear lessened but always returned for Lettice could not believe she was so fortunate. She had convinced herself that her happiness would not last.

When she was like that he always sensed what she was thinking and would reassure her, but it did not help.

Why should he want to be bothered with her when he could have any woman he wanted? she would ask. He would tell her that she was the only one he cared for, who interested him, entertained him, loved … But, too easily, she could persuade herself that he was simply being polite. All she would bring him was trouble and worry … Her worries were his, he had told her. Why should he have the extra burden of another man's children? Her daughters were his, he said. He loved them as if they were his own.

How contrary I am, she told her reflection. One moment filled with joy and optimism, the next bowed down with worry and dread. She glanced out of the window at the sweep of the great moor that lay beyond the garden. Such a precious garden: it needed constant care and attention, wrenched as it had been from the moorland that threatened to encroach and reclaim it – like Hugo with her. 'No!' she said aloud.

From the cupboard she took out the simple linen skirt and long cotton tunic she had made and which she tended to wear here. In it she felt more like the farmer's wife she wanted to be, rather than the grand lady she had been. The silk and satin dresses of that life were tucked into the back of the wardrobe. Simplicity was her aim now, and she knew that Ramsey liked to see her dressed thus.

Downstairs, Phyllis, the young maid, who also helped with the children, had already lit the range. The kitchen was warm as always. The smell of fresh-baked bread filled the air. She whisked the eggs that the hens had laid and from the pantry fetched bacon that had come from Ramsey's pigs. She had learnt to cook a few things, scrambled eggs being one of them, but she would soon do far more for there was no permanent cook. A woman came in from the village and cooked for Ramsey when he needed her. Although the food she made was wholesome it was heavy, and rarely varied from stews and pasties. Lettice had found that her waist was thickening, and she suffered from indigestion, which was most unpleasant.

'Mummy, we want to go riding!' Charlotte burst into the room.

'Good morning, Charlotte.' She smiled at her daughter's enthusiasm, and cracked an egg into the pan.

'Go riding wiv Ramsey.'

'Good morning, Georgina. And you should call him Mr Poldown – it's more polite.'

'But he said we could call him Ramsey – he did, Mummy, honest Injun, he did.'

'Have I caused problems? If so I apologise.' Ramsey had joined them. 'That smells good.' He crossed to the range: the bacon was sizzling in the pan now.

'You're worse than your Labrador,' she teased him. 'And if you don't mind being called by your Christian name then so be it.' She smiled at him, but was already worrying what people would think if they heard the children being so familiar.

'It doesn't matter, you know,' he whispered in her ear.

'What doesn't?'

'What people think. We can weather it.'

'How did you know what *I* was thinking?' She turned the bacon over.

'Because I love you.' He picked up a tendril of hair and lovingly placed it in position.

She smiled at him and hoped he was not aware that she did not share his confidence. She knew that she would be blamed for everything when the gossip started. The woman always was. She suppressed a sigh. 'Oh, look what I've done!' She had just cracked another egg into the pan and the yolk had broken. 'I wanted it to be perfect.'

'I like my eggs broken.'

'You fib.'

'Does it matter?' He leant forward. 'I want to kiss you.' He leant against her and she groaned inwardly with longing.

'Can we see the pony, Ramsey, please?' Charlotte was jumping up and down and, within seconds, her little shadow, Georgina, had joined in.

'What is all this talk of ponies?'

'Yesterday I happened to find two little ponies for sale and, well, I suppose I should have asked your permission?' He grinned at her.

'That was very kind of you. Thank you. I hope they thanked you too?'

'They did. Still, we will eat first, young ladies, and then we shall go to meet your new friends.' The children clattered out of the room to tell the maid of their good fortune. 'I knew how distressed they were to leave their ponies at Cresswell.' They sat down at the table. Lettice had managed to crack and cook one more egg perfectly. 'Congratulations,' he said.

'I've so much to learn.'

'You don't have to, you know.'

'But I want to. Even if I'm not your wife I want to be able to behave as if I am.' She put out her hand to touch his. 'Silly, isn't it? I want to be close to you all the time.'

He squeezed her hand. 'Not silly at all, but if it is then so am I.' He took an envelope from his jacket pocket. 'I've a letter for you.'

From his tone she knew it had to do with Hugo and felt colour drain from her face. 'How did he find me?'

'He hasn't. It's from the detective agency.'

'I can't read it. Will you?'

She felt sick as she watched him open the letter. Then she saw a smile grow. He looked up at her. 'It's time we went to see a lawyer. He has been indiscreet, not once but several times. You have a case against him, my darling. Can you believe it?' He was pulling her up from the chair, and she protested that someone might see them. 'I don't care,' he declared, as he swept her into his arms.

2

Hannah was well organised and worked long hours but for all that she seemed to be getting nowhere. She looked at her desk where piles of paperwork waited for her attention. The problem in working for any government agency, she found, involved a proliferation of forms to be filled in and reports to be made when she could have been far more usefully occupied. This morning she had planned to do some ordering on the telephone. Two months into the war, she had learnt that she must not allow her stores to diminish because it was not always easy to come by everything she needed.

When Oliver and Mortie had asked her to come to Cresswell and help run the big house as a convalescent home she had, at first, resisted. She felt the task was far beyond her capabilities, but a sense of duty, combined with the persuasive abilities of Dulcie Prestwick, had made her change her mind.

'To help run', her brothers had said. Which was untrue – she ran it! Of course, she had staff to assist her but all the clerical work, decisions and planning were her responsibility. There were nights when, although her body was exhausted, her mind whirred with worries and niggles. Her greatest fear was that she might let everyone down.

Although most people were still saying the war would be over by Christmas, Hannah was not sure. So, with shortages beginning, she was already planning for Christmas although it was still two months away. Her men were not going to be deprived, she had decided – that was how she thought of them: *her* men. They would arrive, so young and yet so worn down, shuffling like old men in their dark blue convalescents' uniforms. Some had been shocked into a tragic silence; others' sadness could not be restrained; the hearts of yet more were simply broken. Her duty, as she saw it, was to mend their spirits, after the doctors had mended their bodies. Every morning she would tour her wards with a word for everyone. It was a joy to her when a soldier they had thought would never smile again did so, and she knew that he was on the mend. God alone knew what horrors they had witnessed. She never asked – she had no need to because it was in their eyes. Some eventually talked to her about their experiences, and she would listen to the unimaginable. She knew she would dream about it but she made herself listen. What were a few nightmares compared with what these poor lads had suffered?

It would be a strange Christmas. She had not yet decided the best way to celebrate it, given the circumstances. She had been stockpiling little presents for the soldiers – cigarettes, scarves, mittens. She could look back now and smile at her early plans to attend sewing bees and first-aid lessons. She had little time for such pursuits now and relied on Esmeralda to bring the occasional box of comforts for the soldiers.

They had been caught napping. When the war had begun they had thought it would be some time before they would take in convalescent officers. But the first were trickling through after the battle of Mons. There were six, a comfortable number – two were recovering from minor injuries, two had broken legs, and two more sudden deafness – but within weeks they were full to capacity with fifteen. And the degree of convalescence was changing: only last week two severely wounded men had arrived.

'But we're not equipped to deal with such injuries,' she had protested, to the army ambulance driver.

'That's my instructions, Miss. Two for Cresswell Manor Officers' Convalescent Home.' From his pocket he produced a form and pointed at it with a stubby finger. 'See?'

'That is most certainly the correct address, but I have no professional nurses here, no doctors.' Then she had seen the pleading on one soldier's face. 'Well, we shall just have to muddle through, shan't we?' she had said briskly. 'Whitaker, we should put these gentlemen in the small morning room. It will be quieter for them there. And if you could send for the doctor ...'

Dr Bunting had been a brick. When war was declared he had been preparing for retirement, but had attended with commendable speed. 'We must all do our bit,' he'd said. She had heard that expression so many times since August but each time it moved her. He had been honest with Hannah, had told her that dealing with such wounds was beyond his capability, an expert surgeon was needed, but he would do his best.

That was what they were all doing. And Dr Bunting had continued, for no army doctor came, and the wounded men recovered. One had even gone back to his regiment. That upset Hannah. Had he not done enough? The other was still with them, and would be for some time.

As she bent over her order sheet the telephone rang. It was the call she had been waiting for: the matron of Barlton Memorial Hospital.

'Your request for trained nurses, Miss Cresswell?'

'Yes?' Hannah crossed her fingers and waved them in the air at Oliver who had just entered the room.

'I'm afraid I can spare only one. You will appreciate that we are very busy. Sister Westall is highly competent and has experience from the Boer War.'

'Just the one?' Hannah's disappointment was clear in her voice.

'There is no one else. However, I can send a VAD and one orderly. The volunteer knows nothing and the orderly is little better than a ward maid, but she's very willing. Sister Westall, of course, will supervise them.'

'It's most kind of you, Matron. Should the position change, I trust you will keep us in mind.'

She hung up the receiver. 'One nurse, a volunteer and one orderly are all she can spare, but it's better than nothing.'

'I've been talking to Mortie. He's going to the War Office this morning to discuss our situation. I don't hold out much hope that they will listen but you never know.'

'Mortie was clever enough to get them to agree to his plan. Maybe he has skills in dealing with those in government that we are not aware of.'

'It was certainly a clever move on his part. It has enabled us to put away some of our financial problems for the time being. But when this is all over he will have some difficult decisions to make.'

'Poor Mortie. He doesn't think, does he?'

'No, and then he blames me because he's a bit short of money. Still, Morts is more aware than his father.'

'Did you know that he has been courting Rowan Marshall?'

'The whole estate is talking about it.'

'She's a pretty creature, and sweet, but hardly suitable. I shudder to think what Coral will say when she finds out.'

'Let's hope she doesn't and it blows over. These things usually do.'

'I wondered if you might have a word with him, Oliver. Advise him.'

'That would be disastrous. If he feels we're interfering in his affairs he'll be even more determined to do as he wishes rather than as he should.'

'It's such a worry on top of everything else.'

'He'll see sense eventually, Hannah. In a way I'm pleased – he's been a widower too long.'

At this Hannah gasped. 'You don't mean you think he might marry her?'

'No, of course not. But at least he's showing an interest in the fair sex once more. And it might end sooner than you think. There's a rumour that we might be moved away.'

'Where to?'

'Plymouth.'

'Where's the sense in that? Don't we need guarding too?'

'I suppose they think the docks need more troops. It will be hard on the men – difficult and expensive for them to get home on their pay.'

'Perhaps we could send a cart to pick them up.'

'Do be sensible, Hannah! How long would it take to go there and back? Six, seven hours?'

'Who will help the women?'

'We shall, of course. I promised we'd look after them if the men enlisted. But you will be with them.' Oliver looked at her long and hard.

'No, Oliver, I couldn't possibly – organising this place is taking all my time.' He bent his head to one side and smiled at her. 'You can't get round me like that. Why can't Coral and Mortie come and help?'

'Do you really think they'd be much use to you? They'd make more work not less. And hasn't Coral banned you? Imagine the ructions there would be.' He laughed.

'It's all very well for you to laugh. There's the doctor's wife but her lumbago is crippling her. If only that wretched vicar was married. Of course, there's always the schoolmistress.'

'Can't Melanie Topsham help?'

'I'm sure she would if she could, but she's never fully recovered from that bout of pneumonia and there are persistent rumours that her heart is not strong. Then there's her wretched husband, who's not been well, he's a burden upon her. And she's taken badly to Zeph enlisting. He really shouldn't have – he's too many responsibilities at home. But don't worry, I'll arrange something.' She was puzzled when Oliver laughed again. 'What's funny this time?' she asked.

'A minute ago I was telling you not to worry, and now you're telling me not to. I knew we could rely on you, sister dear.'

Both looked up at a tap on her study door.

'I didn't know you were here, Esmeralda. Should you be?' Hannah asked.

'I am so tired of sitting at home. It's so dull and silly me can't entertain herself.' Esmeralda looked well, and clever dressing minimised her size.

Hannah wondered if it was seemly for a woman in her condition to be seen out and about.

'I came to offer assistance. Honestly, Hannah, I can't just sit at home. There must be jobs I can do where no one will see me and my grotesque shape.'

'Oh, Esmeralda!' Hannah chuckled. 'You could perhaps deal with some correspondence for me. It seems to multiply in the night.' Hannah indicated the pile of papers. 'But should she, Oliver?'

'I learnt long ago that when my wife sets her heart on doing something she will do it whatever I say.'

Esmeralda blushed at the memory of how often in the past she had done just that to meet her father. Not any more, though. She had not seen him for weeks.

'How is your father, Esmeralda?' Hannah asked.

Esmeralda was startled. It was as if Hannah had read her mind. 'I hope that nothing untoward has happened to him with his Germanic name,' she went on. 'I've read such fearful reports in the papers of German properties being destroyed.'

'He has changed it.'

'I didn't know that,' Oliver said.

'Oh, yes. At the beginning of the year. He's using his mother's maiden name and is now Stan Eldridge – not very exotic, is it?' Esmeralda laughed but stopped when Oliver sat down suddenly, evidently shocked by something she had said.

'Eldridge?'

'Yes – he made up von Ehrlich in any case.'

'Are you all right, Oliver? You look quite pale.' Hannah fussed to his side. 'Eldridge ... Now, where have I heard that name?'

Esmeralda noticed that Oliver had clenched his fists.

'Oh, Oliver, I remember,' Hannah went on. 'It was Mortie, wasn't it? Sold someone some land? A Mr Buchan ...'

'Who was in partnership with an Eldridge, if the man Buchan even exists.' Oliver sounded bitter.

'But Mortie said he'd met him and what a nice chap he was.'

'Mortie can lie, you know, Hannah.'

'I won't believe that,' she replied.

Neither noticed Esmeralda sit down. Her side hurt and she massaged it, on the verge of tears. 'Not land again,' she murmured.

'Esmeralda, are you in pain?' Hannah was quickly at her shoulder.

'Just a little. It's just ... I'm so tired of these feuds.' She began to cry.

Oliver was kneeling in front of her, chafing her hand. 'Darling, please don't upset yourself. It's only a little piece of land. What do I care? He can have all of it, if that's what he wants ...'

3

Had there been a war a year ago, Rowan was sure she would have taken no interest in it. She would have considered it had nothing to do with her. Now, though, when war had been declared, her first thought had been for Morts and whether he would be in danger. He had reassured her, but she had listened to the rumours that had taken hold in the village. If Morts was going to be sent away from her, perhaps put at risk, she wanted to be useful too.

'I must do something,' she had told him, as they sat holding hands in the thatched summerhouse, hidden from prying eyes. 'I wish you had never joined the Territorials.'

'But I told you. We'll be on duty locally,' Morts had explained for the umpteenth time. 'It suits the government that we stay near our homes. Then they don't have to find accommodation for so many.'

'But what if things change and they move you away? What if you're all sent to France? If you are, I shall want to go too so that if you're hurt I'd be able to take care of you.'

Morts had kissed the tip of her nose.

'I'm going to find out if I can become a nurse.'

Morts had looked horrified. 'You can't.'

'Why not?'

'I wouldn't want you to. You might fall in love with one of your patients.'

She laughed at him. 'I could never love anyone but you.'

'Are we not lucky to have found each other?' He kissed her again, a long, lingering kiss that made her body ache in the most delicious way. 'But don't worry about me. We won't be sent away. The war won't last long,' he had said.

Emily Sprite did not think her ambition to become a nurse was a good idea either. 'The work is so hard, and not suitable for one of your age and innocence.'

'I need to do something, Emily. I enjoy working here but bundling up flowers doesn't seem important any more.'

'People still need flowers.'

'I'd rather be a nurse.'

Her father's reaction was extreme: 'No daughter of mine will go as a nurse. And I won't be hearing no more about it.'

'Why not?' Rowan was disappointed: she had expected to be praised.

'Those women aren't the type I want you mixing with, and that's that.'

'What's wrong with them?'

'Streetwalkers for the main part.'

'Oh, Dad, that's not so!'

But he refused to discuss it further and her mother agreed.

Only Hannah Cresswell was sympathetic. 'What a splendid idea. You'll make a capital nurse, I'm sure.'

So, Rowan had asked her to speak to her father. She knew he would never disagree with his employer, and he hadn't.

Her interview with the matron had been the most terrifying experience of her life, but she had passed the test and had been at the hospital in Barlton for over two months now. She was an orderly, a long way from being a nurse, but one day she would be, she told herself, when the piles of washing and scrubbing she had to do seemed never ending.

They were a motley crew. Some had a burning sense of vocation – she tended to avoid them since they were rather smug with a holier-than-thou attitude to the rest of them. Then there were the pretty ones, most of whom admitted that nursing was an excuse to get away from home and find a husband. Then there were the society women, who had joined from a sense of duty; they were the laziest. A few, like Rowan, had joined in case their menfolk were wounded.

There were a good twenty of them. The *real* nurses, as Rowan thought of them, were divided into those who welcomed the extra help and those who regarded them as a nuisance.

Most of the time Rowan had worked on the women's ward. At first she had been frightened and hardly liked to touch them because she was afraid she might hurt them. Most had problems with their *womanly bits*, as her mother referred to them. The bodies of some were worn out with childbearing. While she felt sorry for them she could wish they wouldn't cry so much. Most of them missed their children and homes. To Rowan, it seemed pointless to cry: they'd get better sooner if they didn't, she thought. Others welcomed a spell in hospital as a rest.

Then she was moved to the men's ward. It was crowded because wounded soldiers were arriving now. For the most part they were regular soldiers, attached to the regiment in Exeter, which had already seen action. Most were local men and content to be close to home.

She could not remember when she had been so tired. She started at six in the morning and although, in theory, she had the afternoon free, she usually worked through until eight or nine at night.

'Marshall!' the ward sister shouted. She was a fearsome woman, with a moustache that any man would have been proud of. When Rowan had begun on her ward the woman had frightened her witless and made her cry, but soon she realised that it was only her manner and that she treated all the nurses and ward staff in the same way and it no longer bothered her.

'Yes, Sister?'

'Change that apron, comb your hair and check your nails. You're to see Matron in half an hour.'

'Yes, Sister.' Rowan's heart thudded. A summons from Matron could not be taken lightly. She rushed to her room, which she shared with three others, quickly washed her face, did her hair and put on a clean, starched cap. Her stiff apron crackled as she ran down the stairs, trying to think of anything she had done wrong. If she was sacked she would be devastated. Hard as the work was, she enjoyed helping and had discovered a natural talent to care.

She had seen some shocking things: the stumps of a man's legs where the rest had been blown off – bloody and raw, like slabs of meat, they were. The first time she had felt dizzy and feared she would faint but had pulled herself together when she saw the pain and fear on the soldier's face. He was suffering, not her.

It did not bother her that she was more a maid-of-all-work than a nurse. She had resolved that, no matter how long it took, she wanted to be a nurse.

She spent most of her days cleaning the sluices, with their rows of urine bottles and bedpans. Recently she'd been allowed to clean instruments, and the dressings trolleys. Each day Sister trusted her with more.

Apart from the wounds there had been other shocks. She had never seen a man naked before, and was surprised by it. She blushed, then realised she had upset the man and vowed never again to reveal how she felt.

If she was about to be told she was no longer needed, she would have to find another hospital to work in. She was not giving up. Nervously she tapped on Matron's door.

'Come.'

Matron was always immaculately turned out – no crease would have dared to mar her navy blue uniform and crisp white apron. Her cap was a gloriously frothy affair of pleated lace. She wore a pair of gold *pince-nez*, and now looked over them severely at Rowan.

'You're from Cresswell-by-the-Sea, are you not?' Matron began.

'Yes, Matron.'

'The manor, as you know, is a convalescent home for officers. They are in desperate need of assistance. I am sending Sister Westall, you and Ferguson. You will leave tomorrow.'

Rowan absorbed the information. Should she tell Matron that Lady Cresswell had banned her from the house? But why should she? This was an order. Uppermost in her mind was the thought that she'd see more of Morts. She could have kissed the woman.

'Have you no opinion?'

'Yes, Matron, of course. That will be nice, Matron.'

'There are one or two things I wish to say to you.'

'Yes, Matron.' Her heart sank with foreboding.

'In my opinion, Marshall, you are a born nurse and you are intelligent, merely under-educated. I have chosen you to go to Cresswell since I think you will gather invaluable knowledge there. I hope that you will continue in this profession and become fully trained.'

Rowan's hand flashed to her mouth to suppress a yelp of joy. 'I don't know what to say, Matron.' She was grinning and blushing at the same time.

'Keep me informed. And good luck.'

She left the room in a daze. To be acknowledged! And by such an important person! It was far more than she had ever dared dream of. She was not too sure about working with Sister Westall, who was a bit of a martinet, but all the senior nurses were like that. If she ever became one she was determined never to be so fierce with the young trainees. She did not know Ferguson – she'd have to look out for her.

She tripped back to the ward. She'd be sorry to leave here – she had learnt so much – and to say goodbye to the patients, most of whom she'd become fond of.

The three women were squashed into the back of an army lorry driven by a soldier who, evidently, was not used to the cumbersome vehicle for they lurched along the main road from Barlton in fits and starts. They were sharing the space with a pile of equipment, which, at every jerk, threatened to collapse on top of them.

Rowan sat quietly, feeling as though she was in the way. Ferguson and Sister Westall were talking animatedly to each other, discovering whom they both knew and shrieking with excitement when they found an acquaintance in common. They both spoke with a cut-glass accent and moved with a confidence that Rowan envied. After a perfunctory greeting, neither had thought it necessary to speak to her, so she sat in silence and wondered why, since they were all doing the same work, they should think themselves superior to her.

Rowan had only seen Sister Ann Westall as a tyrant so it was strange to watch her being pleasant, as if she had a switch inside her that she could turn on and off at will. Rowan estimated that she was in her late twenties – old, in her opinion. She was in mufti, which made her look less striking, but she had a nice face, albeit dull-looking, frizzy hair. Ferguson was called Sylvia and was beautiful. Her cream complexion made Rowan aware that her face had been tanned by the sun when she was gardening. Sylvia had large grey eyes, and shiny dark hair. Like many fair-haired people, Rowan longed to be a brunette, and her own hair was a mass of curls, which she found difficult to control. Sylvia Ferguson's was sleek and held immaculately in place. She was only slightly older than Rowan, who offered up a silent prayer that she never met Morts. If she did, and Morts fell in love with her, she would hate it but understand: what man could resist such beauty?

As the lorry progressed up the long driveway to the house Rowan began to feel uneasy. What if Lady Cresswell was here? Well, Morts would look after her and defend her – if he was about. And then she looked at Ferguson and her confidence seeped away.

They pulled up in the stableyard, which, to her amusement, annoyed the other two who complained that they should have been allowed in at the front. They'll get used to it, thought Rowan, and jumped off the back of the lorry to be greeted by Freddie.

'Rowan, what are you doing here?'

'Come to work, that's what. Are you helping with the luggage? Do you know where they're putting us?'

'Up in the attics. It'll be like old times, won't it?' Freddie began to unload their cases, helped by a stable-boy Rowan had not met.

'You know this person?' Sister Westall asked.

'I used to work here.'

'In service?'

'Yes.' Why had the woman made 'service' sound like something not quite nice?

'Rowan, my dear, I'd no idea they were sending you. What a very nice surprise.' Hannah had appeared and gave her a hug. 'And these ladies are?' She looked at the others.

'This is Sister Westall and Nurse Ferguson – Miss Cresswell.' Rowan made the introductions.

'Sister Westall, we're in sore need of you. The authorities keep sending me wounded when we're only able to accommodate convalescents. No one here has any medical training, you see.'

'There's nothing to worry about now, Miss Cresswell. Lady Sylvia and I will soon have everything organised.'

Rowan was startled. A *lady*! Why could she not have said? That was it, then. She knew she'd lost Morts for ever.

'Are you the daughter of the Earl of Lairg? Then you will know my sister-in-law, Coral.'

'How lovely! She often visits my parents. How absolutely sublime!'

Rowan skulked, feeling even more in the way.

'Rowan dear, would you show Lady Sylvia to her room next to yours? Mrs Herbert thought you would be happy to have your old one back. I shall show Sister Westall her accommodation. Then we will all meet in the small study – you know the one I mean, Rowan – and have tea together.' She bustled away, the stable-boy trailing in her wake with the largest carpet bag Rowan had ever seen.

'Right, you'd best come with me.' She was pleased to see that Ferguson looked most put out.

'You don't mean we're in the servants' quarters?'

'Where else?' Rowan had the satisfaction of saying.

'It's quite a small house, isn't it?' was all she said, as Rowan led the way up the female servants' staircase to the attic rooms.

This annoyed Rowan immensely. For a start it was not true, and she did not like anyone to be dismissive of the manor. 'Hardly,' she snapped.

'Of course, it depends on what you're used to, doesn't it?'

'You're in here.' She opened the door to Mary's old room, which was smaller than hers.

'But it's ghastly. So poky.' Ferguson twirled about in the centre of the room. 'I can't stay here.'

'It's a roof over your head and much better than the nurses' home.'

'But I expected to be treated better among my own.'

'Then you should have a word with Miss Cresswell. It's nothing to do with me. I'll be back for you in five minutes.' She enjoyed saying that – it made her feel more in control.

'Rowan!' Willow was hurtling along the corridor. 'They told me you were back. I'm so pleased. But you've got no uniform on.'

'I'm just about to change. Come and talk to me.'

While she changed her clothes, neatly hanging up her best skirt and jacket, she caught up on the news. Zeph Topsham, she learnt, had enlisted, and not with the Territorials. 'What did he do that for?'

'Mum says to get away from warring women. He had a bit of how's-your-father with that May woman. Dolly was upset and went back to Barlton. Quite a to-do.'

'Poor Dolly.'

'Poor Dolly, my arse. She shouldn't have stayed away so long, that's what Mum says. But Melanie's taken it bad. With two sons in the army, she worries, and it's not good for her ticker. She's been quite poorly. Mum's having to work more.'

'I saw Freddie, he hasn't joined up then?'

'Miss Cresswell says as her needs him here too much. Nice excuse, if you ask me. Mind you he's got flat feet too.'

'Has he? I can't say I ever noticed.'

'As long as it don't get in the way of you-know-what!' Willow giggled. 'You're not still …'

'Promise not to tell anyone? We're getting married next year.'

'But that's wonderful. Why is it secret?'

'He don't want his mum to know. Apparently she don't approve of us Marshalls.'

'Why ever not?'

'Common, her calls us.'

'And what about Freddie, what's so special about him, then?'

'Don't ask me. Rowan, you look like a real nurse.' Willow gazed admiringly at her uniform.

'I wish I was. But one day I shall be.'

'And Morts?'

'I hardly ever see him now,' she lied. The less that anyone knew about it the better.

'I said it would never last.'

'But he didn't get in my knickers – so there!' She was grinning. It was good to be back.

A few minutes later, Rowan led Ferguson along the passages and down several staircases to the ground-floor study, which had once been the estate office. She knocked on the door. Having shown Ferguson the way she went to leave.

'No Rowan, I invited you too. You're an important part of our team. We've much to discuss.' Hannah shepherded her in.

As Rowan shut the door she thought she would burst with pride.

4

A month later Rowan's dream of seeing Morts regularly had not come true. He was not there when she had arrived because he had been sent to Plymouth. He'd been wrong about the authorities' plans for this group. Alarmingly, his letters to her had ceased. She convinced herself rapidly that he had found someone else and forgotten her. She had written twice to let him know where she was, but there had been no reply. She had been surprised by that – she would have thought he had the manners to let her know his intentions. She had tried to be angry with him, and failed. She was hurt, but she could not forget about him, let alone stop loving him.

Now she lived in fear for him, that next time he was moved it would be to France. She had heard rumours that some Territorials had been sent to Salisbury plain to train for combat.

She had been afraid before but since she had come here she was even more so. 'It's carnage,' one young soldier had told her, then promptly burst into tears. Rowan had not been sure what to do or say. Finally she listened to her instincts: she put her arms round him and hugged him. A young girl of sixteen consoling an officer of barely twenty – she was overwhelmed by the responsibility and knew she was grasping only a fraction of the horror he had witnessed.

'Marshall, it has been reported to me that you have been over-familiar with one of the officers. You do realise you could be dismissed for such an offence?'

'I was not being familiar with him, Sister Westall. I was trying to stop him crying.'

'You had no right to. You might be found in a compromising situation.'

'I don't think so.' She was incensed.

'Don't argue with me, Marshall.'

'Then what am I to do if I see one of them as distressed as he was?'

'You call for me.'

'But you weren't there.'

'Marshall …' Sister Westall said threateningly.

When she returned to her duties Rowan was seething. There had been
only one other person in the room at the time: Sylvia Ferguson. She
must have reported her to Sister Westall. The stuck-up bitch!

'Was it necessary to sneak about me to Westall?' She confronted
Ferguson at the next opportunity.

'I did no such thing.'

'When Lieutenant Feltham was distressed, you were the only other
person there so you must have told her I tried to comfort him.'

'Then you should learn to behave in a seemly manner and it wouldn't
be necessary, would it?'

The days ran into each other. Men she thought she would never forget
quickly became a distant memory within a day of them leaving.

It angered her that people were not told the truth. It was all brass
bands and triumph but she knew, from the broken men she dealt with,
that war was nothing of the sort. And the men sent here were not among
the worst cases – they went to the big hospitals. The soldiers who came
to Cresswell were convalescing after surgery, or had what the authorities
deemed *minor* injuries. How, she would ask herself, could a bullet going
through you be considered minor?

They were all to be pitied, but just recently they had had two young
men who could not stop shaking: they could not fight because they
could not hold their guns. Cowards, some called them; mad, said others.
Rowan thought their minds had been damaged by their experiences just
as others' bodies were hurt.

She was lonely. There was no chance of her and Ferguson becoming
friends – Ferguson had made it clear that she wanted nothing to do with
Rowan, and spent her free time with Sister Westall or Hannah. In the
evenings Rowan tried to see Willow and the other staff, but by the time
she came off duty she was so tired that she often fell asleep as she sat
with them.

'They work you too hard. Best have another slice of my pie.'

'I couldn't, really, Mrs Gilroy.'

'You need to keep your strength up. Cocoa?'

'That would be lovely.' And Eve was across the kitchen and boiling the milk before she had finished the sentence.

'Miss Cresswell told me that Alf says you never go home, these days.'

'I know, Mr Whitaker, but there's never time. I've only had a couple of afternoons off and I slept all the time.'

'They're going to have to get more nursing staff, aren't they? With winter upon us, you all risk being ill.'

'Miss Cresswell keeps trying to get more.'

'Now the nights have drawn in and the men can't sit outside, the pressure on the house is too much. The floors are scuffed and I had to remonstrate with some men who were throwing darts at a board – and missing. Call themselves officers and gentlemen!'

'Oh, Mr Whitaker, they are, but they get bored here.'

'Better than being in the trenches.' Eve Gilroy put the cups of cocoa in front of them. 'Tell me, is that Lady Sylvia being pleasanter to you?'

Rowan pulled a face. 'I don't think she knows how to, Mrs Gilroy.'

'Rowan, you shouldn't speak like that of your betters.'

Rowan snorted. 'If she's better than me I don't want to be her. She's lazy and sly and stuck-up.'

'She's a lady.'

'Then she hides it. Miss Cresswell's a lady and she's always friendly and polite.'

Whitaker coughed. 'It's highly commendable of her to do the work she's doing.'

'As it is that our Rowan volunteered,' Eve commented, in a tone that did not allow for debate.

It was raining. It seemed to have been raining all month, as if the heavens were weeping for the many dying men. Rowan was waiting in the kitchen porch, an old umbrella in her hand, for the shower to ease so that she could dash home. She had been feeling guilty about her parents, and the cook's comment had made her determined to visit them the next time she was free.

Then a figure dashed across the yard. She couldn't see his face but she knew it was Morts. She did not want him to notice her or the hurt in her eyes. She turned to go back into the house but the door was stuck. As she struggled with it his voice said, 'Let me,' and his fine, elegant hand appeared and deftly turned the handle.

'Thank you,' she said, in a muffled way, keeping her head down and her hat pulled low, while all the time her traitorous heart was beating with excitement at his closeness.

'Rowan?'

'Hello, Morts,' she said, in as lighthearted a tone as she could muster.

'What *are* you doing here?'

'I'm here as a nurse – well, an assistant, really.'

'How long have you been at Cresswell?'

'Over a month. As I told you in my letter.' She hoped she sounded dignified.

'What letter? I received no letter.'

'Oh, really, Morts, you can do better than that.' She stepped out into the rain and walked quickly across the yard.

'Rowan, stop. Listen.'

She was almost running when he caught up with her and grabbed her arm, the rain lashing them. 'I had no letters from you. You must believe me. I've been miserable with worry.'

'So miserable that you didn't bother to write to me.' She shrugged off his hand and set off again.

'But I did.' He was following her. 'I wrote you many times.'

She stopped abruptly so that he banged into her and apologised. She wiped the rain off her face. 'I haven't had a letter from you in weeks. I told the secretary at the hospital to forward any mail to me here but none came. I've been so miserable, I truly have.'

'Then what's happened? I thought you'd met someone else – taken a shine to a dashing cavalry officer.'

'*I* thought *you*'d met someone. I couldn't sleep at night.' She said this even though at night she was so exhausted that nothing stopped her sleeping. 'Actually, I sleep like a top.'

'Oh, my darling Rowan! You're so funny.' And there in the yard, for everyone to see, he picked her up and twirled her round so that she had to hang on for dear life to her soaking hat. 'Where are you going? Stay and talk.'

'I can't – I've got to visit my mother. I hardly see her.'

'Can I come too?'

'If you like.'

She felt ridiculously proud sitting beside him in his motor-car, which was silly since she had been in it before. But now they were at the manor. She longed to meet Sylvia Ferguson so that she would see her with Morts. Unfortunately, with all this rain, there was little likelihood of her being outside.

'And very smart you look in your uniform, Mr Morts.' Her mother had sat them down in the kitchen at the inn with tea and her seed cake, which no one could resist.

'I still don't feel like a proper soldier.'

'How is everyone?'

'Young Sol Pepper's doing well. He'll make corporal soon. And Herbie Robertson is the best shot we have. My uncle's doing well too. In fact, we all are. It's a bit dull, though. Sentry duty mainly and endless marching. I've never understood why the army set such store by marching. Mrs Marshall, this cake surpasses any I've ever eaten before.'

Flossie acknowledged the compliment. 'And what do you think of our Rowan?'

'You must be very proud of her, Mrs Marshall. The men she cares for are most fortunate. And doesn't she look smart in her uniform?' He looked at her with such love that Rowan glanced nervously at her mother to see if she had noticed.

'The news from France isn't good, is it?' was all Flossie said.

'There weren't enough in the expeditionary force, but the recruitment is going well. Lord Kitchener wants a million and a half men. We're lucky our countrymen are so patriotic.'

'Or in need of the money,' Flossie said.

'I'm sorry, Mrs Marshall?'

'More cake, Morts?' Rowan interrupted, and glared at her mother.

'How's your grandmother?' Flossie enquired.

'I've not had time to see her yet – I only got here an hour ago.' He grinned at Rowan. 'But I doubt there's much change.'

Rowan felt uncomfortable, as if she didn't belong here any more. All she wanted was to be alone with him for the few precious moments she had left before she was due on duty.

'Let's not go back yet,' he said, when they had taken their leave. 'Let's go to the summerhouse.'

She needed no second bidding.

They were late. Rowan was flustered as she stood in the hall at Cresswell Manor, rainwater dripping off her umbrella. She could not have chosen a worse time to return with him for Sylvia Ferguson was walking down the main staircase, immaculate in her tailored uniform. She paused at the sight of them. Rowan turned her back, aware that Morts had seen Ferguson, and made a fuss of removing her sodden coat.

'Aren't you going to introduce me, Rowan?' she heard the hateful voice say.

'This is Ferguson, Morts. I work with her.' She had no intention of doing it properly.

'Sylvia Ferguson, actually.' She held out her hand in the slow, languorous way that Rowan hated yet admired. 'Our parents know each other I don't know why we've never met.'

Morts shook her hand. Rowan dared not look – she didn't want to see the expression of interest that must surely be in his eyes. She stood awkwardly, knowing she should go but afraid to leave him.

'You're wanted upstairs,' Ferguson told her, and Rowan turned to go.

'Wait a minute, Rowan. I want us both to go and see Aunt Hannah.' He took her hand, politely excused himself and led her towards Hannah's office.

'Morts, what a delightful surprise!' Hannah welcomed him with a kiss.

'Aunt Hannah, Rowan is missing some letters,' he said, when the pleasantries were over. 'They would have been forwarded here from Barlton Memorial Hospital. Do you know anything about them?' he asked, in a clipped, stern voice. His aunt blushed. 'As I thought. I would like her to have them now.' He held out his hand. Rowan did not know what to do with herself – she was embarrassed, scared and proud, a mixture of confusion.

Hannah took a key from the bunch on her desk and opened a drawer, took out a small pile of unopened letters and handed them to Rowan without looking at her.

'Thank you,' Rowan said.

'And the ones that Rowan put out to be posted to me.' He held out his hand again. The process with the drawer was repeated. He took possession of two envelopes. 'Thank you, Aunt.'

'I did it for the best, Morts. For both of you.' She looked close to tears.

'We will decide what is best for us, not you, Aunt Hannah, if you don't mind.'

If Rowan had dropped dead at that point she knew she could not have died happier.

'Esmeralda, I'm so pleased you popped in – I need to talk to some-one. I've done the most dreadful thing.' Hannah sat down behind her desk. She looked haggard.

'You, of all people, do something dreadful? I can't imagine such a thing!' Esmeralda laughed as she smoothed her skirt, adjusted the large woollen cardigan she was wearing as camouflage, and sat down in the armchair set in front of Hannah. 'Oh dear, you're being serious. Forgive me for being so flippant.' Now Esmeralda was worried too.

'I thought I was doing it for the best.'

'Of course you did,' Esmeralda cooed, and thought that when people said that, they meant they had been interfering.

'It's Morts. I fear he's making the most dreadful mistake and I was try-ing to protect him.' Hannah gazed out of the window. Esmeralda waited patiently. She was aware that a confidence couldn't be hurried. 'I inter-cepted and hid some letters he had written to a young woman, and some from her to him …' She trailed off into silence.

Esmeralda waited. 'But why?' she ventured, when it became clear that Hannah would say no more without prompting.

'He is too interested in her and it would not be right. Not for him. I thought if I took the letters they would both think the other no longer cared and forget each other.'

'And they didn't?'

'No. They met here, and Morts realised what must have happened and asked me and, of course, I could not lie.'

'Of course not.' Esmeralda wished Hannah had not chosen her to con-fide in. Her sympathy was already with the young lovers. 'And who is the young woman, if I might ask?'

'She's a nurse.'

'Well, I don't see a problem.'

'She was once a maid here.'

'Oh.'

'At the time I thought it was a flirtation. But Coral was suspicious and dismissed the girl. I thought that was a mistake – it simply made them more determined. And you know what men are like. No doubt he would have tired of her if Coral had not acted so hurriedly. Inadvert-ently I encouraged them by giving her employment in my greenhouses, sufficiently far from the house for them not to meet, I thought. After all, when has Morts shown any interest in gardening?' She laughed hollowly. 'And he was so rarely here. But they met again – perhaps he sought her out, I don't know … I'd no idea. Which was naïve of me.' She was talking quickly, as if she had been bottling up this tale and needed to rid herself of it.

'Which maid?'

'Rowan Marshall.'

'She's very beautiful, so it's hardly surprising.'

'But she's not suitable to be his wife. I was worried for Rowan too …' she added.

'It seems harsh, though … I mean, if they love each other. Have you forgotten that I was regarded as unsuitable – why, Oliver and I had to elope …'

'That was more to do with your father than with Oliver's family.' Hannah almost bristled. 'And you had been brought up to know how to behave.'

'And there are times still when I feel that I am an outcast.'

'Not as far as I am concerned, I assure you.' Hannah looked distressed. 'Who?'

'Coral and Lady Penelope.'

'No one would ever suit either of them.'

'Perhaps Rowan could be educated.'

'I doubt that would be possible.'

'Morts is an exceptional young man. As far as I've gathered, he has shown no interest in anyone else since his wife died. If he has found love again, he won't give it up easily.'

'But what will Coral say?'

'It's Morts' life, not his mother's.' But she hoped she would not be there when Coral found out.

'But his duty is, first, to his family and his responsibilities. You can be so exasperating at times, Esmeralda.'

'Because of my own unsuitability, I expect.' She laughed to let Hannah think that she was joking. She had no intention of arguing with her.

'Perhaps if I hadn't hidden the letters …' Hannah said wistfully.

'We shall never know, shall we? I'm sure you meant well.' The three most depressing words in the English language, she thought. 'But if he's determined to be with her then we should help her.'

'You don't think he *is* thinking of marrying her, do you?'

'I thought that was what we were discussing. I'm sorry – if he was considering taking her as a mistress, you would hardly be worrying.'

'Esmeralda! I never expected to hear you speak of such matters.' Hannah was evidently embarrassed at the turn in the conversation and shifted papers on her desk abstractedly.

'I'm sorry, I didn't mean to offend you. Let's talk of other matters. Let's worry about Morts later. Are you still planning your gardens? Oliver was wondering.'

'No. I can't. This is hardly the right time to concentrate on such things.'

'Then how are you?'

'Overworked.' But she smiled. 'We have fifteen officers now, but since another delivery of beds has been made the numbers will increase again.'

'Word has travelled of how well you care for the poor men.'

'It's difficult, but I'm enjoying it. And I feel bad about it – how can I enjoy others' pain? Life is so complex, isn't it?'

'Very.' Esmeralda shuddered at the image Hannah's comment produced in her mind.

'Are you cold? You shivered.'

'It's nothing. Someone must have walked over my grave.'

'Don't say such a thing! How are you? I should have asked before I burdened you with my problems – but you seem positively blooming.'

Esmeralda had caught a hint of regret in her voice. 'I'm very well, thank you, though the way Oliver behaves you would think I was an invalid. He treats me like a piece of china. I tell him I'm restless and need not sit around like a turnip.'

'He's looking after you because he loves you.'

Esmeralda didn't agree with that. Although she enjoyed the fuss Oliver made of her, she thought it was the idea of the baby he loved, not her.

'Does he get back from Plymouth often?'

'Every weekend. I'm in charge of the estate during the week, not that I'm very good at it. All the letters and figures make my head reel. He says they might be moved to Salisbury plain after Christmas.'

'Oh …' Hannah paused. Then, 'How is your father?' she asked.

'I don't see him any more.'

'I trust you have not had a disagreement?'

'Oliver is still so grumpy about that piece of land Papa bought from Mortie. There's so much – does it really matter who owns which little bit?'

'It's unreasonable of Oliver to expect you to cut ties with your father.'

'He doesn't. I feel that I should be loyal to my husband over all others.'

'That's different. But I would give everything I own for five minutes with my own dear father. All I have left, it sometimes seems, is little Cariad, and she grows so old.' The dog, who was always with her, wagged her tail and fell asleep again.

'It's hard when they die, isn't it? I thought I would never stop crying when I lost my Mr Woo, but now I have Blossom and all is well again.' Esmeralda was glad that the conversation had moved on to a safer topic.

'I can't even think about ... you know ...' Hannah gazed fondly at her dog. 'It will be a strange Christmas,' she said suddenly.

'Won't it? Will Coral and Mortie be here?'

'Don't tell anyone, but I hope not. Coral didn't just ban Rowan from the house, she banned me too.'

'But you have the authorities behind you. She won't dare ask you to leave.'

'I trust you're right. It would be horrible if I had to desert my dear officers. Are you here to help me?'

'I am. Any letters – that's all I'm any good at and then not very. But, also, last week there was a young man here who couldn't see. I said I'd come back to read to him.'

'That will be Captain Roger. How kind of you.'

'I thought he'd be most suitable for me since he won't be able to see my condition, will he?'

Esmeralda had read to Captain Roger – a charming young man whose acceptance of his blindness, caused by a shell, was humbling. It did her good to come here and see their suffering: it made her take stock of her own life. It was not the perfect one she had hoped for – Fate and Petroc had seen to that – but even then it would never have been perfect because she loved Oliver far more than he did her. Someone had told her once that equal love never existed in a partnership, that one party always loved more than the other. If it was true, it was sad.

Every day she fought with herself over what to do about the truth and the baby. Logic told her she should keep it to herself, as Lettice had advocated. But something else said she should confess.

Esmeralda was about to leave for home when Lettice arrived, fresh-faced and happier than she had seemed in years. 'My dear, you're glowing. What has happened? Where have you been?'

'I would tell you if I could, but I must keep my secret for the time being. The wonderful news is that I am to be separated from Hugo. He does not object – in fact, wishes it to be so.'

'How confusing! I'm not sure if I should be happy or sad for you.'

'Happy, please. I know I shall be a pariah in society, but I don't give a fig for that.'

'But what about your girls? When they come to marry, won't their chances of a good match be ruined? Excuse me, Lettice, but I must speak my mind, even if I have to say disagreeable things.'

'I'm glad you feel you can. It means you are a true friend. They are young, and when they marry it will not matter what their parents did or didn't do.'

Esmeralda nodded as if in agreement, but she was far from sure. She couldn't see society changing that much. And Lettice had never seen how cruel it could be, as one who was on its outskirts could.

'Hugo has a new love and I'm happy for him, if it gives him the contentment he could not find with me. They wish to marry, but her father would never countenance her husband having been divorced. So until he dies they have to play a charade.'

'How calculating and cold it makes her sound. Are you returning home?'

'Not yet. I came to see Aunt Hannah to ask if I could help. I've done a course in first aid and I might be of some use to her.'

'She will welcome you with open arms. But when you've seen her, join me for tea. There is something I wish to discuss with you.'

'Not about the ...'

'No, nothing like that. I've taken your advice.'

While Esmeralda waited for Lettice she wondered where Ramsey was. When Lettice had run away, Oliver had guessed that she had joined him. He was angry with his niece, but Esmeralda could not be, not where love was an issue. She did not share Lettice's belief that Hugo had acquiesced so easily and was sure that trouble lay ahead. He might not want his daughters, but he would take them if he thought it would make Lettice unhappy.

The door opened and Lettice came in. 'Aunt Hannah is overjoyed, just as you said she would be. I've arranged to come on three days a week. I can't leave the girls for longer than that.'

Or Ramsey, thought Esmeralda.

'I've a plan,' said Esmeralda. 'Morts has fallen in love with one of the maids.'

'Rowan. I feared as much.' Lettice was duly shocked. 'How could he be such a fool? Mother will be beside herself.'

'I know, and I think it is so sad. The poor girl can't help being what she is, but what if we change her?'

'What do you mean?'

'We could help Rowan. Teach her how to speak, dress. After all, we were taught when we were young, weren't we? If we do that, people will not be nearly as horrible to her, will they, if Morts decides to stay with her?'

'There are times, Esmeralda, when you shame me with your thoughtfulness.'

6

Dolly had been feeling guilty about Melanie, which, in the circumstances, seemed unfair. She should be Zeph's responsibility, not hers. But Melanie was the children's grandmother and had always been kind to her, so she should go and see how she was – not that she would stay, oh, no.

'Why are we going to Cress? I don't want to go.' Apollo, who had been playing chess with one of his schoolfriends, was reluctant to leave his game.

'Because we have to. Del, change your pinny, that one's filthy. We'll go for the night and be back here tomorrow. Flossie Marshall has written to tell me that your granny isn't well.'

The train journey distracted the children. Dolly gazed out of the window, but did not see the passing landscape. She was still seething with anger at Zeph. Not only had he betrayed her with May, he had joined the army. He hadn't deigned to mention his plans to her – he'd thought only of himself, not his responsibilities. How was she supposed to manage on the pittance he was paid? Now her business, which he so hated, would be a life-saver. And it was not just her and his children he had let down but his mother too. She used to think Zeph was the least selfish man she could ever meet, but not now.

As it was, Sunday was the one day in the week when she had time to catch up with her household chores. It was a wicked thing, but this war had doubled her business overnight. Maids had left their employers in droves and gone to work at the factory in Barlton or even further afield – she'd heard of several who had gone to the munitions factory at Woolwich, wherever that was – so never a day went past without her acquiring new clients. Even Miss Cresswell had called upon her, asking for nursing aides. Yet although she was making more money than she had ever thought possible, it did not stop her being annoyed over Zeph's paltry contribution to the family upkeep. Despite her increased earnings she was still short of money. Not only was she supporting them all, she was having to find the money for the rent on the house in Barlton, *and* to repay Sir Mortie for the cottage – Zeph's harebrained scheme. She hated going there now, remembering the betrayal that had taken place under its roof. But she had no choice: she was not prepared to go back to her mother's and have her snooping into her affairs.

She and Zeph had not rowed over May – Dolly had managed to control herself, even though she had murder in her heart. It was more dignified and it confused Zeph. She knew he would have liked her to scream and shout at him, but she wouldn't give him the satisfaction.

'There! Isn't it nice to see your old home?' she said, with false jollity, as she unpacked the basket of food she had brought with her.

'It's cold.'

'Of course it is – what else would you expect in December? I'll light the fires and it'll soon warm up. Then we'll go and see your grandmother. Now, stop fighting, please.'

The children complained all the way to the inn and she couldn't blame them. She loved Cresswell, of course, but life in Barlton was far more interesting with much more to do. Whatever happened between her and Zeph, she never wanted to live here again.

'Hello, anyone home?' Dolly called, as they entered the inn.

'Dolly, you came!'

She was puzzled at the urgency in Flossie's voice. 'I only decided last night. I've been so busy but I felt the children should see their grandmother – it's been a month since I was last here.'

'I sent a telegram this afternoon.'

'It must have come after we left. Flossie, what is it?'

Flossie glanced at the children in a way that made Dolly's heart turn over. 'Go and see if you can find some toys you left here,' Dolly said to them. 'Go on, Pol.' She used her sternest voice.

Once they were alone she turned to Flossie. 'Is it Melanie?'

'It's Timmy. He's missing in France.'

Dolly clasped her hands together. 'Missing? That doesn't mean he's dead, does it?'

'No, but apparently it's serious. According to Alf, we're not being told the truth – soldiers' conditions are dreadful and they're dying in their hundreds.'

'So, Alf's an expert now?' She spoke sharply on purpose: she hated all the uninformed gossip that swirled about them, these days.

'He talks to people. He helps up at the big house and finds things out. And being rude to me won't help!'

'I'm sorry, but these days you don't know what to believe. How's Melanie?'

'Taken it bad, she has. I had to call the doctor.'

'What about Richard?'

'Useless as always. I doubt if he even knows what's going on.' Flossie fussed about her kitchen. 'I need help here! I have my own family – I can't do it all myself.'

Dolly felt as if the walls were closing in on her. 'Has anyone thought to tell Zeph and Xenia?'

'I sent them telegrams too last night. There's been no reply.'

'Typical,' Dolly said, under her breath. 'I'd best go and see her.'

As she climbed the stairs Dolly's mind was in turmoil. Flossie had meant that she should come back and care for Melanie. Well, she wasn't going to. How could they expect it of her? She hadn't told anyone about Zeph and May, but anyone with any sense would have worked out what had happened.

'Melanie, I'm so sorry. What a worry for you.'

'Dolly, you came!' Melanie was lying fully dressed on the eiderdown.

Dolly was shocked by her appearance, and busied herself with the fire, which had burnt low. 'It's not that warm in here.' Melanie seemed shrunken. Her face was wan and her eyes pink. 'He'll turn up, your Timmy.'

'I didn't even know he'd gone to France … I didn't say … goodbye to him.'

'He should have come to see you.'

'He's cross with me … All my children are.' She paused between sentences to take a deep breath.

'Oh, come. That's not true,' Dolly said even though she knew it was. 'I hear you're not well.' It was a futile remark to make when Melanie was fighting for every breath. 'What did the doctor say?'

'I have to rest …' She made a noise that Dolly interpreted as a derisory laugh.

'Then you must.' Dolly poked the fire unnecessarily – it was burning quite well now. 'I'll be here all tomorrow. We go back on the evening train.'

'That's very good of you …' The effort of talking was really too much for her. 'I was sorry about Zeph … and you …'

Tears formed in Dolly's eyes.

'Fool ... You deserve better ... You're a good wife ...'

'I shouldn't have left him alone with her. It was partly my fault.' Had she really said that?

'You work for ... your family ...'

'Look, Melanie, whatever happened between Zeph and me doesn't affect how I feel about you. And talking isn't helping you. You should be resting. Let me help you get into bed properly.'

Her mother-in-law settled, Dolly went back to the kitchen. 'She's so thin, Flossie. I'd no idea until I helped her into her nightie. She's skin and bone.'

'Worry – that's what's done it.'

'She seems so tired.'

'She's that, all right.'

'Have you some broth? She's promised to try to eat some.'

'She'll try, but she won't manage it. I tell you, Dolly, I'm worried sick. If something happens to Zeph, as well as Timmy, it'll kill her.' And, to Dolly's horror, the indomitable Flossie began to cry.

'There, don't take on so.' She tried ineffectually to comfort her. 'You get along home. We'll be here tonight.'

'I haven't seen my family for days. I got a girl in to do the bar, and my Oak's been helping.'

'What would we all do without the Marshalls? You're always there when we need you.'

The bar checked, the children tucked up in bed, Dolly sat with Melanie while she slept. She hated to see her like this: she'd always been so strong. She tried to imagine how she would feel if her own son was missing on some battlefield in a far-off country. She wouldn't survive. If anything happened to either of her children she wouldn't want to live. She couldn't desert kind Melanie now.

Leaving the children with Flossie, Dolly caught the train to Barlton on Sunday morning. As it clattered along she was impervious once again to the passing scenery. She was busy planning and thinking.

'I didn't expect to see you again.' May greeted her on the doorstep of the small cottage on the outskirts of Barlton that Zeph had taken for her and for which Dolly now paid.

'The feeling is mutual. Aren't you going to invite me in or do we conduct our business here on the step for all and sundry to listen?'

May held open the door for her.

The cottage was small and dark. Good, Dolly thought. 'My, but you've grown,' she said to Charlie, who, ignorant of adult problems, had welcomed her with enthusiasm.

'Do you want to sit?'

Dolly took a chair by the small table and May sat opposite. Charlie proceeded to show her his toys. 'I've come to ask your help,' she said, without preamble. 'Melanie is seriously ill. Timmy has been reported missing and we all know what that can mean.'

'Oh, the poor woman.'

'I can't leave her but I have my business, which, with my husband away in the army, I need to continue. You are intelligent and *normally* honest.' She allowed herself a small smile at the barb. 'I was wondering if you would run the business for me.'

'Me?'

'Just while Melanie needs me. For a wage, of course.' Everything came down to money.

'How much?'

'I shall return each Friday to pay everyone and do the books. So, for five days, I suggest ten shillings.'

May snorted. 'A pound and I might consider it.'

'That's too much.'

'Ha, well.' May stood up. 'It's you needs my help.'

'I'll give you twelve and sixpence. You must be in need of money.'

'On the contrary, I'm thinking of returning to my parents' home. They have begged me to go.' She walked to the door.

Dolly was aware that she was being shown out. 'Melanie is gravely ill.'

There was a long pause. 'For her, I'll help.'

'Thank you,' she felt obliged to say. There was no point in rocking the boat now.

An hour later Dolly had explained the running of her business. She arranged for May to keep an account, told her which clients she had to treat with kid gloves, went through her system for docking wages in respect of any breakages. She said she would arrange for a telephone machine to be installed – she had been considering having one for some time: far more people had them in their homes now and the present situation had made the decision for her. 'No private calls, but if you have any problems you can contact me.'

'There's just one thing, Dolly.'

Dolly paused. 'Yes?'

'Thank you for paying the rent on this cottage.'

'I don't pay it for you but for Charlie – he's done no wrong.' She left for fear she might say more and ruin her plan.

As she sat on the train back to Cresswell-by-the-Sea, she wondered if Melanie would ever know what it had cost her to do that. But there had been no alternative. May was bright and educated. She could be polite and Dolly's richer clients would appreciate her. But Dolly didn't like having to ask her help. When she next saw Zeph she would … Be happy to see him safe and well. That was the problem.

As the train arrived at the halt, she picked up her account books, which she had brought with her. She would not let May know the extent of her success.

7

Every day Rowan ended up washing the bedpans and urine bottles, emptying the bins and doing the other dirty work. There was never enough hot water so her hands were raw and weeping from cracks. Sylvia Ferguson's were never dirty, let alone chapped; she was usually to be found sitting on an officer's bed flirting outrageously, which shocked Rowan to the core – she had never seen such blatancy. If she ever behaved like that her mother would box her ears.

She collected the bags of soiled dressings from the special bins that stood behind a screen in each ward. They had to be emptied regularly or they began to smell. Then she had to line the bins with old newspapers. She took pride in this task, as she did in all things. She made sure the paper covered the white enamel interior completely. Then she had to wash her hands again – and how the carbolic soap stung!

She took her cloak from the linen cupboard. It was dark blue, lined with red, and when she swept it round her it was as warm as any fancy fur. Carrying the bags of old dressings, she made her way to the boiler room where Sol Pepper's Uncle Denzil, called out of retirement, would burn them in the huge boilers, which were never allowed to go out. As she opened the heavy door, she remembered how, as a child, she had loved to come here in summer. Old Sol would open it and hundreds of bats would swoop out, making angry little cries at the disturbance. She had loved to watch them flying through the air in their graceful dance. She'd never been afraid of them, which was odd because she screamed if she saw a mouse.

'Kettle's on the boil,' Denzil said, as she entered with her burden. He had got into the habit of making her a cup of tea whenever she came in, which she never refused. It also gave her the chance to sit down, if only for five minutes, which Sister Westall never allowed. He stepped forward and took the bags from her. 'Bloody hell! These get heavier and heavier.'

'They're sending more men with open wounds now. Apparently there are too many for the hospitals.'

'Over by Christmas, my arse.' Denzil spat in contempt. 'Here, take a pew. You look worn out.'

'We need more staff. They've sent us another two, and there's Fanny Petty – she's as strong as two of us put together – but it's not enough.'

'Fanny Petty? Can't say as I ever heard of her. Not from these parts, then?'

'No, from Barlton. She was in the clink with Miss Cresswell. She does some of the nights for us. Nice woman, not like some I could mention.' She took a sip of the orange-coloured tea. It was sweet and, as her mother would say, strong enough to stand a spoon in. 'Of course, Miss Lettice comes and Mrs Oliver, but it seems to me that the gentry get all the praise and do none of the work.' She looked ruefully at her sore hands.

'I hear Lady Sylvia's a looker.'

'She's that, all right, but idle with it. Flirts with the men something shocking and then it's "Oh, Lady Sylvia, what an angel you are, what would we do without you?"'

'Still, I suppose if she cheers them up she's doing something. If her's not pulling her weight, why don't you complain? Say you're not going to do it all.'

'I wouldn't want to make trouble.'

'Don't see why not.'

It wasn't all misery, though, Rowan thought, as she made her way back to the house. Although she had a few minutes ago been almost complaining about Lettice and Esmeralda, she was in fact, to her astonishment, making friends with them. Perhaps that was an exaggeration, but they had taken her under their wing and were teaching her so many things she hadn't known before. She'd always thought she knew how to walk but she didn't, according to them. 'Imagine you're carrying a ewer of water on your head,' Esmeralda had advised, which Rowan had thought silly. But when they congratulated her enthusiastically on how much better she carried herself, holding her head high, she watched herself in the mirror and saw that they were right.

They had spent hours telling her how to eat – something else she thought she'd managed quite well for the past seventeen years. But she hadn't. Now she knew how to take soup. 'But why do I have to push the spoon away from me?' she'd asked.

'So you don't drip it down your best dress,' Esmeralda had explained.

'There's always a logical reason for the rules of etiquette,' Lettice added.

'Even though they're sometimes difficult to fathom,' said Esmeralda.

She was told never to put her elbows on the table. That at table she must speak first to the person on her right, then on the left. This made her smile – in the servants' hall, or at home, everyone was too interested in eating to talk to each other. They told her she must never say 'pardon', rather 'what', which was a puzzle too, since her mother said that was rude and would box her ears if she ever heard her say such a thing. When she asked why, she was told they did not know – which made it even odder. But, to please them, she listened and learnt but did not think she would take their advice.

She enjoyed talking to them about clothes since they brought some of theirs for her to try on. Looking in the mirror – they called it a looking-glass – she was thrilled by her transformation. 'Well, look at me!' she had said, which made the other two collapse with giggles. They told her she must never dine with her shoulders bare. Since she never 'dined' this was useless information, as was the knowledge that she must never wear diamonds before luncheon, which was regarded as vulgar.

Still, they were only being kind and it amused her when she wasn't working.

Whitaker was making his sedate way along the kitchen corridor at the same time as she was. 'How are we this damp day, Rowan? Shipshape, I trust.'

'Very well, thank you, Mr Whitaker.'

She had to admit that everyone was nicer to her now that she was no longer a maid. Perhaps it was because people depended on her to a degree so they had to be pleasant. She liked that idea.

Off the drawing-room, now one of the main wards, there was a small anteroom, which had been turned into a linen room with hastily erected shelves, which tended to wobble because they could not be secured to the wall as the tapestries hung behind them. One of Rowan's fondest dreams was that they would collapse on Sylvia Ferguson and she would be smothered by goosedown pillows. Here, the staff could have a cup of tea and sit for five minutes, if Sister Westall was off duty. Ferguson was ensconced in the only chair, leafing through a copy of the *Lady*. For once she noticed Rowan, and even smiled at her. What did she want? Rowan wondered as she began to change her shoes.

'I met Morts properly today and he's divine.'

Rowan dropped her shoe. 'He's here?'

'Arrived this afternoon. But there's no need for you to get excited, he's hardly likely to notice you, is he, not when I'm here?'

Rowan ignored this.

'It will be nice to have a whole man here rather than the cripples we have most of the time.'

'That's a horrible thing to say!'

'It's the truth. In this last batch there's hardly a whole man among them.'

'By the way,' Rowan had tied her laces, 'tomorrow you can take the dressings bags to the boiler room. I do it every day, and the bedpans and bottles. It's time you did a bit more.' She was changing out of the blue apron she wore for cleaning into a crisply starched white one.

Ferguson laid down her magazine. 'I beg your pardon? And what are you intending to do about it? I can assure you I didn't come here to be a scut. Not when you're about.' She laughed, in her false, tinkling manner.

'Come on, it's time to serve tea.' Rowan had finished dressing and this time she was confident that Ferguson would be close behind her. Serving the men their tea was one of the few tasks she apparently enjoyed.

She was still smirking, no doubt because she thought she had won. But Rowan had meant what she said. She would complain. Why should she put up with the woman's idleness?

Half an hour later she was returning from the kitchen with one of the kitchenmaids, who was helping her with the large tea urn they'd had to fill. As they struggled along the top corridor she saw Sylvia Ferguson standing, hand on hip, bosom pushed forward provocatively talking to someone who was sitting on one of the window-seats. 'There she is, flirting again. It's all she ever does,' she complained to the maid. As they approached, Rowan heard a man laugh and nearly let go of the urn's handle. It was Morts. When they reached the pair her eyes were full of tears. She could not look at him and averted her head. 'Rowan,' she heard him call, but ignored him. She wanted to go somewhere and hide. She had always known this was inevitable, but that didn't help.

The urn deposited in the ward, Rowan scuttled off to the safety of the linen cupboard and squeezed herself into a place between the window and the shelves; she often hid there just to be alone. Five minutes later the door opened, startling her. She relaxed when she saw it was Fanny Petty.

'Lawks. What's the matter? You've been crying. Who's upset you?' Her large form virtually filled the doorway. 'Tell me what it's about.'

'Nothing.'

Fanny shut the door purposefully and leant on it so that no one else could enter. '"Nothing" never brought on tears like that.'

'I'm fed up. I'm always on duty with Nurse Ferguson and she's so lazy. I do all the dirty work while she just chats to the men and flirts …' It sounded so lame, yet how could she add that the woman was about to break her heart?

'Have you spoken to Sister Westall about her?'

She shook her head. 'What would be the point? Westall and Ferguson are thick with each other. She wouldn't hear a word said against her.'

'You need to tell Miss Cresswell. She'd see what's what straight away.'

'I can't.'

'Why ever not?'

'Because she doesn't like me.'

'I've never heard such nonsense. You go and see her, that's my advice.' She collected the pillowcase she had come to fetch and bustled away.

It did sound like nonsense, she knew, that Miss Cresswell didn't like her. But she could not explain about Morts and the letters. Keeping her precious letters had been cruel so Miss Cresswell must dislike her enormously to do such a thing. She sat up straighter among the blankets – red, she'd been told, so that blood would not show. She brushed back her hair and adjusted her cap. Moping wasn't going to help her. If he had finished with her, he couldn't have truly loved her. 'Better to find out now rather than later,' she said aloud. But for all her brave thoughts she knew it was going to be hard. She had tried not to love him and failed. How did you stop loving someone? She knew that, after Morts, she would find all other men wanting.

8

Dolly sat beside Melanie's bed, she was getting worse by the hour. She was afraid of being alone in the sick room. What if her condition worsened, what if she died, what would she do? In a way, she thought, Melanie had already gone from them. Most times she was deeply asleep and proper conversations with her were a thing of the past. She regretted all the things she had not said to her; she should have expressed her love and gratitude more. Now it was probably too late.

She looked up as Muriel, the nurse they now needed to help them, entered the room. She moved almost silently, used to being with the sick. 'Thanks for relieving me,' the nurse whispered.

'I don't mind sitting here for longer if you want to take a nap.' This was not true but she felt she should offer.

'No. I had a good sleep earlier, thanks to Flossie. You run along and get some rest yourself.'

'Well, if you're sure. You'll call me?'

'Of course.' The nurse sat herself in the armchair across the room from the invalid. She removed her knitting from a bag beside her, adjusted the lamp and settled down for her vigil. 'Go,' she said kindly to Dolly who was dithering by the door.

Dolly was convinced she would not sleep but exhaustion won over concern and soon her eyes became heavy.

It was pitch black when she was awoken from a deep slumber and found herself sitting upright in bed. What had disturbed her? She listened. There was nothing. She lay back on the pillow to try to sleep again but found she was too wide awake. Then she heard it, a vague shuffling noise. She was quickly out of bed and slipping on her dressing gown. She tiptoed along the corridor but both her children were sleeping peacefully. Quietly she pushed open the door to Melanie's room. Muriel was still in the chair but with her head back, snoring lightly. That, no doubt, was what she had heard. Melanie did not stir. Should she wake the nurse? No, she decided. She'd get herself some hot milk and then relieve her.

Dolly had almost reached the kitchen when she heard a chair scrape. She blew out the candle, tilted the candlestick forwards and crept towards the door. Through a crack she could see the faint glow of a light. Abruptly she pushed it open. 'Hold your hands up, I have a gun,' she said, as fiercely as she could manage, aiming the candlestick. In front of her, cowering with fear but, for all that, brandishing a knife, stood Timmy, Zeph's half-brother.

'Christ, Dolly, you gave me a fright!'

'And you think you didn't scare me? What the hell are you doing here?'

'I didn't know where else to go. I was starving.'

Dolly looked at the mess he had created; a loaf of bread had been torn apart, the wedge of cheese hacked at, pickled onions were strewn across the table. 'There's some soup in the larder. You look as if you could do with something hot inside you.'

'I was afraid of making too much noise.'

'Afraid of what?' she asked as she went to fetch the soup. 'What have you got to be afraid of?' she repeated as she returned. 'I expect you'd like a cup of tea too. Still, am I pleased to see you – even if it is the middle of the night. What's the time?'

'Could you just shut your trap for one minute and heat the bloody soup.'

She swung round. 'I beg your pardon? Who do you think you are?' She found him standing menacingly behind her, the knife thrust towards her. 'Timmy, don't be silly. Put that thing away. What has got into you?' Realisation began to dawn. 'Oh, Timmy, you weren't missing. You …' She was not sure how to continue with the knife between them. She put the saucepan on the stove.

'Deserted? Is that what you were going to say? Couldn't quite get the word out, could you?'

'No, it's just …'

'Just what? Don't give me any lectures. Don't get pious with me. Whatever you think or say, you won't know what you're talking about.'

It was then she saw the bleakness in his eyes, and the fear. 'Timmy, I'm so sorry. But …' What should she say to him? 'Had you best not give yourself up?'

'And be shot? Talk sense woman.'

'Then why did you run away?'

'If I told you, you wouldn't believe me. Not unless you'd been there. Where's Zeph?'

'He enlisted.' She began to stir the soup. 'He felt it his duty.'

'Bloody fool.' To her relief he sheathed the knife and sat down on the chair, where he slumped with exhaustion, saying no more. When the soup was hot she poured it and gave it to him. He drank it noisily and with relish, evidently impervious to its heat. She sat opposite him.

'You can't stay here. We've a nurse who has two sons at the front. She wouldn't …' She stopped again as another conversational pitfall opened in front of her.

'You mean she's likely to report me?'

'I don't know, I hardly know her. You'd best stay at our cottage.'

'What cottage?'

'Zeph and I are buying a cottage on the estate.'

'With Mother's money?'

'Please, Timmy, don't start that. Not now. I'm glad you're here. Your mother is very ill. If I can get the nurse out of the way you'll be able to see her.'

'I don't want to.'

'But it would mean so much to her. She's been asking for you.'

'You gone deaf? I don't want to see her.'

'I don't know how to say this, Timmy. I'm sorry, but we think she's dying.'

'We all have to die.'

'Timmy!'

'I need money.' He ignored her shocked disapproval. 'Can you get me some? After all, you've both had enough.'

'I can't, I've nothing to spare. It's hard enough—'

'You can.' He did not let her finish. 'Else, I'll slit your bloody throat.'

'How much?' He looked as if he meant it. She decided not to argue with him.

'Fifty pounds.'

'I have no way of getting such a huge sum.'

'Please, Dolly. Help me.' Now his expression was pleading. 'I've a mate can get me on a boat out of here.'

'I'll see what I can do.'

He stood up. 'Which cottage?'

'Briars. But don't light the lamps. Everyone knows I'm here.'

After he had left she slumped on the chair and felt weak with relief. She had never liked him, now she loathed him. Still, sitting here wasn't going to solve anything. She cleared the food up and had finished just as Muriel appeared. 'Have you had visitors?' she asked, pleasantly enough.

'No.'

'I thought I heard voices.'

'Oh, that was Richard. He's gone to bed.' She hoped her guilt did not show on her face. 'I found you asleep. Do you want me to sit with Melanie?'

'No. I just nodded off for a minute. I'm awake now.'

In the morning, Dolly asked Flossie to care for the children. 'I'm sorry to bother you, but I need to see the bank manager today. I'll be as quick as I can.'

'Always money,' she heard Flossie mutter.

At the bank in Barlton, she removed five pounds of her precious savings from her account. Her interview with the manager was a dismal failure.

'I need this loan … for family reasons,' she added.

'Forty-five pounds is a considerable sum of money, Mrs Topsham.'

'I'm aware of that,' she said. 'I have shown you my figures.' She pointed at the ledger open in front of him on the desk.

'They are excellent – as always. But if they were even better, it would make no difference.'

'Then loan me twenty pounds.'

'I might consider such a sum.'

'Good. When may I have it?'

'When your husband has signed the papers.'

'But he is away at the war.'

'Perhaps when he is sent on leave?'

'I need it now.'

'Unfortunately you cannot have it when you want it.'

He looked so supercilious that she had to struggle to keep her temper. 'Then I might have to consider going to another bank.'

'We should, of course, regret it if you did so, Mrs Topsham – you are a valued customer. But I can assure you the answer would be the same at any bank. You would not be able to borrow without your husband's signature.'

'But that is *my* money. I earn it. It would be me paying it back, and the interest.'

He shrugged and held his hands wide. 'It's the way of the world.'

'Then the world is wrong!'

She gathered her bag and ledger and, without another word, hurried from his office, close to tears of anger and frustration. It was so unfair. What was she to tell Timmy? He meant nothing to her, but for Zeph and Melanie's sake she had to help him. As she rushed out of the front door, dabbing at her eyes, she cannoned into a man on the steps.

'Madam, I'm sorry.' The man removed his hat and gave her a courteous bow. 'But you are crying! What has happened?' he said with concern. 'But I know you …'

'Mr von Ehrlich.' He made her feel even more flustered.

'Are you not Zeph's wife?'

'I am.'

'Then let me assist you. Perhaps some refreshment.' And placing his hand under her arm, he led her across the road towards the Victoria Hotel.

'You know my daughter, Mrs Cresswell?' he asked, once they were settled.

'I sometimes see her. I wouldn't say I knew her. She's a lady.' She was glad she had said that, for he smiled and nodded with evident approval.

'But you must hear things said about her?'

'Sometimes,' she answered, puzzled as to where this was leading.

'How often do you see her?'

'She is often in Barlton. She likes to patronise the local traders. She's good like that.'

He smiled at that.

'Not that we've seen much of her recently, you understand.' She wasn't sure if it was polite to mention her condition to a gentleman.

'No doubt. Then I wonder if you would do me a favour. Nothing irksome.' He smiled at her. 'Let me know everything you hear about her. And when you see her let me know how she looks.'

'Of course I will.' She was happy to agree.

Chapter Eight

December 1914

1

It was all very well for Mr von Ehrlich, or Eldridge, or whatever he chose to call himself these days, to ask her to keep him informed about his daughter, thought Dolly, but how could she?

Dolly should have been checking the cellar at the Cresswell Arms, but instead, she was sitting at the kitchen table, mulling over this particular problem. It was unlikely that she and Mrs Oliver would bump into each other, and improbable that, if they did meet, they would have anything to say to each other.

She should never have agreed to his request – but she had needed the money, for Timmy. She did not want to get on the wrong side of the man, for she sensed that he had a fiery temper. In any case she did not like the look of the scar that snaked across his cheek.

She picked up a sharp knife and began to scrape away at the block of rock salt in its wooden box. It was a task she enjoyed – she would hack away at it and rid herself of frustration. The other problem was how to pay him back?

It was odd that he had agreed so easily to her request. He had taken her for coffee at the Victoria, a grand place if ever she'd seen one and, over their cups, had asked her why she had been crying. She felt this was rude of him since he hardly knew her. She had told him she had a family debt, of twenty pounds, that with Melanie so poorly she could not bother her and was at her wit's end. To her astonishment he had asked no further questions, but had taken out his soft black leather wallet and handed over the money. She looked at the folded white notes and was immediately on her guard. She was about to tell him she wasn't that sort of woman when he had said, 'I know Xenia,' and pressed the notes into her hand. 'For her.'

The memory made her dig harder at the salt. There was only one conclusion: all the rumours that her sister-in-law was a kept woman were true. And at some time, if not now, von Ehrlich had been Xenia's protector.

Half of Dolly thought this shocking, while the other was consumed with curiosity and admiration. The last time she had seen Xenia she had been overwhelmed by envy of her lovely clothes, her jewellery and the elegant way she held herself. Most of all, she had respected her self-confidence. Now everything about her seemed even more glamorous and exotic. If she was sinful she looked remarkable prosperous on it.

When she had finished the salt she went to see Melanie and found her asleep. The poor soul did little but sleep, these days. Then, from her own room, she collected a capacious canvas bag. Quietly she made her way to the back porch, and took down her coat from the peg.

'Don't tell me you're going out in this weather?' Flossie had appeared in the passage.

'Melanie's fast asleep.' Flossie was bound to notice the bag.

'Going shopping?' Flossie nodded at it.

'No … Some clothes for …' For the life of her she couldn't think of a single poor family's name.

'The church?'

'Yes, the church.' How false she sounded. She wished Flossie would go back to her kitchen.

'Why don't you wait till the rain eases off a bit? I shall think you've a lover if you keep on like this.'

'A spot of rain never hurt anyone,' Dolly said. With that, she put on her galoshes, picked up a large umbrella and set out.

Although it was only half a mile to the cottage it seemed further as she battled through the driving rain. When she went in Timmy was standing in the kitchen, pointing a gun at her, looking scared to death. 'Put that thing away,' she ordered.

'How was I supposed to know it was you?'

'If it wasn't me, killing someone isn't going to help you, is it?' As she spoke she was divesting herself of her coat. She frowned at the puddle of water she had shed on the stone flags.

'It'd make me feel safer.' He grinned but she could smell his fear. 'Did you get the money?'

'Only twenty five.'

Timmy thumped the wall with frustration. 'I need fifty pounds.'

'If wishes were horses beggars would ride. Do you want it or not?'

He held out his hand and she gave him the notes. 'Thanks,' he said, in a disgruntled tone. 'It'll have to do.'

'It will! If it hadn't been for Mr Eldridge – Mr von Ehrlich, he used to be – you'd have only got—'

'He knows? Did you tell him?'

'Of course I didn't! I'm not a fool.'

'Then why did he give it to you?'

'He didn't. I've had to borrow it. But you'll pay me back some day.'

'As soon as I can.'

Empty words, Dolly, thought. 'I don't want to be in debt to him,' she said.

'I said I'd pay,' he muttered through his teeth.

Aware of the gun, she decided to change the subject. 'He said, "I know Xenia. For her," then gave it to me. As if he was paying off a debt.'

'Hardly, if he wants it back.'

'It was the look in his eyes ... Wistful.'

'I don't care why he gave you the money.'

'I didn't think you would,' she snapped. 'If you weren't Zeph's brother I wouldn't help you. Anyway, I've clothes of Zeph's for you. You can't go around the country looking like a tramp.'

'He's taller than me.'

'I turned up the trousers.'

'Did anyone see?'

She sighed in reply. She had done them sitting beside Melanie. The nurse must have seen her sewing but had said nothing. Perhaps she hadn't registered what she was working on. And Flossie had commented on the bag.

He took the trousers, shirt, jumper and jacket with bad grace. 'You're so ungrateful, Timmy. Why won't you go and see your mother? I could get the nurse out of the way for a bit.'

'Mother might talk, I told you.'

'And she might die.'

'Then there's no point in telling her, is there?'

'You're a cold fish, Timmy Topsham.'

'And you're a nag, Dolly.'

'But not a coward.'

'What would you know?' he said angrily.

'You liked prancing about in your uniform when there was no danger but it's different now, isn't it?' The words were out before she knew it, but he had annoyed her so much. At least it would be no hardship to say goodbye to him. She had no idea what Zeph would have to say about her helping Timmy – there was no love lost between the brothers.

The rain had eased when she walked back to the inn, and she had still to find out about Esmeralda Cresswell. The only solution she could think of was to write to Mr Eldridge and pretend she had seen her. What a sorry state of affairs that her own father didn't see her when she was having her first child. She wondered what had caused the rift.

But only a few months ago her own life had been free of sadness and spite. Now they were always with her.

'Dolly, a word please.' She had been met on the stairs by Muriel. 'We should send telegrams to Mrs Joynston's family.'

'You don't mean …' Dolly's legs buckled although she had been expecting this for days.

'Steady, dear.' The nurse took her arm. 'We don't want you falling and hurting yourself, do we? She's weakening fast. I don't think it will be long now.'

'Would they let Zeph home from the army?'

'Perhaps, in the circumstances. We can but try.'

Dolly was not sure that she was ready yet to see Zeph.

'If only we had good news of Timmy for her,' the nurse said. 'At least she would die happy. It's tragic that she doesn't even know whether he is alive or dead.'

'Yes.' Dolly stiffened. 'I must go to her.'

She went up the stairs and into her mother-in-law's room. 'Melanie,' she whispered. There was no response, but she hadn't expected one. 'Melanie,' she tried again. 'I've news of Timmy.'

Melanie's eyes opened. 'Dolly? Is it you?' she rasped. 'Always here …'

'And why not? You've been like a mother to me.' She took Melanie's hand. 'We've got to get you better.'

'Not now, Dolly. So tired …' Her eyes closed.

'Melanie. Please listen.' Dolly glanced over her shoulder to check that she was alone. 'It's Timmy …'

Suddenly Melanie's eyes, which, a moment ago, had lacked all expression, were alert.

'He's alive.'

'Are you sure?'

'Yes, I've seen him. Right as rain.'

Melanie's sigh was almost a groan. But when she closed her eyes again, she was smiling.

The following morning, Dolly was staring dolefully into her tea when Nurse Muriel entered the kitchen. 'Have you sent for your husband as I suggested?' Her starched apron crackled.

Dolly wanted to cry. 'No, I haven't.'

Muriel sat down beside her. 'Might I ask why not, when he is sorely needed here?'

'Because … I don't know where he is.' Dolly was ashamed that she had to confess the truth to her.

'His regiment will know.'

'I don't know which regiment he joined. He left without telling me.'

'I see. Does anyone know? Flossie, pehaps?'

'How can I ask and have her know too – let the whole world know that I have no idea where my husband is?'

'But if you don't you'll have to live the rest of your life knowing that he didn't see his mother before she died because of your pride,' Muriel said gently.

Now the tears tumbled down Dolly's cheeks, and she fumbled for a handkerchief. 'Excuse me. I never cry usually and now I can't stop …'

'Perhaps you didn't have anything to cry about, my dear. Now it must seem as if your whole world is collapsing. Too much responsibility for any soul.'

Sympathy was the last thing she needed. The tears increased to a flood. Muriel crossed to the range and put the kettle on.

'What's the matter?' Flossie had appeared, and her tone suggested exasperation.

'Dolly?' Muriel asked.

'I can't …' She buried her face in her handkerchief.

'Then I will, for my patient's sake. Flossie, do you know where Zeph is?'

'That I don't. He left without a by-your-leave.' She glared at Dolly. 'She must know.' Muriel shook her head. 'She doesn't? Well I never. They've had a right falling-out, I can tell you. Melanie was hoping it would all get worked out.' At this Dolly howled even louder. 'But Melanie must know …'

'I fear she is past asking.'

Now Flossie was fighting the tears. 'I'd always thought he went to

Exeter.' She gulped. 'I'll get my Alf to see what he can find out, and Miss Cresswell will want to help. I'll go and see.'

Muriel made the tea and laced both cups with brandy from the bottle that always stood on the dresser. She waited patiently for Dolly to compose herself. 'I'm sorry I had to tell Flossie, but this is not a time for secrets. Drink this now, while it's still hot,' she said, when Dolly had quietened.

'I don't know what came over me,' Dolly said.

'Sometimes it does you good to cry and let the misery escape.'

Dolly blew her nose noisily.

'Too many worries, that's what.' Muriel patted her hand. 'I hope you told Melanie that Timmy's alive?'

Dolly's mouth fell open with surprise, which she was not quick enough to disguise. 'I don't know what you mean.'

'You do, my dear, and I quite understand. No doubt he told you not to tell but I'm hoping you have.'

'But how ... ?'

'I heard the voices. I know Richard's and when you told me it was him, I knew it wasn't. I saw you shortening men's trousers, and you've been running errands when you'd not left the house for days previously. You're obviously worried out of your mind too.'

'What will you do?'

'Nothing, of course.'

'But I thought—'

'You thought that, with two sons in the regulars, I would disapprove and report him. Dolly, if the same thing happened to one of mine I'd hope someone would help him.'

'But he's a deserter.'

'He must have had a reason. What do we know of what goes on in France, tucked up safe as we are here?'

'I never asked him because I don't like him.'

'So you had to help – you couldn't let personal feelings get in the way, could you? Don't worry.' She patted Dolly's hand. 'Your secret is safe with me.'

Just as no one knew Zeph's whereabouts, they didn't know Xenia's either, so Dolly, well wrapped up against the bitter weather, had driven a pony and trap to Courtney Lacey. Now, having argued with the butler, who wanted to deny her entrance, she was waiting nervously to see 'Stan Eldridge'.

310

'Not more money, Mrs Topsham?' he asked, as he entered the room with what she hoped was a benevolent smile. 'Or perhaps you have come to repay me? In which case your speed commends you.'

Dolly looked anxiously at the austere but handsome woman who had accompanied him. 'Miss Beatty is my confidante. You may speak freely.'

From the look that passed between them, she was a lot more to him than that – disgusting at their age, Dolly thought, and surprising with all she'd heard about the woman. 'Unfortunately, I haven't come to repay you. Not yet,' she added hurriedly. 'I'm hoping you might tell me how I can get in touch with Xenia Topsham.'

'How should I know where she is?'

'Because you mentioned her when you gave me the money. "For Xenia", you said, or some such.'

'I knew her many years ago.'

He was lying. Last Christmas, as Dolly knew, Xenia had stayed only hours with her mother, then come here. 'I need to find her,' Dolly told him. 'Her mother is dying.'

'Again?'

His coldness shocked her. But if he knew that, it proved that he did resort to lying. Which gave her more confidence. 'She got better last time.'

'And now?'

'I fear not.'

'How sad. She's a fine woman. Intelligent, too, even if she did marry my useless secretary. At least, she *thought* she did.'

He was confusing her. Dolly stood up. 'Should you remember Xenia's address, perhaps you could let me know.' She turned to leave the room.

'And my daughter?' he called after her.

'Blooming,' she said, with as much spite as she could muster.

She got back into the trap and whipped the pony into a fast trot. What could he have meant? '… even if she did marry … at least *thought* she did …' was Richard a bigamist? She certainly wasn't going to tell Melanie that – even if the poor woman could hear her. But if she died without making a will and Richard inherited everything, it would matter a lot. 'Oh, Zeph,' she shouted, as she bowled along, 'I need you.'

As Dolly sat by Melanie's bed, holding her hand as she had done for the last hour, she was full of sadness. Melanie, she knew, had been a good mother, yet she was dying without her children around her. Mavis, her own mother, crept up behind her. 'Any change?' she asked.

'No.'

'Any news of your Zeph?'

'He's in France,' she snapped. She hated saying it: she could no longer pretend he was safe in Exeter. Alf had found out that he had been sent there.

'And that flighty Xenia?' Mavis gave a disapproving sniff.

'I haven't been able to find her.' In fact she had, but she was not about to tell her mother – Mavis was too much of a gossip. Dolly would tell no one that Stan Eldridge had sent a note saying Xenia had no desire to come. She wished her mother would go away – she was far too nosy. This pulled her up sharp: what had she just been thinking about mothers? There was no difference between her and Xenia. She patted the seat beside her to make amends, but Mavis said, 'I've got to go and get your brother's supper.'

'Isn't he big and ugly enough to get his own?'

'Our Bill works hard and needs his food. I'll come back after.'

Dolly took her mother's hand. 'Thanks,' she whispered.

She supposed Mavis was right: life had to go on. At least she would know she'd done her best for Melanie – but if it hadn't been for Dolly Zeph would not have cleared off.

Melanie's face was ravaged by illness; you would never know now that she had once been pretty. Dolly had had no idea that it could take someone so long to die – it was as if she was still fighting to stay alive. She found herself wanting Melanie to get better but also to die quickly so that the sadness would go with her.

Melanie struggled for each breath, which was followed by a silence, as if her body was fuelling itself for the next. Dolly was not sure which was worse to listen to.

Suddenly she felt dizzy, and it was then that she realised she was breathing in time with Melanie and the silent gaps were getting longer.

At last Melanie gave a long sigh. Dolly waited for the next breath. But it did not come.

And then she knew.

Melanie was dead.

3

Robert Robertson had been to measure Melanie for her coffin. As the estate carpenter, and thus coffin-maker, he was used to seeing those he had known lying dead, and it did not usually bother him. But with Melanie he was upset. She had been taken too soon and her life had been so hard. He vowed to make her the best coffin he could.

He hadn't liked the way young Dolly had queried the cost. What sort of woman was she, putting money before respect? He'd do it for nowt. That would shame her.

'Money mad, that Dolly is,' he said to his brother, who had taken over as grave-digger as the regular man had the fever.

'Who can blame her, though? No one knows who Melanie left everything to. She's two little 'uns to feed – and what if Zeph gets hisself killed? Who'll care for they then?'

'That's a good point.' Robert sucked awhile at his pipe, thinking hard. 'But for all that she should have hid her concern.' He watched his brother. 'I'm glad to see you ain't put her close to that there husband of 'ers. That would never do.'

On the estate feelings were mixed about Melanie's passing. Some were sad at the death of a kind woman, but others still could not find it in their hearts to forgive her good fortune in inheriting the inn.

'What will happen to the inn now?' Esmeralda asked her husband.

'Hopefully it will go to her children. In fairness Zeph should have it, as he was the only one who appeared to care about it and for Mrs Joynston. If he and Timmy are dead, though, Xenia will claim it and Dolly will resist her. Perhaps, even, Melanie's husband will take it over and then everyone will be dissatisfied. Is Lettice to be here this weekend for the funeral?'

'I don't know,' she replied. She herself had been wondering. If Ramsey was at home nothing, normally, would separate her from him. Esmeralda believed that Oliver still did not know his niece was living with him, and dreaded him asking her outright. Sometimes she wondered if he did know but didn't ask to save her lying to him. If he hadn't heard what was going on, it was little short of a miracle in view of the gossip in these parts.

She longed for the baby to be born, to hold it, look into its eyes, to know the child she already loved ... but fear continued to stalk her. She hoped the little one was unaware of her turmoil.

'Why did you sigh?'

'Did I?'

'As if you had all the troubles of the world on your shoulders.'

'I can't imagine why.' She had to tell so many lies. What would happen if she told him? He would throw her out, no doubt about it. And then she would have no one for she could never again trust her father.

'There's talk on the estate that someone was in Zeph Topsham's cottage for a couple of nights recently.'

'Really?'

'A couple of men were walking past and thought they saw someone move at one of the windows.'

'Were they sober?'

'Very.' He laughed.

'A tramp, perhaps?'

'His brother Timmy, more like.'

'Surely not. It would have been foolish of him to come here where everyone knows him. But if he did, the poor man must have been desperate.'

'He's a traitor and should be shot. I wish I'd known sooner – I'd have flushed him out.'

'Oliver, how can you be so harsh?'

'Many of our brave men are being killed in France.'

'Perhaps he was afraid. I know I should be. I hate loud noises and they do say that if you listen carefully you can hear the guns in France.'

'Fanciful nonsense! And don't you think that most of the soldiers are afraid? Yet they don't run. It's no excuse.'

'It's every excuse,' she said, almost to herself.

'I beg your pardon?'

'It was nothing.'

Melanie's funeral was simple but dignified. The coffin was on a farm cart decorated with holly and evergreens and the mourners followed the cortège as it wound at a slow pace from the inn to the cemetery along the lane that joined Cresswell-by-the-Sea to the estate.

Richard Joynston and Melanie's father, with Dolly behind them, followed the wagon – Dolly had almost hoped Richard would be too drunk to come, but somehow he had pulled himself together. For the first time in years, he walked upright and seemed to be grieving genuinely, but he got scant sympathy. He should have treated Melanie better. But now it was too late.

314

Dolly held her children's hands as they walked. She could hear whispering from those who lined the route as they doffed their caps, and fell in behind them. Many were remarking on the absence of Melanie's mother. 'The one thing I'm not is a hypocrite,' Mrs Beasley had said, when the funeral was being planned. 'I had little time for her in life so why would I in death?'

There were times when Dolly thought she would never understand the family she had married into.

Finally they arrived at the grey stone church. All who lived on the estate were baptised, married and buried there – from the Cresswells to the humblest retainer.

The Cresswell family had done Melanie proud. Of course, Mrs Oliver could hardly be expected to attend, with her baby due any day, but her husband was there, with Miss Hannah, Miss Lettice and Mr Morts. Sir Mortie was absent but then, Dolly thought, in the circumstances, perhaps that was for the best. Most of the indoor servants had put in an appearance, led by Whitaker, whose fine baritone voice contrasted well with Mrs Gilroy's contralto. The church was packed.

Zeph, Dolly said to herself. She thought of him long and hard so that wherever he was he would know perhaps what was happening. As the organ played the introductions to the first hymn – 'The Day Thou Gavest, Lord, Is Ended', Dolly knew she wouldn't be able to sing a word without breaking down.

That night, at Lees Court, Esmeralda's baby, Marigold, was born. As one life had ended, another had begun, she thought. She gazed at her baby in the ornately frilled cradle. She loved Oliver deeply, but the love she felt now for this tiny child was all-consuming.

'Oh, Oliver, just look at her little fingers. She's so perfect. I'm sorry she wasn't a boy.'

'But I have everything I could wish for in her.'

She watched her husband bend over the baby. And saw him fall irrevocably in love.

4

In the past Eve Gilroy had been accustomed to put her feet up during the afternoon – years of cooking had taught her the sense in resting whenever she could – but not any more. Not since the arrival of Sergeant

Bob Turner. There was no way she wanted him to think she was getting on in years, for a finer, more upstanding, man it would be difficult to find. A gentleman, too.

The sergeant had been wounded at Mons. Not, as he had explained, that he had been fighting. He had been in charge of the field kitchens, and a pan of boiling water had tipped over his right leg and foot. When the burn had turned septic, he had been sent back to Blighty.

'And when that happened it would have been hard to find a happier man. War is a dreadful business,' he had told them. Eve had admired his honesty. It would have been easy to pose as a hero – they would have been none the wiser – and it was brave of him to admit that he was glad to have escaped the horror in France. Sergeant Bob was indeed a most superior being. Whitaker, however, was less impressed.

Bob still had a limp, which was worse on damp days, but he had been sent to help Eve with the catering for the ever-increasing band of convalescents at Cresswell. She welcomed him as a colleague. They now had between fifteen and twenty soldiers, as well as members of the family, who came and went, the household and medical staff. There had been days when Eve cooked for fifty. Hilda was still in Whitby and it was almost too much for her alone, with only the kitchen- and scullerymaids to help her.

Now, with Sergeant Bob, work was a pleasure, and she had someone to talk about her favourite subject: food.

Although in the field he had been more of an administrator and overseer, here he was content to roll up his sleeves. He had confided to Eve that when he retired from the army he wanted to open a café of his own. She dreamt of them running it together – a genteel place, with an appreciative clientele … Torquay or Lyme Regis might suit.

Some days she sensed that Whitaker's nose was out of joint. For so long, he had been the only male of consequence at Cresswell and he did not seem to like the presence of another. It was rather how she had felt over the last couple of years with Hilda in the kitchen. With Sergeant Bob, though, Eve had found an equal, and she did not mind sharing her kitchen with him.

More than that, and this was her secret, she was sure she had found love. Not that she had said anything about her feelings – it would not have been proper. He had to make the first move. But she had hope: first, he was single and, second, she had caught him looking at her in a way that made her feel all hot, excited and almost skittish.

The only inconvenience in this new state of affairs was that she couldn't have Gussie Fuller visiting, and had to find time somehow to see her at Lees Court. Gussie could not meet the sergeant until the situation between him and Eve had been clarified.

'You needn't come here every time, Eve. I don't mind popping over to you. We should take it in turns.'

'The truth is, Gussie, I like to get away. I'm so busy I never see anywhere but my kitchen. It's a joy to be out and about, if only for an hour.'

'You should put your feet up more. I'll visit you next week.'

'Don't put yourself out, my dear friend. You're doing me a favour in letting me come to you.'

Eve and Sergeant Bob were planning the menus for the following week. They liked to do this on Wednesday, put the order in on Thursday, and everything was delivered on Friday. While he wrote out the lists, Eve rolled pastry for the steak and kidney pies she was making for lunch – it was the only time she missed Hilda, who, she had to admit, had a light touch with pastry.

'Were you close to the lady who died?' the sergeant asked, as he put away his pen.

'Melanie Joynston? I knew her, but she was more of an acquaintance than a friend. And with her running the local hostelry – well, I never went there. An unmarried lady can never be too careful.' There seemed no harm in reminding him now and then of her status.

'Of course.'

'Some people, these days, claim friendship long before they should.' She wished she hadn't said that: he might think she was putting a barrier between them, the last thing she wanted to do.

'Friendship is an honour to bestow, don't you think, Eve?'

Such sensitivity, she thought, as she agreed. They had been on Christian-name terms for the past week. It had seemed so right – in fact, she always called him *Sergeant* Bob, *her* name for him. But every time he said 'Eve' she wished she could put out her hands and clasp it to her with his breath still on it.

'Many claim friendship on a nodding acquaintance,' he went on.

'Not me,' she said.

'No, I couldn't imagine you—' He was interrupted by Whitaker's arrival. He stopped in the doorway and sagged against the frame.

'Good heavens! What's the matter, Edward?' Eve dropped the flour sifter, which fell off the table and rolled underneath it. She rubbed the flour off her hands on to the cloth she always had tucked into her belt and rushed across the kitchen to him.

Whitaker's face was ashen and drawn. He was opening and shutting his mouth but no words came forth. 'There, there, Edward. Eve's here.' Slowly, she led him to the table. His weight made her lean dangerously sideways and she stumbled. The sergeant rushed across to relieve her of her burden.

'Willow!' she yelled. The startled kitchenmaid appeared at the scullery door. 'Get Sister Westall here this instant! Edward, sit down and get the weight off your legs.' He'd had a stroke, she was convinced. 'How are you feeling?' she asked. Still he could not speak.

Willow reappeared. 'Sister says she's busy. She'll come when she has a moment.'

'Who does she think she is? You go back and tell her she's to come this minute!'

Willow stood motionless, her mouth open. 'Stop looking so gormless! Go and tell that woman to come here immediately – and get Miss Cresswell. Tell her I need her. And not a word to another living soul!'

They eased Whitaker on to one of the chairs. 'Now, a nice tot of whisky is what's called for.' But there was no whisky bottle on the dresser so she poured him a glass of cooking brandy, then one each for herself and Sergeant Bob. 'This'll warm your cockles.' She placed the glass in front of Whitaker and it was then that she noticed, crumpled in his hand, the buff paper of a telegram. 'May I see?' she asked, but he did not respond. She tried to prise it from his fingers but it seemed he would not let it go.

'What's the matter, Mrs Gilroy?' Hannah asked, as she came in, followed by Willow, who was agog with curiosity. 'Oh dear, Whitaker, what's amiss?'

'I think he's had bad news, Miss Cresswell. He's holding a telegram but he won't give it up.'

'Whitaker, have you had bad news? Let me see.' He gave her the telegram and began to struggle to his feet. 'No, Whitaker, I insist you remain seated.' Hannah spread out the telegram and began to read it. Half-way through, she, too, sat down. 'My poor dear Whitaker. Is there anything I can do for you? Should I get the doctor? Here, drink this.'

Whitaker looked up at her, his eyes filled with misery. 'Oh, Miss Cresswell, what shall I do?'

'You are a man of great courage, Whitaker, but today is not the day to think of what next to do. I shall call the doctor to come post-haste. You need a sedative. Can you manage if I give you my arm?'

'I am—' But no one discovered what he had intended to say for Whitaker gave a terrible groan. 'Forgive me, please,' he mumbled, through the tears that had begun to fall. He hauled himself out of the chair and, somehow, ran from the room.

'Oh, Miss Cresswell, what's happened?'

'It is the most dreadful news, Mrs Gilroy. Hilda is dead.'

'Dead?' It was Eve's turn to sit down abruptly. 'But how?'

'The Hun. There's been a bombardment from the sea on Whitby. Many others have died too.'

'Oh, my Gawd! How awful.' Eve fanned herself with her oven-cloth. It never rained but it poured, she thought. Whitaker was single again and how long could she keep that news from Gussie?

Chapter Nine

Christmas 1914

1

Rowan looked at the drawing-room ward with satisfaction. It could not have been better decorated. A tall Christmas tree stood in front of the large window that overlooked the rose garden. It had been brought in from the grounds and was covered with glass and wooden ornaments, and the candles in their little silver holders would be lit as dusk fell. A sparkling angel, in shimmering silver, was positioned on the top. She felt like a child as she gazed at it.

She hauled a screen from the side of the ward and stood it round a small table at the far end of the room.

'Hiding from us, are you, Nurse Marshall?' a man called.

'I've got secrets I don't want you to see.' This was met with much oohing and aahing. She always felt awkward when they called her 'nurse', when she was only an orderly. She was sure it annoyed the proper nurses but there was nothing she could do about it. 'You're as good as they are,' one had whispered to her only yesterday. She opened the tapestry bag Miss Cresswell had given her and began to sort the contents into piles.

Miss Cresswell had amused everyone earlier by asking the soldiers' permission to hang the tree decorations: 'I purchased them some time ago in Germany and I don't wish to offend …'

'Good things as well as bad have come out of that country,' someone had said and they had all agreed.

Rowan thought it had been wise of Miss Cresswell to ask; she'd read about the dreadful treatment meted out in England to Germans and some whose names just sounded German. People were changing their names, and leaving their shops or homes because mobs had terrorised them. German grand pianos had been thrown out of windows. Even Lady Coral had sorted through the volumes of music and removed all those by German composers. Then there were the awful tales you heard of young Belgian girls being mutilated and babies killed. In Barlton a poor Dutchman had been beaten because of the way he talked.

Poor Whitaker had cause to hate the Germans, losing his wife as he had. The Germans were hated even more after Scarborough, Hartlepool and Whitby had been shelled from the sea. She hoped the British soldiers would soon win and that the war would be over. Along with everyone else on the estate, Rowan had been relieved that Hilda's funeral had taken place in Whitby. Two funerals in a month was at least one too many.

Rowan began to stuff socks that Miss Cresswell was using as Christmas stockings for the men, and which they would keep. She had learnt that soldiers set great store by a good thick pair of woollen socks – as soon as Queen Mary had asked for three hundred thousand pairs, everyone had knitted like mad. She had assembled a pile of the little gifts Miss Cresswell had been accumulating – cigarettes, matches, chocolate, hand-kerchiefs, pencils and rubbers – and now she shared them out so that no one got more than anyone else.

It had been a horrible month. Although Morts had reassured her that he hadn't been flirting with Ferguson, she found it hard to believe. Then he had come for Melanie's funeral but she had not been able to see him because Sister Westall would not let her have time off. It had been agony to know he was near, and not be able to see him for more than one hurried kiss. He had said he hoped to come this evening but he did not know when. If she could steal away, they would meet at Emily Sprite's cottage. She had gone to Exeter to be with her fiancé and Rowan still had a key – not that the door was ever locked.

Without doubt, Sister Westall was the meanest-hearted woman she had ever met. It had been Willow's birthday last month and the Marshalls had invited everyone to a party at the Cresswell Arms, but she had not been allowed to go.

'How your mother can contemplate holding a party in a house of mourning, with her employer hardly in her grave, amazes me,' Sister Westall had said.

'They thought it would cheer everyone up, and Mr Joynston agreed.'

'How very strange.'

'It's not Willow's fault that Mrs Joynston died.'

'Take your cheek to the sluice, Marshall!'

She could go days without seeing her sister – they were so busy. But perhaps that was no bad thing. She and Willow had little in common now. Willow did not understand her feelings for Morts and Rowan could not understand why her sister bothered with Freddie.

Then poor Zeph had arrived on compassionate leave but long after his mother's funeral – it had taken Dolly ten days to contact him. Honestly, thought Rowan, it was as if the army had never heard of the telegraph.

321

He had been beside himself with grief, her mother had told her – she had heard him sobbing at night.

'Marshall, you've no time to sit mooning.'

'Yes, Sister. But I wasn't – I was doing these stockings for Miss Cresswell.'

'There's cleaning to be done. Leave that for now.'

She packed away the presents in the big bag. She didn't want any of the men to see them and spoil the surprise.

As she walked the length of the drawing-room ward she was aware of the men's admiring glances. It made her proud. If she was a little bit pretty and it cheered them up, she was doubly proud. As usual, Sylvia Ferguson was sitting on one of the beds chatting to a handsome young lieutenant, who had arrived yesterday. It was a rule that no one sat on the bed, yet she flouted it every day and no one said a thing!

Still, Rowan was in no mood to be cross. Morts was coming home today. In a few hours he'd be with her. The thought of it made her feel as if her blood had turned to honey. On top of that Lettice had promised her another lesson in table etiquette. That was odd: she had so little time to herself, but if Lettice or Esmeralda summoned her, Sister excused her immediately. Because they were like friends to her, she always thought of them by their christian names, not that she ever called them this to their face. When Esmeralda's Marigold had been born, three weeks ago now, Rowan had given her a little matinée jacket that she had made in her scant spare time and had received a lovely thank-you letter. She kept it under her pillow because it smelt of lilies.

She envied Esmeralda her baby. How lovely to have such a distraction from the war. What it would be like to have Morts' baby? She stopped herself. She had vowed not to think about him in that way. It could never be. She had made a rule that whenever she saw him she must just enjoy the time she spent with him. There could be no future for them.

In the bathroom, which had been made into a sluice, she began to scrub down the dressings trolleys with a phenol solution. Afterwards she would buff them dry – Sister liked the trolleys to gleam. She looked with distaste at the pile of bandages she had to wash. It was a horrible task, but it had to be done. At least when it came to rolling them she could sit down to do it.

She looked up when the door opened. 'A message for you from Lettice Hamilton. She can't give you your lesson today,' Sylvia Ferguson informed her.

'Do you know why?'

322

'She didn't say and, of course, I wouldn't dream of asking. Have they not taught you that?'

Rowan chose not to answer but wished she would go.

'I don't know why they bother.'

Again she did not respond.

'Do you?'

'Because they're kind,' she finally spoke.

At this Ferguson laughed – a pretty sound, which she knew the men loved. 'Kind?' she said. 'You're even more stupid than I thought. They do it because they find it amusing. Didn't you know?'

Rowan's throat ached as she fought back tears of hurt. She concentrated on filling a glass jar with cotton wool. 'I don't believe you,' she managed to say.

'I've heard them laughing about what a peasant you are.'

'You lie.'

'Don't you dare tell me I am a liar!'

'And don't you dare be so rude to me.'

'Well, it's the truth. They shriek with laughter about you and how incompetent you are.'

She was on the point of leaving the room when she stopped. 'By the way, such excitement for me. I've received a *billet doux* from the dashing Morts. He wants an assignation.'

How could such a lovely laugh issue from someone so spiteful? Ferguson waved a letter in the air and Rowan saw Morts's distinctive handwriting. Then, in a flash, she was gone.

The ache in Rowan's throat now hurt as badly as if a lump of stone was lodged in it. Had she not always expected this to happen? She had always told herself it could never last. Of course he would prefer one of his own class. But how could he be deceived by a pretty face? She knew that Sylvia Ferguson would hurt him one day. If only she could warn him.

But she could not. He would be embarrassed by her now and wish he had never said the lovely things to her that he had. He would want to concentrate now on his new, more suitable love.

She balled her chapped red hands and wanted to scream. But she couldn't. She was not going to let Ferguson or anyone else see her distress.

'I'm sorry, Miss Cresswell, but I'm not feeling well. I wonder if I might go home.'

'You certainly look peaky, Rowan. I do hope you're not coming down with anything. If you leave now, though, you'll miss the carols and other festivities.'

'I know, and I'm disappointed. But if I am ill, I don't want the officers to catch it.' Rowan waited. Half an hour ago she had felt like running away and not telling anyone where she had gone. But her growing sense of responsibility had made her come to Hannah's office.

'That, of course, is true. But do you need to go home?'

'I want to see my mum.' Rowan knew she looked as if she was about to burst into tears again.

'Yes, of course you do.' Hannah sounded flustered. 'But, really, you should be asking Sister. She's in charge of you all.'

'I couldn't find her,' she lied.

'Well, I don't know what to say. Still, if you can't find her …'

'I'll be better tomorrow if I can go to bed now.' Another minute and she would be crying, she knew it.

'Have a hot toddy and wrap up warm. And here …' Hannah opened a drawer in her desk and took out a beautifully wrapped box. 'A little present, which I had intended to put under the tree but you might as well have it now. Perhaps it will cheer you up.'

Rowan did not go back to the ward. She had brought her cape with her, certain that Hannah would excuse her. Now she wrapped herself in it and, clutching the box, let herself out of a side door.

First she went round to the stables. There was a small crack in the wall of the clock tower. It was where she left messages for Mort to let him know what time she would be free. She had already placed her note there this morning, telling him she hoped to be away by eleven. She retrieved it and put it into her apron pocket. She did not want anyone to find it. Most of all, she didn't want Morts to know she had planned to be waiting for him.

She set off towards the cottage. She needed to be alone, with no chatter about her, to control the misery that was threatening to swamp her. And no one was going to know how she was suffering.

Hannah was concerned. She knew why Rowan had come to her rather than Sister Westall – the girl was afraid of the woman. Hannah was puzzled. Why was she so unpleasant to Rowan? She had always found that kindness ensured co-operation. Sister Westall had made two other orderlies' lives so miserable that they had walked out, leaving a drastic staff shortage. The girls worked for next to nothing, they were all volunteers, and desperately needed. They should be grateful to them, not upset them. Perhaps she should search for another sister to replace Sister Westall.

Then there was Sylvia Ferguson. Hannah had talked to the matron at Barlton Memorial Hospital, who was also having difficulties with the VADs. 'They volunteer, but they don't want to do any work. Too highborn, in my opinion,' Matron had complained. 'They see themselves as angels of mercy but don't want to get their hands dirty – although I've a couple who shouldn't be described like that,' she added. 'But most of them are merely looking for husbands.'

That discussion made Hannah feel better about her attitude to Sylvia Ferguson. While the girl was charming to her, Hannah knew she could turn it off at any moment. She knew, too, that she was unkind to Rowan, probably because Rowan was the more beautiful – vanity was so dangerous.

'She's lazy, far too superior,' Fanny Petty had reported to her, 'and she's making poor Rowan's life a misery. We'll lose Rowan if we're not careful and that would be a shame. I've been telling her she should train as a nurse. She's good.'

'What do you think I should do?' Hannah asked. Fanny had become a faithful confidante.

'Get rid of her,' Fanny had said.

'So many problems, Cariad, my darling,' she said to the dog, who was in her usual position at her feet in the well of her desk. Cariad's tail wagged and Hannah looked at her with affection.

There was a tap on her door. 'Come,' she called, and adjusted her cap. She still felt a sham in her matron's uniform, but she had worn it since someone had suggested it would give the men confidence in her.

'Miss Cresswell?'

'I am.'

'Medical Officer Frobisher Fellowes.' He gave a small bow. 'I've been ordered here – too much of an old crock to go to the front.' He grinned. 'I'm at your service.'

'A doctor! How wonderful!'

'Such a gratifying welcome.'

'I *am* in need of professional medical assistance. We are receiving the occasional officer with a still-open wound and—'

'They haven't told you?'

'Why does my heart sink?' Hannah smiled at him. He was a most attractive man, grey-haired but upright. She judged him to be well into his fifties. Most of all she liked his voice, moderated and deep. Voices were so important, she thought inconsequentially.

'Since the grave losses at Ypres, I'm told you'll be seeing more wounded not less. Some will need surgery.'

'But we have no facilities here. As it is, we're understaffed for the number of walking wounded we already have.'

'Which is why I'm here. I'm told you have a racquets court and I'm to decide whether it can be converted into an operating theatre.'

'Good gracious!'

He laughed at her astonishment. 'I assure you, they don't intend to knock down any walls – but it will have the space we need. And you would acquire more medical staff.'

'And you?' Suddenly she needed to know if he would be staying.

'I shall be your medical director.'

'Most satisfactory,' she heard herself say. Had she been younger she was sure she would have blushed. 'But why Cresswell?'

'As I'm sure you're aware, the plan is for the wounded to be moved as close to their homes as possible for the sake of their families.'

'All the officers here have connections in Devon and it's a comfort to them to be near home. It gets worse, doesn't it?'

'Sadly so.'

'We all thought it would be over by Christmas, but it isn't.'

'I don't think Kitchener and the other generals ever thought that. I fear that conscription will be introduced soon.'

'And will you and your family be requiring accommodation? I could talk to my brother about cottages ...'

'No, no. A small room here would suit me. I have no family. I'm a widower.'

'I'm so sorry,' she said, but she could not have heard better news.

The front door of Cresswell Manor slammed and a sword that had hung on the wall for centuries crashed to the floor. James, the young footman, skidded to a halt, too late to fulfil his duty.

'Where's Whitaker?' Coral Cresswell demanded shrilly. She looked so fierce, with her staring eyes and flared nostrils, that the footman was dumbstruck. 'Have you no arms? I'm not accustomed to opening the door myself.'

'I say, Coral, calm down!' Mortie had followed her in, but his suggestion fuelled her rage.

'I'll deal with this,' she shouted at her husband. '*Where is Whitaker?*'

The footman gulped and mumbled, 'Whitby.'

'What do you mean, *Whitby*?'

'He's gone.' He was goggle-eyed with fear.

'Where's Whitby?' She was screaming at him now.

'Leave this to me, Coral. Now, my good chap, what are you trying to tell us?' Mortie asked.

'Mr Whitaker's wife has been killed in Whitby.'

'Killed? What business had she to be there in the first place?' Coral snapped.

'When was this?' Mortie asked.

'On the sixteenth, sir. I don't know when he'll be back.'

'This is so inconsiderate,' Coral fumed. 'And at Christmas too!'

'Who's here?'

'Just Miss Cresswell, sir.'

'What is *she* doing here? Where is she?'

At that moment Hannah appeared, alerted by the commotion, with the major at her side. 'You! What are you thinking of? I told you never to set foot here again.' Coral pointed her umbrella threateningly at Hannah.

Hannah stepped back as the major moved forward as if he was about to defend her. They apologised in unison as they collided.

'Coral, I thought you knew I was here. I have been since September.' She looked accusingly at her brother. Mortie looked down at the floor. 'You didn't tell her, did you, Mortie?'

'No,' he said, almost in a whisper.

'That was too bad of you, Mortie. I mean—'

Coral lunged at Hannah, caught hold of her cap and wrenched at it.

Hannah put up her hand to protect her head and Coral slapped her face.

'Madam!' the major remonstrated.

'Coral!' Mortie grabbed his wife and held her by the upper arms, but she struggled and fought him, spitting and scratching.

'It's your fault! You're responsible! If he dies it will be your fault!' she shrieked at Hannah.

'What have I done?' Hannah's voice was anguished.

'It's Felix! My baby! He's enlisted and all because of you, you evil, shrivelled, barren bitch!' At which point Coral fainted.

In the kitchen a gaggle of staff had met. 'You've never heard anything like it! Poor Miss Cresswell. Scared witless, she was. Her ladyship was like a mad thing. I tell you …' The footman was regaling them with the scene he had just witnessed. 'And the major rushed to the rescue.' He was evidently enjoying being the centre of attention.

'Did he now?' Eve smiled.

'But why?' Philomel Herbert asked.

'Attacking Miss Cresswell? She needs locking up! Is Miss Cresswell hurt?'

'Shook up, more like, Mrs Gilroy.'

'I'm not at all surprised at Master Felix running off to war. It's the sort of thing he would do – not giving no one else a thought. But why should her ladyship blame Miss Cresswell?'

'And at Christmas too. Thoughtless boy.' Eve returned to mixing the pancake batter. 'And as for her ladyship not knowing about Whitaker? She must have known!'

'Her didn't even know where Whitby was.'

'Typical of her sort. Only London counts for her ladyship.'

'You don't approve of your mistress, then, Eve?' Sergeant Bob smiled sardonically.

'She's hardly here, but when she is don't we know it! She upsets every-one with her tantrums. It's not good enough.'

'I think she's mad,' said the footman.

'It's not your place to comment on your betters. What would Mr Whitaker say about that?' Eve admonished him.

'What would Mr Whitaker have to say about what?' a voice asked from the back door.

Eve ran across the kitchen. 'Edward! You're back! Oh, come and sit down, do. You must be tired out, travelling all that way.'

'I felt I had to be back for Christmas. That I would be needed.'

'Well, we're all glad to see you. And you can all stop gawking now. Have you no work to do? Willow, make a pot of tea for Mr Whitaker and bring it along to his room. I'll see to this, Phil.' She picked up Whitaker's bag and led him along the passage to his pantry.

'It's good to be back among friendly faces.' He sank wearily into his worn leather chair.

'Not so friendly this afternoon.' Eve explained about the scene upstairs. Then she said, 'I feared you wouldn't return.'

'Why not? This is my home. Whitby's a pleasant town and bracing, but I know no one there. This is where my friends are.'

'Oh, Edward, what a lovely thing to say.'

'And what is the news here?'

'James heard we're to become a proper hospital.'

'Never!'

'Yes. An army doctor arrived this afternoon and we're to expect more patients. Still, it's not too bad at the moment – all those who could go home for Christmas have been sent on their way and we have only eight officers left.'

'And the sergeant?'

'I don't know how I managed without him.'

'Has Miss Lettice returned?'

'I've heard tittle-tattle that she's over Widecombe way with that friend of Mr Morts. It's not right, with those young children. I don't know what her husband's thinking.'

'It's hardly our place to speculate, Eve.'

'Well, you did ask,' she pointed out.

'And Lady Penelope?'

'No change. I think it's laziness ails her.'

'And how is Gussie?'

'I've hardly seen her. She don't come here and I haven't the time to go gallivanting across the park.'

'Mortie, I'm so sorry,' said Hannah. The local doctor had just left: he had given Coral a sedative and ordered her to bed.

'It's not your fault. He's done what hundreds of young boys are doing.'

'But he's too young.'

'Lied about his age. Still, I'm proud of him. Gone to fight for king and country. It's what a young fellow should do.' Mortie spoke with conviction. 'I don't know why she's taken so against you, Hannah.'

'She's worried out of her mind and has to blame someone.' Hannah was relieved that Mortie did not know that her indiscretions had caused Felix to run away. 'But wouldn't you think the authorities would see he was too young?'

'He's a big lad and probably a convincing liar too. Also, Hannah, people can be bribed. Where are Lettice and Morts? Is Oliver coming?'

'Esmeralda is still confined to bed – but Oliver said she was trying to persuade the doctor to let her come. Marigold is a dear child. I suppose Lettice is with Hugo, and Morts is due at any hour. How long will you stay, brother?'

'I suppose it depends on Coral. I can't put up with the noise she makes, don't you know?'

'Oh, Mortie, you *are* precious.'

4

Lettice sat on the floor in front of the fire. Beside her were two sacks she had made from red felt on which she had embroidered the names of her girls.

'This is, without doubt, the most wonderful Christmas of my whole life,' she said to Ramsey, who was sitting smoking a pipe and watching her wrap the children's gifts.

'It hasn't even begun.'

'Oh, but it has. Just listen to them.' The girls were chattering in the bedroom above. 'I don't know when they'll go to sleep. Charlotte is beside herself with excitement.'

'You are the most beautiful woman I have ever seen.' He stroked her cheek with his forefinger.

'Oh, Ramsey! I'm not! I border on plain, as my mother always told me.'

'You're beautiful to me.'

'Then love has made you blind.' She smiled at him.

'I think not. You were beautiful to me before I loved you. Love may have enhanced it, but only a little.'

'Ramsey! And there was I thinking you'd fallen in love with me at first sight!'

He slid from the chair and joined her on the rug in front of the inglenook fireplace. There, he kissed her, long and hard.

They broke away from each other.

'I loved you the minute I met you,' Lettice told him.

'But you are wiser than I.'

'Of course. I'm a woman.' She sighed and leant against him, enjoying the muscular feel of his body, its warmth.

'Is it truly your best Christmas?' he asked.

'I've never felt so light-hearted, so full of anticipation. And my little ones have never known such fun.'

'What about all the luxury? You could have gone to Cresswell, you know. I fear you will miss your family.'

'The arguing, more like. In any case, you're my family now.'

'I'm always afraid that one day you will wake up and find you miss that life. I'll never be able to replace all that you have given up—'

Lettice placed a finger over his lips. 'I shall never leave you.'

Dolly was sewing. She had sent Flossie home early to be with her family, and was glad of the peace and quiet. She was tired. She had done every-thing she could think of to lift Zeph's spirits but his grief at his mother's death had changed to utter bleakness. Melanie had left no will and he was angry with her as well as bereft.

'I don't blame her,' Dolly had said, hoping to make things better.

'I do.'

'She was probably afraid to make one,' Dolly ploughed on. 'Some reckon that if they make a will, they'll die.'

'Dolly, you're making things worse with your prattle.'

He hurt her when he spoke to her like that, especially when she was trying to help. She inspected the petticoat she had been making for Cordelia, all lace and frills. She could understand his anger, but he was behaving as if he was the only one affected by Melanie's failure to make her wishes known. It posed problems for her too. Now everything – the inn, Melanie's cottages, her money, the stock – was Richard's.

Should she tell him what she thought Stan Eldridge had said, that Richard was a bigamist? But she'd no proof. She needed to find out the truth.

'Is it quiet tonight?' she asked Zeph, as he entered the kitchen from the bar.

'Most have gone up to the big house. Sir Mortie's back and they're looking for their gifts.'

'Will they do it this year?'

'I doubt Sir Mortie even knows there's a war on.'

When Zeph had returned from the front he was not the man he had been before the war. He must have seen things that had affected him deeply. She had asked him once about what he had been through but he had turned on her with such bitterness that she had not tried again. He had to return to his regiment on Boxing Day.

'Zeph, there's something I have to tell you. Two things, really ... Important things ...'

There was no interest in his eyes. 'Yes?' he said.

'May Snodland is working for me in Barlton.'

His eyes were hooded with suspicion now.

'When I came here to care for your mother, I asked her to help me with the business.'

'That was good of you.'

'It wasn't. I was at my wits' end, and she's good at organising the women. Fortunately I only have to see her once a week. But now I shall have to go back to work, with Richard owning this – unless he wants us to stay. Have you asked him?'

'I wouldn't ask him for anything.'

'Zeph, I'm not sure I can carry on helping her and Charlie. Your army pay isn't enough and—'

'You must do as you wish. And the other thing?' It was as if he no longer cared what happened to May yet at one time she had been so important to him.

'There was something else?'

'Timmy came here.' Now he was interested.

'He ran away—'

'You mean he *deserted*?'

'I didn't ask – he was afraid—'

'We're all afraid. You should have reported him to the police.'

'But he's your brother!'

'No longer. Where was he?'

'I put him in our cottage. He was only there for a couple of days, while—'

'You're a fool, Dolly.'

'I did what I thought was right.'

'You were about to say more.'

'I had to go to the bank. He needed money to go to Canada to your uncle. I didn't have enough. I happened to meet Stan Eldridge, Mrs Oliver's father, and borrowed from him.'

'At what interest?'

'There is no interest.'

'That man doesn't give anybody anything without something in return.'

'He asked me for information about his daughter. But I can't give him any. I never see her. I've written him a couple of notes full of lies about her and the baby – but I haven't even seen the child. I'm afraid he'll find out what I'm doing and want his money back. And I haven't got it. He frightens me.'

'How much?'

'Twenty pounds.'

'And where am I supposed to get that sort of money from?'

'We could ask Richard.'

'I'm not begging favours from him.' Zeph stood up so abruptly that his chair fell backwards with a clatter.

Left alone, Dolly sighed. She didn't know what she had hoped for, only that it hadn't happened. She loved Zeph still, she knew, but she feared that he had no love left for her.

5

Rowan had lit the fire in Miss Sprite's cottage and sat huddled on the floor. She remembered, as a child, sitting with her father and watching pictures form in the burning wood. But no matter how hard she looked tonight, there were no pictures. Perhaps you had to be a child to see them.

Beside her on the rug was an untouched plate of bread, cheese and a pickled onion. She did not know why she had prepared it since she hadn't been hungry.

It was one thing to make herself think how she could conquer her feelings, quite another to do it. It would be so much easier if she could hate Morts, but she was as likely to do that as she was to stop herself breathing.

She had been warned enough times about him – she remembered the concern on Melanie's face when she had told Rowan of her own mistake. Should she tell Morts how spiteful Sylvia Ferguson was? But he wouldn't believe her – as she hadn't believed those who had told her he would hurt her.

His cowardice made her cross. He should have had the courage to write to her and tell her it was finished – she'd have respected him then. The little spurt of anger made her feel better momentarily. But she couldn't hold on to it.

'Oh, Morts, I do love you.' And she knew that if she ever loved again it would never be like this. 'Never!' she said aloud.

'Never what? Are you going to eat that bread and cheese or can I have it? I'm starving.'

'Morts?' He had made her jump.

'Don't look so surprised. Of course it's me. Have you been at the brandy?' He sank on to the floor to join her. She moved away from him to distance herself.

'My sweet one, what's the matter? You're behaving as if you don't want me near you.' She sidled further away. 'Darling, what happened?' He came towards her, hand outstretched. 'Please tell me. What have I done?'

'You know.'

'I don't know anything. I expected a welcome from the woman I love, not have her back away from me.'

She pressed her hands to her ears. 'Don't say it. Don't lie to me.'

'I'm not.' He sat back on his haunches, puzzled. Then his expression changed. 'You've met someone else,' he said wretchedly.

'I haven't! What do you take me for?'

'Then tell me – or we shall resolve nothing.' Tears sprang into her eyes. 'Darling! You must tell me! What is it I've done?'

'How could you – and with *her* of all people?'

'*Who?*'

'*Lady* Sylvia – that's who.'

'I don't know what you're talking about.'

'You wrote to her – I saw the letter. She made sure I did.'

'I swear I've *never* written to her.'

'She showed me the letter,' she said stubbornly.

'Are you sure it was for her? I wrote to you yesterday to say I would be late. I swear on my life that was the only letter I wrote. I would not want to correspond with her. I don't even like her.'

'You don't?' she said, in a tiny voice.

'Why should I look at her when I have you, the most beautiful woman in the world?'

'But she's lovely.'

'Attractive, yes.'

'You see?'

'She's jealous of you – she wanted to hurt you.'

'But she said you'd arranged to meet her tonight. I went and took my message out of the hole in the clock tower.'

'So that was why it wasn't there. Oh, my sweet love, I was so frightened when I found no note – I thought someone else had claimed you. I wanted to die.'

'Don't you ever dare die! Don't you ever leave me! You have to promise – I couldn't live without you.' She went to him at the speed of quicksilver and fell into his arms.

He covered her face with kisses, then her ears and neck. It was her hands that went to the buttons of her blouse. 'I want you to take me, Morts, so I can always remember.'

'I can't! It's wrong!'

'How can it be when we love each other?' Her hands were at his trousers and she slipped her hand inside. He groaned as she touched him. 'I want you in me,' she said. 'I want to know ...'

At the manor, the nurses and orderlies, with the choir from the village, made a line led by Hannah and Sister Westall. Slowly they climbed the great staircase, their lanterns aloft, singing 'Silent Night', the lanterns swaying as they entered the ward. The men sat up as the procession passed by, and all were weeping.

Chapter Ten

Christmas Day 1914

1

Lettice had been up for over an hour, preparing the lunch. The goose was ready to put into the oven and now she was peeling the potatoes. It was extraordinary how much she had learnt in such a short time. When she had come here she could play the piano, sing, embroider, paint in water-colours and manage a large house. Now she could milk a cow – even though she need not since there was a dairymaid – iron, starch and dust. She never scrubbed because Phyllis did that and Ramsey would not have liked her to. Best of all, she was learning to cook, which she enjoyed. Once more she consulted her newly acquired *Mrs Beeton's Book of Household Management* to check how long it took to roast a goose. She was determined that everything would be perfect. Christmas Day would be a disastrous day to fail.

Now she took the cutlery through to the dining room. She looked with satisfaction at the shine on the long table – she had polished it with a mixture of beeswax and vinegar, which Phyllis had shown her how to mix. She wanted the room to look festive for the children when they awoke, although nothing she did could make it compare with the grandeur that was Cresswell at Christmas. There would be just the four of them. She had suggested that Phyllis should go home to her own family – as a treat, she had said, but really she wanted to be alone with Ramsey and the girls.

She had made friends with Phyllis – another new experience. She had never befriended a servant before but in Phyllis she had found someone willing to teach and help her, without judging her. They spent hours chatting and laughing together. It made her think of Rowan in an entirely new way.

Just recently she had allowed herself to pretend that Charlotte and Georgina were Ramsey's own children. Recently she had allowed herself to dream that one day they would have a little girl of their own and perhaps a son. She had even chosen names: Abigail and Thomas. Not that she had confessed it to Ramsey – he might think it silly of her.

No, he'd never be so unkind.

Ramsey could not have been a better father if he had sired the girls himself. He had infinite patience, played with them and always had time to listen. He loved them, it was plain to see.

She placed the swan centrepiece she had made from papier-mâché on the table. In the middle she arranged the Cox's apples she had brought down from the attic where they were stored in sweet-smelling pristine rows on brown paper. Then she added a few nuts and some little parcels, wrapped in gold and silver paper, that contained more little gifts for her daughters. Finally she fetched Ramsey's silver candlesticks, and pushed the candles into them.

Once, possessions had been important to Lettice – a crack in a plate and a whole dinner service might be thrown away, a spot on a chair and the upholsterer was summoned. Nothing could be frayed or shabby – everything gleamed and shone. Now she did not see imperfections.

She owned nothing – but, then, when she had lived with Hugo, she had owned nothing. Apart from her jewellery, everything was his and he had never stopped reminding her of it. Hugo. She could think of him now without rancour or bitterness.

'Merry Christmas, my darling.' Ramsey stood in the doorway.

'I feel like a child again – I'm so excited!'

'You look like a child, not an elderly mother.' He grinned at her and she pulled a face at him, then tripped across the room and hugged him. Suddenly there was a loud knock at the front door. That was unusual: everyone used the back door.

'I'll see who it is,' Ramsey said.

Lettice finished the table with a scatter of golden pine cones. She stopped dead when she heard shouting, which was followed by an almighty crash. She rushed into the hallway.

Ramsey was prone on the floor, blood pouring from his nose. A man was standing over him, heavily wrapped against the weather, his hands still balled into fists.

'Hugo!' Lettice swayed with shock. 'What have you done? Oh, Ramsey!' She knelt beside him, fumbling for a handkerchief to stem the bleeding. She looked up at her husband. 'How could you?'

'I've only done what I should have done months ago. Where are my daughters?'

Her blood froze in her veins. 'They are not here.'

'Don't lie to me.' He lifted his foot as if to kick Ramsey.

'I'm not.' Her nerves were shrieking but she wouldn't let him see her

337

fear. 'They're at Cresswell.' Stay calm, keep your voice down, don't wake them, she told herself. She put her hands behind her back so he could not see they were shaking.

'How strange when the butler there told me they weren't.' He smirked.

'I told you—'

'Mama!'

'Mama!' Her daughters were clattering down the stairs, dragging the red felt sacks she had made for them.

'Go back to bed,' she shouted.

'Come here! Do you remember your papa?'

Both children stood still, wide-eyed with surprise.

'Come here, there's good girls,' he coaxed them.

'Don't touch them.' Swiftly she placed herself between Hugo and the children. They were not smiling now: instead, tears brimmed in their eyes.

'Get out of my way,' Hugo ordered. 'Brown!' he shouted.

The front door was pushed open and a man even larger than Hugo walked in. 'There.' Hugo pointed at the children.

'No!' Lettice screamed and scooped them up, one under each arm. 'You can't have them!'

'They're mine!'

'They don't even know you.'

Charlotte and Georgina were screaming.

'They will learn. Get the girl,' he said to Brown, and to Lettice: 'You can release them to me with dignity or I shall take them from you.'

'You will have to kill me first.' She was half aware of Ramsey's groans as he began to get to his feet. 'And what do you want with them?' She spoke as normally as she could to distract him from Ramsey's recovery.

'They are mine and I don't wish you to be happy.'

'But we can both have—'

'There's no point in discussing this further. I have made up my mind.'

'But—'

'No more.' He raised his hand and smashed his fist into her face as she had known he would one day. She was not surprised. As he hit her again she accepted the inevitable. The children were crying with terror. Charlotte had wriggled out of her arms and was hitting her father, screaming, 'No! No! No!'

Suddenly Ramsey erupted into a mass of whirling arms and lashing feet. But when Brown reappeared he was knocked once more to the ground and the man kicked his head.

'Take them,' Hugo ordered the girl who had appeared.

'*You?*' Shocked, Lettice watched as Phyllis swooped down and picked up the protesting Charlotte. 'I thought you were my friend.' Nothing, she knew, could be worse than this. But it was. Hugo slapped her again, hard, knocking her head against the wall, and ripped Georgina from her arms. Then he walked out, Brown following him.

The bright red sacks lay on the floor. Lettice picked them up and ran out into the yard, just as her children were being pushed into Hugo's motor. She ran towards it. The girls were beating at the windows, calling to her. 'At least let them take these.'

'They won't be needing your rubbish.' The motor car was put into gear and Lettice stood, helpless, as it turned out of the gate.

She had been right to doubt that she could be happy.

2

Zeph would be leaving tomorrow to go back to the war. Dolly longed to comfort him but the barrier between them seemed impenetrable. And her patience was wearing thin. No matter what she did or said she annoyed him. In fact, everything annoyed him – if the children were noisy he became querulous, if they were quiet he accused them of ignoring him.

His indignation that she had helped Timmy did not go away. He brought it up at the least provocation – and he refused to discuss the debt she owed Eldridge.

She sighed as she began to cook the children's breakfast.

'I didn't expect to see you today,' she said, when Flossie bustled in.

'Too much excitement, too much noise at home. I came here for some peace and quiet.' She laughed as, up above, Dolly's children squealed.

'They're going to be sick before the day's out.' Dolly beat the scrambled eggs.

'Is that for Zeph?' Flossie indicated the eggs.

'No, he's gone to Briar Cottage.' To get away from me, she thought.

'To tell you the truth, I came here because Christmas won't be the same without dear Melanie. I thought I'd feel closer to her here.'

'I keep thinking about her.' Dolly could not admit that it was with

339

mounting anger. 'Now you're here, can I ask your advice?' She pushed the pan of eggs to the back of the range: she'd cook them when the children came down.

'Ask *me?*'

'Melanie didn't leave a will,' Dolly stated.

Flossie pursed her lips. 'I can't say I'm surprised. Making wills is a hard thing to do. But she should have, with her owning so much. I suppose his nibs gets it, lock, stock and barrel.' She nodded towards the snug where, since Melanie's death, Richard had slept. 'Don't seem right. But if he goes on as he is, he'll be joining her sooner than he thinks. Still,' she tied on her voluminous pinny, 'I can't help you with that sort of thing. It's beyond me.'

'Zeph's worried sick about what he'll do for money.'

'It's not as if he's been left high and dry, is it, not with the annuity?'

'What annuity?'

'You don't know? I *am* surprised. Perhaps I'd best not mention any more.'

'You must, now you've started,' Dolly insisted.

'I meant the one left by old Sir Mortimer to Melanie. If my memory serves me right, upon her death another was to be purchased for her children for their lifetime. But Zeph must know all about it.' She sharpened her boning knife.

'Oh, he does. I thought you meant another one.' Dolly was too proud to tell Flossie that she knew nothing about it. Why hadn't Zeph told her?

'It's a huge sum even if Xenia and Timmy share it. It's not as if you're going to starve.'

'We're fortunate.' She thought it politic to say so. 'No, it's something else. It was something someone said to me. I didn't have the wit to ask what he meant. I haven't dared tell Zeph in case I'm wrong – and I don't want to raise his hopes, what with Melanie dying and Christmas ... It's just ... Well, this person hinted that Richard was a bigamist.'

Flossie dropped her knife. 'Never!'

'That's what I thought. Spiteful gossip, I expect.'

Flossie sat down at the table and Dolly joined her. 'And you didn't tell Zeph?'

'I wondered if Melanie had ever said anything to you?'

'Not as such. But he gets letters, you know. Never showed them to Melanie. It annoyed her. She never knew who they came from. When she asked, he said they was from a friend. I told her to find them and read them but she wouldn't, said it would be wrong to snoop ...'

So, you think there might be something in it?' Dolly could feel hope and excitement returning.

'I'll cook him breakfast if he wakes up, I'll keep him here. You go and have a look.'

Dolly tiptoed past the snug. She could hear Richard snoring loudly. She climbed the stairs gingerly and pushed open the door to Melanie's bedroom. She had not been here since her death, and it was still filled with her presence, as if she hadn't left them. 'I'm sorry, Melanie,' she whispered. Now, where to look? She knew there was a trunk pushed under the bed. She pulled it out. She expected it to be locked but instead it swung open. Richard in one of his fuddled states must have forgotten to lock it. Inside she found some books and old photographs. She flicked through them. Richard as a bridegroom with Melanie. Then Richard as a bridegroom again, this time with a pretty young blonde. Someone had written a date on the back but no names. She slipped it into her pocket. She picked up a book, and found what she had been searching for – a pile of letters. She took one at random.

'My darling Richard,' it began. There followed some family news, and then, 'Dicky and I miss you very much. How much longer before we see you again?' It was signed 'Edith'. There was no date. Was Edith the bride in the photo? Had Melanie once said he'd been married before? She couldn't remember. She put the letter into her pocket with the photograph. Quickly she leafed through the other envelopes but there was nothing more from Edith. There were letters from his bankers, from an employer, and one that might have been from his mother. She replaced them in the trunk, then pushed it back under the bed.

When she went into the kitchen Flossie looked up expectantly.

'I found these.' Dolly showed Flossie the photograph and the letter.

'I don't think Melanie said he'd been married before. I'd have remembered that.' Flossie had to sit down again. 'Well I never did. What are you going to do?'

'Talk to him, I suppose.'

'Shouldn't you tell Zeph?'

'I don't know.'

'Well, it's his business. He might not like you taking over.'

'I'll think about it.'

'If he's off to the war tomorrow you haven't got much time for that.'

'It is the strangest thing, Flossie. But I could have sworn that Melanie was in the room and guiding me.'

'She probably was,' Flossie said in a matter of fact way.

Dolly left Flossie in charge of the children and walked rapidly towards Briar Cottage. As she approached she could see smoke rising from the chimney. He must have lit a fire to air the place. She shivered as she remembered the last time she had waited for Zeph in the cottage. It had been the night she had found out about May, nearly five months ago.

'Zeph,' she called. He was in the parlour, in his chair, staring at the fire. She saw he was crying. 'Oh, Zeph, darling, what is it?' She rushed to his side, knelt on the floor and took his hand. 'Tell me! Tell Dolly.'

'Such a mess I've made of everything ...' he started.

'What a mess we've *both* made of everything.'

'No, it's my fault. I was unfaithful. I had no right to treat you the way I did. I was feeling sorry for myself and you were a good wife but I didn't see it.'

'Then why are you so angry with me all the time?'

'I'm not. I'm angry with myself and what I've brought us to. Now I don't even have enough money to pay your debt. I can't see the point of going on, Dolly. I've nothing. I shall have to depend on you again.'

'No, you won't.' She took out the photograph and the letter and explained her suspicion. 'I'm not proud of what I've done this morning. And maybe I'm wrong about Richard. But we'll only learn the truth if we face him.'

'We'd better get it over with straight away.' He got to his feet, took her hand and led the way. He walked more purposefully than he had since his return from France.

The interview with Richard was brief. Although Dolly was angry with him she pitied him. He looked so ill and she was sure his grief for Melanie was genuine. Zeph produced the letter and the wedding photograph. Richard looked at it and shrugged his shoulders. 'It proves nothing,' he said, but not aggressively.

'We know that, but we'd like to think you'd be honest with us. In any case, we can check the records and find out for ourselves,' Zeph said firmly.

'How did you find out?' he asked.

'Mr von Ehrlich, as he once was, told me,' Dolly replied.

'He always gets his revenge one way or another.' Richard smiled sardonically. 'I suppose you want me gone?' Suddenly he seemed very old, and defeated.

'Why did you do it?' Zeph asked.

'I meant no harm. I hadn't seen Edith in years – and when we were together we did not get on. I was deceived into marrying her – I'd almost forgotten about her.'

'But the child?'

Richard laughed. 'There was no child. It was a dog. I loved your mother, Zeph, and without her …'

'How can you say you loved her when having deceived her you continued to do so? You've been stealing from her all these years, haven't you?'

'A little, here and there. It was hard having to ask her for every penny. And I'm a weak man.'

'Would you have cheated Zeph and the others of their rightful inheritance?' Dolly asked.

'I like to think I would have come clean. Shall you go to the police, Zeph?'

'No. My mother wouldn't want me to. But I'll need you to sign a confession.'

'I'll do anything.'

'I don't want you to come to harm. Find somewhere to live and give Dolly your address. She'll send you a small sum each month to keep you from the workhouse.'

'I don't deserve such kindness.'

'I'm not doing it for you, I'm doing it because it's what my mother would have wanted. As far as I'm concerned you can rot in hell.' Zeph stood up and left the room.

'You've a good man there, Dolly.'

'I know. Pity his mother didn't have such luck.' Without saying goodbye to Richard, she followed her husband.

'Well, I shall have my hands full looking after this place on my own,' she said, when she joined him.

'We could sell up.'

'And have Melanie haunt us? No, thank you. I was proud of you in there and she would have been too.'

'I wanted to hit him.'

'But we've got what you wanted and it's helped me make my mind up. I've been doing a lot of thinking since I came to look after Melanie. The Mays and Richards of this world can't destroy us. We're stronger than them. We had a good marriage and we shall again. We'll work together to make it so. I'm going to give up my business.'

'You don't have to, Dolly. Not for me.'

'If there's hope of a second chance for you and me, I'll give it up gladly. But there's to be no more secrets from each other. Anyway, with the men at war, the women who used to work for me have other things to do. Some have gone as hospital orderlies, others to the factories. I don't know how much longer I can go on anyway.'

'There's something I must tell you now. We've a substantial annuity, even when it's shared with Xenia and Timmy.'

'I know about it.' She was relieved that he had told her himself. 'Why didn't you tell me before?'

'I needed you to come back to me because you wanted me, rather than my money.'

'Are you calling me a gold-digger?' Her heart plunged with disappointment.

'No – forgive me. I didn't mean it in that way. I meant we had to make our decision with nothing on the table but our feelings.'

'Well, I love you, Zeph Topsham!' For the first time since his return Zeph smiled, then his arms went round her and he was kissing her. The past disappeared in a flash.

3

Rowan lay in the narrow bed in the little room at Emily Sprite's cottage and turned to look at Morts beside her. She had dreamed of love, imagined love, but nothing could have prepared her for the wonder of the reality.

She wondered if she looked different now that she was a proper woman. Would everyone know straight away what she had done when they saw her? She supposed she should feel wicked, but something so lovely and so natural couldn't be sinful.

Morts stirred in his sleep and she held her breath. She didn't want him to wake yet. She wanted to savour last night a bit longer.

Now he had had his way with her he would finish with her, she thought. She was prepared for it to happen, and she didn't regret what they had done. If he was to leave her for another, if he was to go to war and be ... At least she would have her memories of him, the feel of him within her, his smell. She would remember all that had happened last night, every movement, every whispered word, even when she was an old lady.

Strange that she hadn't noticed the crack in the ceiling before now. She could see it clearly in the daylight. Daylight! She had overslept! They would have sent to her mother's for her. Everyone would know, she thought, with mounting fear.

'Merry Christmas,' he said.

'I didn't know you were awake.' She felt shy suddenly, which she hadn't during the night. She supposed she had been wanton. What a lovely word.

'I love you.' He kissed her.

'I adore you.' Her arms were open for him as he caressed her, then took her with such power and strength.

When they had finished he wanted them to stay where they were. 'No. I can't.' She sat up. 'I shall be skinned alive. What's the time?'

He felt for his pocket watch, which he had laid on the floor. 'It's nearly ten,' he said. 'Listen – there's the bell for Matins.'

'Oh, fiddle!' She was scrambling out of bed.

'Wait a minute!'

'I can't. I'm late for work.'

'You're so late that another few minutes won't make much difference.' He pushed her back against the pillow and stood up. She lay admiring his muscular body as he padded across the room to his clothes. He took a little box out of his jacket pocket and returned to the bed. He knelt down beside it. 'You know I love you?'

'Yes,' she replied. For the time being, she thought.

'And I will always care for you.'

'Do you feel the same about me after last night?'

'I love you even more for the gift you gave me.'

'You can still respect me?'

'Of course. I know this is the wrong place to say this, that it should be different ...' Her heart was pounding. He was about to say that they could not meet again.

'Will you marry me?'

She stared at him, uncomprehending.

'Well, will you?'

'I didn't hear what you said. I was thinking—'

He laughed. 'Well, that's put me in my place. I asked if you would marry me.'

'You don't mean it?'

'Darling Rowan, I'm not in the habit of saying things I don't mean. Will you honour me?'

'We can't!'

'Why not? Give me one good reason.'

'Your family.'

'And another?'

'My family.'

'I'm not asking either of them to marry me, just you.'

'But I need permission.'

'And I shall ask for it, and if your father won't give it we shall simply wait until you are of age – or elope to Scotland.' He clicked open the little blue leather box to reveal the most beautiful solitaire diamond she had ever seen.

'It's lovely. But we can't. You can't marry someone like me! It's just not what people do.'

'I'm Morts, not *people*. We love each other. We want to be together. I know it will be harder for you than it will be for me, but I can help you, and Lettice will too.'

'Could we keep it a secret?'

'Is that a yes?'

'I suppose it is.' She wanted to cry when he placed the ring on her finger.

'But I want no secrets. I want the whole world to know.' And, laughing, Morts kissed her, and once more they made love to each other.

Rowan felt sick with nerves as they approached her parents' house in Cresswell-by-the-Sea. Morts had held her hand tight all the way there as if he was afraid she might run away.

It was the usual bedlam in the Marshalls' house when they entered. If anything it was even noisier than usual as the children played with their toys. 'Are Mum and Dad here, Oak?' she asked.

'You're in trouble,' he said, with sibling relish. 'Everyone's been looking for you. Apparently that sister's very angry.'

'Are they in?'

'Dad is. Mum's gone to the inn.'

He sauntered off. 'Do we go and see him together?' she asked, hoping he would go alone.

'I don't know. I wasn't scared until now. See what you've done? You've frightened me too.'

'Is that you, Rowan?'

'Yes, Dad.' She pushed open the door to the crowded sitting-room.

'You lot, out! I need to talk to your sister,' Alf said. 'Where have you been? I've had that sister here looking for you, stuck-up old biddy if ever I saw— Sorry, Mr Morts, I never saw you there.' He was immediately on his feet.

'What did Mum say?'

'She don't know. I didn't tell 'er. There was rumpus enough without your mother joining in.'

'It's my fault, Mr Marshall. You see, I bumped into Rowan and I wanted to ask her something and we both lost track of the time.'

'Well, you'd best be doing the explaining to that old trout, Mr Morts, begging your pardon. But our Rowan's in a lot of trouble. Staying out all night. Telling lies …'

Morts grabbed Rowan's hand. 'There's something I want to ask you, Mr Marshall. Will you do me the honour of giving me permission to marry your daughter?'

Alf sat down abruptly in the chair he had just vacated. 'You want to do what?'

'We want to get married, sir.'

'You can't.'

'I know Rowan is not of the age of consent, sir, but if you would—'

'Are you in the family way?' Alf looked at her suspiciously.

'Sir, I can assure you she is not. I love your daughter. I want to marry her and care for her. She is very precious to me. I promise you to love her always.'

Alf looked close to tears. 'Put like that … But what will your mother say?' he asked Rowan.

'That it'll end in tears. But we want to prove her wrong.' Rowan was determined now.

Alf shrugged his shoulders. 'There's not much I can say … It'll be hard for our Rowan but, then …' He put out his hand and shook Morts', then hugged his daughter. He coughed noisily. 'I'd best get some water,' he said, and rushed from the room.

'Should we go and see your mother?'

'I'd rather not. Let Dad tell her. He's good at calming her down.'

'Then it's my parents next.'

'Do I have to come?' Rowan's courage had left her. She was pale and frightened.

'Yes. We face them together. There's nothing they can do to stop us.'

Rowan was not so sure.

4

Once Morts had informed his parents of his engagement, Coral's screams reverberated against the aged wood panelling and wafted up the stairs. No one missed them. The horses in the stables lifted their heads and Cariad scuttled for shelter in the study, where Hannah, excluded from the family Christmas celebrations, was catching up with some overdue paperwork.

'A family drama?' Major Fellowes had just entered the room. 'That proves it's Christmas.'

'I fear my nephew has become engaged.'

'Unsuitable, is she? An actress or of that ilk?'

'Oh, no, nothing like that.' Hannah laughed. 'She comes from a very respectable family on the estate.'

'A servant?'

'Yes.'

'Well, at least she'll know you as a family with all your foibles and understand what she's taking on.'

Hannah's head jerked up sharply, but he was smiling. 'It will be hard for her,' she said. 'She will never be accepted – not just by certain family members but by the estate workers.'

'Maybe she won't want to be. Why should she kow-tow to those who don't approve of her? I wouldn't. And if others are jealous of her good fortune, they would not make reliable friends, would they?'

'Of course, what you say is true. But how can she, a child of the estate, become the mistress one day of this great house? The servants will laugh at her, and society will snigger.'

'Provided the wages keep coming, I'm sure the servants will learn. And if she's intelligent, she will learn how best to handle them. How old is she?'

'Just seventeen.'

'Even better. She'll be malleable.'

'I hope you're right. I try to be egalitarian but sometimes it's so difficult.' She sighed.

'I like your honesty.' He smiled at her ... in a different way from before. 'You remind me of a dear friend of mine, Dulcie Prestwick. She looks at things in the same sane, logical way. Come to think of it, she will be of immense help to Rowan – if the child weathers that assault from my sister-in-law.'

'The poor girl. Anyway, the reason I popped in was to wonder if you will do me the honour of joining me for luncheon. We have much to discuss. But I suppose you will be with your family.'

'My sister-in-law has banned me.'

'Then it would seem you have much in common with the bride.'

'Whatever next?' Eve had to sit down from shock at the news. 'Rowan's a pretty little thing but it'll never work.'

'I agree, Eve. It's a tragedy for the family. I feel for her ladyship.'

'What does Lady Penelope say?'

'No one's dared to tell her in case she has a seizure.'

'What's Flossie thinking of, giving her permission?'

'She didn't – it was Alf. She's furious with him – they've had words. She agrees with us. Apparently she said, "It'll end in tears." Never a truer word.'

'Still, there's time. A long engagement will sort them out, especially when they're parted. They'll both meet other sweethearts.'

'No. I overheard Mr Morts with his father. He's already arranged a special licence.'

'I don't know what the world's coming to, Edward. Time was when people knew their place.'

'Good luck to the young people, I say,' Sergeant Bob put in. 'Love conquers all, doesn't it, Eve?'

'Just so,' Eve simpered. 'Did I hear you saying Mr and Mrs Oliver were coming for luncheon? Whatever next? And her just delivered of a baby.' She congratulated herself on having neatly diverted the conversation.

'I gather from Gussie that Mrs Oliver is in fine spirits,' Edward said.

'You've seen Gussie? She never told me,' Eve said.

'She delivered me a small Yuletide gift.'

Eve gave an almighty sniff of disapproval. 'She never gave me anything.'

'An oversight, I'm sure,' Whitaker said diplomatically. A bell rang, summoning him to the front door. 'That'll be Mr Oliver and family,' he said, and went to welcome them.

'Ask if we might see Miss Marigold,' Eve called after him. 'And, Willow, you needn't think you can skive off work just because your sister's got ideas above her station.'

Hannah was interrupted once more in her attempts to work. 'Come,' she said. 'My dear Esmeralda! Should you be here? Oliver, the wing chair.'

'We thought it best to come and see you, Hannah. Hugo has turned up and has behaved abominably.'

'Oh, Oliver. How?'

'Lettice, the foolish girl, has been with Ramsey Poldown.'

'Dear me, no!' Hannah had to sit down quickly. 'How could she?'

'She's in love,' Esmeralda explained helpfully.

'That is no excuse for flouting all the rules of society. Lettice has ruined herself. What are we to do, Oliver?'

'I'm not sure what we can do. Hugo is within his rights. She took the children and no man could countenance his offspring being raised in such unsuitable circumstances. He has removed them from her by force.'

'The poor child!'

'He beat her and Ramsey.'

'I can understand his violence to the man, but not to his own wife.'

'As soon as Christmas is over I intend to go to London and take advice as to our course of action. I hope that his violence might stand against him.'

'But, in the circumstances, who could criticise him?'

'I hope he joins the army and is killed!'

'Esmeralda! what a wicked thing to say!' Hannah remonstrated.

'He doesn't love those little girls. He's only taken them because he hates Lettice. He's wicked!'

'Esmeralda, don't upset yourself! It will do you harm.'

'I'm as fit as a flea, Hannah, just angry for poor Lettice. She's in a dreadful state, crying, unable to eat or sleep. Ramsey is beside himself. He worries that if he has to go to the army she might harm herself.'

'She must come and live with me. I'll care for her just as I did when she was a child.'

'Dearest Hannah, we hoped you'd say that.' Oliver kissed her. 'And what about Morts? Foolish boy.'

'He's a man and quite capable of deciding for himself,' Esmeralda said firmly.

'Quite,' said Hannah, who noted how confident Esmeralda had become. It pleased her.

'And Rowan is highly intelligent, you know, simply not educated. I think she will surprise everyone.'

'I hope you're right, Esmeralda. Shall we all go for luncheon?' Oliver suggested.

'You go. Coral won't allow me to join you,' Hannah told him. 'Not, in the circumstances, that I mind. I fear it will be a fractious meal. Morts has insisted his fiancée should be there.'

'The trenches would be preferable to Coral in full cry!' Oliver roared with laughter.

The family had met before luncheon in the library, which now acted as their sitting-room. A scared-looking Rowan had sought out a window-seat as far as possible from Morts' mother.

'You can't, Morts, it's as simple as that. How could you even contemplate it? The shame! I forbid it!' Coral's voice rose with each sentence.

'If you don't quieten down, Coral, you'll burst a blood vessel, and I don't want to miss my luncheon,' Mortie said reasonably, but it was doubtful that his wife had even heard.

'Are you behind this?' Coral turned on Esmeralda, who was, on her doctor's orders, lying on a *chaise-longue*.

'I knew nothing.'

'I don't believe you.'

'I'd prefer that you didn't call my wife a liar.' Oliver was on his feet.

'The housekeeper tells me that Esmeralda and Lettice have been giving this creature lessons in etiquette.'

Rowan blushed to the roots of her hair.

'Yes, we have.'

'There! What did I say?'

'It was obvious to us that Morts adored her. We were trying to make things easier for Rowan.'

'You treacherous viper!' Coral spat.

'But whatever Lettice and I did, it made no difference to Morts – who I consider a wise and lucky fellow.' Esmeralda was pink with emotion and exertion.

All of the shouting had woken Marigold, who began now to cry. Oliver was first at her side and she subsided as soon as he spoke to her. The nanny was summoned to remove her.

'You're an underhand minx, aren't you?' Coral had turned her attention to Rowan, who looked as if she was confronting a poisonous snake. 'You inveigled your way in here to ensnare my son.'

'If I knew what "inveigle" meant I might be able to answer you,' Rowan said, with spirit. 'I didn't ask Morts for anything. He asked me.'

'Are you in the family way?'

'No, I am not.'

'Mother!' Morts sat down beside Rowan and put his arm round her.

351

'How much do you want? Mortie, make her an offer.'

'I shall do no such thing. Pretty little gal, if ever I saw one. And a bit of peasant blood will do this family no end of good.' Mortie sounded calm enough, but his colour showed that he was angry – with his wife, though.

'If you continue to insult my fiancée, mother, I shall walk out of your life and you will never see me again.'

'*Fiancée!* You've lost your senses. The shame!'

'You are the one who is behaving shamefully, Mother.'

'I shall have it stopped!'

'You cannot, Mother. Mr Marshall has given his permission. I am of age. It is my life and I shall marry whom I choose.'

'Disinherit him, Mortie. Cut him off without a penny.'

'I can't do that, as well you know. And even if I could, I wouldn't. Good luck to them, say I.'

'Oliver – you're a trustee! Stop his allowance. See that he inherits nothing.'

'I agree with Mortie. And since you aren't speaking to Hannah, you can't ask her opinion, can you?'

'This is insufferable! Wipe that grin off your face, Oliver. You all see this as a jolly jape but to me it is a tragedy.' She began to howl.

'It's because of January, isn't it, Morts?' Esmeralda asked kindly.

'Partly.'

'What about January?' Rowan asked, but she was afraid she already knew the answer.

'We're all off to Salisbury Plain.'

'That means you'll go to France.' She was ghostly white.

'Perhaps not.'

'You can't go to France! Felix is there – I can't risk losing both my sons! Mortie! Do something this minute!' Coral demanded.

'Please, Sir Mortie, do something to stop it – please, I beg you!'

Neither Coral nor Rowan was aware that at that moment they were in agreement.

5

The rhythmic boom of a drum attracted Rowan Cresswell's attention. Curiosity getting the better of her, she stopped pouring her early-morning tea and approached the window, which was a good ten feet high. Every inch of the glass gleamed in the bright January sunshine. She positioned herself by the heavy curtains of blue and gold brocade so that she could not be seen as she was still only half dressed. Below, the shrill chatter of women sounded like a flock of starlings approaching their roost. They were standing at the roadside waving flags. Now she could hear cornets, trumpets, cymbals as well as the drum.

They had one more day. One more precious day before Morts, too, had to line up behind the regimental drums. Ever since Christmas Day she had been begging God to stop the fighting and spare her husband.

How could those women be happy? How could they be rejoicing when their loved ones were leaving and might never return?

The last few days had passed in a blur of emotion. She had been in such a state, happy yet unhappy, courageous yet afraid, confident and yet certain she should not be marrying this man.

'What if I make his life too difficult?'

'You won't.' Esmeralda had reassured her.

'What if he's ashamed of me?'

'He won't be.'

'What if I'm ruining his life, as his mother says I am?'

'You aren't. You will add to it.'

The ceremony had passed in a blur. She'd been aware that both mothers were crying, of Coral cutting her dead and her own mother hugging her. She could barely remember the good wishes heaped on them, only the words of criticism. She had felt shy with those she had known all her life.

There was no time for a honeymoon, but three days ago Morts had brought her to the Victoria. Once she had longed to work here as a maid, and now she was occupying the best suite.

She remembered their lovemaking. It was even better now – because they were married or because they were familiar now with each other's bodies?

'You're up early, my sweet.' Morts had entered the room, resplendent in his officer's uniform, a proper khaki one now.

'I wish you didn't look so handsome. It makes it harder.'

'I know, my love. Now, promise me, take any problems straight to Esmeralda or Hannah. I don't think Oliver will be going to France. He's too old.'

'Lucky Esmeralda.'

'Are you listening?' He smiled at her. 'If my mother comes to stay I suggest you go to Aunt Hannah or to Emily's cottage – they will look after you. There's no point in exposing yourself to mother's fury.'

'I wouldn't want to be at the manor without you. Emily Sprite has welcomed me.'

'And one more thing, my darling. This won't have been necessary but, just in case, I've made certain that you will be secure and looked after for the rest of your life.'

'Dear one, don't say it, please. I can't bear to think of being without you.'

'Maybe you have a little life in there.' Gently he touched her stomach.

'Wouldn't that be wonderful? Then you'd always be with me. Are you afraid?'

'Only a fool wouldn't be. And I'm angry that now we are one we must be torn apart. But I'm excited too. I want to do my bit. And now, my sweet, get dressed – we leave in two hours.'

'Where?'

'To catch the train.'

'But you don't go until tomorrow.'

'I lied. I thought it for the best. I didn't want our last night together spoilt with unhappiness at the prospect of parting.'

'I should have known.'

'I wanted to protect you. That's my role now.'

Ramsey had woken early that morning with a start. It was still dark and bitterly cold. He listened in the darkness but could not hear her breathing. He fumbled for matches and a candle. The bed, beside him was empty. Fear clutched him. Had she gone out into the bitter cold, was she wandering the moor? The last week had been agony for both of them. He had thought she would never cease crying.

He lit the lamp and holding it high he ran down the stairs. Beneath the sitting-room door he saw a strip of light. He felt the fear ease. He tapped at the door. There was silence. Slowly he opened it. She was sitting upright on a hard chair in the middle of the room. At her feet was a valise, secured and no doubt packed.

'Lettice. What are you doing?' He spoke gently not wishing to startle her. 'Lettice?' She did not answer. He knelt in front of her. 'My darling …' He looked up at her, putting out his hand to take hers but she moved it away abruptly. 'Lettice …' He placed his hand under her chin and turned her face towards him. 'Sweet one …' The eyes that looked at him were those of a dead person. She opened her mouth but no words came out. 'It's all right, my darling. I understand what you want to do.'

The station was a hive of activity. Esmeralda stood with the other wives looking about her for Rowan. A woman approached her. 'Lettice, is it you?'

'Esmeralda. How are you?' Lettice spoke in a strange hollow manner as if she was speaking by rote.

'My dear one, are you ill, what are you doing here?'

Lettice did not answer. 'She feels she must return to her children.' Ramsey had joined them. He spoke in the way of someone trying to control their voice.

Esmeralda took hold of her hand. 'You don't look well enough to travel. Are you sure you want to go? You can come and stay with me.'

Lettice merely shook her head.

'It's kind of you, Esmeralda, but it is best she goes.' Esmeralda looked shocked by the sadness of Ramsey's expression. She put out her hand and touched his.

'Is there nothing you can do? she asked.

'I have consulted everyone I can think of. They all say the same, that she should return to Hugo. I shall accompany her until she's safe.'

''But what if …' she managed to stop herself from voicing her fears.

'You can think of no nightmare that I haven't already.'

'I'm so sorry.' She kissed Lettice. She watched as the forlorn creature, Ramsey at her side, climbed onto the train. It was barbaric, she thought. How could she return to her husband when he evidently hated her so much?

What if Oliver ever hated her as much? What if he could only look at her with loathing. What if he beat her and turned against her. She could not abide it. Perhaps Lettice was right. Perhaps it was better if she never shared her fears about Marigold with another living soul.

Now Rowan was standing on the station at Barlton. Morts was leaning out of the window of the train and she was hanging on to his hand as if she would never let it go. She smiled but her heart was breaking. He must remember her smiling for him, not crying.

The whistle blew and the guard raised his flag. A great cloud of steam issued from the engine. As it moved, so did Rowan, walking at first, then running to keep up. Finally, he had to let go of her hand. She ran the faster, waving for him. She could not see him now – the tears were too thick – but she continued to wave. As the train snaked out of the station, she felt as if she was watching her life go with it.

'He'll come back to you,' Hannah said.

'We have to be brave for them.' Esmeralda took her hand.

'I don't feel brave.'

'But you will be.'

'I want him back, Esmeralda.' Tears poured down her cheeks and Esmeralda put her arms tight round her. 'Oh, I want him back!'

She watched as the train disappeared. Angrily she wiped the tears away. He would be back! She would *will* him to return to her.